PRAISE FOR CHRISTOPHER RICE

Bone Music

"A stellar and gripping opening to the Burning Girl Series introduces the tough, smart Trina Pierce, aka Charlotte Rowe, who survived a childhood of murder and exploitation to discover there might be another way to fight back . . . Readers will be eager for the next installment in Rice's science-fiction take on *The Girl with the Dragon Tattoo*."

—*Booklist* (starred review)

"*Bone Music* is a taut and gripping thriller that's as bleak and harsh as the Arizona desert. It never lets up until the final page. Rice has created a great character in Charlotte Rowe."

—Authorlink

"A simply riveting cliff-hanger of a novel, *Bone Music* by Christopher Rice is one of those reads that will linger in the mind and memory long after the book itself has been finished and set back upon the shelf."

—Midwest Book Review

A Density of Souls

"An intriguing, complex story, a hard-nosed, lyrical, teenage take on *Peyton Place*."

—*Publishers Weekly*

"A chillingly perverse tale in which secrets are buried, then unearthed . . . very earnest plot."

—*USA Today*

"As gothic as one could expect from the author (*The Heavens Rise*) and son of Anne Rice, this tale of evil vegetation that feeds on the blood of those seeking revenge for past wrongs is gruesome . . . there are dark thrills for horror fans."

—*Library Journal*

The Heavens Rise

"This is Rice's best book to date, with evocative language, recurring themes, and rich storytelling that will raise the hairs on the back of the neck. It rivals the best of Stephen King at times and sets a standard for psychological horror."

—*Louisville Courier-Journal*

"A masterful coming-of-age novel . . . Rice's characters are complex and real, his dialogue pitch-perfect, and his writing intelligent and strong. He builds suspense beautifully . . . amid enduring philosophical questions about what it means to be human."

—*Publishers Weekly* (starred review)

"Christopher Rice never disappoints with his vivid people and places and masterful prose. He will hold you captive under his spell as his images and emotions become your own."

—Patricia Cornwell, #1 *New York Times* bestselling author

"Christopher Rice is a magician. This brilliant, subtly destabilizing novel inhales wickedness and corruption and exhales delight and enchantment. Rice executes his turns, reversals, and surprises with the pace and timing of a master. *The Heavens Rise* would not let me stop reading it—that's how compelling it is."

—Peter Straub, #1 *New York Times* bestselling author

BLOOD
ECHO

OTHER TITLES BY CHRISTOPHER RICE

BLOOD ECHO

A BURNING GIRL THRILLER

CHRISTOPHER RICE

Text copyright © 2019 by Christopher Rice.
All rights reserved.

Published by Thomas & Mercer, Seattle

www.apub.com

Amazon, the Amazon logo, and Thomas & Mercer are trademarks of Amazon.com, Inc., or its affiliates.

ISBN-13: 9781503904354 (hardcover)
ISBN-10: 1503904350 (hardcover)
ISBN-13: 9781503904330 (paperback)
ISBN-10: 1503904334 (paperback)

Cover design by M. S. Corley

Printed in the United States of America

First Edition

For Liz Berry,
who helped name this one,
and Jillian Stein,
who made the last one so fun to write

I dreamed about the creek again last night.

Of the way Daniel Banning used to reach out and push aside the thick branches of the eastern hemlock trees that always intruded upon the rocky path. Even then, I thought they looked like Christmas trees.

Because yes, the two serial killers who raised me for seven years always made a point to get a Christmas tree. After I was rescued, and my father trotted me out to reporters whenever it could earn him a dime, my interviewers would all get stuck on this detail. They couldn't believe the Christmas trees were decorated with reflective silver balls and bright red bows Abigail ordered from a catalog. Why not human bones?

Maybe if there'd been some warped religious motivation behind the Bannings' crimes, the reporters could have bought it. But there was no religion in the Bannings' house. Only their twisted brand of loyalty and their deep, abiding love of the natural landscape around their farm.

To hear Abigail tell it—and this is always challenging given that so much of what she's said from prison has been a lie—the Bannings did what they did to make their marriage work. Not just work. Thrive. In other words, Abigail assisted with her husband's abductions and rapes because it was the best way to hang on to her man. It wasn't a grotesque hobby, or an addictive adrenaline rush. It was an essential ingredient of their marriage.

I believe that she believes this.

I also believe that when Abigail Banning entered the root cellar so she could cut the throat of their latest victim after her husband had defiled them for days, she took pleasure in it. But it was the pleasure of an avenger; she blamed those women for her husband's sick, violent appetites, and so she stamped them out as if they were a pestilence. Women like my mother, who'd never met the Bannings until her car broke down one night on a rainy mountain road with me in the back seat.

Abigail's motivation wasn't religion, but loyalty; a disgusting version of it, to be sure.

*I was never able to stomach watching any of her TV interviews until recently. Even now, I can only manage to get through a few minutes of each one. A few months ago—the eighteen-year anniversary of my rescue—*Dateline *ran a two-hour special about the murders, for which I, once again, refused to be interviewed. But I found it on the internet later, and I made it as far as Abigail's preening assertion that Daniel could still make passionate, tender love to her even after raping their victims repeatedly; that he could do this because she allowed him to rape their victims for days on end.*

Enough interviewers have jumped down her throat in the past that she's learned to stop short of saying what she really means: let your man find a way to feed his worst appetites and he'll be yours forever. Even worse, her words imply that every man, deep down, has appetites as sick and twisted as Daniel Banning's.

This is the same woman I remember walking behind me, her arms out protectively, as I splashed through the pools of that creek. A woman who could develop that kind of motherly affection for the child of someone she'd murdered is capable of warping concepts like love and loyalty into something that makes decent people recoil in horror.

Everyone has their own definition of love, I guess.

I just wish I could forget Abigail's.

After I was rescued from the Bannings' farm, after my father sold the rights to my story to horror movie producers who would go on to imply I had participated in the murders, I would sometimes wish the Bannings had killed me, too.

Then I could have joined my mother as one of their beloved and cherished victims and not this grim survivor forever tainted by their warped paternal care of me. The country could have grieved for me instead of leering at me while my father lined his pockets.

I would have forever been little Trina Pierce, brutally snuffed out by the side of a mountain road, and not Burning Girl, who Abigail instructed to place the belongings of their victims into an incinerator and hit the "On" switch. Burning Girl, a living question—can you spend years receiving the loving attention of two brutal murderers and not be infected with their evil?

But it was selfish, I soon realized, to wish for my own murder.

It was selfish because in the end I was the reason the Bannings were caught.

If a deliveryman hadn't recognized me from an age-progression photograph, who knows how much longer their killings would have continued?

So I'm glad I lived.

I'm glad they were caught.

And I'm glad I have a new purpose today.

While I've been stunned by the levels of secrecy Cole has been able to maintain so far, I'm still convinced that the work I'm doing is going to get out. Maybe it won't be exposed all at once, but pieces of the truth might start to surface. And unlike the years I spent on that farm, I'm not going to let other people twist the story of my involvement.

If the time ever comes to tell this story, mine will be told in full, and by my own hand.

But that time won't be coming anytime soon.

For now, the world has no idea what Burning Girl has become.

I

1

"Veg tanned, right?" the girl asks.

When Richard Davies nods, she smiles and goes back to running her index finger along the dark leather wallet's burnished edges. Then she turns it over in her manicured hands, furrowing her brow.

It's kind of cute, Richard thinks, *that she's acting like a leather expert, given she looks about nineteen.* But maybe that's how they train them at the Seattle Leather Company: *Pretend like you just spent five years working in a tannery. Whatever you do, don't act like you're a University of Washington student who's too good to shovel hash in the cafeteria.*

She's never seen him before, he's sure.

But he's been watching her.

The day before, he followed her from the store back to her dorm.

Her name's Stephanie, and she wears her salon-perfect, sunflower-colored hair in a precise ponytail that sits high up on the back of her head. He's willing to bet her corporate-looking outfits are store policy. But combined with her apple-cheeked, doe-eyed face, they make her look like some lady lawyer's kid dressing up in her mom's work clothes.

If he had to bet, he'd wager her parents are both tech billionaires who live out in Medina. Maybe her daddy or her mommy invented some stupid app that charges five billion people five cents a day, and now they're putting their daughter through the motions of college just so they don't feel like failed parents when she finally raids her trust fund. As for the few shifts a week she puts in trying to get downtown shoppers to buy overpriced leather products, she probably tells all her rich friends she only took the job because she likes being around nice things.

Maybe he'll take her.

She's not what he normally looks for in a woman. Lately, though, he's been thinking about trading up. He's been getting good. Much better than when he started. Adding a few challenges to the process will keep the whole thing from feeling like work.

Maybe. Soon.

But for now, the store's his focus. The store and its glass shelves of cheap, bullshit chromium-tanned leather goods, all of which will end up looking like old sponge less than a year from now. But not before some fool who doesn't know any better walks out the door with them, several hundred dollars poorer.

To get himself in the zone, he always needs a store, preferably with a female employee. Doesn't matter if they look young and sweet like the girl before him now, or older and more world-wise, like that sour bitch he visited over at Cole Haan last time. Just as long as his satchel or his leather belt draws their attention. It doesn't matter if they're genuinely interested in his leather or just hoping to warm him up for a sale.

What matters is that when he offers to show them the wallet, they take it in their hands and run it through their fingers like Stephanie's doing now.

God, he loves this sight; the sight of an innocent woman's fingers traveling over the grain of his handiwork. He's not hard yet, but he's got all the symptoms. The tightness in his balls, the shortness of breath, the hot flush down his neck.

The store's empty except for the two of them.

She's left the glass door to the street propped open; maybe to invite customers in, or, more likely, because the landlord controls the heat and it's one of those confusing Pacific Northwest days when blasts of sunlight alternate with sudden, drenching downpours, so that when the sun returns, reflective puddles blind you in every direction you look.

He hates days like this. Days that can't decide what they want to be.

He prefers the oppressively gray ones, when the clouds and the treetops conspire to give you comfort and protection. This kind of day—erratic, jumbled, confused—is usually a sign from the earth. A sign that you should slow down, take your time. Not commit to a course of action until the sky's made up its damn mind.

A delay is the last thing he wants when he's getting into the zone.

Who are you kidding, friend? he asks himself. *You're not getting yourself in the zone. You're just acknowledging you're already in it.*

"You seriously made this yourself?" Stephanie asks.

He nods, smiles, as if he's immensely proud of himself, when really, he's trying to imagine the expression that would contort her pretty little face as she took a shot from his Weatherby Mark V. It's always there, he knows. He can usually hear the music a woman's agony will make the first time he looks her in the eye; the tension in her smirk, the half smile she gives him under batting eyelashes, the soft, teasing sounds she makes under her breath—they're all pretty good indicators of the type of sounds that will come ripping out of her as soon as one of his bear traps snaps shut around her ankle and she realizes she's completely and entirely his.

But Stephanie's lucky.

He prefers a different kind of prey.

Stephanie's life, her bearing, her privilege, it all speaks of harmony.

He prefers the women who walk Aurora Avenue at night. He prefers to hunt parasites spun off by a world out of balance, a world that ignores the clear and comforting dictates of the wild. A world that doesn't know stillness and focus and calm like he does. A world that's fast losing the patience to take the thirty days required to vegetable-tan leather like the wallet Stephanie's now passing back to him, her smile fading at the sight of whatever she's noticing in his expression for the first time.

"What kind of animal is it?" she asks.

Well, Stephanie, she told me her name was Crystal, and she offered to blow me for fifty bucks. What kind of animal does that sound like to you?

"Guess," he says.

"I don't know. Goat? I saw this guy on YouTube who makes leather out of goats."

"I don't work with goats."

Pigs, he thinks. *Cows, maybe.* But truth be told, he wouldn't insult any member of the animal kingdom by comparing them to the type of women he hunts.

Too much anger in my tone, he thinks. Stephanie's staring at him now like this whole exchange is something different than she thought; something she doesn't have a frame of reference for. Because she's nineteen and spoiled and learned about life from YouTube.

That's got to be it. It can't be his appearance that's upset her. At least, he hopes not.

After his first hunt, he realized it'd be a lot easier to draw in prey if he lost the wolfman beard and the sideburns. He preps himself now with grooming products bought from the big redheaded woman who sells organic bath products a few stalls down from where he sells his vegetables at the Pike Place Market. They're pretty sissified, but at least they smell like plants and not some old French lady.

"Well, it's amazing, whatever it is," she says. "I'm not sure we have anything that good, but if you get tired of making your own stuff . . ."

It's perfunctory and lazy, this pitch. She's sensed something about him she doesn't like, and now she's just punching the clock, doing her best to hurry him out of the store. This annoys him, but he doesn't kill when he's just irritated, so she's safe. *And therein,* he thinks, *lies the essence of why I'm such a good hunter.* He doesn't shoot at everything that moves.

He smiles and nods and heads for the door, but in his mind, he's saying, *Goodbye, Stephanie. You have no idea how lucky you are. Or what a fan you are of human flesh.*

Count your blessings, he thinks. *It's time to hunt.*

2

The charity luncheon his mother has dragged him to is being held inside what's supposed to be an art museum, but Cole Graydon thinks the place looks more like a villain's lair from an old episode of *Miami Vice*.

He's more annoyed at how many damn tables the organizers of this event have managed to cram inside the concrete column–lined main hall of the Claret Fine Arts Center.

From the expressions around him, he can tell he's not alone.

Some anticapitalist social justice warrior would no doubt get a kick out of this, he thinks—the richest, best-dressed people in San Diego County trying not to reveal how uncomfortable they are now that they're jammed cheek by jowl into a sea of flower-festooned tables that barely allow room for the harried waiters rushing to refill glasses of wine and champagne.

But Cole's trapped, too, and so he's not getting a kick out of it at all.

Maybe it's a deliberate strategy on the part of the . . .

What is this damn charity lunch for, *anyway?*

He makes a bet with himself. If he can figure out the cause du jour before the first speaker takes the podium, he'll give himself a little reward. That means ignoring the program tucked under one side of his bone china salad plate—a cheat sheet if there ever was one. Behind the podium, there's a logo that's supposed to represent something. It's spotlit, even though fierce Pacific-reflected sunlight streams in through the nearby glass walls. The logo looks like a bunch of inter-locking silhouettes. He's not sure what they're supposed to represent, but they seem vaguely familiar. His best guess? Two dolphins trying to fight their way free from some scrambled eggs.

"You remember what this is for, right?" his mother asks.

Shit, Cole thinks. She must have noticed him studying the stage.

"Kids?" he says.

She flattens her napkin across her lap and stares into space as if he hasn't spoken.

He's tempted to lighten the mood by saying that if she wanted to exert effort to look like the wife of a dead president this afternoon, he would have preferred she pick Jackie O over Pat Nixon. But his mother's willing to laugh at everyone except herself, so, in the end, the remark would only lighten the mood for him.

"Cancer?"

"Yes, Cole. It's a benefit for cancer. We're raising money for cancer so that it can, you know, do a better job of killing people."

"Now you're being churlish."

She gives him a blank look, as if she's deciding whether to be offended.

Jesus Christ, he realizes, *my mother doesn't know what* churlish *means.*

"OK, what?" he asks. "Spoil the surprise."

"Your high school."

Cole nods, takes in a deep breath, both small gestures intended to hide how colossally pissed off he is by this revelation.

My high school? I am busy running one of the largest pharmaceutical companies in the entire world, which, by the way, has the added burden of funding your Saudi royal lifestyle, and you drag me here during my few precious hours of time off for a fund-raiser for my fucking high school? Which, by the way, already has enough money to put a gold toilet in the faculty lounge!

But he knows the deal.

If he doesn't make some effort to show up for his mother's busy social calendar, she eventually turns her full attention to Graydon Pharmaceuticals, and his record there hasn't exactly been spotless. Of course, hers would be far worse, if his father had left the running of the company to her.

Which he most certainly didn't.

"I take it you don't approve?" his mother asks.

"Of my high school?"

"No, of course not. I'm just saying you probably feel as if I dragged you here today, and so now I need to be punished with looks."

"We were driven, not dragged. Who doesn't like being driven?"

"Cole. Be serious. Every now and then you need to do something that isn't about work. Especially if your idea of work means raiding our venture capital fund to buy some useless resort in the middle of Big Sur."

Our *venture capital fund?*

He bristles at his mother's sudden possessiveness of a company about which she knows almost nothing. Giving her a spot on the board was his late father's strategy for making her feel included; that's all. But since his father's death, she's managed to add a few too many of her beach club pals to the board's recently vacated seats. For the most part, they're just like her—insanely rich dilettantes in need of hobbies that make them feel important. The idea that they might start developing strong opinions about how he chooses to invest the company's leftover cash sets his teeth on edge. The idea that they might find a way to work in concert, and against him, is too unnerving to contemplate.

And if they had any idea who I really bought that resort for . . .

Priority one, he reminds himself: make sure the only reason his mother, her lackeys, and the entire board should ever hear the name

Charlotte Rowe—or Trina Pierce, or Burning Girl—is because they've been up late watching true crime shows on television.

"Mother, come now. There's no such thing as a useless resort," Cole says. "You, of all world travelers, should know this. You practically have permanent rings around your eyes from all the cucumber slices you've worn."

"Not really?"

"No, of course not."

"Good. So there's going to be a spa?"

"We're making room for it."

"There better be. It's in the middle of nowhere, Cole."

"Big Sur is not nowhere."

"It's hardly the South of France is what I'm saying. I mean, it's all . . . trees and cliffs, isn't it? Just the pictures make me carsick."

Cole needs the entire board, his mother included, to stay convinced his purchase of the Altamira Lodge five months ago truly was an impulse buy and not part of a top-secret project that could put their company on a path to glory no one could have predicted just a few years before. That path, however, is sure to be twisty, the stops along the way already involving a fair amount of law breaking and unexpected deaths. But as his father taught him long ago, you can't have progress at a company like theirs without a fair helping of both.

"I won't be expected to *go*, will I?" She sips champagne, gives him a long, searching look. Her expression smacks of irritation, but there's some veiled curiosity there as well. This is the longest conversation they've had about the Altamira Lodge since he assured the entire board he could improve the roadways leading to it, guaranteeing them some sort of reasonable return on their investment. "I'm afraid of heights, and the damn thing's on a cliff."

"Mother, rest assured, I will never try to take you anywhere you're not comfortable."

It's not really a smile she gives him next. But it's close. And Cole's reminded once again that their relationship consists primarily of the two of them finding ever more eloquent ways of asking to be left alone.

His cell phone vibrates in his pocket. The text is from Ed Baker, his security director.

Richard Davies just left a leather store. Countdown clock activated.

He types back,

Bluebird?

The response:

In costuming.

Cole feels like he's breathing more deeply than he has in weeks.

"I have to go," he says, rising.

"Cole." His mother doesn't sound all that disappointed or surprised.

"Sorry, duty calls."

"Picking out new linens," she says, "or approving a new drug trial?"

"A bit of both." He lifts his untouched champagne flute and sets it down next to hers.

"Fine. But never say I don't at least attempt to be part of your life."

"I never ever do." He kisses her on the cheek, then hurries from the room just as the first speaker takes the podium.

3

The motel where his mother destroyed their family once and for all isn't there anymore. It's been replaced by a storage facility that promises the cheapest rates in town. But Richard Davies can still feel a churning in his gut as he drives past it, a feeling that starts out as nausea but turns into a kind of caffeinated excitement that has him tapping his fingers against the steering wheel.

If he hadn't started hunting, it would be all sickness and nothing else.

In the beginning, he was careful not to cruise Aurora Avenue North before dark. But he's grown more confident over the years, and now he's comfortable driving through the dreary warehouse-filled streets when they're barely dusted by twilight.

He's reclaiming a piece of himself every time he visits. A piece of his father, too. Reclaiming the essence of what was pure and good about his family before it was destroyed by the rot in his mother's soul.

That's why, even though the Pacific Motel is long gone, he still needs to feel the magnetic tug of the land on which it stood. He doesn't slow down much, just enough to suck in a few breaths of the tainted air so his lungs can cleanse it with his new wisdom.

Before his first and second hunts, he made it a point to remove his license plates. Back then, he was more worried about his truck being captured on a security camera than he was about a traffic citation. But he's got enough experience now to know the real worst-case scenario—getting pulled over for driving without plates while he's transporting prey.

He could give two shits about being busted for solicitation.

Who's going to judge him? The deer who visit his farm? The other vendors at Pike Place Market, who can't remember his name? (Which, by the way, is exactly how he likes it.) At worst, an arrest for something that petty would mean he'd have to find another hunting ground. That would hurt, given his historical connection to this grim avenue of broken-down whores, but he'd make do.

He's pulled five prey from this place in three years. He's well past the point of restoring his father's honor and into . . . something next level. He's not sure what, but he's a little afraid of it, because it comes with urges that are harder to control.

The manifesto, he reminds himself. *Put your focus back on the manifesto.*

He's only outlined a few pages of it, but more passages come to him every time he visits here.

The beginning of the end of a man is when they come for his land.

His destruction is hastened when his woman seizes this opportunity to blame him for her weakness.

Once it's written, he'll upload it to some blogging site but won't actually post it. If law enforcement ever comes for him, he'll tap a button to make the post live. Not a bad end—sharing his father's real story right as he goes down in a hail of bullets just like a character out of the paperback Westerns his dad used to love. Before he lost everything.

But right now, the manifesto serves a more important purpose.

It's a place to channel his energy when the urge to hunt comes on too soon and too strong. Or when he gets crazy ideas about taking a girl like Stephanie.

Before his first hunt, he researched dozens of the mavericks and outlaws the world has called *serial killers*, and he could trace their downfall to two things: their impatience and their need for attention. And he vowed he wouldn't fall victim to either.

But he couldn't predict then how he'd feel once he advanced.

Once he became good.

In the beginning, the thought of following a hunt through from start to finish seemed so momentous, he could envision no greater goal. But after a year of handling his exquisite work in the solitude of his cabin, a childish desire for recognition began to set in.

That's when he started visiting the stores. And now, it looks like those visits have inspired a craving for younger, prettier victims. Women in whom the flaws and weaknesses of his mother have yet to fully blossom.

But the most dangerous urge has been harder to control.

He's tired of waiting six months.

He doesn't doubt this delay has been key to his success, though. Six months between hunts keeps him from becoming a regular on Aurora Avenue North, which keeps the cops and whores from chalking up the disappearances of his victims to anything other than an overdose or a woman who somehow left the life.

Having the cops looking out for his type of truck would be bad. But a bunch of whores spreading the word to their diseased sisters that his truck could mean the end of a girl? That could seriously jam him up, here or anywhere else he chooses to hunt.

He doesn't have money for another vehicle; he's spent way too much on the other implements of his hunt. And he doesn't need hesitant bitches slowing down his extractions with a lot of bullshit negotiation through the open car window.

In and out quick. That's how it has to work.

Six months.

In and out.

That's how it'll be tonight, he's sure of it.

And he needs to remember what got him here. The patience, the deliberation, the control. Even if he does think Stephanie's firm young skin would make an amazing belt.

4

"Is there time to get me to Seattle?" Cole asks as soon as the door to the control center hisses shut behind him.

"No!" his security director barks. "You shouldn't even be *here*."

Ed Baker's standing a few feet away, arms crossed, looking at Cole as if he's an annoying distraction and not his boss. Cole shoots the man who was his late father's security chief a withering look, then turns his attention to the two sunken rows of surveillance stations lighting up the otherwise dim room. There was a time, a few months earlier, when it felt to Cole like Ed was his only real loyalist. All that changed with the sudden reawakening of Project Bluebird, and they're long overdue for a conversation about it. Right now, they've got work to do.

Their backs to him, the techs continue to ignore his arrival.

As instructed by Ed, Cole thinks. *If I let Ed have his way, we'd all be wearing stocking masks so we couldn't testify against each other later.*

A few days before, this place had been home to just two people watching a constant feed from several tree-mounted cameras angled at Richard Davies's farm and its long, rutted driveway. With their target on the move again, there are now twice as many techs monitoring three times as many screens.

It's not the first time one of Davies's road trips has sent them scrambling to add resources. It's the third.

Cole's hoping for a different outcome this time. Whether he's sipping Balvenie in his home office or pacing the back of this chilly windowless room, he's not interested in spending another few days watching Davies sell vegetables at the Pike Place Market while making as little conversation with his customers as possible.

But the visit to the leather store is new.

It's the escalation they've been waiting for.

It's the escalation I've *been waiting for, anyway,* Cole thinks. *Ed wants to shut this whole thing down.*

The surveillance center sits in the basement of one of Graydon's never-used satellite office buildings. His father only bought it to give prying eyes the illusion that Graydon hadn't moved all of its laboratory research offshore. Even if his dad were still around, it probably would have stayed as empty as it is now. Their neighbors are cold storage facilities and small office parks for companies that prefer the relative anonymity of Otay Mesa, an arid stretch of San Diego right next to the Mexican border.

Save for the yards of steel fencing and a guardhouse at the parking lot's one entry point—a guardhouse that wasn't manned up until a few months ago—the exterior of the building is nondescript. From the air, the place looks like a U made of bone. The outer walls are mostly long, uninterrupted stretches of heavily tinted windows and bands of concrete painted so white they're blinding on a sunny day. Which in this part of the country is pretty much every day. Nothing about the exterior gives a hint of the labyrinth of never-occupied laboratory spaces and office suites constructed inside.

It's in this hyper-air-conditioned, lightless bunker, with its thick layer of carpet underfoot and its walls reinforced to withstand both electronic surveillance and a bomb blast, that Cole feels less like a spoiled, privileged fraud and more like a daring innovator pursuing a grand vision that would have made his father proud.

He turns his attention to four of the newly installed LCD screens now showing live feeds.

The leftmost screen, which is slightly larger than the others and hung vertically, displays Richard Davies's pickup truck as a green dot moving through a black grid of streets that represents Seattle.

To the right of it, two screens broadcast alternating aerial feeds of Davies's truck captured by the small cloud of microdrones trailing him from an altitude of about three hundred feet. The expensive little buggers will monitor Davies's every move, but only when there's enough open sky for them to make quick course changes without smacking into a building and convincing the people inside that Earth's been invaded by alien nanobots. The weather forecast must have improved; there's no operating them in high winds or a consistent downpour.

Right now, the microdrone cloud's offering up four different angles from around the same fixed point: the front of the truck, the back, the passenger side, and the driver's side. They alternate with a rhythm that's just a beat or two shy of headache inducing.

Another screen shows the feed from a shoulder-mounted cam on a conventional tail—if a guy who's been trained to kill in a dozen different ways can be considered conventional. Because the camera's got massive zoom capabilities, there's no telling the actual distance between the tail's vehicle and Davies's truck.

Cole could ask; the tail's in constant radio contact with one of the techs seated before the row of screens. Or he's supposed to be.

He knows what it's like to put one of these things together on the fly, and he's not going through that hell again.

Cole studies what he can see of the neighborhood Davies is driving through.

"He's scoping?" Cole asks.

"Too early. The streetwalkers don't come out until after dark." The tech who answered him is Asian and tomboyish, with a neat pageboy cut and a heavy sweater to protect her from the blasting

AC. Her lower lip tenses. Does she regret speaking up without being called on? Cole's grateful for it; she made it clear, without meaning to, that Ed has brought everyone in the room up to speed on their target.

Good. So Ed's only being an obstinate jerk when I walk into the room.

"Scouting locations, then," Cole says.

"Possibly," Ed answers. "If the file is reliable, he's taken girls from this area before. Not sure why he needs to get the lay of the land again."

Ed's use of the word *file* sounds acidic, probably because the file came from an intelligence source he didn't vet and select. An intelligence source Cole hasn't yet shared with him, or anyone.

"It's been six months," Cole says. "Things could change. Buildings get torn down."

"Yeah. Real estate's booming round these parts."

"Newly abandoned buildings, then. Burned-out lots. They're all good abduction sites."

"Sure," Ed says as if he isn't and doesn't care if he is or not.

"It's another escalation, for sure."

Nobody answers him.

Maybe if he'd phrased it as a question . . .

Ed's desire to keep Cole inside a plastic bubble, completely removed from the workings of Project Bluebird 2.0, is possibly protective loyalty. But it's completely unworkable in the long run, and it worsens Cole's concern that Ed might deliberately throw the project off track while Cole's not looking.

Either way, he'd like his director of security, formerly his mostly loyal and steadfast employee, to relax. Just a little.

Even if everything they do in this room is entirely illegal. And possibly unethical.

It's only unethical, Cole tells himself, *if Davies doesn't turn out to be a butcher of women. And besides, when Ed answered to my father, he was no stranger to the unethical.*

"The link to your home server is secure." Ed's so close to him suddenly, Cole jumps. The man looks like a version of Mr. Clean that could take out ten guys in a bar fight, but he always smells like Ivory soap and Listerine.

"Why are you whispering?" Cole asks.

"It's called professionalism."

"Oh, OK. Is this you apologizing for your insubordination?"

"If you're doubting my work, then I—"

"I don't doubt the link is secure, Ed. I wanted to be here. This is my operation."

"I still don't think it's a good idea," Ed whispers.

"I still didn't ask." The bite in Cole's tone causes Ed's cheeks to turn red.

"Fine. Can I ask you something, then?"

Cole just glares at him.

"How'd you find this guy?" Ed asks.

"It's a little late for that, isn't it?"

"For you, maybe."

So Cole had identified Richard Davies, organic farmer, as a potential serial killer without using a "digital services team"—their polite code for the black-hat hackers handpicked by Ed. So goddamn what. That means less work for Ed. He should be pleased. Grateful. Less mouthy. Instead he's—

"Bluebird's coming online," one of the techs says. He's a pale-skinned, baby-faced nerd boy with a buzz cut and librarian glasses.

"TruGlass?" Cole asks.

"No. Audio," the tech answers.

"Can you bring her up?"

"On headset," Ed says, walking to his desk chair.

"No," Cole answers.

Several of the techs glance his way for the first time.

"I'd like everyone to hear her so we can all appreciate the magnitude of what we're doing here. Of what she's about to do. For us."

Ed's eye roll suggests he considers Cole's words no more genuine than a politician's stump speech.

Worse, the baby-faced tech looks to Ed for permission to comply. Then he notices the glare he's getting from Cole and spins back to his station without further delay. A second later, he gives Cole a thumbs-up.

"Charley?" he asks.

"Yes."

"You're on with me and the control room, so measure your words carefully."

"Hello, everyone," she says.

5

Charlotte Rowe's even tone sends send a ripple of new energy through the room, something between wonder and nervousness. The techs all look up from their computer screens at the same time—this must be the first time they've heard the voice of the woman they've been told to call Bluebird.

"How are you feeling?" Cole asks.

"It's too big, Cole. I can't wear it."

"The earpiece?"

"Yes."

"OK. Is your ground team with you?"

"We are." The woman who speaks next sounds as though she's standing just an inch or two away from Charlotte inside their transport truck. "With respect, we think she's being too cautious here."

Cole notes that Ed didn't warn him his voice was being broadcast to Charlotte's entire ground crew. There have been so very many things he's had to note about Ed lately, so many of them sour.

"It's in keeping with the specs I approved?" Cole asks.

"Absolutely," the ground tech answers, "it's matched to her exact flesh tone."

"It's lumpy," Charlotte says.

"Isn't it the size of a pea?" Cole asks.

"It doesn't feel like a pea," Charlotte answers. "It feels like a marble inside my ear."

"Well, I can't see it and I'm looking in her ear right now," the ground tech says.

"We still think he skins his victims, right?" Charlotte asks.

There's a new tension in her voice. But it's her words that shock everyone in the room.

Ed stops swiveling nervously in his rolling chair.

The female tech who spoke up earlier drops her hands to her lap.

Even Cole feels his breath catch.

"Is that a yes or a no?" Charlotte asks.

"That's our assumption, yes," Cole answers.

"OK," Charlotte continues, as if she's indulging all of them, "then it's reasonable to assume that at some point, either before or after he takes me, he's going to examine my flesh. Or some part of it, at least. Does that sound right?"

"I'd say that's . . . probable," Cole answers.

"OK. Then what do you think he's going to do if he suddenly comes across several hundred thousand dollars' worth of technology sitting inside my right ear?"

Try several million, *Burning Girl.*

But Charlotte Rowe is alluding to another possibility without saying so explicitly.

Tonight, she will be posing as the same type of sex worker they believe Davies has abducted and murdered five times over the past three years. Which means that to make his introduction, Davies will first pay for access to her body. What she allows Davies to do and for how long will be entirely up to her. Which means, in order to accomplish tonight's mission, she's being forced to think of herself as a piece of meat. Literally.

"If you don't wear the earpiece," Ed says, "then we have no audio connection to you."

"So?" she asks.

"It means we can't warn you if we see something you don't."

"You weren't in my ear last time and things went OK."

"Define *OK*," Ed says.

"Ask Frederick Pemberton. He's on death row."

"And you're a free bird, thanks to the cleanup job we did," Ed says.

"Define *free*."

"Ed," Cole says.

"What?"

"Step out."

Ed just stares at him, then his eyes widen, and he sits forward with his elbows on his knees, frowning at Cole as if he's a cat who just dragged a dead animal inside the house. "Excuse me?" he whispers.

"I said step out of the room. Now."

The emotion drains from Ed's face, then he gets to his feet and leaves. If it were possible to slam the bank vault–style door behind him, he might have, but it's far too heavy. Once Ed's gone, Cole feels a pang of regret. But just a pang.

Ed just drove them dangerously close to an uncomfortable truth at the very moment Cole needs peak focus from everyone.

For Cole's security director to express any opinions on Charlotte's past performance was colossally stupid. For starters, five months ago they'd been monitoring her without her consent. Worse, she'd been deceived into taking Zypraxon by Bluebird 1.0's lead scientist, who decided to start posing as Charlotte's therapist after Cole shuttered the original project and denied him access to his labs.

When the dust finally settled and the full consequences of Dylan Cody a.k.a. Noah Turlington's betrayals became clear to everyone involved, Cole gave Charlotte what he considered a reasonable deal, with a pretty good exit plan, if she chose that option.

But he'd hardly call it fair. Reasonable, but not fair.

Fair is for kindergarten.

In the end, she'd agreed to keep working with them. So he wasn't about to let Ed's former-cop ego and loose lips screw up the fragile peace he'd established with the woman the world once knew as Burning Girl. The same woman who now happened to be the only human on the planet in whom Zypraxon actually worked.

"Ed's going to sit this one out, Charley. I apologize for his . . . insensitivity."

"Your call," she answers. "And thank you."

"And the earpiece is *your* call."

"Good, 'cause I'm not wearing it."

Cole pulls his iPad from his satchel and opens the PDF of Richard Davies's case file.

"How about we do a little quiz to get you ready? I assume you've read Davies's file."

"Five times."

"OK. Then spell his last name for me."

"Really?"

"Just a little verification that you're doing what I asked. That's all."

"D-a-v-i-e-s. Not David. Davies."

"Excellent. And where was his father's farm located?"

"Cashmere, Washington. It's east of the Cascades."

"Correct. And what happened to Richard's family when he was nine years old?"

"His father shot his mother three times in front of him and then turned the gun on himself. Richard was doing his homework on the other side of the motel room they were living out of. Police believe that after they lost the family farm his mother's meth addiction became worse and his father forced her to start prostituting herself on Aurora Avenue North. The night of the murder-suicide, Richard told police his father was angry because his mother came home with less than her usual take."

He listens carefully for any sounds of sympathy in Charlotte's voice, but she sounds like she's reciting sports statistics. And when her voice does waver, it seems due to distraction, like she's studying her reflection to see how convincing her costume is.

"It's a sad story," he says.

"A lot of us have sad stories. We don't have to turn them into horror shows."

"Good point."

Charlotte clears her throat, then starts speaking again. At first, Cole's got no idea what she's saying—until she gets to the third name. "Shayla Brown. Deborah Clover. Maryanne Breck. Patrice LaVon. Janelle Cropper. Shouldn't you be asking me about them? Given that, you know, I'm about to become one of them?"

"You're not going to end up like they did."

"Missing, you mean?"

"You know what I mean."

"Still, it might be a good idea to quiz me about the victims instead of trying to figure out if I've developed some sort of identification with a psychotic killer just because we both had shitty childhoods."

He considers arguing with her but decides against it for two reasons. One, he'd then be guilty of the same thing he just gave Ed the boot for doing. Two, she's right.

"Touché," Cole mutters.

"A suggestion from your lead scientist perhaps?"

Cole feels his chest tighten and the pit of his stomach go cold.

"We will never solicit suggestions, tips, or advice of any kind from Noah Turlington when it comes to you and your psychological well-being. And I can assure you, he's not present in this room right now, nor will he ever be."

"Noah, huh?" she says. "Not Dylan?"

"A condition of his reemployment is that he's to use his birth name at all times."

"You call me by the name I picked."

"You've earned the right," Cole says. "He's done quite the opposite."

It never occurred to Cole that Charlotte might assume Noah would be present in the control room. Maybe that explains her quick temper with Ed. Or maybe it's the fact she's about to do something no human being should be able to do, and for the second time in five months.

The baby-faced male tech says, "Her TruGlass feed's coming online."

A few seconds later, a previously dark screen lights up with a jerking point of view on the cargo bay of a container truck that's been soundproofed and carpeted. There are several flashes of darkness—*blinks,* Cole realizes—then a few glimpses of Charley's ground team members scuttling to get out of her eye line. Costume racks flash across the screen, then a vanity and makeup table.

She takes a seat, and a second later, thanks to a prototype on loan to their operation from a family friend, Charlotte Rowe is staring into the mirror—and directly at everyone in the control center—by way of a pair of contact lenses that broadcast crystal-clear images of everything their wearer sees via an encrypted satellite connection.

The costuming job is perfect.

It helps that Charlotte lost fifteen pounds for tonight's perfor-mance, introducing sharp angles to her face that suggest the first stages of a serious drug habit. Her eye makeup's so heavy a john will assume she's trying to hide dark circles or a full-on black eye left by a vicious pimp. But it's what they've done to her hair that Cole finds most striking. He figured they'd opt for some shiny costume wig. Instead, they've thinned out Charlotte's actual hair unevenly and then sprayed it down so that it looks like she's been clawing at her scalp for days and is just now trying to hide it with some cheap hairspray.

Cole's only direction to the ground team was to costume her in keeping with the other missing women. And apparently that's exactly what they've done. Charlotte Rowe, a healthy, fresh-faced twenty-something, has been turned into the kind of haunted, prematurely aging streetwalker you'd see in a grainy black-and-white photo shot by a photojournalist.

"Well?" Charley asks.

"I think we're good," he answers.

As soon as it's out of his mouth, he expects her to make a biting remark about his inappropriate use of the word *good*. Instead, she gives him a thumbs-up, suggesting she considers the two of them teammates.

For now, at least.

"Cole?"

"Yes, Charley."

"How'd you find this guy?"

The same question that encouraged him to kick Ed out of the room.

With her, he doesn't have the same luxury.

"Trust me," Cole says, "he's a bad, bad man."

It takes her a second to grasp the significance of his last four words. They're the same ones Charlotte said to Frederick Pemberton five months earlier, right before she squeezed his right hand hard enough to crush every bone in it.

The stern look she gives him doesn't quite indicate trust.

But it doesn't indicate a desire to quit, either.

6

It's cold out, but Charlotte's grateful for it. She's been practicing the symptoms of drug withdrawal for weeks now. The shivers are the hardest to fake. Now she won't have to.

Her pantyhose are new, but they've got precisely placed runs made by a razor blade, so they do little to protect her legs from the damp chill. The tiny jacket they've put her in—dark denim, stained with cigarette smoke and some dabs of spilled beer—barely covers her lower back, much less her butt.

As for the rest of her outfit, maybe it's a skirt. Maybe it's shorts. Maybe it's that thing they call a skort. She doesn't care, so long as she doesn't stick out from the other women working Aurora Avenue North.

It's not her first time in Seattle. Her father made her do a couple of public appearances here as a girl. But it's her first time in this part of town, a desolate stretch of urban eyesores that prostitutes and law enforcement call a track, a place where motorists can still summon a streetwalker to their car window with a wave.

In this digital-driven era, when sexual connections both legal and not so legal can be made at the press of a button, only the most desperate sex workers still prowl the streets—the ones who move from payment for services rendered to their latest fix with the speed of basketball players crossing a court.

This is the group Richard Davies has been targeting for three years.

Allegedly.

Two blocks away, a short, pear-shaped woman in a similar getup walks hurriedly along the sidewalk, a cheap glittery purse swinging at her hip. Charlotte slows her steps. Right now, she's more afraid of having her cover blown by an encounter with a territorial working girl than she is of Richard Davies.

A plain brown Toyota Camry with tinted windows rolls past her and slows to the curb right next to the woman. The Camry's passenger-side window powers down. The woman turns to it instantly, recognizing a familiar call. Charlotte takes a deep breath.

The brown Camry's just one of several cars she was told to look out for—members of the ground team who will do their best to make sure that by the time Davies rolls up, Charlotte's the only offer available. If they're already at work, that means Davies is close.

She reaches into her purse and takes out the burner phone they gave her. It's set to vibrate and she didn't feel it buzz, but she checks the display just to be sure. It's loaded with a series of fake text messages from a fictional pimp. They're disguised as directions, some of them laced in vague threats that aren't too over the top. None of them is meant to direct her movements yet. Those will be written in an agreed-upon code she's memorized.

where u at? Slow your walk to a stroll.

R u working? Turn right at the next intersection.

Luv u girl, but need u to score. Turn left at the next intersection.

need intel. how's the street? Cross the street immediately.

i'm talking 2 u. Davies's truck is within sight. Stop immediately and hit a sales pose. Visible from the curb. Close to the nearest light source.

why u never listen? Start walking again in the direction you were headed until you get further instructions.

This strategy, combined with ground team members tying up all her competition, is intended to corral her and Davies into the same channel like cows to the slaughter.

Yes, the earpiece would have made it easier, but so what?

The worst thing that can happen tonight is she doesn't get taken.

But if her cover is blown, there's no getting close to him again. If he doesn't abduct her, then she doesn't get to lay eyes on his kill spot. Then she doesn't have proof he's anything other than a creepy asshole. So even if she does get triggered somehow, she won't have cause to go full Zypraxon on him, other than Cole Graydon's assurances that he's a bad, bad man, and how good are those anyway?

Cole's never lied to me, Charlotte tells herself. *Manipulated me. Invaded my privacy. Treated me and the people I love like pawns in a chess game. Withheld information. But Cole's never flat-out lied. Yet.*

The next gust of cold wind brings drizzle that needles her legs.

If the rain starts up again, the microdrones can't operate, and that's not good at all.

There's another gust, dryer than the last one.

That's better.

She puts the burner phone back in her purse, alongside the fake ID for Sara Ann Wakeman, a twenty-six-year-old high school drop-out and meth fan from Clarkston, Washington, who doesn't exist except in Charley's imagination.

Serial killers, for the most part, don't interview their victims. Once they've got you in their clutches, you've become a prop in their sadistic fantasy. They aren't interested in acquiring information about you that will distract them from the sick role they've forced on you. A john, on the other hand, might engage his chosen girl in a little preliminary chitchat. That's why Charlotte had devised an extensive backstory for Sara designed to poke at Richard Davies's psychological pressure points.

Sara's father cramped her style, so she ran away from home after stealing some of his cash. She wants to be an artist; she's always been good with a BeDazzler. Every now and then, when Sara's running low on funds, she calls the old bastard and cries into the phone for twenty minutes until he breaks down and sends her some money. He always caves. What a loser! Men are so *obvious*. Especially dumb dads.

Over the past few weeks, Charlotte's spent as much time researching the history of Washington State and towns like Clarkston and Cashmere as she has the lives of streetwalkers. In her heart, Sara's got a longer story. A deeper, more complex story that put her on the path to victimhood by age seven. But Charley's not out to change Davies's thinking. She's out to stop his killings in their tracks. So, the version she'll present of Sara is shallow and crafted.

Weaponized.

At Cole's request, she wrote up a dossier on her chosen alias— two thousand words, thank you very much!—a day or two after he gave her the file on Davies. For prep, the psychiatrist on Charley's ground team had put her through a dozen interviews about Sara Ann Wakeman's past.

They weren't just interviews. They were rehearsals.

Acting comes naturally to her for someone who'd never spent a day in the high school drama club. God knows, when she was young she had to put on enough performances as the star of her father's traveling carny show about her gruesome past. So many that the first thing she did after she fled to her grandmother's at age sixteen was find ways to work with written words. In privacy and silence. She edited, but never wrote, for her new high school's literary magazine and newspaper, two activities that cut down on her contact with other people and allowed her to use language to make the world seem more orderly and knowable.

But after her grandmother died and she won the lawsuit against her father, giving her a modest portion of the money he made off her when she was a girl, she decided to take a cross-country road trip, alone, to visit the graves of everyone the Bannings had murdered during her time on their farm.

A few days in, she found herself alone in a roadside café in Amarillo, Texas, eating some of the best chicken-fried steak she'd ever tasted, struck by the realization that if she wanted to she could change everything about herself. Not in terms of wealth or her profession—the lawsuit hadn't given her *that* much money—but in terms of how she walked into a room. How she talked. How, in each and every moment, she chose to just *be*.

Should she change her accent?

Should she glare back at strange men instead of turning away from their unwanted attention?

Should she laugh uproariously when she thought a joke was funny instead of biting back her guffaws for fear of drawing too much attention to herself?

It suddenly had felt as if her entire identity was composed of choices meant to please or repel the people who'd been in her life. And who was left? Her grandmother was dead. Her only close friend was the lawyer who'd won her lawsuit against her dad. And she'd given herself a new name meant to protect her from the Bannings' obsessed fans.

If she was free to roam, maybe she was also free to pretend.

And so, when the waitress brought her bill that afternoon, Charlotte became Sammy, a college student from UCLA who'd dropped out to move in with her boyfriend in Miami and was maybe going to work with animals because she really loved dogs and cats but probably dogs more if she had to make a choice.

God, it had felt good. Like scratching an itch. Finally, she was someone whose past wasn't draped in murder and loss.

At a Cracker Barrel in Lubbock, Texas, she donned a New York accent and explained to the family seated next to her how her parents had money and they'd bought her a car and told her to go on a road trip through the South because she was turning into one of those Northeast bigots who thought everyone south of Kentucky was an inbred fool. The family was from Dallas, so their eyes lit up as she described what they clearly thought was a worthwhile venture. They even offered to buy their new friend, Heidi, some dessert. Heidi declined. That would be taking things a little too far. She wasn't out to swindle people.

Charlotte told herself these tissues of lies were the only way to discover who she truly was underneath. After a week of pretending to be someone else to strangers, she was confident the fundamentals of her character would pull back against the fake accents and the made-up stories, revealing who she was meant to become before her mother was slaughtered and her life derailed.

She's never been a drinker, but she imagines that the joy and freedom she felt during those few days of lying to waiters, waitresses, and other road trippers were similar to what an alcoholic feels while they're on a good run.

There were no rules, no limits. Along the way, she realized that most of what she'd done from moment to moment throughout her life was just a habit that could be unchosen with enough forethought.

But the insight she craved never came.

The true Trina Pierce, or Charlotte Rowe, or Burning Girl, wasn't finally coaxed out of hiding by all the lies, demanding to be seen and recognized once and for all. Worse, Charley could no longer ignore that most of the anecdotes and pieces of trivia she'd used to construct her false identities had come from her grandmother's close circle of friends back in Altamira, California, the same ones she'd abandoned because just a glimpse of them around town made her smell her grandmother's perfume.

By the time she'd reached New Orleans, the first stop in her gravesite tour, she was overcome by a sense of loneliness so acute, she pulled over to the side of the road and wept for the first time since Grandma Luanne's funeral. Maybe it was just guilt over having lied to so many people. Or maybe what she'd really coaxed to the surface was her grief for her grandmother, still raw and beating like a second heart a year after the remarkable woman's death.

She's not that lonely anymore, thank God.

One of the unexpected perks of Dylan Cody's—*Noah Turlington's*—deception was that it drove her back into the bosom of the only place she'd ever considered a hometown.

That's where she reunited with Luke Prescott.

A different, better version of Luke than the one she knew in high school.

But thinking of Luke now isn't a comfort. It only reminds her of how close he was the last time she did something like this. This time, having him nearby wasn't an option. This time he had to stay in Altamira while she prepped and practiced and waited for Davies to escalate. Cole made that clear. And she didn't fight him on it.

Maybe she should have. Despite the number of people currently monitoring her every move, she feels surprisingly alone.

She's got a dozen unwritten text messages to Luke floating around in her head still. Right before she stepped from the back of the transport truck, she almost broke down and sent him one. But her support team would have seen, and then they would have reported it. And besides, she and Luke made an agreement before she shipped out: If she did get in touch, he'd only want to ask questions she couldn't answer. *How was she* would lead to *where was she*, which would careen into *how much longer*. Why put themselves through that torture? No communication was better, they agreed.

It doesn't feel that way now.

She's afraid. Not of dying, but of what she'll see when she enters the belly of the beast. And she's afraid of what will happen to her sanity in the long run since she's barred from talking about any of it with Luke once she's home.

The phone buzzes in her purse.

i'm talking 2 u.

She almost curses.

Instead, she starts for the nearest lamppost, turns to face the street, and leans against it.

A glance to her right. No sign of the pear-shaped woman or the brown Camry.

She returns her attention to the street, and that's when she spots Richard Davies's brown pickup truck headed straight for her. The headlights blind her for an instant, then she can see again.

The truck's slowing down.

7

Richard can't get a good look at the girl until he powers the driver's side window down. That's when she uncrosses her arms and steps forward.

She's too young, he thinks. Not a kid. He wouldn't even pull over for a kid. She's just not the age of his usual prey. Not as broken down.

"How yah doing, mister?" There's a defiant tone in her voice, and her expression's searching and a little hard.

Not nearly as desperate as what he's used to.

Not like Mom. But before this little whisper in his ear can make his stomach swim with sickness, another one answers it. *More like Stephanie. She thinks she's too good to be out here. Too good for you. That's interesting.*

"I'm good," he answers. "How you doing?"

"All right. It's kinda cold out. What you looking for?"

"Nothing complicated. Car stuff."

She steps closer, leans her head in through the window. "I don't know much about cars, but I'm willing to learn about you, handsome."

Oh, you'll learn, bitch.

"How's whatever fifty bucks'll get me sound?"

She takes her time considering this. She probably wants to charge more. Probably thinks she's worth it, but she's reconsidering because he's not twenty pounds overweight and doesn't reek of body odor. "Oh, it'll get you something good," she says with a smile that looks more genuine than the last one.

"You need some of it now?" he asks, playing the part of the good, honest, decent john.

"Nah. Payment for services rendered's just fine."

"You need to see it?"

"You seem like a reliable guy."

He unlocks the doors. "Hop in."

She does. When he takes his foot off the brake, the nerves in his legs are tingling with excitement, and there's a stirring in his groin similar to the one he felt when Stephanie handled his wallet. "You new around here?"

"Kinda. Yeah."

"Where you from?"

"Far enough away." She turns and gives him a grin. He can't tell if she's telling him to mind his own business or trying to pass herself off as some kind of free spirit. "Dad kinda cramped my style, you know?"

"How's that?"

"Just . . . bullshit. Expectations. That kind of thing. I mean, he's some fucking dirt farmer. What does he know about *life*?"

A lot more than you do, you stupid little whore.

"Dads can be a pain," he says.

"You're telling me. But it helps if they've got a bad hiding place for their cash, if you know what I mean. Helps you get the hell away from 'em."

He tries not to grit his teeth. He does it sometimes when he's angry and sometimes when he's excited. One time he even cracked one.

"How 'bout over here?" he asks, pointing to the alleyway up ahead.

"Whatever's clever, handsome."

8

Cole's feeling a sudden burst of performance anxiety so strong he might as well be the one inside Richard Davies's pickup. Then he notices something on the screen monitoring Charley's vital signs. "Why is her pulse dropping?"

"It's not abnormal." The tech who answers, the balding one with the fine-boned face, hasn't said anything up until now, probably because his work just started a little while ago. He's in charge of monitoring Charley's vital signs, and out of some show of respect for her privacy, they kept that particular monitor dark until she stepped out from the back of the transport truck.

"She just got in a car with a serial killer. I'd say a *drop* in heart rate's pretty abnormal. Give me her blood ox."

The balding tech nods, taps keys on his computer. The boxes displaying Charley's vitals shift and change size so her blood oxygen reading can pop out to dominate the lower left quadrant.

96%, it proclaims in Day-Glo orange.

Normal, especially when Cole considers what it might reach before the night's over.

Blood trackers have been circulating through Charlotte's body for months. To the control center and to a central lab facility farther away, they transmit a constant stream of data about almost every chemical interaction happening in her bloodstream. Protein levels, white and red blood cell counts, you name it. The second any of her levels become abnormal outside of a testing period, Cole gets an immediate call from the lab.

Someday this kind of technology will be implanted in anyone who can afford it, alerting them to see a doctor the minute they show even the slightest sign of heart attack, stroke, or generalized pathology.

For now, no one can afford it. Except Cole, which is why he injected it into Charley a few months before. So far, the data compiled has proved one remarkable fact again and again—Charlotte's body remains unchanged even after multiple exposures to Zypraxon.

"She's breathing deeply," the med tech says.

"Yeah, I figured."

"No, I mean she's making an effort to. It's not her usual pattern. It's almost . . . meditative."

"She's meditating. In a car. With a serial killer."

"So she can stay focused maybe?" The female tech speaks more confidently now that Ed's out of the room.

Charley's trying not to trigger, Cole realizes, and a chill goes through him.

She's alone in a car with a psychopath, and she's got something in her veins that allows her to tear through five boa constrictors at once with her bare hands, but she's making sure not to use it until the time is right. The last time Charlotte did something like this, she got so caught up in her strategy for hooking a killer she forgot the most important thing she needed to do—be afraid. Frederick Pemberton had knocked her unconscious before he could scare Zypraxon into working its magic. Now, Charlotte's trying to re-create her old mistake for a very simple reason: she doesn't want to burn up her three hours of Zypraxon time before she gets to Davies's kill site.

For maybe the hundredth time in the past few months, Cole thinks, *You really are something, Burning Girl.* Even though he'd never use that dreaded nickname to her face.

The microphone they implanted in Richard Davies's steering column is giving pretty decent audio. But he asks them to check it anyway. The connection's good.

Davies and Charley aren't saying anything.

Good, Cole thinks. *Breathe, Charley. Just breathe.*

Davies turns the truck into an alleyway.

The truck slows to a stop, but the engine's still running.

On the TruGlass feed, Cole watches the truck's headlights wink out.

"How's this?" he hears Davies ask.

Davies appears on the monitor. A dark shadow, one side of his angular face fringed by a distant streetlight.

"Yeah," he hears her say.

Davies makes a subtle jerk of the head.

A nod, really.

A gesture.

Directed at his crotch.

The TruGlass feed jerks slightly, then it begins to slide down Davies's shadowy torso.

It's so quiet inside the control center suddenly, Cole's sure he can hear the earth settling outside the room's subterranean walls. The female tech lowers her gaze from the displays overhead to the monitor in front of her—just stats and metrics for all the surveillance devices involved in tonight's op. She's looking away without looking away.

Cole wishes he could do the same.

He wanted to talk about this part with Charlotte. Come up with some sort of game plan. But Charlotte refused. *We need an abduction,* she'd said. *I'll do whatever gets us there.*

9

Shayla Brown's mother used to collect Beanie Babies.

She died when Shayla was seven, Charlotte remembers, leaving Shayla only some credit card debt and her collection of big-eyed stuffed animals. Right after the newly minted orphan moved in with her aunt Margot, her only living relative, Margot installed some shelves right next to Shayla's new bed so the girl's tiny inheritance could watch over her while she slept.

On the one-year anniversary of her last phone call from Shayla, Margot posted a picture of the stuffed animals on her Facebook page alongside a school photo of her niece taken when the girl was fifteen, a year before she shot heroin for the first time and became hopelessly lost to everyone who loved her.

Charlotte runs these details about Davies's first alleged victim through her brain again and again as she undoes the top buttons of his plaid shirt with her teeth. She's not just trying to delay the inevitable; she wants to frustrate him so he accelerates the proceedings.

Maybe he makes his girls blow him, but she doubts it. A killer as methodical as he is, she can't see him wasting a bunch of time in this dark alley. And she can't see him getting off on something as simple as a blow job.

He grips the back of her head and pushes her gently toward his crotch. But he hasn't unzipped his jeans. That's her job, apparently.

She breathes deeply.

There's no tingle in her skin.

No tremor deep within her.

No bone music—the sure and unmistakable sign that the Zypraxon in her system's been triggered.

She unbuttons his jeans.

Janelle Cropper was a C student. But she'd memorized the name of every type of bird that passed through her uncle's neighborhood. She'd bird-watch from the front window of his house outside Portland for hours on end while her mother turned tricks. Until she became old enough to fight off her uncle when he'd come to her bedroom drunk. Around then, her uncle made it clear she couldn't live there anymore. That was the last time any of Janelle's friends ever saw her. When they were interviewed by the local paper for a piece after her disappearance, they all agreed they hoped she was watching birds, this time in peace. But to the reporter writing the piece, Janelle was just another local girl lost to drug addiction, not the victim of a serial killer.

Shayla. Janelle. Maryanne. Patrice. Deborah.

Their stories are all similar. Broken homes. Guardians turned abusers. Heavy drugs before they're out of high school. The same barrage of spirit-breaking obstacles before adolescence that only a detached and suspiciously self-satisfied observer would consider easily overcome.

Charlotte says their names to herself, remembers the smiles in their old childhood photos. Then she unzips Richard Davies's jeans, releasing a little swell of boxer shorts underneath. Just then, Davies's grip on the back of her head tightens. But he doesn't force her face into his crotch. It's a different pressure. Like he's steadying himself. Keeping his balance while his other hand . . .

Sensing what comes next, she forces herself to take a deep, slow breath through her nostrils.

Then she hears a quick, sharp sound like a tiny car whizzing past on a miniature highway. Her right calf explodes with pain. It's some sort of tranquilizer dart. He's fired it into her leg. She doesn't feel bone music in response. Doesn't feel anything like a trigger event caused by this sudden, fierce stinging impact.

She controlled it. She's proud of herself. And even though she's the one going limp, the last thought Charlotte has before darkness closes in around her like a shroud is, *Got you, fucker.*

10

"What was that?" the tomboyish tech whispers.

"Tranquilizer dart," Cole hears himself say.

He knows the sound well. Remembers the insectile concert they made as they went whizzing one after the other into Project Bluebird's first test subjects, whereupon they did absolutely nothing to stop those Zypraxon-filled trained killers from chewing on their own hands like they were fried chicken breasts.

He closes his eyes, forces himself to focus.

The TruGlass feed's gone dark, indicating that Charley's eyes are shut, but a human tail is crouched at each mouth of the alley. Their shoulder cams have night vision, but the microdrones don't, so the overhead angles make Davies's pickup look like a mood-lit art piece surrounded by a sea of oil. Parked in the shadows of the surrounding block is enough firepower to start a small siege—stationary green blips on the GPS map that's also tracking Davies's truck.

Baby-Faced Nerd Boy's in charge of the camera feeds. He's alternating between the two shoulder cams until Davies pops out of the driver's side of the truck, holding a hog-tied Charlotte in his arms. Nerd Boy switches to the rear view because the truck's closer to it.

Silently, they all watch Davies place Charley in the cargo bay, then snap its cover shut over her as though he's transporting a bag full of newspapers he doesn't want to blow away.

"Blood ox is still ninety-six," the white, balding med tech says. "Pulse rate's dropping."

"I can see her vitals, thank you," Cole says.

"Ground tail wants to know if they should respond," the only female of the group says.

"To *what*?" Cole snaps. "We've got an abduction. And right on schedule."

The med tech says, "Pulse rate's still dropping, consistent with a sedative."

"I can see her vitals. Thank you."

"She's *not* triggered." It sounds like the med tech's speaking through clenched teeth. At least he didn't turn and shoot Cole an accusing look.

"I know. That's how she wants it."

"Seriously?" asks the baby-faced nerd.

So I've got the whole peanut gallery to answer to now, Cole thinks. *Well, fine, maybe they'll learn to listen to me, and not just Ed.*

"Yes. That's what the breathing was about. She doesn't want to burn up her Zypraxon time pretending to be passed out in the trunk of his car. She wants to get to his kill site first."

Davies's truck starts forward, headed for the opposite end of the alleyway.

The microdrones lurch, then follow its path.

"All right, follow positions. Alert the team outside his farm. Once he leaves the city, the microdrones are useless because we won't have enough light sources. Put your focus on the tracker inside his truck and our ground tails." The female tech begins quietly relaying Cole's instructions to everyone listening on the other end. "And remind the ground tails they can't go up the mountain. The road's too isolated. They'll stick out."

She mutters into her mic, then turns to face Cole for the first time. "They'd like me to remind you they're skilled in evasive and surveillance driving and they'd—"

"I don't care!"

She bows her head, clears her throat, and turns to face her computer again. For a few seconds, all he can hear in the room is their collective heavy breathing and a low mutter of radio traffic from the ground teams muffled by the techs' headsets.

"Look," Cole says, steadying himself. "I know this is not like anything you've ever done before. But we've got enough men and firepower to pull her out at a second's notice if it goes wrong. So I need everyone to take a deep breath and stay objective. This is a field test, and nothing more. Got it? It's a field test."

"Got it," the baby-faced nerd says.

But the woman and the med tech just nod.

They're not calmed, Cole can tell. And that should be his job, shouldn't it?

"Names," he says.

The med tech looks at him for the first time.

Baby-Faced Nerd Boy follows suit.

"Tran," the woman says without turning. "Shannon Tran."

"Where are you from?"

"Stockton, California."

Cole locks eyes with the baby-faced nerd, realizing that the guy's actually pretty cute. If they ran into each other at a hotel bar and the guy did something outwardly gay—whatever that is these days—Cole just might buy him a drink. "Tim Zadan. I was born in Stockholm, but we moved to Boston when I was four."

"Love Boston," Cole says. "Don't love the winters, but love the town."

"Uh-huh," Tim says, then turns his attention back to the camera feeds.

Cole finds the med tech staring at him.

"Why are we doing this?" the tech asks.

"Because pretty soon I was going to start calling you guys by nicknames, and I don't want to sound . . . impolite."

Smart as you guys are, you're all about to freak and I can't have that, so play along, nerd.

"But we're not supposed to—"

"I know what Ed said, but he's not here. What's your name, friend?"

"Paul Hynman. South Carolina, mostly. Then San Diego. Then Virginia."

"Military family?"

Paul nods.

"Great."

"Not really," Paul says. "I switched schools every five minutes."

"Seems like you turned out OK."

Paul Hynman just glares at Cole as if whatever set of circumstances landed him in this secret subterranean room taking orders from Cole doesn't exactly qualify as OK.

Serves me right, Cole thinks, *expecting to chitchat with some science geeks.*

When all three of them return their attention to their computers, Cole's quietly relieved.

He looks at the feed from the ground tail's shoulder cam, and the relief leaves him instantly. The feed is shaky and occasionally blurry. Without the microdrones and their godlike view of everything that happens below, Cole now feels as if he's sealed up in the back of Davies's pickup right beside Charley.

11

Maybe she'll try climbing a tree like the second one did, Richard thinks, *or maybe she'll start begging for her life like the fourth.*

This is his favorite part—when he's safely perched inside the deer blind, waiting for his prey to regain consciousness and find herself lost in a sea of shadows and thick forest. Even better, tonight he's got snow and ice to play with. That's why he took off her shoes before stringing her bound wrists to a tree branch about six and a half feet off the ground.

Once, only once, did one of his prey undergo a startling, admirable metamorphosis upon waking up and realizing how fucked she was. One minute she was shuffling and disoriented and confused. The next, she tore off a branch the size of her arm and used it to beat a path through the darkness as if she expected a bear to explode from underneath a nearby bush and was ready to fight it to the death. That was the same one who tried to keep climbing the fence even after she realized it was electrified at a strength that could stun a cow.

That wasn't pretty.

But he doesn't bring them here to make them *pretty*; he brings them here so they can have a chance to find some deep reservoir of inner strength before he removes their sickness from the world.

What will this one find within herself?

Will she cry out for the daddy she betrayed?

Richard watches her through night vision googles as she sways gently in the frigid winds. It's another world at this altitude, which is how he's always liked it. Any spot where the earth kisses the clouds is a special place, a place where primal truths reveal themselves to those who've acquired the wisdom of solitude.

The course he's built is as big as he can make it, though it's barely an acre. But when you're having trouble seeing, it might as well be the Hundred Acre Wood. It's full of holes and baited with bad hiding places. The deer blind's not that well camouflaged, and most of them are able to make it out after a few minutes, which is how he likes it. And then there are the traps.

The first time he practically lined the fence with them. But upon reflection, it didn't seem like the makings of a fair fight, so he'd knocked it down to three. One is close to the string-up spot, its placement a reward for the prey who doesn't panic the minute she wakes and start running in mad circles. The ones who take their time to get a sense of their surroundings, to let their eyes adjust to the dark.

The other's close to the farthest section of fence, designed to punish the bitch who foolishly assumes escape is an option and just starts running for her life. And the third's right in front of the deer blind, should she be stupid enough to try to approach him directly.

His favorites are the ones who try to hide.

Because he likes finding them.

Which one will this one be?

Young and confident, skin firm like Stephanie's.

She might be a fighter.

She might be . . .

She's awake, he realizes.

He almost missed it. A few seconds before, she was swaying in full forty-five-degree rotations, her torso and face coming into view. Now her movement's been reduced by half. Probably because she's tensed her right forefoot so it creates a little drag on the snow. Awake, and trying to get her bearings, without letting him know it.

That's a new one, he thinks.

12

Charlotte can see the bear trap. The giant steel jaws have a subtle glint in the branch-filtered moonlight. Maybe they're fringed with ice. She can't tell.

She figures the placement's designed to punish a victim careless enough to lean against the tree trunk in an attempt to catch her breath.

She focuses on it, hoping the sight will flood her system with fear. It's not working. All she feels is silent, quivering rage.

Anger's not enough to make bone music. What she needs is stark terror. A sudden shock.

And that's not as easy to come by when she knows trained mercenaries are perched in the woods nearby watching her every move.

Davies hasn't tied her wrists tightly; she can get free if she wants. And he'd love her to try, she's sure. He wants her to run, beg, suffer.

But what she needs is something that will trigger a sense of powerlessness so total it unleashes Zypraxon's impossible power.

I know too much, she realizes. *I let Cole tell me too much about the operation, about how safe I am, about how nothing could go wrong. And now, something actually is wrong. I'm too safe. Too protected. I need . . .*

"I see you, lady," Richard says from somewhere in the shadows behind her. "Not moving much anymore, are you? Don't be looking for a way out 'cause there isn't one. This is gonna be about you digging deep and finding out what you're really made of. And if you're lucky, you'll find something stronger and better than you've ever been."

"How many?" she asks.

"What?"

"How many women have you done this to?"

He lets out a small, self-satisfied laugh. "I don't get interviewed by whores, sweetie. How about you focus on what you're gonna do next?"

She manages to wriggle her wrists free from her restraints. The loose coil of rope smacks to the snow right as her knees do. There's a vague structure nearby, some sort of hunting blind. It must be where his voice is coming from.

They all went through this. Trapped in the middle of nowhere, a psychopath addressing them from the shadows like they were feeble children. But the thought brings no terror. Just more anger.

Only a split second separates the puff of air above her head and the deafening crack of the rifle shot. Gooseflesh coats her skin. Has she been triggered? But it passes, leaving a ringing in her ears and a body that feels woefully normal, nothing like the bass beat deep inside her bones that tells her Zypraxon's in full bloom.

Does he always fire a warning shot? Maybe it's his way of showing them what a good hunter he is. Or maybe she pissed him off.

"I'll give you a three-minute head start. Then it gets serious."

The way she can see it, there are two strategies.

One: piss him off and see if he'll fire closer, if not right into her leg. They've got lab tests galore to prove that a sudden shock on the order of a bullet wound would be more than enough to trigger her. But the wound itself is another story. If it's bad enough, if it strikes an artery, wreaking untold havoc inside her in the seconds before Zypraxon's unleashed, there's no telling whether the drug will heal the initial damage fast enough for her to recover in time to keep fighting.

The second option's more of a sure thing, but it's more frightening.

"*Three minutes*, you fucking whore!" he shouts. "Three minutes and then we find out if you're worth anything underneath that sack of flesh you've been selling."

Charlotte gets to her feet and runs. She's not sure if the bear trap she spotted earlier is out of his sight line or not. Either way, there's no hesitating. As she nears it, she's hoping the prospect of what she has to do next will trigger her, but it doesn't. So she runs right up to the trap and sticks her foot into the middle of it.

13

Richard hears a sound like a giant guitar string getting plucked.

What doesn't come next is the harsh metallic clang of the jaws snapping shut against each other like they do when he tests the thing with a plank. Instead, there's a soft thud that tells him the trap's caught flesh and bone.

The woman lets out a high-pitched grunt.

But that's all.

No gasping. No shrieking. No begging for mercy.

He squints into his night vision goggles.

Probably best that she hit the thing right away, he thinks, *given what a mouthy little bitch she turned out to be. Teach her some humility. But shouldn't she be screaming at least?*

Just silence and the thick rustle of ice-clotted tree branches in the cold wind.

He scans the darkness. There's no sign of her. She's got to be lying flat. There are enough gaps in the foliage that if she were trying to make a run for it, even crawling on all fours, he'd catch a glimpse of her after a few seconds. But he's not.

So she's pressed to the ground, either dead or knocked out from the pain. That would be a new one. Knocked out from the pain, that one he'd believe.

Killed by the trap alone? Doubtful.

Amid these thoughts, he's feeling something he's never felt before during a hunt. Confusion. More than that, he realizes.

Fear. A sense that for the first time in his hunting grounds that something is . . . not right.

And now he's hearing his father's voice, tone shaking with anger the way it always did when he had to tell Richard something the boy needed to hear. Telling him he should have listened to his instincts when he first laid eyes on her—too young, too arrogant. Too much like pretty Stephanie of the Seattle Leather Company. And now he's feeling strangely shamed and small and—

Jesus Christ. I gotta go wake this bitch up or this is gonna be no fun at all.

"So, girlie," he says as soon as his boots hit the earth. "Let me explain something to you about how this works. There's no escape, really. I mean, I might have fun letting you try, but you won't, so why not try listening for once?"

He raises the Weatherby Mark V so the rifle acts like a boat's prow as he pushes through the branches. He's cut back most of the really low foliage, but there are still a few branches at eye level and he doesn't want them slapping the night vision goggles and amplifying their screwy effect on his depth perception.

"If you just go on and accept what this is gonna be, then maybe you'll learn a few things about—"

What he sees next he assumes is a trick of the night vision's green flare. For starters, the bear trap's not only empty, it's broken. His mind has trouble wrapping around the word, but there's no other word for it. The thing must have misfired and come apart. But if that's the case, why is one entire jaw missing?

"Hey, fuckhead."

He spins so fast the goggles jostle. His vision's gone hazy, crooked. Is he hallucinating? If so, there's no time to process it, because the woman says, "Catch!"

There's no sound, but the force that explodes in his left shoulder feels as powerful as a rifle blast. For a second, he thinks he shot himself. But that's impossible. He's still holding the rifle aimed straight in front of him.

Fiery pain shoots up the left side of his neck and coats his chest. He's been hurled backward several feet. Whatever projectile the woman just threw at him pierced him with enough force to pin him to the tree trunk behind him. And there was only one thing out here the bitch could have hit him with—the bear trap's missing jaw. But that's impossible. The whole thing's fucking impossible.

He tries to move. He can't. He's pinned to the tree.

Through me, he realizes. *Straight fucking through me. Whatever she just threw, it went straight through me and pinned me to the goddamn tree.*

Too late, he realizes he's completely forgotten about the rifle in his grip, that he's even raising his left hand to reach for whatever's torn through his left shoulder. That's when there's a deafening explosion followed by a burst of pain in his right foot so intense piss warms his underwear. And that's when Richard Davies realizes he literally just shot himself in the foot.

The next thing he feels is the gentle tug of the woman pulling off his night vision googles, followed by a soft thud when she tosses them to the ground.

14

If any of the techs doubted the momentousness of tonight's test, those doubts probably evaporated as soon as Charlotte Rowe used a single overhand throw to send one jaw of the bear trap shooting through the air with the speed and precision of a tennis ball fired out of a practice machine.

Cole feels as gratified by the stunned expressions on their faces as he is by Charlotte's sudden transformation.

Shannon Tran says, "Ground team would like to know if—"

"Not yet," Cole answers. "Let her play."

15

Charlotte sinks to a crouch several feet from Davies as he tries to suck breath through snotty nostrils.

She's waiting patiently for him to look up from the shattered stump of gore that used to be his right foot. If she has to, she'll wait all night.

Zypraxon doesn't trigger mood changes. It doesn't remove remorse or accountability. Anything she feels in this moment comes from her true self, so her delight in his condition is her responsibility, and if she leans too far into the feeling, whatever she does next will be her responsibility as well.

"I'm disappointed in you, Richard."

"Wh-whut are you, you *fuck* . . . you *fucking* bit—"

"I guess I'd hoped for more. I guess I thought you'd learn something about yourself when I took your toys away. Discover who you really are inside the sack of flesh, or whatever bullshit you just shouted at me while you were safe in your little hunting blind and I was out here freezing to death."

She has his full attention now. He looks doped up suddenly, like he's going numb from blood loss.

"Oh, wait," she says, "silly me. This *is* who you really are. A whiny crybaby who can't fight for shit the minute he loses his weapons."

He's shivering, so maybe the stony expression is a ruse. She can't see much blood where the bear trap's pinned him to the trunk, but the foot's another story. If she had to guess, the blood's flowing fast and free enough that he might not survive the cleanup operation Cole's planned.

"How many?" she asks.

"I'm dead."

"Excuse me?"

"I died, didn't I? Been dead all day. Everything's . . . wrong. Everything about you was wrong. Shoulda never picked you up. But you found me, didn't you? 'Cause I'm d-dead and that's how you found me, 'cause you think you some kinda angel but really you're just a demon bitch."

"That would make this hell, Richard."

"I'd believe it. How else would you know my name?"

"How many people have you killed?"

"You think I'm gonna answer to you?"

Charlotte stands and snaps a branch the thickness of her arm from a nearby tree with one hand. She snaps it in two, then clears the twigs from both halves with a single quick slide of her fist. Both motions sound like popcorn popping in a microwave. If that wasn't enough to frighten Davies into compliance, she takes both broken halves of the branch and begins rubbing them together. She's practiced this move countless times in the lab but never out in the frigid air like this. She did a version of it the second time she was triggered, only she used steel rebar and the goal was to create sparks, not flame. Now, both ends of the branches are glowing; then the embers turn to flames.

Goggle-eyed, jaw slack, and spilling drool, Davies looks up into the fire.

"How many women have you killed?" she asks.

"Five," he says. "Was gonna be six."

"Yeah, well, I'm not what you expected, am I?"

"I ain't talking about you."

"Who are you talking about, Richard?"

Davies's leering, drooling mouth crooks into something close to a grin.

She holds one torch close to his face, blows the other out with a puff of breath strong enough to rattle the branches nearby.

"I said *who* are you talking about?"

It's a slight gesture, maybe the best he can do. He nods in the direction of the woods behind her. *Was* going to be six. *Was*. Which means . . . Memories from five months ago assault her as viciously as the bear trap did. There'd been some hope that she could rescue the captive Frederick Pemberton was holding, but they'd been too late, and the images that greeted her inside his walk-in freezer would never leave her. But now . . .

If she'd been wearing the earpiece, no doubt Cole would have ordered the ground teams to move in as soon as he heard Davies mention anything like a captive. But TruGlass offers no audio, and since no one's bursting through the trees behind her, they've got no mics planted in the area. In short, they've got no damn idea what Davies just told her. The plan was for her to confirm his kill site, then locate evidence linking him to the other murders, not just the attempt on her. Once she did both, Cole would order the ground teams in so they could move her out and drug Davies within an inch of insanity. That way, he'd look and act like a babbling fool by the time the authorities arrived and discovered him badly injured, paces from gruesome evidence of his long murder spree.

But a live captive? This changes everything. Cole will insist on leaving her where she is for the police to rescue, she's sure. He certainly won't want anyone else seeing what Charlotte can do.

Which means who knows how many more hours of terror for the poor woman. Of darkness. Of anticipating further torture. A fate just like the one suffered by her mother before Abigail Banning cut her throat.

Yeah, I don't think so.

"Promise not to move?" she asks.

"Fuck you, demon bitch."

Charlotte reaches out and presses ever so gently against the exposed tines of the bear trap jaw; it's enough force to drive it deeper into the tree trunk behind him. In response, Davies moans like a frightened cow.

"Where is she?"

Davies mumbles something inaudible amid his groans. She drives the flaming end of the torch into the earth, right in front of his crotch. He cries out, then realizes she's suffocated the flame.

"Where is she?" She's eye to eye with him.

"T-tannery . . . by the house. Not the barn. Far-farther away. She's in the cellar."

When she starts digging inside the flaps of his waffle-print coat, he lets out a series of stuttering whines. "Be still or you'll hurt yourself," she says.

She doesn't find a key ring in his pockets; instead she finds it attached to a hook on his belt. With a slight tug, she pulls the entire hook free.

She's on her feet now, running past the deer blind. After another minute or two, she comes to an access gate in the electric fence. She rips the cover off the power box, revealing a switch. She's had extensive lab practice on performing small, everyday maneuvers after a trigger. So far, it's proven to take a mixture of deep breathing and visualization. *Thread the needle, thread the needle, thread the needle.* It works, and she's able to cut the power to the fence with a gentle flick of the wrist that doesn't tear the switch plate in half.

The woods beyond the fence are much thinner than inside Davies's hunting ground. After a few minutes, she spots his house, which allows her to orient herself on the map she memorized. The property isn't technically a farm, even though that was the shorthand Cole used for it; the region's too sloping and mountainous to allow him to seed anything beyond a few winter-stripped vegetable gardens and a greenhouse that looks far too exposed to contain the implements of murder.

As she runs toward the tannery—a converted garage—she feels a slight sense of alarm that she's put so much distance between herself and Davies so quickly, but the words that keep thrumming through her head are, *Not another minute. If he's got a woman held captive, she's not living in terror another goddamn minute.*

The worst that could happen is that Cole's men might come streaming out of the woods to intervene before she can reach the captive. Which, in the end, wouldn't be so bad.

The tannery's got a padlock. As much as she wants to tear it off, that'll look suspicious to the authorities, so she takes the time to find the right key, and when she does, she pushes the door open into shadows.

She's reaching for the light switch when she hears a small, sharp click. It's answered by a flashing red light somewhere deep within the darkness before her. There's another sound, more distant.

Laughter, she realizes. *From out there. Richard Davies is laughing at—*

The deep, heavy thump she hears next reminds her of the time she was driving on the freeway in a rainstorm behind an eighteen-wheeler toting two decks of automobiles, and a strong wind blew into the plastic wrap enshrouding the cars with enough force to punch a giant hole through the other side.

Then, in the instant before fire comes roaring toward her, Charlotte feels something she's never felt on Zypraxon before.

Terror.

16

It sounded like everyone inside the control center screamed at once, but only two of them are on their feet now: Cole and the med tech, whose name he's already forgotten.

He should have known something was wrong the minute he saw Davies shaking with laughter on the ground team's shoulder cams. But he figured the sick fuck was just losing his mind, and how could that be a bad thing given their cleanup plan?

Then came the explosion—fierce and white hot. Chemical, Cole realizes.

Rigged.

Now they're watching the roof of the tannery tumble back down to earth in a fiery cascade.

Whatever happened, Davies sent Charley into a trap, and for some reason, she fell for it.

Where is she?

Even though he's so far away that Charley was previously just a tiny figure inside his shoulder-mounted cam, the sniper who's been watching over her is knocked backward a few feet by the explosion. He manages not to lose his balance. His shoulder cam holds a fairly consistent angle on the burning tannery and the pieces of wall that went flying out from the blast.

But there's something that didn't come flying out from the blast. Charley.

A second later, it appears that the fire consuming the tannery's remains has intensified. Then Cole realizes that's not quite right.

Part of the fire is walking toward them.

Upright. Steady. Not flailing or weaving or running in panicked circles.

"Jesus fucking Christ," the med tech whispers.

And that's when Cole sees Charlotte's vital signs. Her blood ox is 200 percent, normal for a trigger zone. Her heart rate is 250 beats per minute, also normal for a trigger zone.

Normal for the abnormal, Cole thinks.

And that's what's not normal.

Whatever explosives were rigged to blow inside the tannery, they were powerful. So powerful she should have at least lost consciousness, or been blown backward off her feet in the direction of her tail. But instead, she's fully consumed by flame and walking a steady path out from the tannery's perforated, burning shell.

If she's regenerating on the spot, it's impossible to make it out on the night vision tail cam. The flames have made it something akin to an old 1980s video camera angled at a nest of bright lights; it's all a smear of white.

For a second, Cole thinks everything might be all right and that they've just completed a test of Zypraxon's power they would have been far too frightened to try inside a lab.

Then Charlotte, still burning, collapses to all fours.

II

17

There are little indications along the way that it's a dream.

The steps to the beach aren't as steep or jagged as they are in real life. The crescent of mud-colored sand at the bottom looks deeper and wider than it did the last time she visited. But Bayard Rock's still off-shore like always, the same lumpy obelisk of stone that she's gazed at meditatively on countless afternoons. Whitecaps are breaking across its western face, collapsing into something that resembles beer foam as it gurgles toward shore.

This is a dream or a memory or something in between.

It feels like she could wake herself up if she wanted.

But she doesn't want to because Luanne is there.

Her grandmother walks several paces ahead of her, the ocean wind threatening to whip her mane of straw-colored hair free from its loose ponytail.

When Luanne glances back and smiles, Charlotte sees she's the same age as when Charlotte moved in with her as a teenager. That was the moment in time when their faces looked most alike—softened by the same curves, the same baby fat–padded cheeks that offset that sometimes hard glint in their narrow eyes, the same small button nose Luanne passed to her daughter, who in turn passed it to Charlotte.

The next thing Charlotte knows, they're sitting together on an expanse of coastal rock that has the quality of cooled magma. Glistening tide pools surround them. Luanne has a pail next to her for sand dollars and seashells.

Just over her grandmother's shoulder, she can make out the promontory where the new resort is taking shape, a resort that wasn't even an idea back when her grandmother was alive. A resort now being funded by Graydon Pharmaceuticals as a show of exactly what, she's not sure. When they first bought the abandoned property, Charlotte thought they were trying to frighten her, raise a monument to their dizzying financial power and relentless surveillance right in her backyard. Now it seems more like compensation.

These thoughts, this recognition that the long dead and the brand new are colliding in her mind, are bringing her dangerously close to waking, and she doesn't want to yet.

Because Luanne is here.

"I wouldn't try getting inside their heads, sweet pea," her grandmother says.

Charlotte thinks she's talking about the resort. About Cole. His massive company. But her grandmother's not finished. She keeps talking as she sinks her hands into the tide pool between them. "Sure, they'll have a story, but that's all it is. A story. A story they made up. If you really want to know evil, it's not enough to just look evil in the eye. You've got to bash its head up against the wall and see what comes spilling out. That's messy, girl. Real messy. You sure you have what it takes for that, Trina?"

Luanne gives her an inquisitive look, even as she keeps digging into the tide pool.

"I'm sorry," she hears herself say, but what she really wants to say is, *My name's Charlotte now, Grandma. Will you call me Charlotte, please? It will make me feel like you're alive again.*

"What are you sorry for, honey?"

"I let him trick me. There wasn't anyone there."

"I know, honey. You wanted to set her free, but she wasn't there, and she'll never be there. Because she's here."

The skull Luanne pulls from the tide pool is clean and perfectly preserved. Salt water pours from its empty eye sockets. With the certainty Charlotte only possesses in dreams, she knows it's her mother's, and for some reason, it makes perfect sense that Luanne's been keeping it here all this time, waiting for the right moment to present it to Charlotte like a gift.

She takes it in her hands and studies it and waits for the bone to transmute memories of her mother—memories she was never granted—into the flesh of her bare, dripping hands. The part of her that's close to wakefulness feels she should be horrified, but inside the logic of this dream, there's no greater gift her grandmother could have given her in this moment, and it fills Charlotte with something like warmth.

"But that's not the only reason you ran, sweet pea," Luanne says with a gentle smile.

Charlotte just stares into her eyes.

"You *let* him trick you. You let him give you something to run to. Because if you hadn't turned your back on him, you were going to break his neck."

18

Charlotte wakes with the sense that her mother's skull is resting somewhere in bed with her. She reaches for where she thinks it might be and ends up grabbing a handful of bedsheets. Not quite as thin and scratchy as hospital issue, but close.

The bed's edges are surrounded by some kind of zipper, the lower part of a plastic biohazard tent. The rest of the tent's nowhere in sight.

A shadow steps forward.

Several bars of soft light—one at floor level, the other about waist-high, and the third close to the ceiling—start to fill the room, transforming it from a cube of darkness into something closer to a private room in a nightclub, then something a little brighter but still classy looking, like a waiting room in a high-end spa. The institutional blandness all around her is revealed to be a design scheme of the kind you find inside those celebrity-built mansions featured in magazines. Everything is clean and white, the stainless steel fixtures gleaming and polished. The walls, she sees, are upholstered.

It's a padded cell, she corrects herself. *The padding's just really pricey.*

Cole steps through the door between a viewing area and the rest of the room, dressed in one of his typical long-sleeved collared shirts and black slacks. As usual, the shirt's blue. The shirt's always some shade of blue. The one time he wore green, she commented on it and he actually cracked what seemed like a genuine smile.

He's not smiling now. In the tense silence, she notices the window across the room is actually an LCD screen, its view of snowy mountains computer generated.

"How long since . . ."

"Eight hours," he says quietly.

She wouldn't have been surprised if they'd told her it had been a week, but maybe that's due to whatever drugs they're pumping into her. She's got two IV ports feeding into her right arm.

"What are you giving me?"

"Antibiotics mostly."

"For what?"

"You had wounds when the medics got to you, and they were bad. You just didn't have them for very long. So our primary concern was infection. As for pain, we didn't know if we should be treating any. You weren't responsive, but we didn't know how you'd wake up so we socked you full of the good stuff. How are you feeling?"

"Weird dreams."

"Pain?"

She shakes her head.

"I'll start pulling you off." He turns in the direction of what must be a hidden camera and makes a slicing motion across his throat. Since he doesn't explain himself any further to whoever might be watching, she assumes the person's listening in as well.

There's something she's never seen before in his expression. Maybe it's just concern, or maybe it's fear. But the past eight hours have rattled the typically unflappable Cole Graydon down to his bones. Parental concern. That's what's suggested by his furrowed brow and the way he occasionally chews his lower lip. The way he's studying her with uncharacteristically wide eyes.

He's a numbers guy, she thinks, *and I am his most expensive project. That's what I'm seeing on his face right now. Concern for an investment.*

"How'd you get me to California so fast?" she asks.

"I didn't."

"So I'm not in California?"

"Nope."

"Sometimes I have trouble wrapping my head around how rich you are."

"My company, you mean."

"You do all right. I've seen your spread in La Jolla."

"When?"

"Some magazine. I can't remember which one. *Architectural Digest*?"

"Don't believe everything you read in magazines."

"I don't. But pictures don't lie."

"Sure they do. If you pass them through the right hands first." Cole smiles. "What happened, Charley? Did he tell you he had someone in the tannery?"

Maybe. Or maybe I ran because my grandmother's ghost is right—I was about to break his neck.

"If you'd worn the earpiece, we could have told you he was lying. We weren't picking up any heat signatures."

"It's not like you picked up on the trap, either."

"The bear traps?"

"No. The one that blew up."

"There was some disagreement about how deeply we should risk penetrating his property before . . ."

"Before I was on it?"

Cole nods, but he's looking at the floor.

"Because you thought there was a chance he wasn't really a killer, and you didn't want to invade his privacy?"

"We'd already invaded his privacy and then some. And I never thought he wasn't a killer. Next time, we'll do more groundwork first."

"I'm confused, though."

"Call it a draw. You made a bad call by running into the tannery. I made a bad call by not having it inspected more closely by a ground team."

"That's not what confuses me."

"What, then?"

"Who has the power to disagree with you? Aren't you running the show?"

He studies her for a few seconds, but she figures he's not seeing her, only the words he's going to say next. Or not say next. "I was swayed by a strident voice. I won't make that mistake again. I'm sorry."

Because it's the first time she's ever heard him say the last two words, it takes her a minute to swallow them.

"I'm sorry, too," she whispers, "for running. It was . . . thoughtless."

Cole nods, looks to the floor. He's not going to rub her nose in it. That's good.

So this is what a draw feels like.

"Next time you wear the earpiece," he says.

"So there's going to be a next time?"

He's clearly startled. Does he think she's threatening to quit?

"It was our first time doing this. Together. I didn't expect things to go perfectly."

She nods, but she's wondering how he'd react if she tried to back out now.

Five months ago, he'd made her an offer—she could walk away from this forever, ensuring the total destruction of Project Bluebird once and for all, but on one condition: Dylan Cody a.k.a. Noah Turlington would have to die. Occasionally she lies awake at night wondering if she only chose option B to spare Noah's life. But it's just a nagging fear that usually passes after a moment or two of self-reflection.

Shayla Brown. Deborah Clover. Maryanne Breck. Patrice LaVon. Janelle Cropper.

That's why she's doing this.

And don't forget Joyce Pierce.

Thinking these names brings another to her lips. "Richard Davies?" she asks.

"Dead. We were a little too concerned with you. He bled out."

"From what I did to him, or did the explosion—"

"You stopped him, Charley. That's all that matters. I'm not going to indulge any sort of misguided guilt around any of this."

Because you got the vials of paradrenaline you expected, and whatever else you took from my body while I was sleeping.

"So you just scrubbed the whole place and nobody's going to know what he did?"

"If anyone does try looking for him, which given the way he lived, I doubt they will, he will have gone missing and his farm will have burned to the ground. That's correct."

"So the families don't get . . . anything."

"Most of those girls' families were hotbeds of abuse. What do you think they deserve exactly?"

"Someone cared. Someone always cares. Just because they couldn't work miracles doesn't mean they don't deserve to know what happened to those women. My grandmother went over a decade without knowing what happened to me and my mom. It almost killed her."

"If that's how you want to describe getting sober and becoming one of the pillars of her community, then fine."

"Someone deserves to know what happened to those women. Someone deserves to know that maybe they would have gotten off the streets one day, but Richard Davies took that chance from them."

"Well, next time let's do a better job of wrapping things up, then. My plan was to send him to a nuthouse or prison, just like Pemberton. But you had other ideas."

She wants to argue with him, but all things considered, he's being charitable. If he wanted to, he could put Richard Davies's death squarely on her shoulders. Instead, he's sort of loosely tying it to her left ankle. And his.

"Speaking of next time," she finally says.

"I'm listening."

"I knew too much. About the operation. That's why I had to stick my foot in the trap. I couldn't get triggered."

"OK. Next time we'll keep you in the dark."

"No. Next time there needs to be *actual* dark. I need to know that I'm . . . not safe."

"Let's not get ahead of ourselves."

"It isn't going to work any other way, Cole. You can't take the fear away and expect me to be afraid."

"Fear is in the mind. We'll find a way to train your mind to be afraid again."

"How are we going to do that?"

"Well, it didn't take much for Davies to send you running straight into a trap. Maybe you're equally suggestible in other ways."

His patience is thinning. She can hear it. And so can he, apparently, because his shoulders sag and he takes a deep breath that might just be for show. But she wouldn't be surprised if he actually needs it.

"Besides, we don't have trouble triggering you in the lab," he says.

"We can't count on every serial killer we target to play with my phobias the way you do in a completely controlled environment. And that'll probably stop working after a while, too."

"Why?"

"Because when we started lab testing I was afraid of you, too."

"And now you're not?"

She smiles.

He smiles back, brow raised. "Between the lab testing and last night, we've got a lot to work through. A lot to process, both in terms of data and . . . procedure. I'm not going to rush you into the field again until we do a full accounting of everything."

"Fair enough. How much longer do I have to stay here?"

"Another twenty-four hours at least. If you show any signs of infection, longer."

"OK. And what about Luke?"

Cole just stares at her. "What *about* Luke?"

"Has anyone been in touch with him? Just to let him know I'm OK."

"Your boyfriend is not our priority right now."

"I told him I'd be gone three weeks. It's been five."

"Then stop giving your boyfriend arbitrary timelines about our top-secret operations."

"A condition of our deal was that you would allow me to have my life when I wasn't working for you. Luke is part of my life. I'm not kidding myself that we're not under constant surveillance every minute I'm in Altamira; I'm just saying that after what I've done for you in the past twenty-four hours, maybe somebody in this billion-dollar fortress of I don't know what in the middle of I don't know where can send a text message to my boyfriend telling him I'm alive."

Cole approaches the bed. In his expression, she sees the same man who ushered her into his own private helicopter five months earlier and issued a series of proclamations that changed her life forever.

"You can act like the hapless victim of my big, bad, terrible, heartless company as much as you want, Charley. But let's not forget that what we've built here, *together*, is a system that allows you to systematically execute human monsters like the ones who killed your mother."

"It's not my plan to execute them."

"Fine. Torture them, then."

"*Stop* them. And if we built this system together, then tell me how you found him."

"What?"

"Tell me how you found Richard Davies."

"Get some rest, Charley. We'll talk about this when you're more . . . together."

Cole's almost to the door to the viewing area when she says, "It's Bailey, isn't it?"

Cole goes still before his hand can reach the doorknob.

A few years earlier, Luke's younger brother, one of the most wanted cybercriminals in the United States, went into foreign exile, severing all ties with his brother after using his considerable skills to track down a slimeball who'd defrauded Bailey and his fellow classmates out of the tuition they'd paid to a small community college.

To find the bastard, Bailey hacked a satellite.

An actual satellite that circled somewhere above the earth.

His only mistake?

Believing the FBI would be grateful for his assistance.

When Luke and Charley reconnected after her return to Altamira, Bailey, who had apparently been monitoring his big brother's conversations for months, decided to make his presence known to them. Digitally, of course. The help he offered led Charlotte and Luke right to the front door of a madman. Meanwhile, Graydon Pharmaceuticals had been impressed by his work. When all was said and done, they offered to use their powerful connections so that Bailey could return home without the FBI on his back.

But Bailey had refused, and Luke's feelings had been hurt all over again.

Now Charlotte can't help but wonder what will happen to Luke's feelings if he finds out that Cole made a different offer to Bailey than the one he conveyed to them.

And Bailey accepted it.

"Sounds like Luke should be more of a priority to you than you realize," she says.

"No." Cole turns to face her but stays rooted near the door. "In fact, his brother's condition for working with us is that we don't involve Luke at all."

"I doubt he's concerned for Luke's safety. He just doesn't want to take orders from him."

"He won't have to. And neither will you."

"I'm not taking orders from Luke."

"That's correct. You're taking them from me."

She's not quite sure what to say to this, or if she should say anything at all. It feels like he's baiting her into a fight to distract from these revelations about Luke's brother.

"Meanwhile," Cole says, "I don't actually take orders from Bailey, so I'm going to ignore his demand that you not discuss his new position with his brother. However, I'd like to strongly suggest some wording you can use when you do."

"OK."

"Put it like this. Would Luke rather his brother be safe, in an undisclosed location, answering to me? Or would he prefer him to have stayed on a Russian troll farm working alongside people who may or may not have swayed a United States presidential election?"

Jesus Christ, she thinks.

"You still haven't told me how Bailey found Davies."

"He doesn't discuss procedure."

"I've heard. But still . . ."

"Still what?"

"Given how well you probably pay him, I figure he probably runs the broad strokes by you, at least."

"I *am* ordering you not to discuss this part with Luke."

"Agreed."

"I'm serious, Charley."

"So am I."

Cole clears his throat and approaches the bed again. "Bailey is a genius. Where the rest of us see endless strings of code, he sees a world without walls, and he's willing to look into just about any corner of it provided he's searching for someone he deems morally suspect enough."

"That's a pretty good description of what he did for us with Pemberton."

"But what he lacked then was raw computing power. I've given it to him. In spades. And he's used it to put the full force of his highly sophisticated mind to use. For us. For you."

"This is going to be one of those conversations that uses the word *algorithm* and I'm going to have to pretend I know what it means."

Cole ignores her. "Within the first seventy-two hours, Bailey identified sixty-five people who were purchasing significant amounts of materials that could be used to dispose of human bodies but who had no legitimate reason to be purchasing those materials."

"Materials?" she asks.

"The materials you need to melt down flesh and bone."

Charley swallows. In her mind's eye, she sees a glittering digital net stretched across a map of the night-dark country. Sees it laced with red threads where it catches the cybertrails of anonymous psychopaths who believe they're working in secrecy. That's probably not how it works, in a visual sense anyway. Still, the idea of it fills her with something that's either excitement or stark terror. Probably both.

"You put sixty-five people under surveillance just to find Davies?" she asks.

"No. We still have them all under surveillance. Davies popped first."

"What does that mean? Popped first?"

"It means he started acting suspicious right away. And he ticked all the boxes of a typical serial killer profile. An angry white male loner with a traumatic past. And then, of course, there was the fact that he'd invested heavily in a personal leather-tanning operation but for some reason had never made any effort to sell or present the fruits of the labor to the world. So once Bailey gave me the signal, I devoted resources to tracking Davies on the ground. And the rest is history."

"What about the other people under surveillance? How did you eliminate them?"

"We haven't eliminated them, Charley. We're still watching them. For all we know one of them might be the next Richard Davies or Frederick Pemberton."

He falls silent, maybe giving her time to process the enormity of this. Or maybe he's bragging. Either way, she's impressed.

"You realize what the purpose of this is, right?" he finally asks. "I mean, aside from giving you targets."

"Untold billions for Graydon Pharmaceuticals?" she asks.

"We're not waiting for the horror movie idiots to get our attention by writing letters to the local paper. We're not targeting the ones who are so desperate for media attention they'll escalate to incompetence by their fifth kill. We're targeting the quiet ones. The effective ones. The ones who are content to work slowly and steadily year after year, who might be responsible for an untold number of missing persons cases to which no one's connected them yet. We're targeting killers like the Bannings, Charley, who killed for almost a decade because they knew better than to leave a single body by the side of the road, including yours.

"Even better—and I do say this with some amount of pride, so forgive me if my chest is puffing up a little bit—we're devoting a level of resources and attention to serial predators that no aboveboard, legitimate corner of law enforcement will ever give them. And do you want to know why? Because most of them don't kill enough people fast enough. That's why you've got some boutique wing of the FBI devoted to hunting them that only springs into action every now and then.

"When it comes to resources, dollars, manpower, *human*power, the people who make those decisions make them based on how many bodies pile up and how fast. They don't have a metric for what it means to die by the hands of a sexual sadist. Or to have a loved one who does. But I'm different, Charley. I do take those things into account. For *you*. And for me. And that's why, together, we've built a system that marshals the resources typically reserved for tracking terrorist organizations and applied them to lone human monsters who stalk the night like sharks cruising the deep sea."

"What does that make me?" she asks.

"A hook," he says.

"OK. Are you eating them, then?"

He laughs quickly, nervously. Maybe the thought frightens him. "I was trying to be respectful of your personal ethics. But honestly, if you want to act more like a harpoon every now and then, you won't get any complaints out of me."

Cole smiles, pats the edge of the bed. "Get some rest. If you're not running a fever in another eight hours, I'll let you go." He's almost to the door when he says, "And in the meantime, I'll find someone who can send your boyfriend a text."

Dead, she thinks once Cole's gone. *Bled out.*

The sound of Davies's cackling laughter still rings in her ears. It chases away anything that feels like guilt. Will it always? Will she have to spend the rest of her life summoning her worst memories of their brutal encounter to keep his death from choking her with guilt? *This might be the price of vengeance,* she thinks. *You have to spend the rest of your life living inside the memories of the worst things done to you so you can constantly justify what you did to avenge them.*

19

If Luke Prescott checks his cell phone one more time, his fellow sheriff's deputy, Pete Henricks, will probably rip it out of his hand. Maybe a little tussle would be preferable to this endless back and forth over whether they'll ride patrol together or separately. It's not like anyone else inside the sheriff's station would notice. Friday nights aren't as peaceful as they used to be. Not since the new work crews rolled in to start renovating the old resort and the term *boomtown* became applicable to Altamira for the first time in its history.

Back in the old days, each weekend night they'd see maybe one or two drunk and disorderlies, tops. Tonight, they had five inside the holding cell by nine o'clock.

Still, Luke's new relationship to his phone seems to have Pete concerned, regardless of what Luke might think. Over the past few weeks—five and counting since Charley shipped out—checking his texts and emails has gone from a regular habit to a jittery compulsion. Which is silly because the two had agreed on radio silence while she was gone.

Luke's every waking moment since she left has been dogged by the dark fantasy that he'll soon get some cryptic summons from Cole Graydon or one of his mercenaries, demanding Luke meet them at some isolated warehouse on the outskirts of town. They'll march into the room with guns drawn and explain in vague platitudes how something went wrong and Charley's never coming back to him or Altamira. Maybe the drug didn't trigger as expected, and whatever psycho they went after this time was able to mortally injure Charley before Cole's men could rescue her.

Or maybe the drug did trigger, but in the end, it finally went haywire, sending Charley into the same orgy of self-mutilation that killed their first test subjects. In both cases, they'll demand he be relocated and given a new identity so they can sweep all evidence of Project Bluebird under the rug. Then they'll monitor him for the rest of his life, ready to assassinate him if he ever talks. And all the while, he'll be left to wonder if their story's bullshit, a cover for the fact that they've locked Charley up in a lab somewhere because letting her run around in the world, with *him*, has proven too risky.

Or inconvenient.

A man as rich and powerful as Cole Graydon can easily move mountains just because one of the mountains annoys him.

They've never threatened anything quite like that, of course, and Zypraxon's successfully bloomed inside Charlotte's bloodstream so many times now, it's hard to believe it would suddenly stop working. But given they still don't know why it works in her—and only her—maybe that part of his nightmare has more fact to it than he wants to admit.

She chose to go, Luke tells himself for the thousandth time. *She chose to work with them. And she chose not to fight them when they said you couldn't help.*

He doesn't want to resent her, but anger's been a steady temptation these past few weeks. Anger can give you a false sense of direction when sadness makes you feel lost. If she'd fought harder for him to join their team, he wouldn't be stuck here in Altamira, arguing with Pete Henricks over whether they should drive patrols together or separately.

Henricks is a few years more experienced than him, but he's hardly Luke's idea of a stellar cop. Or anyone's, for that matter. He used to have a habit of volunteering for the worst assignments, which

Luke appreciated, but that was back when the worst they had to do was separate a drunk couple before a bottle was thrown. Now that Altamira's turning into a burgeoning center of Central California nightlife, Pete Henricks has turned into a strange combination of lazy and smug.

"So where is she?" Henricks asks suddenly.

"Excuse me," Luke says.

They're next to the coffee maker, which is not where Luke needs to be right now. He's already had five cups. And after extensive testing, it's clear that caffeine highs don't make the waiting game any easier. Quite the opposite, in fact.

"Charley." Henricks fills his mug, then slides the pot back inside the coffee maker. "No one's seen her for weeks. People think maybe she skipped out on you."

"People, huh?"

"Look, I notice stuff is all. That's my job."

"And *skipped out* is code for what exactly?"

"Left your sorry ass. I don't speak in codes, pal."

"She's visiting family," Luke says.

"Family?" Henricks says the word like it's a slur. His implication is so obvious Luke can feel it in the back of his throat. Does he think she went to Haddock Penitentiary to visit the woman who killed her mother? She's got some actual family, for Christ's sake, even if you don't count Martin Cahill, her grandmother's former boyfriend, who's probably the best family she's ever had.

Henricks is twice Luke's height, with a flop of brushed-forward blond hair that screams toupee, but he's about a fourth of Luke's width, so when Luke fantasizes about shoving the guy off his feet, it's not hard to imagine him going over backward like his legs have been ripped out from under him.

"Why are we talking about Charley?" Luke asks.

"Well, we were talking about patrols, but you keep looking at your phone so I figured we might as well address the elephant in the room. Not that I'm saying she's an elephant or anything, but you get my—"

"We need to do patrols together, Henricks."

"Why? You like shitty music and wear too much cologne."

"Because we got about five times the nightlife crowd we used to, thanks to all the new business the construction is drawing to town."

"Which is all good when you get down to it."

"Sure. It's also good for drunk and disorderly arrests. Domestic abuse calls. And DUIs. The kinds of calls we shouldn't be handling alone."

"Oh, cool your jets. You just don't know this crowd yet. Come out to the Gold Mine sometime and just hang out, Luke. They're good people, and they're spending money hand over fist. The resort. The tunnel. It's what we've dreamed of for years. Why are you acting like it's a punishment?"

Because I know who's paying for all of it, and I still don't know exactly why he's doing it.

"Be that as it may," Luke says, "we should still up our patrols. Especially on Friday nights."

"OK. Well, we would be upping our patrols if you and I did them separately, because then we'd cover more area. That's how math works."

"You would think so, wouldn't you, Henricks? But if we don't patrol together, you usually don't patrol at all. That's how you work."

Pete's holding his coffee cup close to his chest, as if he's preparing to hurl its contents in Luke's face. But his expression's blank, lifeless. "We have a boss, Luke, and it's not you."

No way is he letting Henricks in on the secret of what's been calling their boss away from the station so much lately. Staying quiet about it means he can't tell the guy just why Mona Sanchez has repeatedly asked Luke to cover during her absences.

Before he can respond with some misdirection, Henricks goes rigid, staring at something over Luke's shoulder.

Luke spins.

At the sight of the woman who just walked into the station, his stomach lurches and then he feels as if he's been struck across the back of the neck. He's seen her around town, but she looks so different, he's sure she's wearing some sort of mask. The swollen cheeks and eyes, the bruised lips—they give her face a rubbery lifelessness that reminds him of the grotesque masks a psychopath named Frederick Pemberton left on statues throughout Southern California a few months before.

But this woman's very much alive, and she's shuffling toward the reception desk, where the night dispatcher, who's so new Luke keeps forgetting her name, is rising out of her seat.

"Jordy . . ." the woman manages, then she grips the edge of the front desk to keep from falling to her knees. And that's when Luke and Henricks take her arms and guide her through the waist-high gate into the bull pen.

"Jordy . . ." she manages again before they settle her in the nearest empty chair.

And that's when it connects. She's the girlfriend of Jordy Clements, the project supervisor for the new tunnel they're getting ready to blast through the mountains on the west side of town, all thanks to Cole Graydon.

Luke can't tell if she's asking for her boyfriend's help or blaming him for her current condition. She smells of dirt and wild things, and her T-shirt's got something on it that might be dirt stains, but there are no leaves or twigs in her long, slightly curly hair. It looks like she brushed it. If human fists did this to her face, Luke hates the thought that she felt obligated to stop and pretty herself up before going to the authorities.

He hates most of the thoughts he's having right now.

The new night dispatcher pushes a plastic cup of water toward her, but she shakes her head, lips trembling, nostrils flaring. "Get Jordy."

"Jordy's your boyfriend?" Luke asks.

She makes a sound that's something between a sneer and a groan.

"You want to talk to him or you want us to talk to him?" Luke asks.

"How about some medical attention, Lacey?" Henricks asks her. Then to Luke he says, "How's that sound? How 'bout we get her over to the urgent care and they can—"

"She's sitting right here, so why don't we talk to her? And you know her name, apparently?"

"Lacey," Henricks says, as if he's ashamed to have the information. "Lacey Shannon."

She shakes her head furiously. The gesture seems to ignite bone-deep pain throughout her neck and shoulders, so she stops abruptly, wincing and sucking breaths through her nose.

"Jordy . . ." she says again.

"What about Jordy, ma'am?" Luke sinks to a crouch so they're eye level. "What do you need us to do about Jordy?"

She raises her head and stares right into his eyes. Given her battered face, it's like being surveyed by a Halloween ghoul.

"Put him in a cell," she whispers.

Henricks straightens. It's like he's recoiling from the woman and the obvious implication of what she just said. He's given Luke more than one speech about how most domestic violence calls are "complicated things" and how there are two sides to every situation. It's clear that the idea of Jordy Clements, a key figure in Altamira's newfound good fortune, being accused of beating up a woman has Henricks's shorts in a knot.

"Jordy did this to you?" Luke asks.

"Why don't we slow our roll a little bit?" Henricks says. "Make this a little more formal."

"Formal?" Luke asks.

Henricks seems to realize he's speaking too casually in front of a possible battery victim. "Let's get her into the interview room."

Luke's about to agree when Lacey says, "Jordy Clements is a bad man with hate in his heart."

Nobody says anything for what feels like a minute. There's conviction in her voice, even though it's a little slurry, but the word choice is odd—it's studied, rehearsed. Not the kind of furious and agonized string of accusations Luke would expect from a woman whose boyfriend just beat on her.

He realizes how many eyes are on them. The night dispatcher, and also the few new deputies Mona called in from county. The old storage room was recently converted into the kind of interview room you see on TV, and so far they've only used it twice. Before the new work crews rolled into town, increasing the town's population by about a third, they'd conducted their interviews right out in the middle of the bull pen, or maybe inside the holding cell if the interview was sensitive. In those quieter, more peaceful days, there was rarely more than one person in the holding cell at a time.

A few minutes later, they've walked Lacey to the back of the station, past the giant fake ficus he brought in to pretty the station up a little.

There's a small clicking sound as they enter the windowless, white-walled room, with its gateleg table lengthwise against one wall. The new camera system is motion activated; it starts recording the visitor's chair every time someone opens the door. Henricks seems to jump at the clicks. No doubt he thinks Lacey's bullshitting them, and now he's realizing the trade-off for getting her away from prying eyes is that everything she says is going on camera.

Lacey settles into the metal visitor's chair with the slow, methodical movements of someone with a sunburn.

"All right," Luke says, "how about you take us through—"

"No." It's the clearest and most forceful tone she's used since entering the station.

"I'm sorry?" Luke asks.

"Put Jordy in a cell, then I'll talk."

"He can't hurt you in here," Luke says.

"*Did* he hurt you?" Henricks asks.

"Put Jordy in a cell."

"Ma'am, we can't just go around arresting anyone who—"

"Henricks," Luke interjects. "Lacey, why do you need us to put Jordy in a cell?"

"So I can talk."

"About what?"

She looks into Luke's eyes again, and the hair goes up on the back of his neck. "About who he really is."

"Have you had anything to drink tonight, ma'am?"

"I don't drink," she says, staring at Luke.

"Any medications?" Henricks asks. "Maybe ones you don't have prescriptions for?"

For the first time, Lacey looks at Henricks. Luke tries to read her expression, but it's not easy, given her injuries. There's a kind of disappointment there, it seems. Or maybe it's guilt. He can't be sure. Either way, she's staring at Henricks with an intensity that suggests if her eyes weren't both in danger of swelling shut, she'd be glaring daggers at him. No matter what happens next, Henricks has lost the woman's trust. Why couldn't he have waited a bit longer before resorting to good cop/bad cop?

"Is that a no?" Henricks asks.

Lacey turns her attention to Luke. "Put him in a cell and I'll talk."

"Yeah," Henricks says, "with all due respect, that's not how this works, ma'am. See, we wouldn't even know what to charge him with because you won't—*Luke!*"

Luke's past the ficus and moving swiftly toward reception when he hears the interview room door slam shut. Then Henricks is right on his heels. The dude's already pegged the woman a liar, so if Luke's going to do anything to get the story out of her, he'll have to take the initiative. And before he thinks twice about the risks.

"What the hell are you doing, Luke?"

"We're going to go talk to Jordy Clements."

"The hell we are. She's a pillhead, Luke."

"And you know this how?"

"Let's just say she's known around town, OK?" Henricks says.

"I've never seen her in holding."

"You don't work every night of the week."

"Oh, OK. So, if I look for an arrest record on her, I'm going to find one?"

"I don't know. Maybe. I'm just saying, slow down."

"Why, because her boyfriend's building a goddamn tunnel?"

"You know how important that tunnel's going to be to this town. Come on."

"Not important enough to let Jordy Clements beat up his girl-friend because you're a chickenshit."

"Luke!"

It was probably too far, calling Henricks a chickenshit in front of all their coworkers, but it's not like any of them are rushing to disagree.

"Are you coming or not?" Luke asks.

"Where?"

"Where is everybody on a Friday night? He's probably at the Gold Mine."

"He doesn't drink."

"What are you, best friends with this guy?"

"I'm telling you, he's known around town. And *this* will be known around town, too, if you make a big stink and there's nothing to it."

"Well, then I should talk to Jordy and find out if there's nothing to it, right?"

"You can't just throw him in a cell without charging him with anything because she said so."

"Who said anything about a cell? I'm just going to talk to him."

"I don't believe that, Luke. You don't just talk. You always . . . do stuff."

"Yeah, like my job. Are you coming or not?"

"I'm not messing around with a guy like Jordy Clements just because your girlfriend walked out on you and you're not dealing with it."

"You're right. You're not messing around with a guy like Jordy Clements because you think rich assholes should be above the law. Don't let her leave that interview room."

Only once he's out of the station and at the door to his cruiser does he realize Henricks never agreed to Luke's final order. And, of course, when it comes to getting in bed with rich assholes, he's a lot guiltier than Henricks. Or at least his new girlfriend is. But for now, no one in Altamira knows anything about that, and that's how he'd like it to stay.

When Luke was a boy, the Gold Mine Tavern was a hole-in-the-wall bar that served halfway decent burgers for lunch, before the same crew of evening regulars would roll in every night around happy hour. Luke's mother visited the place only rarely before she got sick, and when she did, she never stayed for more than a vodka tonic or two. Afterward, she'd come home complaining that it still smelled like stale beer and the conversations were always the same—complaints about work, or the lack thereof, or endless chitchat about whatever new piece of California history the bar's owner, Dan Soto, had hung on walls that already looked like a TGI Fridays devoted to the state's rugged past.

Luke returned home around half a year ago, tail between his legs, having decided that loyalty to his brother was more important than turning informant on the guy just so he could have a shot at his dream job with the FBI. Altamira's new sheriff was an old friend of his mother's, and she'd been happy to hire him. Back then, little about the town and its most popular watering hole had changed much since his youth. On his first few night patrols, he spotted the one bartender on duty closing the place down around eleven thirty, right after the last customer started their long, shuffling walk home.

At the time he probably muttered something to himself about how it was good that some things stayed constant, even if they were just sad, lonely watering holes.

Now, just a few months later, nothing about Altamira, or his life, is the same.

The Gold Mine's front door is fringed by cackling smokers he doesn't recognize. Some of them have driven in from someplace else, drawn by Altamira's messy nascent nightlife scene and the very real fact that the town's tiny law enforcement office is barely equipped to contain it. A couple of them give his sheriff's department uniform a wary eye. Then they do their best to look more sober than they are.

It takes him a second to realize the wall of muscle standing ramrod straight next to the blacked-out glass door is a bouncer.

A bouncer at the Gold Mine Tavern. A year ago, the idea would have seemed as absurd as a Bloomingdale's opening up next to the Copper Pot.

"Can I help you, deputy?" the bouncer asks.

"Yeah. Move."

The bouncer complies, but not before giving Luke a look that suggests that in the new Altamira, bouncers might have more pull than cops.

The music hits him in a deafening wave. It's someone's idea of country, but not his. The band's out of tune and loud, like all they care about is being heard over the crowd at all costs. But everyone's so drunk, they probably wouldn't give a whit if the lumberjack-looking dudes on stage were yodeling a version of "Feelings."

Dan Soto, the Gold Mine's owner, who just a few months ago spent most of his evenings playing cards with his buddies and listening to absolutely nothing happen on his police scanner, is running around behind the bar, sweating through his T-shirt as he frantically works backup for three newly hired female bartenders who are ringing up drink orders faster than Luke can eat tortilla chips. And he loves tortilla chips.

Boomtown.

The word never inspired dread in him before. But that's what it does now.

One of the bartenders pours a shot of tequila into the navel of a svelte young woman lying halfway across the bar, her feet propped on the stool in front of her. Midriff Girl wears a tube top and a licentious smile as a construction worker Luke recognizes from a drunk-driving stop—the guy smelled all right and only had a block to go, so Luke let him off with a warning—leans in and sucks the shot from her belly button while he's cheered on by his drunk friends.

Midriff Girl's got a somewhat pretty face turned cartoonish by heavy makeup. This, combined with her skimpy, skintight outfit, makes her seem alien to Altamira, where blue jeans and sundresses are considered formal wear. No doubt she's one of the new breed of working girl that's moved into town to service the needs of the town's new male population.

Watching the woman almost as closely as Luke is, but from a small table near the opposite side of the bar, is Jordy Clements, the man Lacey Shannon just accused of beating her.

Clements doesn't even look buzzed. The pint glass in front of him is more than half-full. When his eyes leave Midriff Girl and he starts scanning the crowd, he does so with the cool, assessing gaze of someone who feels like he owns the place, which, Luke fears, in another few months, he just might.

After the guy started strutting around Altamira like the new mayor, Luke did a little research on him. Jordy's thirty years old, but the vertical knife-scar on his left cheek that comes dangerously close to his eye makes him look much older. He sports a high and tight haircut that keeps his long forehead exposed. He's got a Marine Corps background, along with an honorable discharge. Luke suspects he landed the gig as project supervisor for the tunnel because his dad owns the company.

There are two different construction crews in town—Clements and Murdoch. It's easy to tell their men apart.

Clements is responsible for building the tunnel to the Pacific Coast Highway, so while its crew is smaller in number, its members are honest-to-God miners. In another few weeks, after they've taken all the seismic readings and rock samples they need, the Clements crew will start drilling and blasting a hole through the heart of the mountains west of town—which means they can't be bothered by claustrophobia, a fear of otherworldly darkness, or the very real pos- sibility of a tunnel collapse. They're rough and tough guys, each one of them capable of taking on the entire Murdoch Construction crew single-handed in a fight.

The Murdoch guys, on the other hand, are mostly itinerant labor. They're building the resort, which at present involves concrete, hammers, nails, and a whole lot of timber. The promontory on which the resort's main building sits sports some jaw-dropping cliffs, so nerves of steel when it comes to heights has to be a job requirement.

Luke's about to tell Dan Soto to put the awful band on break, but just then the musicians start giving an ignored farewell speech. They step offstage to weak applause that barely rises over the din of rowdy conversation. Despite Luke's quick and quiet approach, Jordy senses him coming and locks eyes with him when he's only a few feet away.

"Got some questions for you, Jordy," Luke says.

"Call me Mr. Clements and I'll be happy to educate you, sir."

Jordy's three burly companions know better than to laugh out loud, but they each give Luke their own version of a smirk crossed with a sneer.

"I would, but I don't see your dad anywhere around."

"That's funny." He reaches into his shirt pocket. He pulls out a pack of Camel Lights, shakes one free, and lights it. "You're funny."

Even though smoking inside a bar has been illegal in California for over a decade now, no one seems to care about the cloud of smoke billowing between them.

Except for Luke.

"Jordy, I need you to come down to the station with me. I can either—"

"Not gonna happen. Come on. Have a drink. I'm buying."

"I'm on duty, but thank you."

"Well, have a Diet Coke then, pansy."

"*Pansy?* What are you, a homophobe from the forties?"

"Ah, don't get all social justice on me. We're just trying to have a good time. Right here. In this wonderful bar I am considering buying and expanding because I have fallen hopelessly in love with this town. Smoke?"

Jordy shakes a cigarette half-free of the pack and extends it to Luke. Instead of taking it, Luke snatches the lit cigarette from Jordy's other hand.

"I'm allergic to cigarette smoke," he says.

"Well, that's a made-up allergy if I ever heard one."

"I'm also allergic to women walking into my station with black eyes."

"*Your* station? You sheriff now? What happened to Mona Sanchez?"

"Jordy, get up and I'll follow you out from a few paces and we can do the whole thing nice and quiet. How's that sound?"

"Or?"

"You'll know it when you feel it."

The pretense of good humor leaves Jordy's expression. "I only smoke when I'm annoyed, and you are most certainly annoying me, Deputy Dawg."

Luke drops the cigarette to the floor and stamps it out under his foot.

"You know what this is starting to look like?" Jordy says.

"An arrest in the making."

"Ungratefulness."

"Station's only two blocks away. If you've got nothing to hide, a trip there won't cost you much."

"All I'm hiding is how much you're pissing me off right now."

"Well, then let it all out, Jordy. I love honest conversation."

"Lacey and me are on and off. I set her up over in Trailer City so she could have a fresh start, a nice long way from her pill pushers down in LA. I'm trying to help her. Whatever crap she's pulling with you is my compensation, I guess. No good deed and all that."

"Why help her? Why not just move on?"

"Love is a funny thing, friend. And I've never been one to quit, even when the battle's hard, know what I mean?"

No doubt Jordy's not-so-subtle reference to his military service is intended to distract. But Luke's still stuck on the words *Trailer City*. God, he hates that name. It turns his stomach every time he hears it.

Sure, they used to be empty fields with no mature trees, so maybe it's good they're being put to some kind of use. But the entire expanse of trailers and outhouses and tents has the look of a migrant city in a war-torn nation. And its new residents seem united in the belief that local law enforcement holds little sway inside its new and improvised borders. The whole place will most likely vanish as soon as all the construction's done and the workers have moved on, but Luke's not willing to consider it a free-for-all zone until then, and neither is his boss.

"So why's she lying if you're being so helpful and all?" Luke asks.

"We fight all the time, but I never raise my hand to a woman."

"So how'd she get two black eyes?"

"I'm thinking a rock, maybe."

"You think she gave herself two black eyes. With a rock."

"You ever seen her mad before?"

"She's your girlfriend. Which means maybe you should have thought twice before dropping her in the middle of your temporary housing for your all-male crew."

"Oh, you think she'll be in demand, huh?"

"She's an attractive young woman."

"Want her number?"

"I'm taken. Thanks."

"That's right. I heard. The chick with the serial killer parents. That must make for some weird role-play in the bedroom."

It happens as easily as tying his shoes or opening a car door. It helps that Jordy Clements lacks the physical strength suggested by his constant strut. Also, the guy's just arrogant enough that he didn't see the move coming. Now, Luke's got the prick on his feet and he's managed to cuff him in less than ten seconds flat. He starts shoving him forward through the gawking crowd with the kind of short, determined bursts of force he'd use on a stumbling drunk.

"It's ingratitude, asshole," Luke growls into his ear. "The word's *ingratitude.*"

20

Luke isn't surprised to see the holding cell's still got five men in it, all of them big, grizzled guys with expressions ranging from dazed to regretful. A few of them hold their heads in their hands, a sure sign they're sobering up faster than they'd like.

When Jordy realizes he's about to be locked up with some of his own employees, he sucks in a sharp breath that makes Luke tighten his grip on the man's cuffs. After a light shove that sends him inside the cell, Luke uncuffs the man, then draws the gate shut between them with a louder than necessary clang.

"Howdy, boss!" cries one of the less sober men inside the cell, a mountain of a dude with a scraggly beard the color of the last cup in a gas station coffeepot. "What've I told you about beer after liquor? Sicker quicker!"

"That's backwards, fool," says one of his more sober bench mates.

"You sure you don't want a lawyer, *Mr.* Clements?" Luke asks.

Jordy turns to him, expression impassive. "I won't need one."

Luke nods, then starts down the short passageway to the station's main room.

He's surprised to see his boss heading straight for him through the warren of desks that were mostly empty five months ago. Mona Sanchez is not supposed to be working tonight. Only Luke knows why. She's also not in uniform, which means someone called her in for something.

Henricks, you weaselly prick.

"What are you doing here?" Luke asks, once they're practically nose to nose.

"Nice to see you, too." The flash of hurt in her eyes looks nothing like her usual stony professionalism. Luke instantly regrets his tone.

"Is everything OK?" Luke asks.

"He didn't want me there," she mutters. "He's been throwing up all day . . . and so . . ."

"He's that sick and he *didn't* want you there?"

"He said he didn't want me to see him like that, and he said it about six times, and when I tried to help him clean up he batted my arm away. So . . ."

"So?"

"I got in my car and came back."

As if she didn't already have enough to deal with, around the time the first work crews rolled in town, Mona's long-term boyfriend was diagnosed with late-stage non-Hodgkin's lymphoma. Edward's a lawyer down in Santa Ynez who spends most of his time defending the local Chumash tribe from the endless barrage of legal challenges the neighbors have brought against their casino. For years now, the two have enjoyed a casual commuter relationship, but ever since his diagnosis, Mona's been spending more time in Santa Ynez, helping him navigate the ravages of chemotherapy. Being sent away abruptly by the man she loves, the man to whom she's been giving all her spare time, has got to hurt.

"Why don't you go home and get some rest and I'll—"

"Why don't you tell me why you just arrested Jordy Clements?" Mona asks.

"His girlfriend can help. She's in the interview room. Her name's Lacey Shannon, and earlier tonight she—"

"She's gone."

"To the hospital?"

"No. She changed her mind and walked out."

"*What?*"

Mona raises a hand to quiet him. "Luke, we need to talk about basic protocol with drunks. We're getting a lot more than we used to, and you can't always—"

"She wasn't drunk."

"Henricks says she's got addiction issues."

"Henricks was too chickenshit to go with me to question Clements."

"I heard you, jackass!" Henricks shouts from the coffee maker.

"Good!" Luke shouts back.

"She was slurring half her words," Henricks fires back.

"She'd just been beaten up, ass wipe. We're lucky she could even talk. Who let her walk out of here before she could tell us what happened?"

"Wait, tell you what happened?" Mona asks. "What did she say when she walked in here if she hadn't told you what happened?"

"It's complicated," Luke says.

"Lies usually are!" Henricks barks.

"Why the hell did you let her leave?" Luke barks back.

"There was no stopping her, Luke," Mona says. "Not if she had a change of heart."

"About lying," Henricks adds.

Luke feels his pulse pounding in his ears. He's staring at the shocked expression on Henricks's face before he realizes he's storming through the sea of desks toward the spot where Henricks is backing up against the wall, coffee cup held up against his chest as if it might protect him from whatever's coming next.

"You went back in the interview room, didn't you? You let me go to the Gold Mine by myself, and you came back here and convinced her to walk before I got back with Clements."

"That's bullshit," Henricks whines.

Luke can hear Mona saying his name. She's even grabbing at his shoulder. But as his rage builds, these things feel like the slip and slide of a loose shirt over his skin.

"What is up with you and Clements, Henricks? You guys just fishing buddies, or did he put you on his payroll?"

"*Payroll?* What the hell are you talking about?"

"Maybe you're getting an envelope of cash each week from the Clements crew. And that's why you have such a hard time believing someone with that last name might not be so squeaky clean."

"You're paranoid, Luke. You brought that darkness into your house, and now you're going nuts."

"*Darkness?* What the hell are—"

"Don't come after us just because everything you see's a horror movie now that you're banging Burning Girl."

"You say one more goddamn word about Charlotte and I'll shut your fucking mouth with my—"

"*Enough!*" Mona screams.

The station goes still. Deputy Lewiston, a new hire and former member of Martin Cahill's old contracting crew, looks even more uncomfortable and out of place than usual.

Luke's expecting to be dragged into Mona's office by the shoulder. Or fired on the spot. Everyone else in the department knows he sometimes gets special treatment, and they figure it's due to the long, close friendship Mona and his mother enjoyed before his mother passed away. And they're right. But what they don't understand is that this past family connection means that Mona's just as likely to treat him like a teenager who needs a lesson about losing his temper. On most days, the choice depends on her mood, and right now, her mood's anything but good.

So when Mona walks past Luke and right up to Henricks, Luke is stunned silent.

And relieved.

"Did you allow a fellow deputy to go alone to a crowded bar to question a potentially violent suspect?" Mona asks.

"I didn't approve of the approach he was taking." Henricks's words might be confident, but his tone makes it sound like he's drawing breath through a straw.

"The *approach*? Are you saying Deputy Prescott was planning a violent act, or considering planting evidence?"

"No . . . No, I mean . . ."

"OK, then. Talk to me about this approach you didn't approve of."

"He seemed upset. I wanted him to calm down."

"So in order to ensure calm, you let him go by himself to the Gold Mine?"

The silence inside the station is so thick Luke feels like he's drowning in it.

"It's a yes or no question, Henricks," Mona says quietly.

"Yes."

"Give me your gun and your badge."

"You're firing me?"

"You're under review. You essentially left a fellow officer in a crowd situation with a potentially violent suspect. That's unacceptable and you know it."

As Henricks stares at her, his tongue makes a lump under his bottom lip. His nostrils are flaring like he just ate hot sauce.

Then, slowly—too slowly for Luke's liking—Henricks detaches his gun holster from his belt and sets it on the empty desk behind Mona. Luke breathes easier once the man's set the gun down. Then, as he starts unfastening his badge, Henricks says, "I quit."

"I accept your resignation." Mona collects the gun and badge as Henricks brushes past Luke.

All eyes are on the shamed deputy as he steps through the half gate next to the dispatch desk. Luke doubts the man will leave without getting the last word.

Henricks spins to face them.

"This is the best goddamn thing to happen to this town since . . . ever. And everyone in here's acting like it's the end of the world just because it gave us more work to do. Well, I'm done. I'm done pretending like we gotta turn this whole place into Sunday school or turn back the clock to when we're nothing but a couple horse farms and a shitty diner and an army fort that got smaller every damn year. We're going to drive these people away, we keep acting like this."

"If we don't let them all beat up their girlfriends, you mean?" Luke asks.

"Fuck you, Prescott. Nobody wanted you back here anyway. Your mother's dead and your brother's a criminal. No wonder the best you can do is a serial killer's daughter."

"Get out, Henricks," Mona shouts.

But when Luke says, "Who's *us*?" his quiet tone surprises everyone into silence.

"What?" Henricks finally asks.

"You said, don't come after *us*. Who's *us*, Henricks?"

The man's face reddens and his lips part, but nothing comes out.

"Maybe I am a little quick tempered for a cop," Luke says, "but you sure as hell don't have the temperament to be on the take, loose lips."

Henricks mutters the word *bullshit* under his breath several times as he storms out of the station. Luke figures the fact that he couldn't once say the word while looking anyplace other than the floor is a sign the only bullshit being slung was coming from Henricks.

21

It takes three phone calls to establish that no one matching Lacey Shannon's description has walked into the new late-night urgent care in town or any of the nearby hospitals. That means she's either gone back to Trailer City or left town altogether, and right now, Mona doesn't want Luke investigating either possibility.

Instead, she wants them to sit in her office with the door closed while they both try to catch their first deep breath in five months.

So far, that coveted deep breath is proving elusive. Having Jordy Clements locked in a cell close by does give Luke a newfound sense of control, but he wouldn't call it relaxing.

"I think I'm going to turn into one of those sheriffs who keeps a flask in my desk like on TV," Mona says.

"That's not your style," Luke says.

"Says who?"

"You barely drink."

"Yeah, well, maybe I'll start." After a moment, she says, "I'm going to have to call the county to replace Henricks."

"Fine."

"And maybe get some more people in general."

"Or we could have a jobs fair like everybody else is doing."

"What fine specimens is that going to bring to the surface during this golden moment for Altamira?"

"I don't know. Not everybody who's rolled into town is a bad apple."

"You really think Clements is paying people off?"

"I think we've got prostitutes for the first time. Saw one giving up belly button shots at the Gold Mine earlier."

"I'm not hearing anything about shakedowns, or organized crime."

"Me neither, but still."

"Why don't you get out while the going's good?" Mona asks.

"What?"

"The old Meadows apartment building close to you's still for sale. Price goes up every week, but nobody's touching it yet because it's right by where they're going to start blasting. See if you can get a loan and, presto, once the tunnel's done, you'll be in the real estate business."

"I don't want to be in the real estate business."

"Hell, maybe I'll go in on it with you and we can both get the—"

"*Mona*, come on. This is . . . doable. It's a lot, but we'll figure it out. We'll get more people. We'll manage."

"I'm just tired, is what you're saying."

"Yeah. Something like that."

She plants her elbows on her desk and rubs her face with both hands. "It's hard."

"I know."

"It's hard because it reminds me of your mom. The chemo, the hospitals. And I feel weird saying that because she was your mom, and I don't want to . . ."

"Don't want to what?"

"I don't want to steal your story. What you went through was a lot worse than what I dealt with."

"Not really."

"Luke . . ."

"I'm serious. I was a snot-nosed kid back then. You did all the heavy lifting. Driving her to doctor's appointments, helping her keep track of meds."

"You took care of your brother. That was the important part. You guys called a truce on whatever war you had with each other so that your mom could have a little peace in the end. That was important, Luke. It was important to her. She said so. Many times."

Luke just nods, but any mention of Bailey spears his gut worse than any memory of his mother's final days.

One of the richest men in the world could have cleared his record, allowed him to come home again, and Bailey still said no. He actually chose the life of a criminal in hiding over coming home and being a family again.

"You miss him?" Mona asks.

Mona knows Bailey had to flee the country after conducting an elaborate hack to locate the dean of a small community college who fleeced Bailey and his classmates of their tuitions. But that's just a fraction of Bailey's story now, and no way can he tell Mona the rest of it.

"Yeah, I do," Luke says.

"Well, you've got Charlotte now. That's gotta help."

"It does."

When Luke's cell phone rings, they both jump. He half expects to see some text from Bailey that makes it clear he's been eavesdropping on them via one of the many networked devices in their vicinity. Then the phone rings again, reminding him it's an actual call. The number's unidentified.

"Luke Prescott," he answers.

"Good evening, Deputy," the voice on the other end says.

Cole Graydon.

Luke rises out of his chair and steps quietly from Mona's office. He's aware he's taking steps, but he can't feel his feet connecting with the floor. He's suddenly sweating all over, so much the phone feels slick against his ear. *Not good,* he thinks. *A call from Cole and not Charley means this is not good at all.*

"Good evening," Luke says, but his voice sounds reedy, breath starved.

"Is this a good time?"

"I can always make time for you." *Even though you've never called me on the phone before.*

"Well . . . good," Cole says. "Two things."

"Go ahead."

"Our operation is complete and Charlotte is recovering nicely."

"Recovering?"

"She should be home in a day or two. I'll let her explain, provided you keep those details confidential."

"Of course. But . . ."

Now his vision is spinning, and he feels as if some invisible string that was holding him up by the back of his neck has been cut. All the tension of the last few moments, possibly the last five months, collapses in a single instant. He grips the back of the nearest chair. Only now that his bones have gone liquid can he truly feel the extent to which his fear for Charley calcified his every move for over a month now. He better pull it together before everyone inside the station starts offering him cold compresses.

"But what, Luke?" Cole asks.

"She's OK?" he whispers.

"More than OK. She continues to be her remarkable self."

"Good. Great."

Cole is silent; probably he can tell Luke is trying to catch his breath. He's also blinking back tears, but he's pretty sure Cole won't be able to hear those.

"Is that both things?" Luke finally asks.

"No. Let Jordy Clements go."

Luke is stunned silent.

"Luke?"

"I'm here."

"We're doing important work. Momentous work. And you're supporting us more than you realize. Continue that support by not making mountains out of molehills. They'll ruin everyone's new view. Including yours."

Luke's not exactly sure what the hierarchy is for the strange deals Cole Graydon's put together to bring all this new construction to Altamira. But never in a million years did he think a problem with Jordy Clements would travel all the way up the shadowy ladder to the man who's become the puppet master of both his life and Charley's. (And pretty much everyone in town, even if they don't quite realize the extent of it.)

"We haven't even given him his phone call," Luke whispers. "Who did he call?"

"He didn't call anyone. He didn't need to."

"You've got spies all over town, is what you're saying."

"He's not worth your time, Luke."

"He beat up a woman."

"If that's true, he'll be dealt with. Just not by you."

For a second, Luke feels a surge of relief. Cole Graydon can deal with people far more effectively than any member of the Altamira Sheriff's Department ever could, usually with private armies of mercenaries and surveillance technology that puts the most paranoid conspiracy theorists to shame.

Who knows? Maybe the punishment Cole's got planned for Jordy's going to be way too severe. But Luke doubts it. What he hears is the powerful protecting the son of someone slightly less powerful, someone he might have made a special backroom deal with to get the tunnel project underway.

"Luke?"

"OK."

"Good. Take care."

Cole hangs up, and the next thing he knows he's settling back into the chair in front of Mona's desk while she studies him with as much energy as she can muster, which isn't much.

"Luke . . . ?"

"Charley's coming home soon."

"Oh, good. Where's she been?"

"Visiting family."

"Not her father."

"No, never."

"I didn't think she had much family left."

"Some cousins . . . aunts," Luke lies.

Mona nods. Luke nods.

"Luke?"

"Yeah?"

"Jordy . . ."

"I know," Luke says, more to himself than to her. "We have to let him go."

She feels the wind first.

It's colder than any she's ever felt in town. Then she feels the dull throb of the injuries covering her battered face. There's a new sensation there, not as deep and painful as the others. When she tries to open her eyes, she learns the source—she's been blindfolded.

Now that she's aware she can't see, her body is in a rush to make sense of her surroundings using her other senses.

A length of something—she figures rope—ties her wrists against her back. She can't be sure the same rope is what's securing her ankles together. But there's something else of which she's becoming gradually but sickeningly sure.

She's upside down.

Her hair's been tied back; otherwise she would have realized this right away, but her postnasal drip's running backward, making fire in the back of her throat, and her upper jaw's going sore from hanging at an unusual angle.

The cold, persistent wind grazing her body from inverted head to toe suggests she's inside some sort of vast outdoor space. Now she remembers the mad rush back to her trailer after the asshole cop threatened her. She remembers throwing open the door, already planning in her mind what she would grab and what she would leave behind. Then the darkness inside seemed to grab her, and that's when she realized, too late, that one of them had been waiting for her. Maybe they knew what she'd found, or maybe the other cop, the one who seemed to believe her, had made too much noise.

As soon as she put some distance between her and Altamira, she would have called him, told him about the gift she'd left him. That had been the plan. But she'd always been good at making plans, bad at keeping them.

And now, here she is.

Maybe they're trying to tell her they know about her fall. She wouldn't be surprised if they'd brought her back to the same spot. It was isolated as hell. When she'd gone to visit the place, she hadn't calculated the right time for sunset. The spot was on the eastern side of the mountain, which meant the place lost its good light well before dusk, and she'd found herself lost in shadows quicker than she'd expected. That's why she'd tripped and almost somersaulted to her death.

There's a sharp crack off to her right.

It takes her a second to identify the sound.

At first, she thinks maybe it's a snapping stick. But it's too resonant.

It echoes.

And then there's another sound just like it. Farther away.

Farther down.

Farther *below.*

The sound repeats, and repeats, as the rock bounces down into what sounds like a chasm that travels to the center of the goddamn earth.

Of course, she thinks, fighting a sob. *Of course they'd try to break me like this.*

When they'd all moved to Altamira, they'd driven her over that back road just up the coast because they said the views were beautiful, but it was barely two lanes wide, made of dirt, and there were no guardrails. The drops to one side were so steep she'd actually started screaming in the back seat and begging them to turn around. She'd always been afraid of heights, ever since she was a little girl and her dad took her on the gondola that traveled up the side of the mountain next to Palm Springs. At least her dad had allowed her to shield her face against his chest. But the men who drove her over that twisting mountain road had only laughed at her tears, joked about how they'd take her over the road on a motorcycle so she could really get a sense of its twists and turns. And she'd been forced to cover her head in the back seat and breathe as deeply as she could, imagining she was someplace else, someplace with level roads and better, kinder men.

The blindfold clogs her hot tears.

She's grateful there's no gag, because there's a good chance she might throw up. But if they plan to drop her to her death, maybe choking on her own vomit would be preferable.

Somehow not seeing what she's dangling over is worse than seeing. Much worse. She can imagine the drop goes on forever and at any moment she could plunge face-first into the dark, her bound wrists depriving her of even the most desperate of last-minute attempts to break her fall with her arms.

They think she's weak.

Should she be surprised? She's been a disappointment to everyone. Try as she might, every night before she goes to sleep she sees the expression on her parents' faces when they realized she was stealing pain pills from her grandmother's hospice bed. She sees the look on Jordy's smug, satisfied face every time she came crawling back, begging for forgiveness. Again.

All her life she's been weak. Up until recently, she's only pretended to fight the urge. Only made promises to get her demons under control.

When they let her go, that will change.

Now she'll be strong.

What other choice does she have?

It won't last forever, whatever this torture is. They're trying to find out what she knows, find out what she told the cops. And she didn't tell them anything, at least not in the way they assume.

But this current game will be followed by something worse. Something she might not survive.

A sense of peace comes over her.

She realizes, for the first time in her life, that deciding to be strong doesn't mean you get to decide what you'll endure and when.

All her life she's begged and pleaded and made empty threats to the people who stood in her way. The only way to get through what lies ahead with her dignity intact is to be the opposite of that person. It's her only advantage. If she transforms herself into a person they don't recognize, then they won't know how to control her.

Silence.

The word's always made her feel anxious before. Now it fills her with calm.

She can still talk, but only to herself.

Someone will find it, she tells herself. *They have to. They've got cameras. They'll find it, and then they'll know everything. Even if I'm gone by then.*

Just as Lacey Shannon starts to turn these words into a mantra, another rock cracks against the cliff face nearby and begins its long, echoing plummet.

22

Luke announced the week before that he was sick of cards, so he and the guys who've been gathering at his house every Saturday since Charlotte left have started sampling board games. So far Monopoly's been the only one to meet with their collective approval, but they're still hunting for alternates.

Scattergories and Cards Against Humanity are out. Both made them feel like bougie married couples in the big city who needed giant glasses of merlot to do spit takes with—not four dudes, three with criminal records, brought together just a few months earlier by the world's strangest hunt for a serial killer.

When Trev Rucker, a wiry, heavily tattooed former marine sniper, walks through the door of Luke's house holding up a Battleship box and sporting the most eager smile Luke's ever seen on the guy, Martin Cahill, the group's resident father figure, laughs so hard he literally doubles over where he's standing in the door to Luke's kitchen. Marty's laughing a lot easier than he has these past few weeks. Luke's not surprised. If anyone's as relieved as he is that Charley's coming soon, it's the man who's always been the closest thing Charley's had to a real, loving dad.

Rucker's good buddy Dave Brasher—who's already parked in front of Luke's TV with a root beer and the remote he's just used to mute an episode of some reality show about truck accidents in the snow—turns his head to see what all the fuss is about. His silent laughter causes his giant body to shake like a sleeping dog trying to slough off flies.

"What?" Rucker whines.

"It's a two-person game, Trev," Luke says.

"And you're a goddamn marine," Martin manages between cackles.

"*Dishonorably* discharged," Rucker curses as he tosses the game onto the sofa beside Brasher. "And I didn't serve on a goddamn battleship, all right? Shut up, all of you. What then, charades?"

Luke takes a seat at the dining room table Charlotte made him buy at a flea market in Paso Robles right before she left. She said the ring marks on the hardwood gave it character. When he started getting antsy before her departure, she made him promise they'd refinish it together once she was back. Make it a project. Something to look forward to. Now that he knows she's OK, his fingers aren't sweaty when he runs them over the tabletop. But still, he wants her home.

"Maybe we don't need a game to cut the tension tonight," Luke says.

Marty takes a seat next to Luke. "I didn't think we were trying to cut the tension so much as just . . . you know, trying to be friends, given how hard that is for some of us."

"I know how to make friends." Luke gestures at all of them.

"Learning and knowing are different things," Marty says.

"Thanks, Buddha."

"More like Oprah." Brasher rises from the sofa as if it's the hardest thing he's ever done, which given his formidable size, it just might be.

Soon, they're all seated at the table, no board game or deck of cards between them. A few months earlier, Brasher's Oprah comment might have been a little more cutting. Maybe something that used words like *wuss*, or included some more articulate weaponization of the idea that any exchange of feelings between men rendered at least one of them unmanly. Of late, the group's taste for gendered, if not flat-out sexist, remarks is leaving them. Watching a woman crush a man's entire hand with one of her own does that.

Or maybe the guys hear themselves clearly and learn from their mistakes quickly now because they're always sober. Luke's not really sure. The guys don't talk about their recovery much, even though all three of them met in AA, and Luke's pretty sure Marty's their mentor, or whatever they call it. Sponsor. Though they never lecture Luke about the occasional beer he drinks in their presence.

And God knows, Marty's more than capable of lecturing people when he sets his mind to it.

"Heard you got into it with Jordy Clements yesterday," Brasher says.

"No law enforcement talk at the table," Martin says.

"That's during game play," Brasher whines. "There's no game. What are we going to talk about?"

"Lacey Shannon, any of you know her?" Luke asks.

"She's Clements's girlfriend, I think," Brasher grumbles. "Seems a little on edge, few times I've seen her."

"She a drinker? She ever pop into one of your meetings?" Luke asks.

"Couldn't tell you if she had," Marty says. "It's an anonymous program."

"Never seen her at the clubhouse," Rucker says, then bows his head when he sees Marty's withering look.

"Any ideas why Cole Graydon called and told me to let Jordy go last night after he beat her up?"

This question—and the news wrapped inside it—settles over the table like a thick blanket, and for the next few seconds, it's like they're trying to take deep breaths through it and failing. You could say Charlotte's the one who brought them all together. Or you could say it's Marty, since he's the one who brought Brasher and Rucker into the hunt for the Mask Maker at the eleventh hour. But not really.

Cole Graydon's the reason they're all sitting where they are now.

Cole's the reason Marty, who up until a few months ago was just a small-town contractor whose specialty was hot tub installs and floor refinishing, was made a highly paid key foreman on the construction of the expansive luxury resort, and Brasher and Rucker his two suspiciously well-paid point men. Maybe Cole's buying their silence about what went down with the Mask Maker, or maybe he really does just want to ensure Charlotte's happiness by ensuring the happiness of everyone around her.

If that's the case, Luke wonders, *why didn't he at least let me force Jordy to spend the night in holding? That would have made me very, very happy.*

"Thoughts?" Luke asks.

"Keep an eye on him," Marty says, "but don't make a mess."

"Cole or Jordy?"

"Jordy."

Luke feels like he's been shoved.

It's not the injustice of letting Cole decide which of Altamira's woman beaters gets to walk free. It's that never-minces-words Marty—fierce defender of the downtrodden, the guy who seemed willing to defend Charlotte's honor with his fists when Luke first crossed his path as a grown-up with a badge—is the one saying it's a good idea.

It's that Cole is frightening enough to scare Marty.

"Look," Marty says into the tense silence, "it may feel like we're the only ones who know Altamira might have made a deal with the devil, but other people have got their suspicions. True, they haven't seen the side of Graydon Pharmaceuticals that we have, but still . . . If more bad elements come rolling into town, there's going to be push-back, and then you and Charley can both say something to Cole."

"Unless Cole's the one putting them here," Rucker says quietly.

"Say what?" Marty asks.

"Unless Cole's putting the bad elements here for a reason. Because there's a profit to him."

"He runs a billion-dollar company," Marty says. "He's not messing around in organized crime."

"So that's what you think we've got now?" Luke asks. "Organized crime?"

"No," Marty says as he shakes his head, but he's staring down at his Coke can as if he's not sure his next words are the truth, but he'd like them to be. "No, I think we've got hookers. And I think we've got Jordy Clements thinking he can get away with whatever. And when the resort's finished and the tunnel's built and the roads are done, Jordy and everybody else who's come here for a piece will move on to the next feeding frenzy."

"So the mess isn't permanent, is what you're saying," Luke says.

"Look, this is how it always goes when there's a building boom or an oil strike. Everybody tries to get a piece of the action, and for a while it's chaos. Then the project's done and things settle and the locals are all fat and happy."

"Until they run out of oil," Brasher grumbles.

"The oil's the tunnel and Pearsons Road. Once that's done, we're set."

Only there hasn't been an oil strike, Luke thinks. *None of this is natural. It's all been engineered by Cole Graydon, and they've got no idea what tricks he's pulled behind the scenes to make it happen.*

But there's still a lot of truth in what Marty's saying. Even if the resort goes bust, the tunnel and the widening of the road that leads to it will turn Altamira into a well-placed stop on a safe, new thoroughfare between a heavily trafficked freeway and one of the most beloved scenic highways in the world. For the first time, Altamira will be something more than a name on a freeway sign most people blow past on their way to Los Angeles or San Francisco.

Brasher hears the car first and turns in his chair.

Luke and Marty both jump to their feet at the same time. Then they're all standing in the front yard. A Lincoln Town Car's pulling away from the curb, and a short figure about Charlotte's height is headed up the front walk, toting the same rolling suitcase Charlotte left with. The baseball cap is distinctly un-Charlotte, however. Either her shoulder-length hair's been gathered up under it, or she chopped it all off. This reminds Luke too much of his mother's chemo baldness, and for a second, he actually hopes it's not Charlotte walking toward them but one of Cole's minions whose brought her stuff back ahead of time.

Because that wouldn't be a bad sign at all.

But it's Charley. And when he sees the bright-eyed smile she's giving them, something inside him turns soft, then gives way. Suddenly he's closed the distance between them and she's in his arms, her feet actually coming up off the sidewalk as her suitcase lists to one side behind her.

"Easy, tiger," she gasps, but she doesn't sound like she wants him to let her go. Not yet. So the only concession he makes is to set her back down on the pavement and tighten his embrace a little and lean back so he can see her face.

If the guys weren't there, he'd channel all his relief into a show-stopper of a kiss, but they're already moving forward and ushering them inside, and Marty's asking Charley what she'd like to drink. So Luke's forced to share her for the time being, even though that's the last thing he wants to do.

Then, when they're in the dining room, under the harsh overhead light, he sees it.

He's looking for a ghostly, shell-shocked expression, but what he sees is much different. There's a radiance to her that's distinctly new, and he finds himself rushing to explain it away. Even the blandest food will taste like a delicacy to a starving man, and maybe the fact that he's missed her so much has him regarding every tilt of her chin or cock of her head as if it were ballet. Then he has a darker suspicion—that she's both deeply satisfied and energized by whatever gruesome punishment she meted out against her target, the name of whom she's forbidden to share with him.

But as he studies her, as he guides her to the dining table by one hand while the other guys pelt her with small talk all designed to distract everyone from the fact that they can't ask her questions about where she's been, Luke realizes none of these explanations will suffice. This radiance is in her flesh, her coloring. Even the dome of her forehead looks smoother, younger.

Shouldn't she look the opposite? Exhausted and worn out? *Recovering,* that's the word Cole used. Whatever happened out there, she actually needed some recovery time. And here she is, a day later, looking younger and fresher than when she left.

"When are we refinishing this table?" she asks.

"Didn't know we'd signed on for that project," Marty says.

"You didn't. I'm talking to Luke."

Luke smiles, and he sees, despite her improved appearance, the tension and nervousness that comes from not being able to discuss the operation. It's jarring for all of them, Luke realizes, given what they went through together to get the Mask Maker.

"Figured you'd need some time to rest first," he says.

"Ah, I'm fine."

"Well, we can start tonight, then."

"Not tonight. Just . . . soon."

"Soon." He closes the distance between them, takes her in his arms, then reaches up to try to get a peek under her cap.

"Ew, don't," she says.

"What happened?"

"Oh, it wasn't during. It was before. I thought we were going to use a wig, but . . ."

"Gotcha."

But the way she just trailed off leaves them all awkwardly looking at anything that's not her. Finally, Marty says, "Did you get him at least? Can you tell us that?"

The shadow of something passes through Charlotte's expression as she turns to look at the most important man in her life besides Luke.

"Yeah. We got him."

Marty smiles.

Rucker and Brasher both raise their soft drinks in toast, and Luke pulls her in tighter.

"So," Charley says, drawing him close again.

"So?"

"I've got an idea for my hair," she says.

"Yeah?"

"Yeah, and I figure you might be able to help me with it."

23

The ragged strands of hair they'd left her with fall in clumps around her shoulders as Luke runs the clippers across her head. Some of it lands on the bath towel he's tucked over her shoulders, the rest of it around the legs of the chair he's pulled into the bathroom for this little impromptu haircut. "Maybe the guys shouldn't wait on us," she says.

"You've never shaved your head before, have you," Luke asks.

"No."

"OK, well, it goes by real fast."

"Are these the ones you use on yourself?"

"The clippers? Yeah, but not everywhere." He waggles his eyebrows. She gives him a playful slap on the hip. "What? You're the one who likes things under control down there."

He's been patient with her in the bedroom—he's only the second man she's ever been with, and she can't even remember the first guy's name—but right before she shipped out, their shared anxiety about her imminent departure brought the heat between them to a boil. They went from slow, careful lovemaking to her tying his wrists to the bedposts and saying, "Just give me an hour to see where you're sensitive," to which he nodded enthusiastically. In those last few weeks, her inexperience and curiosity around sex became a kind of expeditionary hunger, and he was more than happy to be explored. Her memories of these last hungry couplings quieted her heart during the long periods of isolation and waiting that followed.

"What do you think?" he asks. "You want to leave a little or go cue ball?" He runs his fingers gently over the straw-colored fuzz.

"That depends."

"On what?"

"What you want."

"It's your hair, baby."

"Yeah, but they're your fingers and the way you're moving them right now is giving me chills, and let's just say I'd like to have a head you enjoy touching now and then."

He sets the clippers down on the counter, bends down, and kisses her gently on the forehead. Since he's got no idea what she's been through over the past few weeks, he's probably trying his best not to rush it. "Only now and then?" he whispers.

"More than now and then."

This time he kisses her on the lips, and suddenly she's rising up off the chair. His arms encircle her, and she feels a surge of desire she's afraid she might not be able to control.

Surviving, she tells herself, *going into the belly of the beast and surviving—that's the turn-on.* But what if he knew? What if he knew that her actions had led to Davies's death? What if he'd seen the rage she'd unleashed on the man, a rage that eventually caused him to bleed out?

Would he still be gentle and hungry with me at the same time?

Luke seems to sense these wandering thoughts during their kiss and pulls away slightly.

"This is weird," she says.

"Making out in the bathroom when you're covered in loose hairs?"

"That's . . . sort of weird, yeah. But no, I . . . I feel good, Luke."

"Of course you do. I'm here."

"Yeah, there's that. But . . ."

"But what?"

"I kinda blew up."

Luke just stares at her, but he doesn't pull away. Still, his serious expression is a bit much for her to stare at while they're nose to nose.

"Blew up how?"

"There was a booby trap at the site. Where we were . . . working. And I walked into it and . . . boom."

For a while he doesn't say anything, but he doesn't let her go, either. She's reminded of the first time he'd witnessed her power, reminded of the way he'd stumbled to the nearest trash can and emptied his stomach into it. Should she expect a similar reaction now? Or is this fear widening his eyes and tensing his mouth and making his chest rise and fall with breaths that look too shallow for his broad frame?

She knows he wanted to be there, and she's afraid he'll try to make the case again now. What will she say? She's probably already told him too much. What's the difference between telling him about the explosion and telling him that Davies didn't survive the night?

Simple. One paints her as a miracle. The other, a murderer.

"Jesus," he whispers. "I wish . . ."

"What?"

"Nothing."

There it is, she thinks. *He wishes he could have been there.* But what would he have done? Sat in some control room, gradually seeing her as less than human.

"But you're OK."

Relieved they seem to be moving on from his unspoken question, she says, "I guess, yeah. They poked and prodded me for a day and ran all kinds of tests. But . . ."

"All right, careful. I don't want you to say anything that will earn you the wrath of Cole."

"I was on fire from head to toe. I passed out right away. But by the time the medics got to me, my wounds were closing. In any other circumstance, they would have been fatal."

For a while they just stare at each other, neither one moving, as they process the profound weirdness of yet another profoundly weird development.

"And you feel . . . better?" Luke asks, eyes wide.

"Healthier," she says. "More energetic."

"You don't think it's because . . ."

"Because what?"

"You enjoyed it?"

The question moves through her like the first chill from a fever.

I didn't enjoying hearing the news that Davies was dead, she thinks, *but I didn't actually shed a tear over him, either. It's like an absence of feeling. Do I have to name it? Can I just let it be an absence?*

"I didn't enjoy the blowing up part," she finally says.

"What was it like?"

"Full system shutdown. I just blacked out."

"We can't get some of the most powerful sedatives in the world to work on you when you're triggered, but at the first sign of a major trauma, you just black out? How does that work?"

"I wish I knew."

"I don't suppose they told you."

"They shared some test results with me. They were general."

"What does that mean?"

"Their working theory is my whole body basically went through what a muscle goes through in the gym. It gets traumatized, and it grows back, possibly a little healthier, they're not sure. Only thanks to Zypraxon it happened almost instantly and all over my body."

"Healthier . . . how?" he asks.

"Red and white blood cell counts are a little better than they were before. Resting blood oxygen levels are improved, like I've done a bunch of cardio. Same with resting heart rate. Everything just . . . a little bit better. That's how they put it."

"Well, if you factor in that all of those things should have been knocked way off-balance by your injuries, it's more than just a little bit."

"True," she says.

He averts his eyes, releases her from his embrace. He starts cleaning the head of the clippers, a tense set to his jaw.

"What?" she finally asks.

"I guess we just have to trust them. I mean, that's the deal you made, right?"

"Yeah, it's the deal I made. I'm sorry if I didn't consult you first. I—"

"No, no, Charley, I didn't mean to sound like that. I just . . ."

"What? You can tell me anything . . . right?"

Even though I can't tell you everything, she realizes. *Wow. Walked right into that one.* But he doesn't take the opening.

"Some things happened while you were gone. Not as big as what you went through, but . . ."

"But what?"

"They're making me wonder about the deals Cole made to get all this stuff going."

"Which stuff?" she asks.

"The tunnel. The resort."

"Well, those are good things, right?"

"Sure. But . . . So I brought in Jordy Clements last night because his girlfriend said he beat her up. Cole called my cell phone and told me to let him go. I'd only had the guy in holding for a few minutes."

"That isn't petty. That's . . . weird. Did he say why?"

"He said I was making mountains out of molehills."

"OK. Did you point out that he's currently developing a drug that could allow women to protect themselves against violence and meanwhile he's telling you to let a guy free who just beat up his girlfriend?"

"No."

"Why not? That's exactly the kind of thing you'd say."

"The old me, maybe. The new me doesn't want to make things worse for you. With him. He said you were recovering. I didn't know what that meant. I just didn't want to be an inconvenience."

"That's not a word I'd ever use to describe you."

"You know what I mean. I've got a mouth on me," he says quietly.

She kisses the mouth in question. "Thank God."

"You're using sex to distract me from my feelings."

"Do you mind?"

"Not really, no."

He returns the gentle kiss she gives him with a more powerful one of his own. Then, just when she feels herself rocking forward onto the balls of her feet, he pulls away. "You think I could have said that to him?" he asks.

"What? The irony thing?"

"Yeah. I mean, am I allowed to say anything to him?"

"He called you, right?"

"To tell me you were OK and to give me an order. I mean, he didn't call to discuss sports."

"I don't think he's into sports."

"That's homophobic."

"No, I just don't think he's into anything that doesn't involve billions of dollars and some form of light world domination."

"*Light* world domination? That's cute. Does it say that on the bottle?"

"I've never seen his pantry. I'm assuming it's spotless and white. Look, you've met him, all right? I have no idea what the guy does for fun besides . . ."

"Run our lives."

"He doesn't run our lives."

"Charley."

"He runs a few weeks of our lives out of every few months."

"A few weeks? You were gone for over a month."

"Yeah, well, most of that was prep."

"All right, careful. Don't tell me too much that's top secret."

Because you don't want me in trouble with Cole, she thinks, *or you don't want to hear about the game unless you can play, too?*

"I'm just saying. When I'm on an operation, he runs our lives. When I'm home, we run each other's lives."

"Good."

She pulls him close. It's like he's got a gravitational orbit around him, and she can't stay out of it no matter how hard she tries. Maybe it's because the bathroom's tiny, or maybe it's because she's so glad to see him. Or maybe it's because the energy surge she's been feeling since she recovered from the explosion has intensified her desire.

She doesn't know. Right now, she doesn't care. What she cares about is that he smells like that woodsy soap he uses, and his chest looks broad and solid enough for her to sleep against while he runs his fingers over her almost shaved head. And those things sound nice. Very nice.

She's still holding him when he says, "Charley, if he's calling telling me who I can or can't arrest, he's running this town. And if he's running this town, then he's running our lives."

"You want me to talk to him?"

"Not yet."

"What, then?" she asks.

"I want us to pay attention to everything he does. Or doesn't do."

"Deal."

"You're not just saying that so you can kiss me some more?" he asks.

"No, if I'm going to resort to deception, I'll be after more than kissing."

"Well, you do kinda need a shower."

"What? I smell bad?"

"No," he says, "you've got hair all over you."

"Good point."

"You want me to step out?" He starts to pull away before she can answer. When she responds by grabbing him by one shoulder, he smiles in a way that makes her neck get hot.

"That's a no," she says.

"One second, then," he says.

He opens the door partway.

"What are you doing?" she asks.

"Hey, guys!" he shouts.

"Yep?" comes Marty's reply.

"Go home!"

Then he shuts the door before they can protest.

24

"Four weeks is a month," Cole says.

He's been swiveling back and forth in his desk chair during Julia Crispin's unnecessarily protracted lead-up to this announcement. Now he stops the chair with one foot, raises a hand to his earpiece as if he didn't hear her right because it's coming loose. It isn't.

"I'm aware of that, thank you," she answers.

Too many people play fast and loose with the definition of the word *irony*, but he's pretty sure his late father's mistress talking to him like she's actually his mother qualifies. He's always considered it a strange credit to his dad's character that he married a piece of vapid arm candy and carried on a lengthy affair with an accomplished woman of substance. But of late, Julia Crispin has become a lot more to Cole than an old family secret.

She's the inventor of TruGlass, the device that allows him to monitor Charlotte Rowe's every move during an op. She was also one of the original members of The Consortium, a secret alliance of defense industry contractors who pooled their resources so they could fund Project Bluebird 1.0 without traces of it showing up on the ledgers of their respective companies. Until Cole pulled the plug after the first four test subjects literally tore themselves apart.

"Then why not just say a month?" he asks.

"Would you also like me to say it in French?"

"You speak French?"

"No," Julia answers, "I'm implying, in plain English, that I don't think it's the number of days or weeks that's bothering you here."

"It's a while."

"These are busy men with companies to run. Philip has meetings in Zurich and Dubai, and Stephen can't get out of the UK for two weeks at the earliest. In four weeks, also known as a *month*, everyone will be free and we'll all sit down at Philip's ranch in Whitefish and discuss what's in front of us."

Cole doesn't say anything. He wants to spin the chair around again, but then he'll catch his reflection in the wall of glass behind his desk, which might confirm his suspicion that he's currently pouting. He'd hoped his former business partners would be more impressed by the footage he shared of Charley's takedown of Pemberton and now her overpowering of Richard Davies. If Julia presented it to them with the fire of the newly reconverted, so much the better.

And yet they're making him wait a month.

"Perhaps you could thank me in French," Julia finally says.

"I thought you said they were impressed."

"They were. The explosive finale gave them some pause, even though I tried telling them that was all part of the test."

"It wasn't."

"I know. And they weren't convinced, so it's a moot point."

"Fine. A month."

"Still no *thank-you*?"

"I was hoping for more excitement," he says.

"They're excited."

"Then why aren't they calling me?"

"You hate Philip. You actually want to talk to him on the phone?"

"Philip hates me because he thinks anyone who doesn't kill, skin, and cook their own lunch every day is soft. And personally, I think men who shoot deer for fun are trying to hide the fact that they have tiny corkscrew penises."

"Don't ever tell him that."

"Too late. Stephen and I get along. Why doesn't he call?"

"You asked me to be your representative in this. If you want to talk to them, call them yourself."

"I just figured they'd be more impressed."

"They're impressed, and guess what? So am I. The operation, the size of it. The resources. You impressed me. So no matter what happens, you can count on me, for sure."

This is, perhaps, the most agreeable exchange he's ever had with Julia Crispin, and he's not quite sure how to bring it to a close. Neither is she, apparently. Because after they both mutter a few more thankyous, she hangs up without saying goodbye.

By day, the glass and steel interior of Graydon's headquarters feels clinical and stark. Around this time of night, however, when most of the overhead lights are off and there's little to reflect off the walls of glass, the offices feel vaporous and limitless.

Cole could enter any room at will, rifle through any drawer he wants, and nobody could do a thing about it. These urges are childish and petty, and he's never once given in to them. But once, at around this hour, he did have sex with Dylan Cody—it's hard to think of him as Noah in his memories—on the carpeted floor of his office, a few feet from where he's sitting now.

He wishes they'd left a scuff mark or a stain. Some tiny artifact of a moment when Cole thought Dylan was a mad genius and their relationship might blossom into an unconventional marriage defined by mutual ambition and the devastating expertise with which Dylan catered to Cole's darker appetites.

But the carpet's immaculate, and the man walking toward Cole's office now has never been a lover. He's no longer what Cole would even consider an ally.

Ed Baker steps through the open door and goes still a few feet from the empty chair on the other side of Cole's glass desk.

So he's figured it out, Cole thinks, *which isn't a surprise given I haven't told him a word about how the Davies operation concluded after I threw him out of the control center.*

"I guess I'm not here for an update on Davies," Ed says.

"There were complications. Your insistence that we not sweep his property in advance turned out to have consequences. Bad ones. I should have overruled you."

"Well, you've been real busy these days, haven't you?" It sounds like a taunt. Ed's entwined his hands behind his back, his shoulders rigid. The surrounding desk lamps are too low to give his bald dome its usual shine. "So what's it gonna be? You moving me to some lab that doesn't exist?"

"You're retiring," Cole says.

For what feels to Cole like a long time, Ed doesn't blink.

"For telling you the truth?" he asks.

"The truth? About what, exactly?"

"You're letting that woman run the show, and it's going to end in disaster."

"I'm sorry. When did you tell me *that*? And when would I have ever asked for your opinion?"

"I was keeping her in check."

"You were drawing her attention to how badly we violated her privacy after one of our former employees slipped her a drug that could have torn her to pieces. And you were doing it at the very moment when we needed her complete participation in an operation we'd been planning for months."

"I disagree."

"Who gives a fuck? You're fired!"

"I thought I was retiring."

"I'm spinning it. For your sake, so don't push it."

"And if I do . . . push it?"

Cole opens his desk drawer, extends a file folder in one hand. It's bulging with pages still warm from the laser printer. Ed forces a dead look into his eyes as he takes it. He leafs through its contents while he stands. Whether he's scanning them or reading them in depth, Cole can't tell. Surely he doesn't need to absorb the details. The figures are impossible to forget. Ed made considerable money selling confiscated guns back to street criminals during his time as a patrol cop on the LAPD, before he vaulted up its power structure later in life.

Ed clears his throat. But he can't look up from the folder. He's like a motorist passing a car accident, only every mangled body is his.

"Your father would never have—"

"People have very complicated feelings about the police right now, Ed. Don't compel me to make this public."

Ed lets out a small, unreadable grunt and closes the folder slowly.

"And what do you expect me to do in my new retirement?" he asks.

"You'll go back up to LA, probably. Use your LAPD credentials to become the security director for a big celebrity. Preferably one who travels a lot and has multiple homes for you to worry about. I'll write you a sterling recommendation if you want."

"And what will this recommendation say?"

"Not one word of what you actually did here. Not one. And if you ever consider saying one word about it yourself, if you ever so much as think about consulting an attorney about the language of your confidentiality agreement, and so help me God, if you ever begin a speech in my presence that begins with the words *your father* again, I will flush your entire LAPD career down the drain, and you'll spend your retirement on a boat in Lake Havasu cursing my name."

"I hate Lake Havasu," Ed says.

"Me too."

"You haven't answered my question."

"Which is?"

"What will my recommendation say?"

"That you were steady, reliable. Loyal. That you stayed up to date on modern security and surveillance technologies. That you were someone I could count on, that my father could count on when he was alive."

Ed laughs. He's looking at the glass wall behind Cole as if there's a punchline spray-painted on it.

"What's so funny?" Cole asks.

"You're firing me because you're afraid I hurt her feelings." Ed's mirth has been replaced by stone-cold anger. "After my *years* of service to this company, you're firing me because you're afraid of how something I said made that crazy bitch *feel*. And if that isn't the most limp-wristed, candy-ass—"

Ed falls silent as soon as Cole rises to his feet, fists planted on the glass desk in front of him. "I'm firing you because I'm sick and tired of your belief that the hundreds of Africans you and my father killed during secret drug trials is somehow less of a blight on humanity than what I'm trying to accomplish with Zypraxon. I'm firing you because you can't take orders from a gay man, and you're worse at taking them from a woman."

"Your sexuality has never had a damn thing to do with my opinion of—"

"Thank you. My limp-wristed candy ass will take that to heart."

"None of us should ever be taking orders from *her*, Cole. Especially not you. That's the point."

"The point of your shitty, insubordinate attitude, perhaps."

"You took responsibility for her when you shouldn't have because you let the psycho formerly known as Dylan Cody fuck your judgment. In more ways than one. So now, you've set up an untenable situation where she's out in the world doing whatever she wants, exposing this company to God knows what risk, and you sit here lecturing me on my attitude!"

"I'm not lecturing you on anything. I'm retiring you."

"Because I pointed out the recklessness of your actions."

"In a manner of speaking, yes. I'm retiring you because if you had your way, Charlotte Rowe would be a prisoner for the rest of her life, and her life wouldn't last very long because of it. I'm retiring you because you're the last vestige of a depraved heartlessness with which my father ran this company, and I want you and *it* gone. And I'm retiring you because I'm determined that by the time my reign here is over, my limp-wristed candy ass will have murdered far fewer innocent people in the name of science than you and my father did during your long, sweet time together."

Ed's smile is slight and coy. "Not all of those people were killed in the name of science."

Cole feels the anger coursing through his veins turn into something icy and solid that seems to slide earthward from the pull of its own sudden weight. He hears wind rushing through a clearing fringed with haggard pines, feels the echoing memory of a fiery pain shooting up the side of his nose and forehead from the spot where one of his front teeth was knocked out.

The only way to keep the evidence of these memories from his expression is to remain completely still, and so he does, even though Ed's smile is growing wider.

"I know who you're referring to." Cole feels as if his voice is coming from someplace far away, propelled through his body by the breath of his father's ghost. "They weren't innocent. Neither are you."

"Are you actually threatening my life?" Ed asks without a trace of fear.

"You have thirty more seconds with me. If you want to negotiate, do it."

"Twice my severance."

"Fine."

"I want to keep the Benz."

"No problem."

"And one other thing," Ed says.

"I'm listening."

"I want you to repeat something after me."

Cole just glares at him.

"Are you ready?" Ed asks. When Cole doesn't answer, Ed starts slowly toward the desk. "I, Cole Graydon, put my father's billion-dollar legacy at risk because I finally found a man who could violate me like I had no value at all, thereby distracting me from the fact that I'm too damaged to have what anyone would describe as a normal human relationship, even by limp-wristed, candy-ass standards."

"Get out before I cut the brake line on the Benz."

Cole's alone once again, only now the emptiness of the surrounding offices doesn't feel liberating. It feels vulnerable to infection by his memories.

Memories of what his father did years ago.

For me, he thinks against his will. *What my father did* for *me.*

The sharp smells of untended soil and pine work in concert to drown out the stink of fear-fueled sweat. The fiery face pain, the eye above his knocked-out tooth that's still watering long after the tears have stopped, and the gentle feel of his father's hands coming to rest on his shoulders as they watched the drug go to work. His father's confident whisper. *"Remember. No matter what happens to you, you will always be my boy."* Together, these memories are like echoes in his blood.

He'd much prefer the memory of being defiled, willingly, on the office floor by a man who was later revealed to be a con artist and a psychopath. But that memory feels remote now—a strange irony, given how well Ed just highlighted the connection between the two.

Once he manages to collect himself, he sits at his laptop and starts composing a bland email to his human resources director, advising the woman of Ed's decision to retire and the terms they've negotiated. He tells her of his desire to promote from within, quickly.

Then, time seems to turn liquid.

He's staring out the plate glass wall at the glowing fringe of mansions lining the southern cliff faces along La Jolla Bay. Their lights seem to twinkle, but it's probably just the curtain of eucalyptus branches brushing against the glass in the ocean breeze.

He's thinking of how much time he and Ed have spent together since his father died. Imagines what it would mean to spend that much time with someone in possession of the same attributes Dylan—*Noah!*—used to cause his so-called error in judgment, again and again and again.

The email sits unsent on his computer.

He adds a line asking that all headshots and related photographs be removed from the applicants' personnel files before they're sent over.

The right candidate for this job will be picked on the basis of his accomplishments, of his résumé, and not, like Dylan, the inviting, wolfish look in his dark eyes.

25

Luke's cell phone is making that skittering sound that tells him it's moving across his nightstand. He ignores it anyway.

There are probably a few things in the world that would be harder for him right now than pulling away from Charlotte's almost naked body.

Damn if he can think what they might be.

It's his day off, a time to sleep in. But still, he's startled when he sees how bright the fringe of sunlight is around the window shade. Is it already past ten?

Not that he should be surprised. Once they'd finished their shower, they ended up going several more rounds between the sheets. If memory serves, they didn't nod out until after two. When sleep did come, it was the kind that crept up on you, knocking you out midsentence because you'd used everything short of caffeine pills to keep it at bay. Hell, he was so excited to have Charley back, he would have put on a pot of coffee and stayed up all night talking to her if she'd asked.

The phone stops vibrating, then starts up again.

Mona. It has to be.

He's right.

"I know it's your day off, but I need you down here for a bit," she says.

"You need me to fill in?"

"No, something else."

"Am I in trouble?" he asks, swinging his legs to the floor.

"I've been looking at videos of Lacey Shannon's interview from the other night, and there's some stuff I'm not getting. Can you come down?"

Not getting, Luke thinks. *What does* that *mean?*

"She walked. I thought we were letting it go."

He spoke too quickly, with too much tension in his voice. The frosty silence from the other end tells him Mona feels the same way. She's got no idea about the call from Cole Graydon. She's probably only heard Cole's name once or twice, if at all.

How do you tell your real boss that your girlfriend's secret boss expects you to shut down a possible law enforcement investigation, especially when your real boss is a sheriff and your girlfriend's boss isn't even an elected official and does nine or ten possibly illegal things before breakfast? There isn't an advice columnist on the planet who could help with this one.

"Maybe," Mona answers, "but Henricks is a different matter."

"What? He's already making a stink?"

"Not yet, but he might. That's why I need proof Lacey walked out because he threatened her."

"Is there?"

"Do I have to send a limo, Luke? I said I need you at the station."

"Sorry. Charley's home."

"That's nice. Tell her you'll be back in an hour or two."

"On my way."

A quick shower and some soft kisses on the back of Charlotte's neck later, Luke is standing in Mona's office staring at a familiar face that makes him nervous.

The last time he saw Dr. Marcia Brewerton was on the front steps of Marty's trailer after she had examined Charley a few months before. Luke had still been reeling from his first exposure to Charlotte's new drug-fueled power, but the good doctor had been clueless. Marty had wanted Charlotte to undergo some kind of examination to make sure her first three exposures to Zypraxon hadn't messed with her heart rate or blood pressure, even if the exam was cursory and the doctor giving it had no idea what Charley had actually been through.

If Dr. Brewerton walked away from that strange afternoon with a bunch of questions, they're not present in her expression now. But she's a focused, stoic woman whose face doesn't betray much emotion. Her pageboy cut looks the same, and while he's not sure it's the same color, he's willing to bet the Ralph Lauren men's dress shirt she's got on is the same style.

Mona's closed the venetian blinds over all her office windows. She's also angled her laptop toward the front of her desk so all three of them can see it.

On screen is a paused image of Lacey Shannon, taken from the video footage of her visit to the station two nights before. The camera system in the interview room was upgraded a few weeks ago, a response to the room's skyrocketing number of visitors. Lacey's bruised and battered face assaults them in high-definition clarity.

"Walk us through that night," Mona says.

Luke looks to the doctor. She just stares back at him.

"Marcia's consulting," Mona says.

Unsure what this means, Luke nods.

He walks them through everything that happened that night after Lacey stumbled into the station. As he repeats the details, his vague sense of alarm coalesces into something else—suspicion. Of himself. He's hearing the story for the first time now that he's repeating it. He's hearing how little information Lacey gave them. How unjustified his arrest of Jordy actually was.

"Did I do something wrong?" Luke asks.

"That's not the reason for this meeting."

And that's not an answer to my question, he wants to say.

Dr. Brewerton finally breaks her silence with, "Nobody hit her."

"Excuse me?" Luke asks.

"Nobody hit her. She sustained her injuries in a fall."

"You've examined her? Where is she?"

"No, I studied the tape, and it's pretty clear."

"There's still no sign of her anywhere in town," Mona says.

"Wait, seriously. You're saying she fell down the stairs? That's like a joke people—"

"Easy, Luke," Mona warns.

"No," the doctor says, "I'm saying her injuries are consistent with someone who fell from a great height and landed on her face."

"She's got defensive wounds on her hands."

"She's got abrasions on her hands that are consistent with someone who threw her arms out to brace herself during a fall."

"Jesus Christ," Luke mutters.

"Excuse me?" Dr. Brewerton asks.

"Don't you volunteer at women's shelters? I mean, you're really coming in here to let Jordy off the hook for—"

"I'm not letting Jordy Clements off the hook for anything. For all we know, he's responsible for her fall. But what I can tell you is that Lacey Shannon did not sustain her injuries in an assault to her face by anyone's fists. Most of what she has are abrasions, and her black eyes don't have a knuckle pattern. So if you're going to investigate what Jordy did or didn't do, you should probably know what actually happened to her."

The doctor's voice doesn't rise above the level of calm during this entire speech, but Luke still feels like he's been disrobed and probed. It might not be her intention, but there's an implication in her diagnosis that cuts to the heart of his efficacy as a law enforcement officer.

He reacted too fast to the sight of Lacey, misdiagnosed her injuries out of ignorance. Went off to get Jordy before he had enough specifics about Lacey's claim. No doubt that's why Mona asked him to repeat everything that's on the tape. If he realizes these things just from reciting his own actions, she won't have to drop the hammer on him quite as hard.

"I apologize," Luke says.

"No need," the doctor says bluntly.

"Marcia, thanks for coming in." Mona extends her hand to the doctor, and she shakes it.

Luke does the same and is relieved when Marcia accepts his outstretched hand without hesitation. "How's Charley doing?"

"Good."

"You know, she's been back awhile now, and I haven't seen her once. Might be good for her to visit a doctor now and then. I'm the only full-time physician in town, right now anyway. At the rate we're going, we might have a hospital in a few months."

"I'll let her know," Luke says.

He doesn't tell her that on the outskirts of town, just north of Lake Patrick, there's an old ranch house that's been converted into a state-of-the-art trauma center. Cole's ordered Charley to report there immediately if she suffers so much as a sneezing fit.

Now, he's alone with Mona and his thudding heart and the frozen image of Lacey's battered face on the computer screen.

"She wants to be our medical examiner so bad she's practically itching for a homicide," Mona says.

"I wouldn't be surprised if we have one soon."

Mona doesn't disagree.

"I fucked up," he finally says.

"You moved a little fast, that's all. And that's not why I brought you in. Not the only reason anyway."

"So you do think I fucked up."

"Well, you did kinda let her blackmail you. You weren't under any obligation to cave to her demand that you throw Jordy in a cell before she talked. But you didn't have to tell her that. You could have fudged the truth a bit. Made it sound like somebody was on their way to get him. Suggest she start talking in the meantime just to get things rolling. That kind of thing."

Nobody says anything for a bit.

"What time did you head to the Gold Mine?" Mona asks.

"About nine forty-five."

"Someone used manual override on the camera system for the interview room just after ten."

"He threatened her, but he cut the cameras before he did it."

"I'm reasonably sure."

"How can we be one hundred percent sure?"

"I don't know."

"What about the general security cameras?"

Mona gives him a confused look. He doesn't blame her. She's had plenty of distractions of late, and the station's been forced to augment and improve what systems they can without consulting her every step of the way. If they don't get a new building soon, the place is going to end up looking like the Winchester Mystery House.

"We have general security cameras now?" she asks.

"We added three in the main room after the brawl last month."

"Do we have one on the entrance to the interview room?"

"No, but I'm pretty sure we covered the spot where the hallway enters the main room."

"Well, shit."

A few seconds later, Luke's sitting at Mona's desk as he accesses the station's general security system cameras.

"I should know this," Mona whispers.

"You've been busy."

"Well, I won't be for much longer."

Luke stops typing, turns to face her. "What does that mean?"

"He says he wants to let me off the hook. For good."

Luke spins in the desk chair. "He's breaking up with you?"

"He's not putting it like that. He says he doesn't want me to suffer, too. His mom says he's lost faith he's going to recover and I should ignore him, but . . . I don't want to talk about it. I need a distraction. Right now, it's Lacey Shannon."

The very thing Cole Graydon told me to let go. Awesome.

A few seconds later, he's found the archived footage of the night in question on all three general cameras. He runs them simultaneously, but they're slightly out of sync with each other, which makes him a little dizzy.

They've got Lacey's sudden entrance, the alarmed looks it earned from just about everyone in the station.

They've got Luke and Henricks leading her to the short hallway that connects to the interview room.

He can't fast-forward all three at once, so he picks the best angle on the hallway and advances to the moment when he came striding into the main room with Henricks nipping at his heels. Then he keeps fast-forwarding, watching as the clock at the bottom of the square advances past 9:40, 9:45, 9:50 . . .

When Henricks appears, alone, the two of them both sit back. Henricks turns down the hallway toward the interview room.

"Is that a hundred percent?" Luke asks.

"Pretty much. But I want to see her come out."

"Not going to be easy to tell what expression's on her face given how beat up it is."

"True, but still."

A few seconds later, head bowed, chewing on the thumbnail of her right hand, Lacey Shannon rounds the corner into the main room. She looks unsteady on her feet, and Luke wonders for a second if maybe she really was drunk. Her shoulder brushes the large potted plant next to her, then she looks toward the main room as if she's embarrassed by her collision with the ficus and wants to make sure nobody noticed it.

Luke was right—her black eyes make it impossible to read her expression.

Henricks doesn't appear behind her. But that makes sense. He knew about the cameras. No doubt he was holding back so he wouldn't look like the one driving her away. There's a restroom at the end of that hallway he could claim he was using. But he'd never be able to deny shutting the interview room camera off. Maybe that's why he quit.

Then Luke sees something that makes him go rigid.

Mona doesn't see it, however. She's just shaking her head at the screen.

With a mouse click, he closes the video.

Shame will follow at some point, he realizes. But right now he feels nothing but adrenaline, and this rush empowers a slew of rationalizations for what he's just done. He's protecting Mona from something she doesn't understand. He's protecting the whole department, small and strapped as it is, from something that could overwhelm its resources in the blink of an eye.

"That's all saved, right?" she asks.

"Yeah."

But you've got no idea how to access the archive, and that's a good thing, he thinks. Then he realizes the reason she can't navigate the system is because she's been so busy caring for her sick boyfriend, and his exhilaration turns to shame. *Well, that was quick,* he thinks.

"All right," Mona finally says, "I'm gonna keep looking for Lacey. I'm gonna operate on the belief that Henricks freaked her into running and she's out there somewhere."

"If she is, what do you think she's going to say?"

"I don't need to get involved in her relationship issues. If Jordy shoved her into a ditch, and she's running, good. But I need her to confirm Henricks is the reason she walked."

"In case Henricks tries to bring a suit or something?"

"Yeah, or in case I need to see if I've got others like him inside my station."

Luke just stares at her.

"Christ, I'm not talking about you, Luke."

His stomach feels like it's got a clenching fist in the middle of it. But he just nods.

"Thanks for coming in," she says. "This cleared up a lot of . . ." Just then her cell phone rings, and he can tell who's calling the minute he sees her expression as she looks at the screen.

"Need me to step out?" he says.

She nods, but it's like her eyes have already joined the upsetting phone call she's about to have with her incredibly sick, possibly soon-to-be-ex-boyfriend.

Luke subtly closes the screen on her laptop as if this is polite and necessary. Necessary for him, perhaps. But it's far from polite.

When he steps out into the main room, drawing her office door shut behind him, he's literally sweating under his collar for the first time he can remember. That giddy confidence that came over him a few minutes ago has turned into a blend of anxiety and dread. Before it can paralyze him, he starts toward the plant Lacey Shannon brushed up against. Slowly, he walks past it. On the surveillance cameras, it'll look like he's just peering down the short hallway to the interview room and bathrooms. If Mona somehow sees this footage later, she'll just think he's retracing Lacey's steps. But as he pretends to look down the hallway, his eyes cut to the ficus.

That's when he sees what Lacey dropped inside the ceramic pot.

Just to complete the lie, he walks down the rest of the hallway, even opens the door to the interview room, in case someone comes out of the bathroom and spots him.

Then he returns to the plant and pretends to study it. He bends forward slightly as he runs his fingers through the fake leaves. Once he's confident he's hidden his left hand from the security camera, he reaches into the pot and removes the flash drive he spotted there a few seconds before.

He stands, shaking the edge of the pot with his right hand, as if he only wants to know why it didn't topple over when Lacey brushed against it. But he couldn't care less. She was brushing against it to make sure it was fake. To be sure no one was going to douse the flash drive with water after she deliberately dropped it into the pot.

Luke turns in the direction of the camera, takes a deep breath intended to make him look both tired and frustrated. All of it a ruse to distract from the fact that he's holding some sort of secret. Slowly, he walks through the station, nodding goodbye to others as he leaves, the flash drive burning a hole in his palm.

She wanted us to have this thing, he realizes. But she was afraid to hand it over until Jordy was in a cell. Whatever's on it is proof Jordy's not who everyone thinks he is. And she sure as hell wasn't going to give it to Henricks after he threatened her. Instead, she got the hell out of there, but not before leaving it behind.

But if that's true, it leaves one big, unanswered question.

Why hasn't she called me to tell me where it is?

26

Charley's amazed at how much they've managed to add to the Altamira Lodge in the month she's been gone. It's Sunday, so none of the crews are at work now, but the roof of the main building's practically finished, and the frames of the adjacent cabins occupying the same promontory are also mostly complete.

Across the highway, they've started razing the newer-growth forest on the lower slopes of the mountain so they can lay the foundations for the additional rows of cabins. Just behind where she's sitting now, the tunnel they're about to build will one day open onto PCH.

If all goes according to the renderings, this entire rest area, with its bed of gravel and spread of tables and benches, is going to be cleared away, along with a chunk of the mountainside nearby.

This rest stop has always been Marty's favorite spot. Years ago he carved Luanne's name into the bench where they're sitting now while enjoying Diet Cokes and greasy sandwiches from the Copper Pot. But if Marty's upset this place will soon disappear, he hasn't mentioned it. Right now they're too busy discussing topics that would probably make the occasional passing motorist's head spin.

"When did they tell you?" Marty asks.

"After I woke up."

"So you didn't see it happen?"

"No."

She figures Marty's suppressing a dozen different questions he knows better than to ask.

"How did he tell you?" he asks. "Like it was your fault?"

"No. He had a very relaxed, professional attitude about the whole thing. He was . . . humble."

"Cole Graydon. Humble. Imagine that."

"He took this attitude that it was our first time going out in the field together, and nobody expected everything to go perfectly."

"So he didn't accuse you of killing the guy. He just told you the guy was dead."

"Pretty much, yeah."

Marty wipes mustard off his chin, chugs his Diet Coke like it's the source of life.

"And you're confident, based on what you saw, based on what he did to you, that this guy was the real deal?" he asks.

"A serial killer? Jesus. Yes."

"All right, then. Bye, freak. Enjoy hell."

She smiles, but the laughter she was expecting doesn't come. Instead, the urge creates a tension in her chest that also gives her a headache.

"I hate that it has to be like this," she says once the ache passes.

"Like what?"

"That I can't tell you guys anything."

"You can tell me anything you want."

"I can't, though. That's not the agreement I made."

"Charley, they set me up with a job I'm barely qualified for. I'm making more money than I ever thought possible. What I'm saying is they've bought my silence, and they know it. But they've only bought it when it comes to CNN and the *National Enquirer*. Not when it comes to you and your sanity."

"I'm sane, I think. Do I seem sane?"

"All things considered, yes. But you're still allowed to have feelings. You'd be insane if you didn't."

"I feel sad that the families will never know what happened to their daughters. That they're going to spend their whole lives like my grandmother spent a big chunk of hers."

"That makes sense."

"But when it comes to him? I don't feel a damn thing. But maybe that's . . . I don't know. Sometimes we think the absence of a feeling is a scab when really it's an open wound."

"That's a good one. Where'd you hear that?"

"You. When I was seventeen. I rolled my eyes because I was a little tired of all the AA speak."

"That's not AA speak. That's Marty speak."

"How would you know? You don't remember saying it."

"Let's not get bogged down in a lot of specifics."

His smile seems genuine, and warm, but it fades quicker than his smiles usually do, and the unanswered question fills the air between them like a smoke cloud.

"Should I feel something, Marty?"

"You're not a cop. You're not a judge. And you're not a lawyer."

She didn't expect this turn in the conversation and knows that if she speaks now, she won't be able to keep the anger from her voice. "I see. So you think I'm playing judge, jury, and—"

"No, no, no," he says quickly, hands out as if he's afraid the bench between them is about to shoot up into the air. "I'm not saying that at all."

"What, then?"

"Charley, you don't experience these people at the level of a case file. You lost your mother to monsters like this guy. You lost your *childhood* to people like this guy. It's like . . . When you talk to guys who've been in combat, they all tell you the same thing. They knew who the enemy was. The enemy was the one who would shoot them if they didn't shoot first.

"That's what you've been in for most of your life, Charley. A combat situation with sick fucks who abduct people off the street so they can use them as their twisted playthings. Everything your dad did to make money off you put you in their line of sight again and again. I mean, Jesus, who knows how many obsessed fans like Jason Briffel were out there waiting to strike?

"My point is, no one who knows everything about you, about this . . . situation, is going to expect you to slow down and humanize them for the greater good of I don't know what. They're monsters, Charley. Human fucking monsters. The Bannings. This guy, whoever he was. None of these people turned to crime because their circumstances were mean and they needed to put food on the table. And honestly, if you ask me, Dylan Cody's not that far off. You ever heard that line about staring too deeply into the abyss?"

"We're supposed to call him by his real name now," Charley says. "Cole's orders."

"I'm happy to say I don't remember what it is."

She doesn't tell him. She likes him not knowing.

And she's not sure she agrees with Cole's directive.

Calling Dylan by his birth name puts him in league with her; reminds her that his family was a victim of the Bannings, too.

"There's another thing," she says. She's speaking before she's collected her thoughts, which makes her nervous. She feels like that's a luxury she lost months ago.

"Yeah?"

"Something about the way we were doing it this time made it easier."

"Well, I bet it's more efficient."

"Totally. But that's only part of it."

"What's the other part of it?"

"There was so much around me. So much support. Logistical support, I mean. It almost felt like I was just the scalpel in somebody's hand, and the hand wasn't mine. If it always feels like that, like I've got no responsibility for any of it, who knows what I might do?"

"Well, as long as you do it to one of those sick fucks, I can't say I'm going to lose any sleep over it."

Will I, though?

She can't imagine this strange new life without Marty in it, and this makes her feel guilty all over again for how quickly she abandoned him after Luanne died.

Still, she sometimes worries Marty's perpetual quest for moral clarity can result in oversimplifications. She remembers eating lunch at this same bench years ago, when she was a teenager, before they made an arduous hike to some old ruined limekilns buried in the redwoods near the top of the mountain. Upon their sweaty arrival, he lectured her for close to twenty minutes about how the limekilns used to work, and he did so with the same casual confidence he's just used to put her mess of feelings into neat, labeled boxes. But sometimes matters of the head and matters of the heart are not as predictable and knowable as old machinery.

Does Marty know this?

Before she can answer the question, her cell phone buzzes. It's a text from Luke.

Need you at home.

She texts back, Everything OK?

Not sure. Need your brain for something.

It's not entirely frightening, but it's not exactly reassuring, either. She writes back, Marty's with me.

Good. I need him too.

27

Cole can't stand the sight of Colorado from the air. It's not the altitude that gets to him; it's the state.

He's never been a nervous flyer. One of his favorite pastimes is gazing out the window as he slices the clouds. But no matter how high up he is, Colorado's mountainous folds always seem ready to swallow whatever plane he's in, disappearing him forever. As the rented Gulfstream descends toward Eagle County Regional Airport, he feels like they're about to land on a stormy sea of conifers and snow and he might need to reach for a life vest at any minute.

He doesn't need a psychiatrist to interpret these feelings.

Colorado is where he suffered life-changing wounds; Colorado is where his father's plan for healing those wounds only made them worse. Not just Colorado, but Stonecut Ridge, the ranch his father built to put him back together again.

It's too far from San Diego to get there by helicopter, so this two-and-a-half-hour flight has been the longest period of time Cole's spent with his new security director since hiring the guy. They've only exchanged a few words. That's a good thing.

Exchanging words with Scott Durham would require that Cole occasionally look at him, and right now Cole can't stand to look at the guy because, despite Cole's best efforts, Scott Durham is most definitely something to look at. And that's annoying. He really did make every effort to pick Ed's replacement based on qualifications alone, but of course, the most qualified candidate walked into his office looking like a fitness model.

But Durham's most important selling point was the small string of letters in his personnel file that only Cole, and previously Ed, would have been able to interpret. EFLEVAL5, an abbreviation for Excellent Flight Evaluation Rating 5, code for some very important facts. Not only had Scott Durham done a fine job working security for Project Bluebird 1.0, escorting the test subjects to the island lab (and asking no questions when none were escorted back) and securing the facility itself. He'd also passed his postpsychiatric evaluations with flying colors. Cole couldn't say that for all the men who worked security for Bluebird. One guy had been so disturbed by what became of the second test subject, they'd had to enter him into treatment and then gently retire him with a nice benefits package.

On paper, Scott Durham was the only man for the job.

"How many are coming to meet us?" Cole asks.

Scott lowers his tablet. For most of the flight, he's been swiping through schematics of Stonecut Ridge and topographical maps of the surrounding landscape, occasionally watching live feeds from the microdrones that regularly sweep the property from several hundred feet up.

"Two SUVs. If I'm reading this right, that takes a third of the ranch's security away from the ranch. For a little while, at least. Are you comfortable with that?"

"The security team probably looks light to you," Cole explains, "because there's something else in place that's going to keep him from running. And it's invisible."

"His TruGlass?"

"No, that's just for monitoring. He's got blood trackers. They're weaponized."

"Does he know this?"

"No," Cole answers.

"Do they give him a warning if he tries to run?" Scott asks.

"Yes, and it's painful."

"I'm not seeing anything in the ranch logs about an escape."

"There hasn't been one."

"So he hasn't . . . felt the burn yet, if you will." Scott's smile is slight, but there's mischief in it, and a hint of sadism. The guy must have already read Ed's written account of everything that's happened since Noah Turlington, who was then going by the name Dylan Thorpe, met a woman who'd recently changed her name to Charlotte Rowe. *So Scott wouldn't mind seeing Noah Turlington punished for some of the sins he committed as Dylan Thorpe; that's a good sign,* Cole thinks.

"There's something that keeps coming up in the logs," Scott says. "I apologize if it's not worth mentioning, but it's so frequent I—"

"Go ahead."

"He wants to shave," Scott says. "After he puts his TruGlass in every morning and does his mirror confirmation, he writes out a different note for us. Some are funny. Some are angry. But the subject's always the same."

Cole remembers the debauched sight Noah treated all of them to when Julia first insisted he wear her prized invention at all times. He wonders if Scott would think that was funny, too.

"Shaving," Cole says.

Scott nods. "We could let him if you wanted. I mean, it's doubtful our guys would get taken out by a Gillette. Also we could give him an electric razor. No blade."

"I don't want him shaving," Cole says before he can stop himself.

I don't want him looking anything like the man who used to reward me with deep, passionate kisses right after he inflicted just the right amount of pain.

"He's learning to go without some things," Cole says. "It's good for him."

The plane touches down on the runway with a brief jolt.

When their feet meet the tarmac, Scott's right next to him, Secret Service–style, a definite change of pace from Ed. The man's over six feet tall, rare for someone with a special operations background. When it comes to Navy SEALs in particular, shorter guys have an easier time making it through BUD/S. It's all about endurance; six feet or more of man requires a lot of oxygen and blood to endure the hardships of running miles in thick sand and treading cold water for hours on end, more than is required by a guy in the five-foot range.

Two modified Suburbans are waiting for them right outside the terminal. They've got tinted bulletproof windows, tires capable of plowing through a blizzard. Cole's barely taken a seat when Scott slides in next to him. Ed would have taken the empty passenger seat in front.

A right turn on I-70 would take them east toward Vail. Instead, they turn left. Then they make a quick right onto a twisty mountain road. They're surrounded by slopes of pine blended with a few dry, exposed limestone faces and some determined patches of snow. A few miles west, the Rockies tumble down into a vast, arid stretch that extends into Utah. This land is where that eventual transition has its subtle origins.

The gate to the ranch used to be the traditional kind you had to get out and pull open. Now it's a sliding electrified panel with an attached guardhouse, connected to miles of new fencing that run the property's entire border.

When Cole was young, the only livestock here were a few horses, and they were mostly ridden and groomed by the staff. His father didn't build the place because he loved animals. He didn't even build it to commune with nature. He built it to give his privileged, delicate son some connection to something greater than himself, and because he didn't believe in God, he was convinced that connection could only be found on the edge of a vast wilderness.

The driver slows down some as they descend the dirt road to the main house.

Cole feels a chest-constricting performance anxiety that could be memory, or it could be assaulting him from the present. He's not sure. In the end, it doesn't matter. He just wants his palms to sweat less, and he doesn't want Scott to notice he's having trouble breathing.

If he had a better place to keep Noah Turlington prisoner, he'd use it. But this is the only property his father left entirely to him in his will. Stonecut Ranch was built for Cole, and it still feels like his despite his loathing of it, maybe because the exterior looks exactly the way it did when he was a boy. The limestone cliffs that cup the far side of the glassy lake still look like the palms of a goddess; the gurgling brook still parallels the side of the dirt road as if it were dug by landscapers.

And there, in front of the house's main entrance, amid precisely placed beds of flowers that are currently just green shoots and buds, is the same slab of obsidian his father put in place right after the ranch was completed. It looks like a tombstone, but there are no dates carved into it. Just a long quote. His father's favorite.

> Look at a stone cutter hammering away at his rock, perhaps a hundred times without as much as a crack showing in it. Yet at the hundred-and-first blow it will split in two, and I know it was not the last blow that did it, but all that had gone before.

> *Jacob Riis*

The stone's evenly split at the top to make it look like it just suffered a strike from a giant's ax.

His father used to make Cole lay his hand briefly against it whenever they arrived.

Cole hasn't repeated the ritual since the man died.

Giant logs along the house's facade soar three stories to support the wings of the expansive A-frame roof. All in all, the place has always looked like a Greek temple Paul Bunyan tried to build out of local materials.

Even after the security team opens the front door for him and Cole walks into the great room with Scott on his heels, Noah Turlington doesn't turn away from the room's windows. They're giant walls of plate glass, really, built to make the most of the stunning views of the twinkling lake and its border of limestone cliffs. But given how long Noah's been held prisoner here, Cole has a hard time believing the man's still enamored by the landscape.

When his father was alive there were enough bronze statues of animals stationed around the great room to make the place feel like a petrified zoo. Cole's had them all removed. But he left the dark wood and leather furniture exactly where his dad placed it. Thank God there were never any antlers on the walls, or skulls, or moose heads to deal with. His father wasn't a hunter. The man's relationship to the wild was subtler, more personal.

Cole remembers lots of long walks and hikes. Whenever there was a flash of frightening movement in the nearby brush that would make Cole want to turn tail and run, his dad would take him by the shoulders and make him wait until whatever had caused the disturbance emerged. It didn't matter if it was a deer or a bear. He was intent on turning his only child's moments of fear into patient wonder, intent on connecting him to a world beyond housekeepers and chauffeured cars and his privileged classmates at his elite private school. Perhaps those things might have been easier to accomplish if the property hadn't sported a multimillion-dollar palace for them to retire to each night, but Cole would never have suggested such a thing. The house and its library were the only things that made his visits here bearable.

Now the house is, appropriately, a prison.

For someone else.

Cole drops a thick spiral-bound file onto the coffee table with a loud thud.

Noah turns and, without so much as a nod, moves to the file and starts leafing through it.

Two members of the house's security team stand sentry by the front door, waiting for Cole to give them their cue. Scott's closer, studying Cole with an intensity that makes gooseflesh break out on the back of his neck.

Standing, Noah flips pages with increasing frustration. "This is . . ." The words leave him as he flips more. "This is just a rehash of the footage. There's nothing . . ." Noah looks into Cole's eyes for the first time. Whatever he sees there causes him to raise the entire file in one hand and hurl it to the floor.

The security team, including Scott, start to move in. They stop when they see Cole's raised hand. Maybe Cole's small but satisfied smile also calms them.

"I was hoping we could talk alone," Cole says, "but if you're in a tantrum-prone mood . . ."

"What do we have to talk about?" Noah asks.

"Since you've made clear you reviewed the footage, do you have anything interesting to say about it?"

"Nothing earth-shattering. I could have given you my analysis over the phone."

"This is more secure, obviously."

Noah's grumble sounds pregnant with unspoken profanity. He throws himself down onto the nearby sofa. Then his focus lasers in on Scott.

"Who are you?" he asks Scott.

"He's my new director of security," Cole says.

"What happened to Mr. Clean?"

"He's moved on."

"Why?"

"I'm not here to discuss personnel issues with you."

Noah glares at Scott. Scott glares back. "I bet the job interview was long and hard."

"Would you like me to stay?" Scott asks. "Or would you like to be alone with Mr. Wizard here?"

"Lazy," Noah mumbles, "I hate lazy jokes. Why make a joke at all? Just make a face, pretty boy. It'll earn you more points with this one."

"Why don't you step out for a bit, Scott? Noah seems aroused to distraction by your presence."

Scott nods, gives Noah a fierce, lingering look, then gestures for the two house security guards to follow him outside.

Once they're gone, Noah says, "This is good strategy. I approve."

"I'm sorry, what?"

"Sleeping with your security director. It gets him more invested in you."

"You used to be direct, Noah. Now you're just crude. Have you had lunch?"

"Come on. You know I don't subscribe to the puritanical separation of sex and profession. Some of the greatest warriors in history fucked their comrades. It's what made them fight to the death for them in battle."

"Not everyone's a warrior."

"You better hope he is. For your sake."

"Noted. I'd like to talk about the—"

"I am. I was, at least."

"For what, though? That's never clear."

"Zypraxon." He smiles. "And paradrenaline. Which you've had preserved since the Pemberton takedown, but you're still not giving me access to."

"You don't own the contents of Charlotte Rowe's blood, and you never will. That's not how this is going to work. Once we get started, your focus will be the drug."

"The drug works because it manufactures paradrenaline in the bloodstream, and so far that process has killed everyone except for her. I can't make a study of one without the other, Cole."

"Your area of focus will be where I say it is, and it will commence when I say so. That's the deal."

"Fine, then. You have the drug's new formula. What do you need me for? If you're going to wall me off from the real miracle in all this, you might as well just bury me in a shallow grave."

"You disappeared for three years. If it takes longer than five months to get the island back up and running, I'm sure you'll be able to handle it."

"How much longer? I'm sick of this place."

"*My* labs, which I built for you, cost millions to operate, secure, and keep secret, and I can't come up with that money overnight, as you well know. If you wanted to put all of this on a timetable of your choosing, you should have consulted me before you involved Charlotte without her consent."

"I did."

"You did nothing of the kind."

"I told you I wanted to test it on women, and you freaked out and pulled the plug."

"We'd already killed four people. I was pulling the plug anyway."

"So what? I still consulted you."

"This is childish nonsense, and it's beneath a man of your intelligence."

"No, you coming here every few weeks with another crumb, pretending you're consulting me when really you're just keeping me from the most important work, that's childish nonsense, Cole. For Christ's sake, at least let me shave."

"What's your opinion of the footage?"

"My opinion? I'd like to know how you disposed of Richard Davies."

"That's not an opinion. That's a question about something that's none of your business."

"My opinion is that nobody should be surprised by her speed of regeneration. It's in keeping with everything else we've learned about the trigger zone. The only reason we've never seen it before is because we've never subjected her to trauma that severe. I don't know how you could in a lab, and I wouldn't recommend it. But obviously the healing agent is paradrenaline, which you still won't let me analyze, even though there was a time when you and I would have killed to get a single vial stable and under control."

"We *did* kill, and we still didn't get it."

"Willing test subjects who knew the risks. The only subject who didn't know the risks survived and has changed the whole game, but people are still treating me like I killed her."

"Actually, we're treating you like you raped her, which is more accurate."

"Oh, for fuck's sake."

"Yes, I understand that psychopaths often grapple with the issue of consent. But hopefully it's clear to you that there were a dozen things that could have gone wrong with what you did to her. All of them horrible."

"And yet none of them came to pass. And you have what you want for the first time. But you're not letting me anywhere near it because . . . I don't know, you have some desire to punish me for the fact that I stopped sleeping with you when you shut down my project."

"I'm not punishing you. I'm giving you time to figure out who you'll need to be when this comes together again. If I put The Consortium back together, if I get the funding and the labs running again, you will be a man among men, a worker among workers.

No more mad rogue stuff. So reflect now on how you'll accomplish that. Because if you treat anyone involved in this the way you treated Charlotte, I will fucking end you, do you understand me, Noah?"

Cole's not sure how to interpret Noah's expression. The glaze in his eyes makes him look both angry and distant, but his thick beard makes the rest of his face harder to read. It's also not a typical posture for him; slouched down on the sofa like a sullen teenager, his hands resting on his stomach. The only clothes he's been allowed are T-shirts and pajama pants, and now they complete the look of a hungover ne'er-do-well, drying out at his parents' mansion. Which couldn't be further from the truth.

"Fine," he whispers. "On one condition."

"We're not negotiating."

"Stop calling me Noah."

There's something in his voice that Cole's never heard before. Pain. Pure pain, complete with a weak tremor and a breathiness that suggests it's threaded with fear. In all the time they spent together, ranging from the intimate to the professional, Cole never heard the man before him use a tone quite like this one. It's ironic given the request, but Cole wonders if this is the first time he's hearing Noah Turlington's voice and not Dylan Cody's.

"I'll consider it," Cole says.

He picks up the file from where Noah hurled it to the floor and sets it gently on the coffee table between them. "This is more than just a crumb. It's got detailed analyses of all her levels for four days after her regeneration. Study it. Make sense of it. Tell me if you see something that surprises you. And maybe then I'll let you shave."

"Thank you," Noah says quietly. But suddenly he flinches as if from an invisible blow. He raises one hand to his temple and bows his head. Cole's so startled his anger leaves him. His first thought—the security team's been listening in, and they've decided to play a little trick with Noah's blood trackers meant to punish him for his attitude.

But Noah recovers too quickly. Suddenly, he's staring at Cole again as if nothing's wrong.

"Are you all right?" Cole asks.

"Fine," Noah says, "just a little headache."

"Take a walk. Get some air."

"I've had my fill of mountain air, thanks. If anything, that's the problem."

"Oh, well. Be grateful. Your problems could be so much worse than that." Cole turns and heads for the door. "I look forward to your report, Noah."

"Cole!"

Cole stops, but doesn't turn.

"How is she?" Noah asks.

"Very happy," Cole says. "She's got a boyfriend now. They're making a nice life together. Peaceful. Stable."

He walks out the front door before Noah can call his name again.

They're airborne by the time the email comes through.

It's from Kelley Chen, who's running lead on the paradrenaline research.

Even though it's only two words long, Cole has to read it several times before the shock wears off.

Complete Elimination.

When he gets to his feet, Scott perks up, but Cole dismisses him with a wave and moves to the sleeping cabin at the back of the plane.

Once he's slid the door shut behind him, he calls Kelley from his sat phone. As usual, she answers without a formal greeting. "It's early, but I thought you should know."

"*Complete elimination* means what exactly?" he asks.

"Exactly what I said."

Kelley isn't one for wild swings of emotion, but there's a tremor in her voice right now. It's excitement; it has to be. Or more precisely, it's her failing effort to suppress it.

"How much paradrenaline did it take?" he asks.

"All of it."

"OK. Well, we have more from the Davies operation we can—"

"No, we used that, too. We're out. We need more."

"You just decided to use the whole batch?"

"The cell degradation was constant with each of the measured doses we used. We couldn't believe what we were seeing, so we just kept going. Sorry. It was exciting."

"I get it. I'm excited, too."

But he sounds dazed, because that's what he actually is.

"As soon as we have more paradrenaline, we can get back to work."

"I understand," he says.

"This could be huge, Cole. Huge."

"I know."

"But it's—"

"Early. I know. I get it. It's one thing to wipe it out in a lab sample, another in a live subject, let alone a human one."

"Still . . . congratulations," she says.

"To you, too, Doctor."

He hangs up. For a while, he can't move. The jet's engines suddenly sound like they're miles away and he's hearing them from underwater.

It's not too soon to say he was right about at least one thing. The potential medical implications of paradrenaline are too significant to let someone as devious and unreliable as Noah Turlington anywhere near them, no matter how brilliant he is. He's got other plans for

Noah. Plans more appropriate to his skill set and his weaknesses. And Noah can certainly work with the fruits of Kelley's research here and there. But not for a single moment will Cole allow him unrestricted access to the dazzling hormone that produced those results.

For the project, it's not a loss. Kelley Chen is just as brilliant as Noah. Also, she's not a narcissistic sociopath with a history of deceit and sexual manipulation. She's a PhD from Stanford and a former dorm mate of Cole's who applies the same obsessive focus to her work today that she applied to her studies back when they were both undergrads. Her background check was ten times more thorough than any Cole had ordered on an employee previously; the results, divinely and delightfully boring.

And she hasn't complained once about being sequestered to Iceland and the lab he's built for her there, even though the place is hardly as plush as The Consortium's island. It's a nice facility, but certain corners had to be cut, given he was footing the bill himself.

If the band ever gets back together.

But Kelley's right.

It's too soon to get too excited.

Too soon to be sure if they've actually discovered a cure for cancer, or just the first fleeting suggestion of one.

28

Charley's getting a crick in her neck from staring down at Luke's laptop, but she's too engrossed to care. Once Luke explained where the flash drive had come from, the three of them scrambled to load the thing into his computer as fast as they could. They've been standing over his kitchen counter staring down at it for several minutes now. "What are these?" Charley finally asks.

"Screenshots from someone else's computer," Luke says.

"I got that part," she answers, "but what are all these arrows?"

"Seismic readings," Marty says.

"What, like earthquake risk?" Charley asks.

"No, they're measurements of the thickness of the rock in the path of the tunnel. They shot seismic waves down through the mountain, and the speed at which the waves came back gave them a sense of what's down there, but . . ." He reaches around Luke and swipes the touch pad. "They're different. I mean, they're the same, but they're different."

"What's that mean, Buddha?" Luke asks.

Marty points to the line across the top of each image. Both alternate between wavy and jagged in the same pattern. "That there's the ground level, sort of. I mean, we're dealing with a mountainous surface, so the word *ground* is relative, but you know what I mean. Point is, it's the same in both. Then these clusters of arrows, those are speed indicators. They show how quickly the seismic waves moved through the rock under the surface. The denser the cluster, the slower the waves travel, the thicker the rock. I mean, this isn't my area of expertise, but it makes sense."

"Makes sense how?" Charley asks.

"Well, it's the type of readings Clements would need to do before they drill. He's got to have some sense of what's down there. Normally you drill boreholes, but they're going through the bottom of a mountain range, so drilling a bunch of holes straight down to try to get samples isn't the easiest. This way he just shoots seismic waves through the rocks and interprets what comes back and then calculates what he's going to need to drill. But one of these has to be fake."

"How do you know?" Luke asks. "They could just be two different attempts that turned up different readings."

"Maybe, but I doubt it. They're too different. In the one on the left, the arrows thicken up a good ways from the bottom. I'm not a geologist, but I've heard talk around town from the crews. The mountains are a bunch of different rock types, and some are easier to drill than others. I'm guessing one of these maps is showing a bunch of metamorphic rock right in the path of the tunnel, but the other isn't. And metamorphic rock, that's tough stuff."

"OK. So if one's fake, is he trying to rip somebody off?" Luke asks.

Charley gets an idea. "Like maybe the tunnel's impossible to build and he doesn't want anyone to know. Could be an insurance thing. He stocks up on a bunch of equipment and then he can't drill, so he's got some kind of claim." She feels pretty satisfied with this theory, but when she sees their blank looks, she adds, "I don't know. I'm just thinking out loud."

"What else is on here?" Marty asks.

He elbows Luke aside, but Luke doesn't protest. She's relieved, once again, to see how well they get along these days. The sense that they were both holding down the home front was a comfort to her while she was away, even if she suspects Luke has more mixed feelings about his role than he's been letting on.

Marty starts clicking through a file folder with no label. More screen caps fill the laptop's display. Most of them look like old photographs of Jordy and Lacey, chronicling their happier moments together. In all of them, they're scantily clad, mostly on various beaches, eyes hidden behind sunglasses. They're a rough-around-the-edges version of someone's idea of an idealized young Southern California couple. Surfboards, open-air Jeeps, bottles of Corona they toast while making goo-goo eyes at each other.

"Oh, crap. Tell me this isn't her personal flash drive and now we've gotta figure what she actually wanted you to see," Marty asks.

"I wish I could tell you that," Luke answers, "but I can't."

"Well, if that is the case, she's certainly not working for any intelligence agencies," Charley says.

"Given recent events, that's good to know," Marty says.

"Not a shock," Luke says. "She doesn't sound like a good candidate for anything except rehab. When Mona called her parents, she said they never wanted to speak to her again because she stole medications from her dying grandmother."

"Addiction's a tricky business," Marty says. "Maybe she's trying to do something right for a change."

Is Marty offended? Is Luke afraid he offended Marty? Or is the sudden silence just a sign they're all chewing over the flash drive's contents? Charley figures it's option three.

"Wait," Luke barks, "what was that?"

Marty was opening pictures so fast he didn't notice the odd one out.

It's not a photograph of Lacey and Jordy in better days; it's another screenshot. The background's white, and the squares filling the screen are so small at first glance she misses their outlines.

Charley leans in to get a closer look. They're chat boxes, clustered together. What looks like a single screen cap is actually a collage of them. Over and over again, Lacey's cropped two exchanges from longer threads and assembled them into a collage. After a second or two of reading, Charlotte can see why; in each crop, the second text box is exactly the same, something that looks like a Bible verse.

The verse is the same every time: *Their work will be shown for what it is because the day will bring it to light. It will be revealed with fire, and the fire will test the quality of each person's work.—1 Corinthians 3:13*

It's followed by a phrase, FIND YOUR FIRE. Aside from being underlined, the words are set off from the rest of the post in light-blue text.

After she confirms the verse doesn't vary, she reads some of the messages to which it was posted as a response.

Her breath catches. The skin around her neck suddenly feels tight.

> NO! His work will not be REVEALED!!! We r his agents. We r his soldiers! ACTION MUST BE TAKEN, be it against the sodomites or the idolaters. Or the abortionists. TO SIT IDLY BY IS TO INVITE THE KINGDOM OF SATAN!

The other messages are similar.

> DEEDS AND WORKS. No one on the threads recognizing value of WORKS and DEEDS! FAITH IS NOT ENOUGH. One must act against those who act contrary to God. MY GOD HAS A FINGER OF FIRE!

Slowly, Marty drags the chat collage to one side of the screen so it's still visible.

But it's obvious he's more taken with the photos of Lacey and Jordy.

The tone of each chat exchange is basically the same. Someone with a screen name that makes no sense to her, probably because she's never been very religious, having some sort of breakdown over gays, abortion doctors, and Muslims and the failure of society to react to the supposed evils of each group. Then, in each instance, someone with a different screen name responds with the exact same Bible verse, followed by a link.

"Find your fire?" Luke says. "It looks like a link."

"Well, I can't click on it because the whole thing's a screen cap," Marty says.

"Where does it go?" Charley asks. "A chat room? It feels like an invite, for sure."

"To what, though?" Marty says. "Are they asking for an argument, or are they trying to get the original commenter to calm the hell down?"

"My God has a finger of fire," Luke reads. "'Find your fire.' I don't know. But it doesn't sound good."

"For whoever the poster's wailing about maybe," she says, "but the poster . . . well, they might consider it a nice offer."

"Wait," Marty says.

It doesn't sound like he's responding to what Luke just said, so she shifts her gaze to the photo he's just opened on the right-hand side of the screen. It's a strange one. No beach, no smiles, no sun. It's blurry and dark.

At first she thinks it's some close-up of a wall; then she realizes she's looking at a man's naked back and right arm as he sleeps. She *hopes* he's sleeping. She's not sure if it's Jordy, but the man's build is similar to the guy in the other photos. What sticks out is the square of lighter skin cupping his upturned shoulder. Not lighter skin, she realizes. A bandage.

She puts her finger to it.

"Yep," Marty says, "saw that, too."

"What is it?" Luke asks.

"An injury maybe?"

"An injury she thinks we should see."

As if he's reading her mind, Marty goes back to the other photos. If they aren't already seeing the connection, they will be shortly.

Lacey didn't just want them to see how much the once-happy couple used to love the beach. She wanted them to see Jordy shirtless; she wanted them to see what was on his shoulder up until she snapped a shot of him sleeping.

Marty was right. In all the beach shots, Jordy sports a large tattoo on his shoulder, and it looks like it's mostly words.

"Can you zoom?"

"I can try."

It only takes a few clicks before they see it, and when they do, Luke rears back from the computer as if it's a coiled snake. They can't even read all the words, but they don't need to, because the name of the Bible verse is tattooed larger than the verse itself. The same verse somebody—Jordy?—used in crackpot chat rooms to try to both calm and establish communication with people who wanted to inflict violence on groups they deemed morally repugnant.

"What the fuck?" Marty whispers.

"So someone's using the same Bible verse in all these chat rooms, and Jordy's got the same verse on his shoulder up until . . . recently, I guess? When was the photo of his back taken?" He clicks on it, opens a new window containing the photo's data points. "Three weeks ago."

Charley says, "We know the photo was taken three weeks ago. We don't know if he had that tattoo removed three weeks ago."

"No, but we know three weeks ago is when Lacey Shannon decided that somebody needed to know that her boyfriend got his tattoo removed," Luke says. "And that date comes after the dates on these chats where the same passage from Corinthians was used.

So if it's Jordy talking to these whack jobs, inviting them to chat or whatever—"

"He's not just inviting them to chat," Marty says, "he's inviting them to *find their fire*. Is that how you ask somebody out to coffee?"

"No," Charley says.

"Find your fire," Luke whispers.

"My God has a finger of fire," Charley repeats.

Nobody says anything for a bit.

"Not smart, using a tattoo on your body to communicate with potential psychopaths," Charlotte says.

"Whether he's smart or not," Marty says, "something happened during these conversations that convinced him he needed to get part of his skin taken off. Must have been major."

"And Lacey noticed," Luke says.

"And thought you should notice, too," Charlotte says.

"This isn't her personal flash drive," Marty says. "Every picture on here is the same. Jordy's shirtless in every one. She's showing us that tattoo."

"And that he had it removed," Luke says.

"OK. So . . . the seismic maps?" Charlotte asks.

The third detail seems to stump all of them.

Then Charlotte feels her face get hot all of a sudden.

"Shit," she whispers.

"What?" Luke asks.

"Marty, what else goes into building a tunnel besides the drills?" she asks.

"Probably something to stabilize the hole with. Equipment to drag away the broken rock you've drilled through. Explosives to . . ."

Marty's face drains of color.

"What, guys?" Luke asks.

"I had it backwards," Charley says.

"Backwards how?" Luke asks.

"Maybe the one that said the tunnel's going to be twice as hard to build isn't the real one," she says. "It's the fake one."

"Because Jordy wants more explosives than he's actually going to need," Marty adds.

"Because they make fire," Charlotte says. "And that's what he wants to give to these lunatics. *Fire.* 'It will be revealed with fire, and the fire will test the quality of each person's work.'"

"Fire purchased through entirely legal means," Marty says.

Luke's the one to finally break the long silence. "Hate in his heart. That's what she said: 'Jordy is a man with hate in his heart.'"

"She wasn't trying to make the case that he was a woman beater. She was saying what she could to get you to throw him in a cell right away. That way she could . . ." Marty swallows.

Charley finishes the sentence for him. "She could make the case that Jordy's a terrorist."

Luke turns his attention to the computer and its mess of open windows.

"Well," he finally says, "does she?"

When the phone rings, Luke yelps in surprise. Marty jumps, but manages to keep his reaction silent.

Charlotte walks to the handset, checks the caller ID.

"Unavailable," she reads aloud.

Luke just shakes his head. Maybe he's already got some sense of who it is, but he doesn't want to believe it.

Charlotte answers using speakerphone.

"This is a very interesting conversation," Cole Graydon says. At first, she assumes he's driving, but the sound of rushing air is too deep and steady. He must be in the air.

"And you've been listening in, I take it?" Charley asks.

"Speakerphone. That's charming."

"Really?" Luke says. "You've been spying on everything we say, and you're gonna bitch about being on speakerphone."

"We do not *spy* on everything you say. We have certain words programmed into the monitoring system that send us an alert. If we receive one of those, *then* we listen to everything you're saying. This is about your safety, guys. Trust me."

"OK," Luke says, approaching the phone, "so which word triggered the system or whatever? *Jordy* or *Clements*? These guys are friends of yours, right? I mean, how else did you get them to build a tunnel in the middle of nowhere?"

"Well, money, for starters," Cole says. "But the word that triggered the alert was *terrorism*."

"I see," Charley says. "So you're afraid there might be a terrorist attack in Altamira, and you wanted to be sure you could evacuate us in time?"

"Let's meet," Cole says. "I'm in the air, but I can redirect to you pretty quickly. I'd like to hear more about what's on this flash drive."

"So you haven't been listening to everything we're saying, but you know about the flash drive?" Luke asks.

"Your conversations are archived. When we get an alert, we go into the archive and review it to see if the alert was justified. OK? Would you like my help with this or not?"

"Depends on what you call help," Luke says.

"For Pete's sake, I'm siphoning enough money and development into your little industry-free town to keep it going for decades to come. What else do you want from me? Weekly puppies?"

"You siphoned Jordy Clements into our town," Luke says. "That's why I'm asking."

Charlotte moves to Luke and places both hands gently on his chest, then she looks into his eyes imploringly. She can only hope her expression conveys everything she's feeling. That she understands Luke's anger, and his fear; that she feels it, too. And that he still needs to shut the hell up. For now anyway. They're not going to get Cole to help by bossing him around.

Eyes downcast, Luke turns away from her. So he got the message. But he didn't like it one bit. Should she be surprised?

"A meeting sounds great," Charley says, "but I'd like to ask for something else, too."

"OK," Cole answers.

"Maybe you could devote some of your considerable resources to finding Lacey Shannon. Obviously she wanted to present this material herself. Maybe she could help explain it to all of us."

Luke opens the refrigerator, takes out a beer.

"I'm not sure that's obvious, but I'll consider it," Cole answers.

Luke wedges the beer bottle against the edge of the counter, then loudly pops the cap off with the side of one fist.

"Stay where you are," Cole says. "I'll land in about a half hour and then I'll call with a meeting place. Somewhere close to you, of course."

29

"What are these?" Cole finally asks. He's looking up at Charlotte from behind reflective sunglasses that make it impossible for her to read his expression.

Next to her, Luke exhales in a loud huff. They've walked Cole through everything on that damn flash drive. In great detail. And now he's going to act like he didn't hear any of it? This is going to be harder than she thought.

Most of the Lake Patrick boat launch is open-air, except for a metal bench at the very end of the dock. That's where Cole first took a seat, leaving Charley, Luke, and Marty to stand between him and the dock's edge like knights delivering reports to their king. They're all inside the halo of shade cast by several rusted metal umbrellas. As always, there's something about the sight of these umbrellas, with their sculpted details and flaking white paint, that makes Charley a little sad; they're evidence someone once thought Lake Patrick would become a recreational haven, not a spot for jerks to dump their trash and unwanted pets.

And for shady CEOs to meet with their secret test subjects in private.

"You really want us to go through it all again?" Charley asks.

"No." Even though it was Luke who gave the presentation, Cole looks straight at her. "I want you to tell me specifically what I'm looking at on this screen. What types of files are these?"

"They're screen caps," Marty says.

"So you haven't been able to follow this link?" Cole asks.

"I thought we said that," Luke says, impatience building. "Didn't we say that? Because I could swear that we . . ." Charley places a hand on his shoulder; he falls silent. But he's right. Cole's being an obstinate jerk, and if he keeps it up, there's only going to be so many more times she'll be willing to silence Luke with a look.

"Screen captures," Cole says again, as if this entire thing is a waste of his time.

"Yes," Charley says, "what did you expect? She doesn't work for the CIA."

"Of course not. She's his on-again, off-again girlfriend with a history of drug addiction who told Luke a lie so he'd arrest him. How could we possibly suspect her motives are anything but pure?"

"We don't know her story about the beating was a lie," Luke says.

"So we know she was beaten up?" Cole asks.

"Or Jordy threw her face-first into a tree by the scruff of her damn neck. Knuckle patterns aren't the point, and you know it."

"No, the point is, Charley needs to be resting and recovering, and instead you've got her all caught up in amateur detective hour."

As soon as Luke's mouth opens, Charley cuts him off. "They're screen caps because she was afraid and didn't have experience with what she was doing. She just grabbed what she could off his computer and ran."

"Screen captures can be altered," Cole answers.

"OK. So we can't trust her because she's not CIA, but now she's able to alter screen caps?" Charley asks.

Her question hangs over them for a few seconds, during which Cole sets the laptop on the bench next to him and folds his hands over his lap. "I am recommending patience and deliberation. That's all. Due process. Remember it? It's something we used to have before social media."

"Due process, huh?" Luke asks. "Awesome. So you're taking this right to the feds?"

"I don't want any of you starting forest fires because of the crazy ramblings of a young woman who lies, abuses drugs, and drops something like this in your lap and then runs for the hills. This flash drive is . . . is a jumble of I don't know. Take away your interpretation and it's nothing."

"Fine," Luke says, "let's find her and talk to her."

"Perhaps *I* will," Cole says with a smile. "I've already started looking for her."

Marty and Luke look as surprised by this news as Charley feels.

"All right," Luke says. "Good, I guess."

"You *guess*? I thought that's what you wanted."

"Well, it's part of it," Luke says.

"Part of it?" Cole asks.

"I'd like to interview her myself, but something about your tone tells me that's not going to happen. What with your concern for due process and all."

"I'm sorry, Luke, but if this is really what you describe, how long do you think the Altamira Sheriff's Department is going to be able to handle it on its own?"

"Well, at least we'd end up contacting the right people. That's probably why she came to us in the first place. But you, on the other hand, you'll probably just . . ."

Luke falls abruptly silent.

Cole raises his eyebrows and smiles. "I'd just what?" he asks.

"I don't know. Throw them all in a cell in some lab somewhere."

"Right. Just like I did Charley when I found out she was the only person in whom Zypraxon actually worked. Could you maybe give me a little more credit here?"

Marty says, "You could stop talking to us like we're nine and see how that goes? Just a thought."

"Ah," Cole says, "Marty and his *thoughts*. Look, I realize this is a highly unusual arrangement, and that it's also new, which means we're sort of figuring things out as we go. So allow me to say, quite clearly, good job! This was the perfect way to handle this."

"I'm sorry . . . *what*?" Charley asks.

"Bringing this to me like this."

"We *didn't* bring this to you," she says. "You eavesdropped on our conversation and made us bring it to you."

"Either way, the end result's the same."

"How's that?" she asks.

The only things she can see in his glasses are her own reflection, the blue sky overhead, and some of the expanse of glittering black water behind her. But she's pretty sure he's staring right into her eyes.

"I'll handle it," Cole says. "You don't need to worry about it anymore." Only then does she realize he's got the flash drive in his right hand. When he notices her looking at it, he closes his fist around it. "I want you to get some rest and find some pleasant, quiet ways to occupy your time. Do you have any hobbies? Sketching? Knitting? Kickboxing? You know, when you can't accidentally kick someone's head off, I mean."

Charley just glares at him.

"There she is," Cole says with a smile, "there's the Charlotte Rowe I know and love. OK. Everyone. Good talk! I'll be in touch."

When Cole stands and starts back up the dock, Charley feels the men on either side of her go tight as guitar strings. She doesn't blame them. The sudden tension in her own chest feels like it's headed for her throat.

"That's it?" Marty calls out.

It's enough to stop Cole in his tracks.

"You're just going to leave him like that?"

"Leave who like what?"

"Luke," Marty says. "Exposed."

"Exposed?"

"Henricks is working for these people, and Lacey's missing. Where do you think that leaves him if they ever figure out Lacey left a gift behind at the station?"

Cole turns to face them, but he doesn't move to close the distance. "You all are safer here than you know. Safer than most people are . . . well, anywhere. I know it sounds cold, but Charley is very valuable to me. And I protect what's valuable to me."

"Maybe," Marty says. "I mean, I think you think that. But what I also think is you brought a terrorist network into our backyard, and you don't want to admit it. Now whether you meant to or not, I don't know you well enough to say. But right now the truth of this thing's staring you in the face, and you still won't admit it's real. So how's that supposed to make us feel safe? It's not, is what I think. That said, here's a suggestion, Mr. Graydon. If you really want to be the lord of this town, start acting like it."

"Or else what?" Cole asks.

"Or maybe your board finds out about everything you're up to here."

"I see. You're threatening me. Well, that's interesting, Marty, because what happens now is if you threaten me, you threaten the lodge, and if you threaten the lodge, you threaten the tunnel, and if you threaten the tunnel, you threaten Pearsons Road, and once all those things are threatened, you've threatened pretty much everything I've done for Charley."

"Aw, hell, no," Marty says. "You didn't buy that resort for Charley."

"I didn't? Who'd I buy it for, then?"

"You did it to show her how goddamn powerful you were before you'd even met. You did it to scare the crap out of her and show you were watching her every move, and now you're stuck with it."

"Give me a break. I could off-load it tomorrow if I wanted."

"Why don't you?" Charley asks.

"Because I'm investing in all of you, and that means investing in your town."

"Or creating a lot of activity that distracts from your spies," Luke grumbles, "and giving yourself a legitimate reason to set up shop here."

"Charley's not a legitimate reason?"

"One you can actually talk about, I mean," Luke says.

"If this town's really an investment now," Marty cuts in, "you can't just let this cancer grow here because you made some backroom deals to get that tunnel built. I mean, dammit, Cole. These psychos are probably going to target your people along with Muslims and women with their own thoughts and whoever else makes their dicks feel small."

"My people?" Cole asks. "Marty, there are only ten of my people in the world, and I barely get along with any of them. Spare me the identity politics, old straight white guy."

"I wasn't talking about you being a goddamn billionaire. That's just a lottery number, and personally I'd always hoped the winners would be more grateful than you seem to be, but apparently not."

"Do I need to stand here all day and listen to insults you thought up in the shower? I'll do it, if it means I never have to hear them again."

Marty laughs bitterly.

"No, seriously. Are we done?" Cole asks. "Because it's not going to change anything I've said. I will handle this. You can go back to your comfortable, normal lives. Lives I guarantee the continued safety of.

In the meantime, consider that if there's a gratitude shortage on this dock, it's on that end."

Charley tells herself not to, but she looks at Luke anyway. His expression shows a battle between shell shock and anger. He's staying quiet for her, and it's tearing him up inside.

He senses her gaze, looks into her eyes. There's a flash of something there that's pleading and frightened and guilty all at once. It makes her remember that moment back in his kitchen, when she put her hands on his chest and stared into his eyes, silencing him with silence. If she doesn't speak up, that moment will leave a wound that will start to fester in no time.

"We don't believe you," she finally says.

"You don't believe what?" Cole asks.

"We don't believe you're going to do anything about this," Charley says.

"Define *this*."

"Jordy Clements is building a network of domestic terrorists across the country, and he's going to use the tunnel project to supply them with bomb-making materials. Lacey Shannon found out, and now she's missing."

"And if I find out there's any truth to that *wild* theory, Altamira will be rid of Jordy Clements, I can assure you."

"That's not enough, Cole," she says.

"It isn't?"

"No. He has to be stopped, and whatever network he's built has to be exposed. And we're afraid you won't do that."

"Why?"

Because you're afraid of exposing all the other shady stuff we're all doing up here. But Luke speaks up before she can give voice to this thought. "Because you told me to let him go," he says.

Charley feels a combination of relief and anxiety. She's been giving voice to his suspicions, she's sure, but maybe she's also given him permission to speak for himself. Or permission to hang himself in front of their new overlord. Either way, it's his choice to make.

"Did you even know why I'd arrested him?" Luke asks. "Or did one of your spies just call and tell you I'd dragged him out of the Gold Mine and, well, he's a Clements, so I had to let him go?"

"You have a tendency to overact," Cole says. "It got worse when Charley left."

"Really?" Charlotte asks. "I asked you to send him a text while I was recovering, and you acted like you couldn't even be bothered to say his name. Now you're saying you monitor Luke when I'm out of town?"

Before Cole can answer, Luke says, "You didn't, did you? You had no idea why I'd arrested Jordy, and you still told me to let him go."

"There were no reports of shoot-outs or bar fights or any kind of violence in Altamira that night. There hasn't been a homicide investigation here in seven years. My assumption was reasonable."

"The report was sitting in the station, and she wasn't going to talk until I had Jordy in a cell," Luke says.

"I had nothing to do with Lacey Shannon walking out of that station," Cole says, but Charley can already see where Luke's headed with this.

"No, you were the reason *Jordy* walked out a little while after she did. And, guess what? No one's heard from Lacey since."

For a while, the only sounds are the water lapping against the end of the dock, the distant drone of a jet plane flying overhead, probably LA-bound, then the insistent buzz of a circling fly that none of them can bring themselves to swat away. Cole's sunglasses still hide his eyes, but his mouth is a tense, set line.

"Before you hold me responsible for a murder," Cole finally says, "we should probably be sure there was one."

"Well, you're about to get right on that," Luke says, "right?"

She's not sure if Cole's stillness is that of a predator waiting to strike or a man trying to hide that taking a single step might send him off-balance.

"Cole?" Charley finally asks.

He turns his head slightly, which makes it clear he's been glaring daggers at Luke from behind his sunglasses.

"I want three," Charley says.

"Three what?" he asks.

"You know what."

"You must be joking."

"I'm not," she says. "We need to protect ourselves. *I* need to protect *us.*"

"You have plenty of protection. Trust me."

"See, that's just it . . ."

"You don't trust me. Yes, I know. And it's very distressing, I promise. But the answer's no. I'm not giving you Zypraxon so you can weaponize a vigilante mission I don't approve of."

"I'm talking about self-defense, Cole."

Cole removes his sunglasses. The look in his eyes frightens her. "I'm afraid," he says with deliberate enunciation, "that it's not always possible to control everything that happens once you've been triggered." She doesn't need skywriting to get his point. He's talking about Richard Davies. "Zypraxon is not a precision-guided missile. It's a cannon. And we must be cautious and responsible with how we use it."

So he's not mentioning the incident—the *murder!*—specifically. Fine. She'll thank him later. Once she stops sweating. He must be satisfied she got his point, because he slides his sunglasses back on.

Next to her, Marty grumbles, "The only reason you don't approve of this vigilante mission is 'cause you can't profit from it."

"Oh, shut up, Bernie Sanders."

"Quite the opposite, in fact," Marty adds. "This little mission might expose who you're really in bed with."

"Since it's clear all of you believe I'm incapable of caring for another human being or following anything one might call a principle, might I suggest the following," Cole says. "Put your faith in the idea that I won't allow anything bad to happen to any of you for the very simple reason that it would entail a colossal waste of my money and my time. When Charlotte isn't working, I want her happy and relaxed. However, it remains to be seen whether the two of you will ever allow her to be either, no matter what I do."

Cole turns and heads off down the dock.

30

Once the Suburban pulls away from the boat launch, Cole asks, "You got everything?"

Next to him in the back seat, Scott nods. He'd already removed his earpiece by the time Cole got back to the vehicle, so Cole wants to be sure he really did listen to the entire conversation via the matching earpiece worn by Cole, the same one Charlotte refused to wear when she took out Davies.

"Tell me about the operation here on the ground," Cole says.

Their driver, Fred Packard, is older than Scott. He's the security director here in Altamira, and he's said very little since their arrival. Paunchy and balding with a wide, easily sunburned nose, he was also one of Ed's old cop friends, hired by Ed, so the fact that he might be pissed about Ed's unexpected retirement has Cole on guard. "We've barely got an operation here on the ground," Fred says.

Cole's too shocked to say anything.

Scott clears his throat. "In a pure manpower sense, it's . . . it's light, sir. Apparently Ed wanted it that way."

"Well, *I* didn't. Jesus Christ. Why is it *light*? She's my most valuable test subject." The words COMPLETE ELIMINATION strobe across his brain so brightly he almost says them aloud. "Who called in the arrest of Clements?"

Scott says, "We've got eyes on the ground, for sure, but those eyes are not attached to people who are strike capable in the event of a real threat. That would require a different type of personnel, and Ed gave the impression it was outside our budget."

"A different type of personnel? What does that mean?"

Scott says, "Ed opted for digital surveillance primarily. He said you already had the equipment on hand, so it made sense. But the manpower, it was getting stretched thin, specifically with the Seattle operation. Unless you started using more outside contractors, and he thought that wouldn't be safe."

"We have men all over the world. How are we suddenly having a shortage?"

"He said he couldn't use just anyone. He said they all had to be briefed on Project Bluebird, and that meant he had to trust them first."

It takes Cole a second or two to realize his splitting headache and spinning vision are the result of the fact that he's not actually breathing. This is beyond Ed having been obstinate, or difficult, or overcautious. This is something else, and he's having trouble admitting it.

"Tell me the Med Ranch is intact," Cole says.

"Absolutely. And it's fully operational. But they're just doctors there, Mr. Graydon. They're not strike capable, either."

Under no circumstances can they let Charley walk into a regular doctor's office or even an ER. Not for a cold, not for a broken leg. While her Zypraxon exposures don't seem to be leaving any telltale traces in her system for now, who knows when that could change? And given the email from Kelley Chen the other day, who knows what might develop inside of Charley's blood? Or what might *never* develop.

"I'm probably not going to want to hear this," Cole finally says, "but what's our response time if there's an attack on Charley?"

"However long it takes a team to get here from San Diego or San Francisco."

Scott barks, "That's an exaggeration, Fred."

"Only slightly," Fred says. "But let me just say this before I get fired. I know that Ed and I go way back, but I'm not some Baker loyalist here. This situation here's a mess, and I flagged it constantly. And apparently he never took it up the ladder like he promised."

"What's the point of a system that monitors everything that happens here if we can't *do* anything about it? What was his plan? Fly a cloud of microdrones into Prescott's house if someone moves on her?"

"He was afraid, sir," Scott says. "Of your mother and the board finding out about all this. He kept talking about silent partners coming onboard, and once they did, you'd have more funding and we could up our game on the ground here, but until then—"

"Bullshit," Cole whispers. "This is sabotage. He wanted a security failure out here so he could make a case for throwing her in a lab forever."

After a moment of brittle silence, Scott says, "I'm not sure I can dispute that allegation, sir."

"Neither can I," Fred says.

"But, sir," Scott says. "With respect—"

"Just stop calling me sir."

"Mr. Graydon," Scott says quietly. "I say this with the utmost respect as your new security director, who only wants to serve your needs. While I disagree completely with Ed's insubordination, there is still a very valid school of thought that letting her live out here is too risky."

I'm starting to agree with you, he thinks. But that's not a conversation he can have with them now. It's not a conversation that should involve Fred at all. Not yet. And it leaves the pesky problem of how to handle the two men in Charlotte's life, who are both being bigger pains in his ass than Charlotte.

"What would it take to get some real security around her right away?" Cole asks.

"It would help if we could assess the nature of the threat," Scott answers.

"This doesn't have anything to do with Jordy Clements. She needs this kind of protection all the time."

"So you don't believe Jordy Clements presents a threat at this time?"

"I think Jordy Clements is a garbage fire, but I'm not sure what type of garbage or how hot he's going to burn. Meanwhile, I think the peanut gallery back there needs to lay off the caffeine and take up mah-jongg. How's that?"

"If there's any way you could be more specific . . ." Scott says.

"Digital services is investigating Jordy now. We'll wait and see what they turn up. But I just stood there and told them they were all safe. And now I find out Ed completely fucked things up here, and on purpose. We have them constantly monitored, but we can't do anything other than call them if something goes wrong? *Jesus!*"

"Just ask for what you want and I'll make it happen," Scott says.

"I want a five-man team, in a van, with Prescott's house in sight at all times until further notice. Whenever she leaves, I want them following her. How long before we can put that in place?"

"That depends on their capabilities," Scott says. "Their skill set, I mean."

"I want them capable of scaring the living shit out of anyone who approaches her with what looks like a bad motive. And if they're not easy to scare, I want them taken out and gotten rid of. How's that sound?"

Scott nods, even though it's clear that once again he'd like Cole to be more specific. Soon he'll learn. This *is* Cole being specific.

"I'd say in the morning at the earliest," Scott says, "unless we scramble guys here from Stonecut Ridge."

"No."

From the driver's seat, Fred says, "Since I'm not getting fired, can I make a suggestion?"

"Yes," Cole says.

"What if we relocate Charley and Luke temporarily, until we've got something better in place?"

Christ, Cole thinks. *Imagine the looks on their faces when I tell them I have to whisk them out of town after all the lectures I just gave them on their safety.* It's not worth it. Not if the source of this stink with Jordy and his angry ex turns out to be a weak fart.

"How long to get at least one person on that house who can see and shoot straight?"

"We can make that happen quickly," Scott says.

"Once we have a team in place, what should they do if they split up?" Fred asks.

"The team?"

"No, the peanut gallery."

"She's the priority. If her men want to act like cowboys, they can do it at their own risk. Do we have an update on Lacey Shannon? Maybe Ed hired her as our new office manager before he left."

Fred laughs silently, but Scott looks serious.

"Her SIM card went dead two days ago," Scott says.

"Dead?"

"No signal at all. Like it was destroyed."

"Two days ago . . . What time?"

"Eleven p.m."

A half hour after I called the station and told Luke to let Jordy go, Cole thinks. *So either Lacey destroyed her own SIM card to avoid being tracked, or Prescott's right and I set her killer free.*

"Freeway's coming up," Fred says. "Which way am I headed?"

"See if the airport's got a hangar or an office I can use."

"I doubt it, sir," Scott says. "It's pretty threadbare, but I'll check."

"Just find me a hotel, then. And let the plane go. I don't want to pay out the ass for it while it just sits there. And bring me my helicopter. That always puts me in a better mood."

"I'm not sure we can find a hotel in the area that's up to your . . . standards," Scott says.

"A motel's fine. I don't need five-star room service. Just privacy."

"For what, if I may ask?" Scott asks.

"A videoconference. I'll also need a secure line on my laptop. Call the office. They can set that up remotely."

Scott nods. "I'll need to say who the conference is with."

"Donald Clements, Jordy's father."

"Forgive me, sir, but wouldn't it be easier just to call him?"

"No. I want to see his face when I tell him about the trouble his son's causing me."

After Cole's team drove off into the rolling golden hills, Luke walked halfway up the dock, as if their departure were pulling him on a string. Now he's standing where he stopped, his back to Charley and Marty.

"I've got an idea," he says.

"What?" Charley asks.

Luke turns. He doesn't look excited, but at least he seems calmer now that Cole's gone.

"Someone who might be able to help us," he says.

"Help us do what?" Marty asks.

Charley has a sixth sense about where this is headed. Suddenly the pit of her stomach feels very cold.

"Find Lacey. Maybe find some stuff on Jordy. More than what was on the flash drive, and maybe a nice sampling of what was so we can make up for the fact that Cole just stole it. So we can give it to the right people."

"Luke," Charley says.

He starts walking toward them. "Now just hear me out. I'm sure there's a way we can reach him. Honestly, I don't think he ever stopped listening in. If Cole's guys are also listening, he probably found a way around them. So maybe if we just stand in my living room and say the right words like last time, he'll—"

"Luke."

Something in her voice stops him in his tracks. His mouth goes slack; he's studying her face with increasing alarm. "Oh, no," he finally says. "What? What happened to my brother?"

"He's OK . . . I guess."

"You guess? What does that mean? Did somebody catch him? Somebody caught him and Cole didn't do anything?"

"No," Charley says, "not exactly."

"Not exactly? Charley. Come on. What?"

It seems to hit Luke in a quick rush, and suddenly he's closed his eyes and he's shaking his head back and forth and he's moving to the bench and taking a seat as if his knees are about to go out from under him. "Oh, no," he mutters, "oh no, oh no. Christ."

"What am I missing here?" Marty asks.

"Bailey's working for Cole now," Charley says.

"Shit," Luke whispers.

"OK," Marty says, "but how is that any different than when he was working for us? I mean, no offense, but Bailey's basically been sleeping and breathing crime since he was a kid."

"It was different," Luke says.

"OK, but how?"

"Because he's *my* brother."

At this snakelike response, Marty holds up his hands and steps back. It wasn't the smartest and most mature reaction on Luke's part, but he's shocked and hurting, and Charley doesn't blame him.

"How long have you known this?" Luke asks.

"Just a few days. Apparently he was living on some kind of Russian troll farm. Now he's not."

"Where is he?"

"I don't know, Luke. I'm sorry."

"What *do* you know?" Luke asks.

"All right now," Marty warns, "it's not her fault."

"No," Charley says, "he's got a right to be upset."

"I'm sorry," Luke mutters. "I just . . . What do you know?"

"He's how they're finding the killers. The ones I go after."

"Oh, OK," Marty says. "Well, he's using his powers for good, then. Maybe they'll use him to find the smoking gun on Jordy and his merry band of shit monsters."

"Uh-huh," Luke says, "and that info will go where and do what exactly?"

Marty doesn't respond; maybe because he just noticed Charley's look telling him not to.

His elbows resting on his knees, Luke stares out at the lake, occasionally brushing his chin with his clasped hands. She hasn't seen him this close to tears in a while. Maybe it's a testament to his character. After all the trauma they've been through, the one thing that still gets to him is Bailey, his only living blood relative.

"My brother." There's a stammer in his voice, but he takes a deep breath and continues. "Every time I try to help him, every time I try to make us a family, he throws it back in my face like it's shit. Like it's *complete* shit. And now this. One of the most powerful men in the world offers to give him a clean slate so he can come home and actually have a family, and what does he do? I mean, what the hell does he do? He goes to work for the guy! He chooses to stay a criminal. He'd rather live in hiding than ever lay eyes on me again."

"Well," Marty says, "he's got a habit of spying on people through their devices, so maybe he's laying eyes on you all the time and you just don't know it."

"Marty, please stop helping," Charley whispers.

"Sorry," Marty mumbles.

"Luke," she says, "we don't actually know if Cole really made that offer to Bailey. It might have been conditional."

"What do you mean?" Luke asks.

"Meaning Cole said you either go to work for me or your record stays the way it is and you freeze to death in Russia every winter."

"Maybe," Luke says. True or not, this possibility doesn't seem to dull his pain.

Nobody says anything for a while. Once again, a sound that should be peaceful, the gentle lapping of the lake water against the sides of the dock, feels as invasive as harsh knocks against a thin door.

"I just need a minute," Luke says. "OK? Can I have a minute to myself?"

Before Charley can say anything, Marty gently takes her arm and starts leading her away from the bench. "Sure thing, podnah," he says. "We'll be right over here when you need us."

They're halfway up the dock when Charley says, "This sucks."

"Hardest thing you ever have to do in a relationship."

"What, telling them what they don't want to hear?" she asks.

"Nope," Marty says. "Giving 'em a minute."

31

The problem with Pete Henricks, Jordy Clements realizes once they've left town, is that he can't focus.

When he first met the guy, he seemed like a pretty good listener. But now that Henricks feels more comfortable in Jordy's presence, he won't shut up, and it's giving Jordy a protracted and unwanted glimpse into the guy's squirrelly mind.

One minute the dude's talking about how when he was a kid he almost drove into that old oak they just sped past; the next second, he's explaining how the women he's dated were all proof that there's a connection between an inability to measure spatial relationships and a lack of emotional discipline. In women, that is.

Maybe he's nervous about this unexpected ride out of town. Or maybe he's just a class-A idiot. Given his behavior the past few days, Jordy figures it's the latter. But he wants to give the guy the benefit of the doubt. For the next hour or two, at least.

Shortly after he got to town, Jordy had some of his guys follow all four of the regular sheriff's deputies for several weeks to see which one might be the most amenable to a new business arrangement. The reports all came back the same: Pete Henricks was the best candidate. A lifelong resident of Altamira and a community college dropout, he was rumored to have declared bankruptcy before getting hired by the department. He also had a rep for explaining to anyone who would listen how common sense was usually the best sense and government usually made a mess of things.

Luke Prescott, on the other hand, was a no go. By all accounts, the guy was an asshole who fancied himself too good for his hometown, probably thanks to his higher education. No doubt his time in San Francisco, Sodom by the Sea, had indoctrinated him in all sorts of diseased ways of thinking.

And boy, had that turned out to be the truth.

He had to give props to the guys who'd warned him off Prescott.

But those same guys had steered him toward Henricks. Should he blame himself for making the final call or take it out on the foot soldiers who steered him in Henricks's direction? That would all depend on what was about to transpire up here in the mountains just west of town.

"You think maybe eventually they'll build up here?" Henricks asks. "Everyone acts like they should be preserved, but the views are rockin', and if there's gonna be more to look at down valley, with all the development and all—hell, I'd build up here if I had the money."

Please tell me this asshole isn't hitting me up for more money, Jordy thinks. *Is he actually asking me for a raise after he fucked up so badly?*

"How long you lived here, Henricks?" Milo asks.

Their driver, Jordy's right-hand man, is almost too large to fit inside his own truck. Milo has a thing about disclosing his height. Like the actual number is a source of strength so long as it's a secret, sort of like Samson's hair if Samson always wore it in a bun. Six foot four, that's Jordy's guess. There was a time, back when he and Milo fought together in Iraq and then Afghanistan, when Milo was all lean muscle; now he's bulk and a bit of bloat, most of it from steroids, but they've turned the man into a human wall, and Jordy likes that just fine. Because that's what Jordy needs around him now. Sturdy, protective walls.

"My whole life," Henricks answers, "you know that. Didn't I tell you that?"

Milo looks in the rearview mirror, probably so he can gauge whether Henricks is actually annoyed. Sunset's a few hours away, but it's already near dark on this side of the mountains, so it's not easy to make out Milo's expression in the deepening shade. But with Milo, it's the eyes that do the trick. There's something that always looks sympathetic about them, even when he's getting ready to bash in a guy's skull. Sympathetic and steady. Strangely inviting.

If Henricks is starting to get suspicious—they've never offered to swing by his place and pick him up before—one look into Milo's steady, welcoming gaze should calm him right now.

"Just got a lot of details floating around in my head, is all," Milo says. "No offense intended, my friend."

"None taken. So listen, we should probably talk about other ways I can be helpful to you guys. You know, since the incident at the station. I'm sure there's stuff I can do. I mean, I don't know if you want me on your crew, but I've got some construction in my background and I'm always up for learning new things. But maybe . . . I don't know, I was thinking . . ."

"What?" Jordy asks. "What were you thinking?"

"I know things didn't go totally as planned, but she did leave, right? I mean, I was able to convince her to walk out so . . . I don't know. Maybe I've got a future with you guys as kind of an ambassador or something."

"An ambassador," Jordy says. "That's an interesting thought."

"You know, like a representative in town. That kind of thing. And I just have to say, again. I mean, I know you've heard me say it before. But honestly, most of the folks in town are really happy you guys are here. You gotta forget about cunts like Sanchez and Prescott. There's no convincing folks like that of anything. But the rest of them, they're easily won over."

"I see," Jordy says. "So what you're suggesting is that you take on a new job for us. That's easy."

Milo gives Jordy a warning look. That's why he needs Milo. He's his balance. His focus. The lens through which the righteous fire in Jordy's soul will soon be unleashed upon the world.

"Oh, no, man," Henricks says. "I mean I'd be willing to do anything just about."

"Just about, huh?"

"Yeah. I mean, I've told you how important I think you guys are. You know that, right?"

"Of course, Henricks," Milo says.

They've left the valley far behind. Slowing down some, Milo takes a sharp left, and suddenly they're traveling a narrow dirt service road Jordy's crew only cut through the brush a few weeks before. Some of the branches have grown in a little, and they thud lightly against the roof of Milo's truck, mostly when the rutted road sends the truck bouncing up into them.

Henricks stares out the back window with a nervous-looking frown. For the first time, he looks afraid.

That's a good thing, Jordy thinks. It indicates the presence of at least one small shred of humility. And given how fucking clueless he's acted over the past few days, some humility about now would be a very good thing.

"Where we going?" he finally asks.

"Found this great view spot up ahead," Milo says. "You can see straight through the mountains, straight to the Pacific. Good place to talk without anybody overhearing us, you know?"

"You guys . . ."

"What, Pete?"

"Seriously, you guys . . . I mean, I don't . . ."

"Hey." Milo hits the brakes, puts the car in park, then turns in his seat to face the passenger in the back seat, all with the smooth authority of a car pool mom; that's how good the guy is. "It's not like that, Henricks. We're just talking. Promise."

"I mean, I know you probably aren't that happy with me right now."

Now you fucking say it, asshole, Jordy thinks.

"Henricks," Milo says with a gentle smile. "Come on, man. Get those thoughts out your head. It's a small town. We just wanted some privacy and some space. That's all."

To his credit, the guy doesn't hesitate or start crying when they all step from the truck. When Milo and Jordy start walking ahead of him, he seems to relax. His only frame of reference for a moment like this has got to be TV shows or movies, so he probably assumes the fact that they're in front of him and not behind him means they aren't planning to shoot him.

And they aren't.

Not really.

Henricks is lucky. He's got choices.

The air's a few degrees colder up here, and they're close enough to the top of the mountain to smell the salty tang of the Pacific. Wind rustles the pine branches, shifts the dense foliage underfoot. Jordy's reminded of what the world could really be like if it were cleansed of pollutants and nonbelievers. Peaceful and tranquil and devoid of those temptations that act like sandpits for good, honorable men. It's the type of world men like him and Milo and the others deserve, men who've been run through the inferno of combat and forced to return to a degenerate country that keeps adding wood to the faraway fires, all without thought to the good soldiers those fires consume, all without respect for the good soldiers who survive those flames.

The foot soldiers in the nearby trees are doing a good job of staying back. Jordy can't see them, and Henricks doesn't seem to be getting any more nervous than he already is, so he probably can't see them, either.

"I'm serious, you know," Henricks says. "I mean, I'm committed, is what I'm saying. You guys are special. What you're doing for us, all the things you're doing for us, I don't take them for granted, and I never will. Never."

"That's real good, Henricks," Milo says. "We appreciate that."

They've reached their destination. Through the branches off to his right, Jordy can see one of the seismic geophone stations they'd set up a few weeks before, a slender pyramid of plywood about Milo's height. The geophone's hung at the apex, pointed down toward the earth. Tucked against a copse of nearby pines is one of the storage sheds they built on-site.

He and Milo have discussed exactly what needs to happen next, but it's not like they've physically rehearsed, so Jordy feels a little flutter in his chest as he pulls his Glock from his holster, and Milo does the same.

Henricks sees both guns, starts saying the word *no* over and over again. Then he realizes that neither gun's pointed at him, and his protests turn to gasps and swivels of his head.

Milo opens the door to the shed, disappears inside, then reemerges, dragging Lacey's hog-tied body like it's a sack of potatoes. There's enough dope in her that as soon as Milo releases her wrists, she collapses to the dirt in the fetal position, gazing at nothing with wet, slitted eyes.

Henricks has raised his hands like a suspect. But he's staring at Lacey as if she's the only thing in his world, as if her bruised forehead and the gag in her mouth and the flex-cuffs on her wrists and the nylon rope around her ankles are all evidence his life will never be the same again.

And it won't be. If he's lucky.

"It's all right, Henricks." Milo's also got his hands up; he's pointing his Glock skyward as he closes the distance between them like a stalking snake. "This isn't what you think it is. Seriously. We've *heard* you. We've heard your willingness and your commitment. So consider this an invitation."

Tears are sliding from Henricks's eyes as he stares at Milo in evident disbelief. "But I . . . but I . . ."

"You what?" Jordy asks.

"I made her leave. She was talking crazy, and I made her leave before she could do anything."

"I know," Jordy says, "but then you quit. You were our man inside the department, and then you *quit*, Henricks. Can you see how that's a problem for us?"

"But I'll do anything . . . I'll do anything, *please.*" The last word unleashes a wrenching sob in the man so pathetic Jordy almost shoots him right there just to have this done with. But that's not how they're doing this. Milo insisted on something different. Given the momentousness of their mission, and how central Altamira's about to become to their operations, they need local men to do more than spy and listen, to jump when they say jump. They need men who *believe*.

That's why Milo reaches up and places the handle of his Glock in one of Pete Henricks's raised hands. Henricks looks up at the gun and his hand as if neither are really connected to him anymore. He lets Milo take his wrist and lower his hand to chest level. Milo nods at Jordy. Jordy lowers his own gun toward his feet and rests it there.

When realization dawns, Henricks goes very still, and then, slowly, brings his free hand to the gun's grip.

"You want me to . . ." Henricks's words leave him, but he's got the gun pointed at the earth a few feet in front of him and in Lacey's general direction, so there's little doubt in Jordy's mind the guy knows exactly what they want.

"She lied, Henricks," Milo says quietly. "She's a lying cunt who told that cop Jordy beat her when he did no such thing. Tell me, how many men have been destroyed by the type of thing she did? But you. You weren't fooled. You saw right through it. You knew better, knew what kind of man Jordy is. You knew he'd never lift a hand to his girl like that. You weren't like Prescott.

"You see, men like him, they believe anyone who calls themselves a victim. They think it makes 'em powerful, you see. But what they don't understand is that when they indulge the lie, they weaken *everything*. Everyone. They think they're being all strong and protective, but really they're just living out some fantasy of being a cowboy that's no better than jerking off alone in their room. But men like you, Pete. Men who can see the truth. Men who think before they act. Men who pause to ask where the bruises really came from. You're the strong ones. *We're* the strong ones."

Jordy's stunned. Henricks is looking straight into Milo's eyes, and it's like all the resistance has drained from Pete's face. Is this shit really going to work? Is Henricks about to become a foot soldier?

Milo reaches down and raises Pete's gun hand until the Glock is aimed directly at Lacey.

"We've got big things planned, Pete," Milo says. "Important things. You could be part of it. I mean, this is way beyond just being our ambassador. I'm talking about being ground zero at a revolution that's going to spread out all over this land. Fear and fire paving the way for truth. The kind of truth only men like us can see. But first . . ."

When Milo suddenly steps away from him, Pete flinches, as if he's been drawing comfort from the big man's proximity, and now that it's been ripped away he feels unsteady.

Milo taps the top of the Glock in Pete's hands, then points to Lacey's prone body as if it were a target in a shooting gallery.

Jordy studies every inch of Pete's body, from the way he holds the gun to the tension in both sides of his flushed neck to the glazed look in his eyes. Is it a settling into a fate, a necessary hardening of the soul, or just paralysis and shock?

But then Jordy realizes that Henricks is looking at Lacey too much. He's not just looking at her; he's looking for something in the way her body's sprawled on the carpet of pine needles and leaves. Big mistake. Lacey is the target, not the revelation. The revelation will be in how he feels once he's disposed of her; once he cuts her vicious lies free of their earthly anchor and allows them to float over the mountaintops before being blown out to sea.

And man, if anyone here should be having an emotional reaction to Lacey's killing, it should be him. She's his girlfriend, after all.

Jordy figures another few seconds of hands shaking this bad and Pete's knees will go next. But instead Pete drops the gun and screws his eyes shut and starts shaking his head as if doing so will make the clearing, the trees, Lacey, and most importantly, Jordy and Milo disappear.

Milo purses his lips and nods at the ground; he seems so disappointed, Jordy almost feels bad for the guy. Maybe he really did think Pete had potential.

Pete's crying now, but at least he's not begging for anything, including his life.

Milo closes the distance between them, wraps his arms around the man. Pete gives in to the hug as if he genuinely thinks this might end with him being given another chance, or at least a chance to run. Instead, in a series of lightning-quick moves accompanied by the quick crunch of breaking bone, Milo snaps Henricks's neck and drops his body to the ground.

Slowly, the other foot soldiers emerge from the woods, seven in all, lowering their guns at the sight of Henricks's body.

Lesser men, Jordy realizes, would probably make a joke to dispel the tension, but they take death far too seriously for that, and so they just stand there, offering up Pete Henricks to the wind and the patches of dark-blue sky with their first dappling of stars, and to a God whose pure will has been ignored so often people have come to view any implementation of his wishes as a sign of pettiness or vengefulness.

32

After what feels like an appropriate amount of silence, Jordy asks Milo where he found Lacey's bracelet. Brushing branches out of their way, Milo leads him past the nearest geophone. A few paces later the pines break, and the ground just ahead turns into a series of granite steps that quickly give way to a plunging slope so steep there's no traveling it on foot.

"It was resting up against that trunk there." Milo's pointing to the trunk of a hearty ponderosa pine a few yards downslope. It's not so thick that the bracelet couldn't have gone easily tumbling past it after Lacey dropped it. But did Lacey drop it? They've still got no damn idea what actually happened during Lacey's first visit here, and two days of trying to beat it and then drug it out of the girl hasn't yielded any clues.

If she fell all that way, she's lucky to have survived. And if she climbed her way back up the slope by herself, she's stronger than he thought.

"So she was snooping around up here and fell?" Jordy asks.

"She wouldn't say, but I checked with all our guys and nobody was up here and nobody pushed her." Milo's trying to hide his frustration, Jordy can tell. Milo's powers of persuasion are intense and effective, but this is Lacey they're talking about, so Jordy's asked him to be less gruesome than usual.

"And we're sure none of our guys did?"

"Nobody knew she was up here. Nobody was here. It was almost dark. If she was up here by herself, for whatever reason, she could have easily lost her footing and taken a fall, especially if she didn't know the area. Maybe that tree broke it."

"That'd explain why her bracelet caught on it."

"Yeah. But it doesn't explain the most important thing . . ."

What the hell she was doing up here in the first place, Jordy thinks. *Checking out the seismic geophones. Making sure they actually existed. Why the hell would she do that? If only I didn't have a good idea. She found something about the fake readings and came up here to find out if we'd actually done any seismic testing at all.*

"The drugs aren't making her talk?"

"Nope. Just zoning her out. I can pull her off and then . . . you know, start up again."

Start beating her again, is what he means. The longer Lacey's silence persists, the more Milo's become convinced something more went down inside that sheriff's station. Something Henricks didn't even know about. That's why he'd insisted on tying up that loose end. Even if the dipshit had quit, he could still have asked for his job back, and in a town this small, maybe the threat of a lawsuit coupled with a call from Jordy's dad would have been enough to get the tiny department to drop whatever bullshit review that bitch sheriff had threatened Henricks with. But given how quickly this had gone to shit, there'd been no bringing Henricks back in half-baked. Not unless he became a real foot soldier.

"All right," Jordy finally says, "so let's review. She comes up here to check out something, we don't know what, but it's gotta be the geophones because that's really all that's up here—"

"Which is not good at all," Milo says.

"I'm aware of that. So because she doesn't know the area, and maybe it's getting dark, she falls. Hard. Maybe lands in that tree right there, face-first. Then suddenly decides she's going to blame her injuries on me and walk into the sheriff's station and tell them I need to be thrown in a cell because I'm beating on her."

"Which might have been easier than trying to explain her injuries to you."

"Maybe."

"Jordy, you didn't try to bring her in on this, did you? It's your call, man, but she's so damn unstable, I just can't—"

"I didn't."

"Well, did she see something? Overhear something?"

Oh, how to answer this question.

The problem, as he figures it, is that almost overnight Lacey went from being a woman who didn't notice anything to a woman who noticed everything. Sure, he'd told her if she went on the pills again, he'd give her the boot, but he hadn't meant it. Not really. He'd brought her to Altamira because he was sure she'd fail again. And he liked it when she failed. He'd grown addicted to the sudden absences that let him do whatever he wanted, followed by the miserable apologies and the begging—begging for *him*. It was always magical, the moment when her need for the pills was replaced by her desperate, frenzied need for him. For his love, his approval. His body. The sex that followed was always explosive. The way she said his name during it, it sounded like a prayer for something she couldn't go without and the invocation of an avenging angel who frightened her down to her bones.

Then the unexpected happened, right after he set her up in Trailer City.

She actually got sober.

Not in an organized, rehab kind of way. In a way that was messy and sudden and left her frazzled, but also as alert and reactive as a Chihuahua. The isolation had worked in a way he'd never really expected it to. Cut off from her roster of sham doctors, she hadn't been able to fill any scrips, and little Altamira wasn't exactly awash in street dealers.

Back in the day, she never would have noticed he'd had his tattoo removed. That's how out of it she was most weeks. And that's why he'd made the mistake with the photos.

He was ninety percent sure that was it. She'd caught him deleting all those old photos of them at the beach, the ones where his shoulder was exposed. And she'd gone ballistic in a way she never did when she was using. Not sobby and messy. Focused, angry, throwing things, and with good aim for a change. Accusing him of turning her into a prisoner out here and then trying to erase their past together.

But he can't tell Milo any of this.

Milo had told him not to use that damn Bible verse to find field recruits. Not to use anything that could be so easily traced back to him. But didn't Milo get it? You don't pick the verses from the Good Book that light a fire within your soul; the verses pick you.

Please, God, Jordy prays. *Tell me there's a lesson here that will only make our devotion to you stronger.*

"This is too much, too soon, friend," Milo says. "We don't even have materials yet, and we've only had sit-downs with four field recruits."

"In four different states, though. That's a victory."

"A fraction of the dozen we're gonna need to make the first wave matter."

"Still, just don't . . ."

"Don't what, Jordy?"

"Don't discount everything too quick, is what I'm saying."

"I'm saying whatever this is, we need to nip this in the bud right away."

"Didn't we, though?" Jordy gestured in the direction of Henricks's body.

"We can't keep her alive forever. There's no bringing her around to this now."

. "I'm not planning on either."

"All right. Then that just leaves . . ."

"Stop baby-walking me and get to it."

"Luke Prescott."

They both fall silent, and Jordy's not sure if he should feel prideful that Milo's nasally breaths sound louder than his.

The nearest mountain peak looks like a jagged shelf of granite turned on its side and wedged inside a giant mound of green; orange sunlight reflects off its western flank. Orange the color of flame.

Milo's right about one thing: This is too much pressure, too soon. Too much messiness before the first bomb's been assembled. Hell, the explosives haven't even been delivered yet. They'll need to be stored, protected, the reserves distributed to their foot soldiers at points throughout the country.

Jordy assumed the hardest part would be finding the bombers most committed to the cause, but that's been easy. Maybe because they've set their goals in the right place. They're after three things that have become a kind of mantra: range, variation, coordination. A gay bar here, an abortion clinic there, a mosque there. All on the same day. A big death toll in each place would be nice, but in the end, it's just a perk. It's the calculation and coordination that will truly strike terror into the hearts of the deviants and the godless, that will convince them that every expression of their twisted selfhood runs the risk of split-second immolation. A web of righteousness, stretched wide, will do more to advance their cause than any single crater in the earth.

"We're not killing two sheriff's deputies in a row," Jordy finally says.

"I didn't say we should."

"Luke Prescott doesn't know anything."

"Why is she so damn quiet, then?" Milo asks. "Why is she acting like she's going to get rescued?"

"You're doping her up," Jordy says.

"I'm jerking her off depressants, then putting her on stimulants to get her gums to start flapping, and it's not working."

"Maybe you broke her," Jordy says.

"Bull. She's hiding something."

"Well, we've turned over her trailer four times and gone through her computer and there's nothing."

Because she went through my *damn computer,* Jordy thinks, *and I'd rather get beat myself than tell Milo that.*

"There are ways to silence somebody without killing them," Milo says quietly. "Honestly, breaking people's more my specialty."

For a while, the two men just stare at each other.

Jordy's seen enough missions go south to know that there's usually, not all the time, but usually, a moment of warning coupled with a moment of decision, and someone makes the wrong choice.

"I fucked up," Jordy whispers. "I wasn't careful enough with my computer. She must have seen something. She'd been such a basket case before, I didn't expect her to get her mind back and start . . ."

Something cold passes through Milo's expression, then he closes his eyes and nods.

"That's the past. Let's talk about the future." His tone's not as forgiving as his expression.

"Do what you think's best," Jordy says.

"With Prescott?" Milo asks.

Jordy nods.

When Milo nods back, Jordy removes his gun from its holster and strides back toward the clearing. His foot soldiers stand in a loose circle around Henricks's corpse. The ones that stick out to him are that kid, Tommy Grover, who always looks like he just smelled something foul, and Manuel Lloya, the ex–car thief from Anaheim; they're Milo's guys, not his, and their presence now is a reminder that loyalties could shift in dangerous ways if Jordy doesn't let Milo put this back on course the way he wants.

All seven men part when they see him coming, but he walks past them, to the spot where Lacey's still on her side in the fetal position, staring into the dope-smeared contents of her mind.

Before she can look up into his eyes, he fires one shot into her forehead.

He turns away before he can be distracted by old feelings.

He'll replace her someday. The world is full of victims waiting to be healed, and Lacey wasn't even the prettiest one.

33

Charley's given Luke a lot longer than the minute of quiet he asked for.

She kept her mouth shut during the ride back to the house. She let him wander outside into the backyard by himself once they got home. Now, it's an hour later, and he's still sitting outside, glowering at the view. In the meantime, she's held her tongue, stayed out of his eye line, done all the things she figures you're supposed to do when someone you love suddenly announces they don't want to hear your voice. It leaves you with no choice but to be assailed by all manner of dark fears about where their little funk might end, but maybe that's just how adult relationships are supposed to be. She doesn't know. She's never had one before.

She had years of experience watching Marty and Luanne go about their relationship with casual ease—spending time together on the weekends, giving the other football fields' worth of space whenever they wanted it. But then there's the specter of Abigail Banning, who through a series of jailhouse interviews has tried to cast her gruesome life's work as a testament to the idea that if you don't help your man indulge his darkest instincts, you'll be alone forever. She knows how repulsive and wrong Abigail is, of course. But she's afraid her early exposure to the idea in practice might have produced in her a neurotic fear that today makes her far more indulgent of Luke's mood swings and outbursts than she should be.

Whatever the answer, she's sick of this routine. She's sick of pacing the kitchen, sick of waiting for Luke to put on his big boy pants and come back inside and talk through his feelings like the modern man he thinks he is, but sometimes isn't.

She'd love to lose herself in obsession over the mysterious disappearance of Lacey Shannon, but with the flash drive gone, that's not really possible. There's always Google and social media, but the wrong search terms will probably set off an alert in some secret Graydon office somewhere, and within minutes Cole will knock on her door so he can explain, once again, what a good person he is for taking away her privacy and serving as a constant reminder the world is run by a largely corrupt cadre of billionaires.

The house around her used to belong to an old classmate of theirs, Emily Hickman. Emily's folks once owned and operated the only drugstore in town, a gleaming white tile–filled place with an old-school ice cream counter and vintage drug ads on the walls. When Charley visited Luke here as a grown-up, she'd been instantly struck by the absence of the cast-iron fence that used to encircle the property, the same one the Hickmans would tie balloons to every time they had a party for their only daughter, which was often.

A few months later, shortly after Charley moved in, Marty and his crew replaced the fence free of charge. It mars the expansive views from the backyard more than the old one ever did, but the spokes are widely spaced enough that it doesn't wreck them entirely. The gnarled oak tree's still there, as thick and solid as it was when they were young. But the old play set's gone, along with the tire swing.

Again, Charley thinks about getting in touch with Emily; maybe dropping her a note about how they live in her old place now and by the way she's shacked up with Luke Prescott and isn't that crazy, all things considered? But then she remembers she's leading a double life. And with the stress of it pitching her boyfriend into a long, brooding silence, new friendships, even basic correspondences, seem like an unacceptable risk.

Still, Emily was one of the few classmates who was actually nice to Charley back when she was Trina; unlike Luke, who'd bullied her almost ceaselessly about her dark past.

They were different people then, she reminds herself. Maybe Emily grew up to be someone not as nice. Kind of the way Luke's grown up to be more mature and reflective, but with vestiges of that old sharp tongue and hot temper. The point, she tells herself, is that those were different times. Memories of them come and go, but mostly they go.

But the longer Luke sits out in the backyard in sullen silence, the stronger those memories become. And the more high school feels like yesterday, the more she fears the return of the Luke she used to loathe.

It's not fair, or rational. He's not acting like the guy he was back then. Not really. More like an injured animal. But deep down, is there really that much difference between the two? And if all this becomes too much for him, will the old Luke return, if only for the purpose of driving her away, cutting himself off?

She's not interested in waiting to find out.

He's got to hear her footsteps crunching the grass, but he doesn't turn or even sit up.

Not good, she thinks.

He's slouched in one of the cheap Adirondack chairs that used to form a ring around his old chiminea. Then Mona dropped by for a visit one day, took one look inside the chiminea's ash- and branch-filled cavity, and asked Luke how long he'd dreamed of starting a wildfire. Luke threw the thing out the next day, and Charley made a mental note: *If I ever need to really get through to Luke, go through Mona.*

Provided, of course, the topic doesn't have anything to do with Graydon Pharmaceuticals.

"This is longer than a minute," Charley says.

"Have a seat." He gestures to the empty chair next to him.

Oooo, can I? she wants to ask, in a voice as sarcastic as the one he used to use with her back in high school. But she knows that's a childish, defensive reaction; she'll save those for later if she needs them.

"I'm not mad at you," he says.

"OK," she says.

Good, she thinks.

"I'm mad at myself."

"OK," she says.

"I fucked up."

"How?"

She's ninety percent sure he's about to say he screwed up by getting involved with her, so when he says, "Cole's right," she sits forward in her chair with surprise.

"How?" she asks.

"The whole time you were gone, I was wound so tight I was ready to pop. Lacey walking into that station . . . it popped me, I guess."

"How does that make Cole right?"

"I handled it badly, and now we've got a mess. Mona thinks the same thing; she just won't say it directly."

"And you think you handled it badly because you were worried about me?"

"Partly, yeah."

"Well, personally, I'm glad you were worried about me. It's nice to have someone worrying about me."

She smiles. He doesn't.

"I don't regret that part," he says. "It's the other part that's got me going."

"What other part?"

"This isn't the easiest thing to say, Charley."

"Well, maybe if you'd just say it, it will be easier."

"You're not going to want to hear this."

"Then say it faster. I don't know. But please . . . just say it."

It's over, she thinks. Whatever this rare, special, unexpected thing between them was, it's over. He's stepping back. Stepping out. Whatever you want to call it. She'd never expected to find someone who could handle her past. Now that her future's twice as insane, how can she expect any man to hold up under the stress created by both? Her mind's spinning with fearful thoughts of what Luke walking away from her could mean, given everything he knows about her current situation. How will Cole respond? But this is a distraction, she's sure. A distraction from the rejection that's about to hit her like a body blow from which no pill can protect her.

"Yes, I was worried," Luke says. "I was worried sick. And the only thing I wanted was for you to come back. But there was another part of it, a part I'm ashamed of."

"Just don't . . ."

"Don't what?"

"Don't give me some speech about how you just want a normal life. If you wanted normal, you should have found yourself a sorority girl."

"Normal?"

"Yeah. Stress-free. Easy. Whatever."

"You think I want a normal life? You gotta be kidding me. I've wanted out of this town since I was a kid. You think I went after a job at the FBI because I wanted to . . . what? Be Father Knows Best and run a feed store? Come on. Charley, I wasn't just worried. I was jealous. I wanted to be there, and not just to make sure you were OK. I wanted to take down another guy like Pemberton."

"Luke, it wasn't the same."

"Even so, I didn't want to be *here*, corralling drunks and counting the minutes until you came back. So at the first sign of something, anything that would make me feel like I was making the world a better place, I jumped at it. But I jumped too damn hard, and now we're in the middle of this crap because of me."

"Lord," Charley whispers.

"What?"

"I thought you were breaking up with me."

"What? *No!*"

"Why didn't you say any of this before now?" she asks.

"Oh, come on. We both knew. Cole said I couldn't be part of the team, and you didn't fight him on it so I backed down."

"I didn't fight him on it because you didn't fight me on it."

"I know, but still . . ."

"Oh, please. We're supposed to read each other's minds now?"

"Maybe not. But we're supposed to know each other, aren't we? I mean, come on, do you really think I want to spend the rest of my life as a sheriff's deputy in Altamira? I came home with my tail between my legs because my dreams were shot and I didn't want to become some consultant with my business degree. And then . . . you and I. We did something amazing. We found that guy, Charley, and you stopped him. And then all of a sudden my job was to stay home and wait for you and not talk about everything you'd done."

"This isn't just about what I said about Bailey?"

"What do you mean?"

"The fact that he's working for Cole now. You've tried so hard to make him be a family with you. I just worry that you think if you go into business with Graydon, too, it'll bring you guys closer."

"It won't."

"I know it won't. I mean, I've been working with Graydon for months, and I've never laid eyes on him."

"It's not about him, Charley. I know it might seem like it, but it's not."

"Are you sure?"

"It's about me. That's why I didn't want to say it. Because it's really just about me and what I want, and it feels selfish. But it's the truth. I want to be part of something. That's what I've wanted all my life. I want to do something that makes the world a better place. But it's too damn easy to give up on that dream, because the older you get the more you realize the world's worse off than you thought."

"You do make this world a better place."

"Charley, don't greeting card this."

"Luke, if you pull over a drunk driver on your shift, you could be saving a school bus full of kids later. You're not giving yourself enough credit."

"You're part of something that could change the world. I'm screwing up basic law enforcement work."

"This wasn't basic. You were being played by someone unstable who'd just discovered a massive criminal conspiracy she didn't know how to handle or even report. You were doing the best you knew how to do. And if you really thought Jordy Clements was a woman beater, good. I'm glad you threw him in a cell."

"You're just being generous," he says.

"That's bad?"

"It's not, I guess," he whispers. "I meant to say *biased*."

"Still. Everyone deserves at least one person who's always biased in their favor."

"Marty?"

"No, my grandmother used to say that one."

"So many sayings, so few of them knitted on things. Missed opportunities all over the place."

"I actually think Cole's idea that Marty start a bumper sticker company isn't that bad. You think we could get him to fund it?"

He laughs, then he brings her hand to his mouth and kisses her fingers. "You're not just telling me what I want to hear?"

"No."

"OK. Will you keep being honest while I ask you something else?"

"Promise."

"What if I asked Cole if I could . . ."

"If you could what?"

"Join the team. Or whatever you guys call it."

Suddenly her right hand feels like he's no longer holding it, even though he just took it in his own. After a few seconds, whatever expression's on her face has brought a stony, distant one to his.

When his cell phone rings, they both jump. "It's Mona," he says.

He stands and walks to the other side of the yard. And after a moment or two, she realizes she's still holding her hand in the air where he let it go, as if she's reaching out to him across the yard.

She's feeling too many things at once to give voice to any single one. But they all have one thing in common: they generate the kind of full-body flush she's always associated with shame. A sense that she'd been suddenly exposed without her consent.

How many times will Luke be able to watch her trigger before he starts to see her as the woman with weapons for hands and not the woman sitting with him now, talking about feelings? How long before he's assaulted by memories of her last hunt every time he tries to kiss her? Will his tenderness disappear? Will he start to touch her like she's made of iron?

Watching her take down Pemberton was one thing. For starters, he wasn't her boyfriend then. They hadn't learned the feel of each other's bodies, become familiar with the sounds of the way the other breathes while they sleep. But the first time he saw Zypraxon in action, he actually threw up. If he joins Cole's team, if he watches her take down monster after monster, will he be able to reconcile both versions of her in his mind, his heart?

She's far from sure, far enough to feel terror at the thought.

If Luke had seen me kill Richard Davies, would he still have helped me shave my head?

He's walking toward her across the grass, pocketing his phone.

"Mona needs me to come in," he says.

"Is everything all right?"

"It's Edward," he says.

"Her boyfriend?"

"Yeah, he's . . . freaking out. He needs her to take care of him, but he doesn't want her to see him this sick and so he's been threatening to break up with her and . . . and anyway, the whole thing's a mess and it's been going on for days. He finally caved and asked her to come over, and with Henricks gone they're going to be short tonight, and I don't want to stop her, you know? The only sort of good thing about it is that it's keeping her from digging into Lacey's disappearance as much as she wants to."

Neither of them say anything for a few long seconds. Neither of them's comfortable with this definition of *good*, it seems.

"Figured I'd go in," Luke finally says. "You know, since we're not supposed to be doing much of anything except having our normal, comfortable lives."

"Luke—"

"Listen, just forget what I said. I don't know, maybe I just needed to say it out loud."

"Luke—"

"I mean, you're right. The Bailey thing. It's getting to me. And Cole taking the flash drive . . . I just. Maybe I'm having a man tantrum."

"A mantrum?"

She can't remember a sound that soothed her as much as his laughter does now.

When he bends down and kisses her on the cheek, she feels like her heart's beating at a healthy, steady pace for the first time in weeks.

"Check in," she says.

"I will."

He's almost to the sliding back door when she says, "And be careful."

"Do I need to be?" he asks. "Cole's got eyes all over town."

Luke waves both hands in the air as if a swarm of helicopters were circling above. Then he turns and drops his pants enough to flash his bare ass to the yard. Charlotte's still laughing and trying to catch her breath when he slides the door shut behind him.

"No," Marty says for the third time.

"What do you mean, *no?*" Charley asks.

It's dark out, but they haven't left the backyard. Charley assumes it's the only part of the house that might be safe from digital eavesdroppers, even if it's not the most pleasant spot at night. There's always the twinkling view. But the new security lights on either side of the kitchen's sliding glass door give off a harsh glare that ends just a few feet from the Adirondack chairs. She can barely make out Marty's face, but if she glances over her shoulder, she'll be blinded.

Just inside the half-open sliding door, her cell phone sits on the nearest counter. She'll hear it if it rings, but hopefully it's far enough away that Cole can't use it to eavesdrop on their conversation.

Whatever, she thinks. *For all we know, they probably put mics in the oak tree while we were sleeping.*

"That's the worst damn idea I've ever heard," Marty says.

"It's not an idea. It's just a feeling, and he needed to talk about it."

"News flash. Nine times out of ten when a man says he's talking about his feelings he's just talking about an idea for how not to have any. And this is a really, really bad idea, Charley."

"How do you know? You weren't in Seattle. Maybe he could help."

"Cole doesn't need Luke's help. Cole doesn't need anyone's help. He's one of the richest men on the planet."

"He needs *my* help."

"That's different. You're special."

"*Luke's* special. He's whip smart, supereducated, and speaks a bunch of different languages."

"You going after Russian serial killers now?"

"That's not the point."

"Charley, you're not hearing what Luke's really saying."

"Fine. What's he really saying?"

"I'm too hotheaded for basic police work, but you should drop me in the middle of an operation so complicated and crazy there isn't even a name for it. And while you're at it, you should expect me to keep my cool while my girlfriend's placed in mortal peril, even though Lacey Shannon's bruises made me lose my mind."

He lets this sit.

It does.

Hard.

"I mean, come on," Marty continues, "that's like the busboy saying he should be promoted to manager because he's so good at dropping dishes."

"That's a little harsh, Marty."

"Maybe, but it's also clear. Which Luke is not right now. Look, he's hurting because he can't accept who his brother really is. I get that, but this is not the solution."

"And how's that supposed to work, accepting Bailey for who he is?"

"Cut him loose. I mean, for Christ's sake, Bailey's why Luke's life was so messed up when you got here. If my little brother's crimes kept me from having a shot at the career of my dreams, I wouldn't be wandering around worrying about my family obligations. Let Bailey be Bailey, is what I say. And that means let Bailey go."

"How's he going to let him go when he's working for my boss?" Charley asks.

"Well, I have a suggestion. Luke shouldn't go to work for the same boss."

She can't argue with him there.

"I don't know," she says. "I think Bailey's only part of it."

"Yeah. I agree. The other part is that Luke's acting just like one of those tools who whines and feels threatened because his wife makes more money than him. And you'd be able to see that if he wasn't lighting up your Christmas tree in the bedroom."

"OK, now you're just being crude."

Her cell phone makes a text chime on the counter. Marty doesn't seem to hear it.

"I'm serious, Charley. Don't let him manipulate you like this."

She gets to her feet and heads to the open door. It's probably Luke, texting her to check in.

"I'm not being manipulated because I'm letting my boyfriend tell me how he feels."

"Fine. But you already let him tell you once. You had the talk and that's great. But the next time he brings it up, that means he's trying to convince you. So distract him or change the subject, or I'll be over here to read him the riot act."

"Oh, what? You're spying on us, too?"

"I'm serious, Charley!"

At the open sliding door, she spins. "Marty, I invited you over so we could relax, not so you could lecture me to death."

"You invited me over because you knew what a bad idea this was, and you needed someone to talk about it with."

"*We* are not talking. You are lecturing. Jesus! What if both of the men in my life chilled out for, like, I don't know, ten minutes? Would the world stop? Would birds fall out of the sky?"

"I'd probably grill some of 'em if they did," Marty says.

"In the BBQ sense, or the 'you don't know when to shut up' sense?"

"Both, maybe. If they were hiding something."

"Charming."

She steps inside the kitchen and picks up the phone. The latest text message reads:

Tell Marty to leave.

She doesn't recognize the number. Who the hell is this?

Who do u think?

Not in the mood for games.

Cole just bypassed me and sent something 2 digital services he wants them 2 review. They won't tell me what it is except it has something to do w/ Altamira.

Bailey. Of course it is.
She types, Don't you hear everything we do?

Not lately. I work in different areas. I've tried 2b respectful.

Of us? Or your new boss?

Both.

Should we be talking? Don't THEY hear everything?

Not right now. I bought us some privacy.

What does that mean?

I kicked yr monitoring system offline.

Won't they notice?

Nope. Looping some archive from last night.

How long will that work?

Not long enough for U2 keep asking questions like this. Or for Marty 2 hang out. Tell him 2 leave please.

Why?

Because we need privacy.

Why???

Why don't u trust me?

Trust you? You and Cole both lied to us, and now Luke knows and he's pissed.

Luke's always pissed. Tell him, he's pissed. Don't tell him, he's pissed. Someday Luke will have to admit no one asked him to run the world but I'm not counting days till then. Tell. Marty. To. Leave.

Point is, trust isn't your selling point right now, Little B.

We can think up dumb nicknames later. Now I have someone who wants to talk to you. If something's up in Altamira, he might be able to help.

"Who are you texting?" Marty asks from the yard.

"Luke." Her breath catches when she notes how easily she spoke this lie.

Who? she writes.

Tell Marty 2 leave x 1000

I have someone who wants to talk to you. The words bring goose-flesh to the back of her neck and a tight feeling to her throat.

One sec.

Marty's standing when she steps out into the yard.

"Everything OK?" he asks.

"How about a break?"

"A break? Girl, we're not dating."

"*Weird!* That's not what I meant. I just need some time to clear my head. You know, without a man having feelings about how another man doesn't have feelings or . . . whatever this has been."

"When's Luke coming home?"

"Not too late. It's not the graveyard shift and it's Sunday anyway, so it's not going to be that busy."

"Are you kidding? They have wet T-shirt contests at the Gold Mine now on Sundays."

"Those are illegal?"

"They're festive. Fine. I'll leave. Just as long as you're not alone all night."

"None of us are, remember?" she says, then she remembers that Bailey just knocked the monitoring system off-line. Still, he's listening in now, so she's not technically alone.

She walks Marty to the sliding kitchen door; then, when he steps across the threshold, he stops and turns. "You know I'm just trying to help, right? With Luke, I mean. The last thing I want is him throwing himself in the middle of something that's already complicated and making it even more complicated."

A brush-off will only trigger another round, she's sure, so she tries the opposite approach: total candor. "And honestly, I don't want my boyfriend seeing what I have to do out there. So you and I are closer on this than you might think."

"He saw what you did with Pemberton."

"This is different."

"Because this guy died." When he sees the look on her face, he says, "Sorry. That was a little direct. I'll go. Just remember, I used to give your grandmother foot rubs before she took a shower, so there's no getting me out of your life. You owe me."

Marty pulls her in for a quick hug that flushes her with guilt given how easily she lied to him about Bailey's texts.

She waits until he completes a wide U-turn that puts him in the direction of the state road, then she closes the door, steps back inside, and looks to her phone.

He's gone, she types.

I saw.

Shock. I figured you'd have eyes everywhere by now.

Yes, and no. Mostly no. Like I said, trying to be respectful.

What changed?
When he bypassed me I got suspicious. Made me think it might involve Luke.

Would it comfort Luke to hear about Bailey's concern, as detached as it is? Or would he just point out what she's thinking now: Bailey's doing this because he's pissed Cole cut him out of whatever cyber-stalking he's doing of Jordy Clements.

Alright, she types, who wants to talk to me?

A second later, the phone rings. She doesn't recognize the number. It doesn't even look like a phone number.

"Hello?"

"Hello, Charley," the man she once called Dylan Thorpe says.

34

She knew this moment would come at some point, but she didn't expect it to feel quite like this. The last time the sound of someone's voice filled her with this many memories in a single instant, the voice was Marty's, and there were years of shared experiences between them waiting to be stirred up by a reunion.

With Dylan, with *Noah*, only three months had passed between their first meeting and the revelation of his betrayal. But in that short time she had experienced a type of intimacy different from any other in her life.

In a daze, she walks to the kitchen counter, powers on her earpiece, and waits for the Bluetooth to connect. Once it's linked, she puts it in her ear and says the most innocuous words she can think of. "Where are you?"

"He's keeping me prisoner at some ranch in Colorado. I think his father built the place. I guess you could say I'm on probation."

"I don't assume they allowed this phone call?"

They didn't, Bailey texts, so tell him not to take forever.

"I don't think so, no," Noah answers.

"How's he doing this?" Charley asks.

"Well, first he made contact through these little lenses they make me wear . . ."

"TruGlass," she says.

"Excuse me?"

"They're called TruGlass."

"Right. Then he started looping the footage so I could write him little notes. And now, this. I'm not exactly sure how he's done it, but I assume he's using whatever monitoring system they have here. It's the first time I've had a conversation with an alarm clock, so it's probably not just an alarm clock. They must use it to watch me in some way. Which is silly, because I'm not exactly getting any visitors."

Boo fucking hoo, she thinks.

"He's a very resourceful guy, your new boyfriend's brother."

Bailey texts. Tick tock.

"He says we don't have much time," Charley says.

"OK, then. Get in your car and drive."

"What?"

"You're in Altamira, right?"

"I am."

"Good. Get on the 101 and head north. Can you do that?"

"I can, but why would I?"

"Bailey thinks there's some sort of security threat there, and Cole's not being as honest with everyone as he needs to be. Am I wrong?"

"In a manner of speaking."

"I'm wrong in a manner of speaking or I'm wrong about the threat?"

"Something's up. We're not sure what. We have a theory. It's not good."

"OK, then. I have something that might help."

"What?"

"Drive and you'll find out."

"Yeah, I don't think so."

"You don't want help?"

"Maybe not from you," she says. "Your definition of *help* frightens me."

"Seriously?"

"Yes, *seriously*."

"Charley, I'm not exactly twirling my mustache at an island compound while I think of ways to make your life difficult. I've been a prisoner here for almost half a year. After you left me at the farm, Cole's men came bursting out of the woods and put me in restraints. Then they injected me with something that could probably kill me the minute I don't do what they want."

"Well, you don't have long to live, then, because you never do what anybody wants."

"Really? Our mutual friend says you had a successful operation in the Pacific Northwest last week. Perhaps you used some over-the-counter Zypraxon you grabbed at CVS?"

You two have been real chatty, Charley texts Bailey.

The response comes back instantly. He's super smart. You should really let him help.

She shouldn't be surprised that a man with half a conscience would be impressed by a man with none.

"Charley, can I just ask a question here?" her former fake psychiatrist asks.

"What's stopping you?"

"Why, when everything seems to be going so well—for everyone except me, that is—why am I still being treated as if the worst-case scenario came to pass?"

"Which worst-case scenario? The one where I might have torn myself to pieces on the drug you said was for anxiety? Or the one where the drug didn't work and Jason Briffel raped me in my own house?"

"I never would have let Jason harm you."

"Sure you would've. If that's what it took to make your drug work. It's a very, very bad idea for you to ever say Jason Briffel's name to me again. Got it, *Noah*?"

The silence on the other end might be the closest he ever comes to admitting fault.

It's not enough.

It never will be.

"I see you've been brought in on the new directive regarding my name," he finally says.

"I don't actually like it, to be frank."

"Then why not call me Dylan?"

"Because that's the name you used to earn my trust, and you're never getting that back."

"Fair enough. I've always wanted to be a Michael, if that works. Or maybe an Edward?"

"How about Dickhead?"

He laughs. It sounds genuine. Then she remembers nothing about him can be taken at face value.

"I like you, Charley. I know you might not believe that, but I really do."

"I wish I could say the feeling is mutual," she says.

"No, it isn't, but that's OK. We can still accomplish great things together. Get in the car, Charley. Let's go for a drive."

"Tell me where we're going."

"First the 101 North. Once you're there, I'll give you the next set of directions."

"You're trying to keep me on the phone with you."

"I am. I've really been looking forward to catching up."

Tick tock, Bailey texts.

She texts back. You initiated this damn call without my consent. If you're not happy with the timeline we're under, you fix it, Little B.

Then, her jaw clenched so tightly she's afraid the bone's going to snap, she grabs her car keys off the console table.

The next text from Bailey reads, I'm cool with the nickname so long as it's LI'L B.

"Bite me," she mumbles.
"What?" the man in her ear asks.
"Nothing," she whispers.

Keep yr headlights off until ur a few blocks away. I just knocked yr car tracker offline and yr tail's so far away they prolly don't have eyes on you.

She obeys, wondering if there's ever going to be a moment in the near future when she's not being bossed around by a bunch of men with personality disorders.

35

"What happened to no babysitting?" Donald Clements suddenly asks.

For the past few minutes, Cole's been describing Lacey Shannon's visit to the sheriff's station, while Donald, in his dining room at his home in North Carolina, stares vacantly at his laptop computer. He's been resting one elbow on the table next to him. This in turn allows him to rest his stout chin on his bear paw of a fist. Every few minutes the video connection gets a little fuzzy, so it's not as easy to read his expression as Cole hoped. The man could either be bored or quietly intrigued; there's no telling. One thing's for sure: he didn't think this call merited anything more formal than a plain white T-shirt.

Cole was hoping they'd speed through this quickly. Like businessmen. Even if the cultural gap between them is wide.

Cole is West Coast Ivy League–educated and an unapologetic bone smoker. Donald Clements hails from a family of coal miners, loves a version of Jesus Cole can't quite get with, and was the only member of his family who became fascinated with how the long tunnels his father, uncles, and cousins shuffled down to work each day were actually built. Cole keeps himself cleanly shaven, sometimes exfoliating twice a day; Donald's silver mustache looks like a single solid metal plate across his long upper lip.

Still, money makes strange bedfellows. Money and the desire to build things. Quickly.

"Babysitting?" Cole asks.

"Yeah. This feels like babysitting."

"I don't remember a discussion of babysitting. Why don't you refresh my memory?"

"You and I, I thought we agreed, we weren't going to ask each other a lot of questions about how to make this work."

"Questions like what?" Cole asks.

"Like why you needed a tunnel of this size in the middle of nowhere."

"*Nowhere?* My resort isn't nowhere. Haven't you seen the renderings? It's going to be wonderful!"

"You could have just widened the mountain road."

"Mountain roads make me carsick."

"It raises questions, is all. Questions I'm not asking."

"Because you know I can pay my bills."

"You're not the only one who pays my bills. The state of California chips in here and there, and I'm sure the deals you made to put that in place are . . . complicated. Point is, the thing's like a bridge to nowhere, and it's not exactly going to make my company front page news, but I've put everything I have on it. For you."

"I wasn't aware you wanted your company to be front page news. You keep a pretty low profile in general."

"I do my work, and I do what it takes to keep doing my work."

Donald's bushy eyebrows form a single white line as he frowns. He leans forward. Cole's not sure if he's doing it to flex his thick bicep or if he just wants Cole to get a better look at the expressionistic painting of a bull rider hanging on the wall behind him.

The motel room has no desk, so Cole's sitting on the foot of the bed, Scott Durham just out of view. Fred Packard's outside guarding the motel room door. They've already made sure the room next to them is empty.

Donald says, "You wanted speed. Clearly, you were under some kind of pressure. Do it fast, and you can do it in a way that's personally profitable. Those were your exact words."

"Not exactly, but close."

"Either way, I took that to mean no babysitting. Now you're butting in to my son's private life. What's that about?"

There's no arguing with the guy, because he's right.

If the gossip about him is true, Cole figures Donald Clements would probably just build some secret side tunnels between Altamira's valley and the Pacific, mainly for the transportation of goods he didn't want to show up on anyone's account ledgers. If the goods ever turned out to involve human cargo, Cole made a promise to himself he'd put a stop to it. But Clements doesn't have a rep as a human trafficker. Just a guy who's richer than someone in his profession should be and has deep misgivings about things like tax filings.

"With respect, your son's private life stopped being private when his girlfriend walked into the local police station and made a claim," Cole says.

"A false claim," he says.

"Do we know that for sure?"

"You're accusing my son of beating up his girlfriend?"

"Did you know about any of this before I called? Maybe you should ask him."

"Parenting advice. OK. That's interesting."

"Try business partner, pointing out a potential exposure."

"My son doesn't hit women. I didn't raise him that way."

"If he didn't, he made her angry enough to lie. To the police."

"You don't have kids, right? You didn't, like, adopt any or anything." The word *adopt* comes out of Donald like something between a hiccup and a low belch.

"I have things that are important to me."

"*Things.* OK. Like what?"

He sees Charley, Marty, and Luke glaring at him as he walked away from them earlier that day. The memory pokes a strange tangle of feelings inside him. Frustration, anger, and a tinge of self-loathing;

if the last one isn't how a parent feels when they let down their kids, it's got to be damn close.

"I want you to move him," Cole says.

"I'm sorry, what?"

"I want you to move Jordy off the project."

Emotion enters Donald's expression for the first time, clear enough that no wavery video transmission can blur it out of evidence. Now he looks dazed and anxious, like someone wondering if they left the stove on at home just as their plane reaches cruising altitude. "I don't have any other projects. Anywhere. I turned down two so I could do your tunnel in record time."

"Maybe Jordy can help you take on another one. Somewhere else."

"What the hell is this? You want me to punish my son for having bad taste in women?"

"No, I want you to punish your son for bringing unwanted attention to a project neither one of us wants going under a microscope."

"Whose microscope, the Altamira Sheriff's Department? What, do they have three people working for them? Come on. She walked out! She didn't even bring charges, probably because she sobered up and realized she was full of it. The only one making a stink about this is *you*."

"She's *missing*, Donald. She's been missing for two days."

"She left. She left like she always leaves because she's a drug addict. And it's not like her family's going to come looking for her; they hate her damn guts."

You've certainly done your homework on Lacey Shannon, Cole thinks. *Or you've just listened to your son complain about her a lot.*

"That's not how it looks," Cole says.

"To who?"

"To anyone who has the presence of mind to ask why a young woman suddenly disappeared a few hours after walking into a sheriff's station and claiming your son was responsible for the bruises all over her face. Right now, that person is me. What happens if the next one works for the *LA Times*?"

"What's done is done. Taking Jordy off the project isn't going to change anything. It'll just look more suspicious if somebody does come sniffing around. And besides, given the nature of our agreement, I'd hope you'd protect him rather than hanging him out to dry at the first sign of trouble."

"My arrangement is with you, not your son. He's been strutting all over Altamira like he owns the place. Everyone in town knows who he is, and if he can't keep his nose clean, he needs to go somewhere where he can."

"I'm not doing it."

"Why don't we table this for now and tomorrow we can check in and—"

"I said, I'm not doing it. My son is a patriot who served this country in a never-ending clusterfuck of a war most people have forgotten about. I'm not going to have his integrity questioned by some little . . ." Donald catches himself.

"Some little what?" Cole asks.

"Let's just say we can do business together, but we're not going to share a beer anytime soon."

"Good. I don't drink after other people. It's a good way to get sick."

"Yeah, you'd know about that, wouldn't you?"

Cole's used to his fair share of vaguely homophobic ribbing in business, but this is something else, and there's no amusement in Donald's expression. Maybe if Cole hadn't seen all those screen captures on Jordy's computer, this moment would seem like nothing. But it doesn't. And suddenly he feels as if he's breathing through a straw.

Donald says, "I meant, because you make medicines and all."

"Yeah, sure you did."

"Look, before either one of us crosses the Rubicon here, let me just lay it out for you, real simple. You make me pull my son off that project, I pull all my men off that project. And if I do that, I start talking to folks about how weird it is doing business with Graydon Pharmaceuticals. How's your board going to feel about that?

"I've done my homework on you, Mr. Graydon. Your track record as a CEO? Spotty at best. Your company hasn't made headlines with a new drug since your father died. So I don't know what in Sam hell this resort is for, but it's important to you for some reason; otherwise you wouldn't have put your ass on the line for it. So let's just work together, all right? And we'll start by you never saying my son's name to me again with anything less than the total respect he deserves from someone like you. Got it?"

Before Cole can answer, Donald reaches for his computer. A second later, Cole's laptop goes dark.

For a while, he just sits there.

Finally, Scott Durham says, "You OK?"

"I'll live," Cole answers.

He closes his computer. It's silly, but the gesture makes him feel like he's enclosing Donald's infuriating parting words inside a titanium box.

"So," he finally says, looking right into the eyes of his new security director, "what's your take on all that, Mr. Durham?"

"I think Bluebird and her crew might be onto something."

36

"Do you have a tail?"

She's been driving north on the 101 for about fifteen minutes, but it doesn't feel like anyone's following her. A few times she's slowed down and let most of the traffic pass. The only holdout's been a lumbering Mack truck. It's still far back in her rearview and looks like it might be towing some kind of livestock.

When Cole offered to buy her a new car, she asked for something that could take almost as much punishment as she can when she's triggered but wouldn't stick out too much in pickup truck–filled Altamira. A day later, he had a brand-new Volvo V60 crossover wagon delivered to her house. It's the color of weak tea, with tinted windows and black leather interior that don't exactly scream *I'm just a hometown girl!* But it's safe, and it drives like a dream.

"How about you let me handle the road?" she says.

For a while she drives in silence, so much of it she starts to wonder if the call dropped.

"You still there?" she asks.

"I am. Our conversation didn't seem productive, so I decided to drop out."

"Well, smell you, Nancy Drew."

"Excuse me?" Noah sounds genuinely puzzled.

"I'm just always amazed by your ability to sound so completely superior no matter how insane you're being."

"I *am* superior. To most people anyway. I'm incredibly smart, and I've made an amazing drug. The majority of people will spend tonight watching some sort of vacuous TV show and wondering if that person they hate at work is going to hurt their feelings again."

"And you'll spend it under armed guard because of your crap judgment calls."

"Oh, please. The tendency of this world to judge geniuses by the standards applied to middle management is going to produce a generation of dullards who think getting out of bed in the morning is an achievement."

"For some people, it is. The ones who've had their lives screwed up by people like you. You used to pretend to care about people who'd been hurt, back when you were masquerading as a psychiatrist."

"I care about helping people. In real, meaningful ways. Not just chatting them up about their perceived issues so that these so-called problems can loom ever larger in their self-obsessed minds. You needed some chitchat, so I gave it to you. It was the only way to get you to a place where you were ready for what I had to offer. And when it was all over, your life was ten times better, thanks to me. Admit that, and it will only continue to improve."

"You know what I think your problem is, Noah Turlington, a.k.a. Dylan Thorpe?"

"Oh, I can't wait."

"You can't see where your life ends and other people's lives begin."

"Good, because if I did, I wouldn't give a damn about helping anyone. I'd just reap the rewards of my own genius. Alone."

"What would that look like exactly?"

"Crime, probably. Lots of it. The profitable kind. I certainly wouldn't allow myself to be held prisoner in this pretend, rustic . . . Christ, I don't even know what this place is. I think it was Cole's father's idea of a hunting lodge, but there're no weapons or trophies in it. Enough about me. How's the lovemaking with your former bully?"

"Maybe you could give me some sense of how long this drive's gonna take."

"Why, so you can come up with ways of avoiding my questions?"

"Is it, like, Salinas long, or San Francisco long?"

"Why don't you just say it?" he asks. "All of it. Say it now, Charley."

"All of what?"

"Whatever you need to say. About me. About all the terrible things I've supposedly done."

"I thought you hated talking."

"No, I hate self-indulgent wound licking."

"I've been honest with you right along. I still believe what I said at the farm."

"We said a lot of things at the farm."

"I think you picked me because you hated me. You thought I profited off the movies and the book and the murders."

"Why would I need to hate you to pick you for this?"

"Because there was a chance I might tear myself apart. Literally."

"No, there wasn't." He says it so casually it's possible he's just being dismissive of the possibility. "I knew you'd do just fine."

He sounds strangely confident, but when has he ever not?

A text from Bailey lights up her phone's screen. FYI, yr security in Amira is a JOKE.

"What?" Noah asks.

"It's Bailey. He says our security in Altamira is a joke."

"Well, for the time being that's a good thing. Because I don't want anyone to see where you're going."

When Julia Crispin's name flashes on his cell phone, Cole tries to suppress a groan. He fails.

Fred Packard's driving them to his living quarters and control center, which he's described to Cole as a tiny tract house they're renting for about the amount of money Cole spends per hour on fuel for his helicopter. Hardly the local command center Cole told Ed to establish.

As soon as he answers, Julia barks, "Who hacked my technology?"

"Excuse me?"

"Someone hacked Turlington's TruGlass earlier today while you were with him."

"And did what?"

"We're still sorting that out. They sent him a text message through the device while he was meeting with you; then as soon as you left they started looping footage to throw us off the scent. Your people missed the first contact, and then my people found the hack. Now your guys are telling me they've ID'd inconsistencies that prove parts of the past few hours were looped."

Cole remembers the sudden splitting headache Noah seemed to undergo right as he was leaving. Is that what Noah was reacting to? An unexpected text message inside his eye?

"Continuously?" he asks.

"Intermittently, it looks like."

"So you're telling me my coverage of Noah has gaps in it?"

"I'm telling you someone on your end hacked my tech! Worry about your ex-boyfriend later."

"*Who* hacked your tech?" He's thinking of their old business partners, Stephen and Philip, and the suspicious one-month delay before they can meet.

"We don't know! Your digital services team just told me about some independent contractor none of them have met, and they don't even know what he does or where he's based. Or if it's a he. Is this *person* behind this?"

To Scott, Cole says, "Contact the ranch right now and make sure they've secured Noah Turlington. I want human eyes on him at all times until further notice. His TruGlass has been compromised."

Scott pulls out his cell phone and starts dialing.

In Cole's ear, Julia says, "We're Fort Knox around here, Cole! My only exposure here are the feeds I run to your team."

"I'm handling this, Julia."

"You better because if I—"

He hangs up on her. "I want Noah in a closet with at least three guns in his face until we figure out what the hell's going on. And if he hasn't already figured out his blood trackers are weaponized, let him know. In no uncertain terms."

When the exit for 198 East appears, Charley turns hard to the right.

In another few seconds, she's speeding west, up a dark road that travels through rolling hills dotted with the occasional oak tree. It's beautiful, open country—by day. At night, it's dark and desolate. If she keeps going, she'll have to wind her way through the deep folds of the scrubby mountains that lie between here and the Great Central Valley, and she'll probably lose cell service while she's doing it.

"What am I looking for?" she asks.

"After three miles, there's a distance to Coalinga sign. About a minute later, if you're going around fifty miles per hour, you'll come to a drainage ditch that runs under the road. It's a short little pass, not a major bridge or anything. As soon as you cross it, pull to the shoulder and park."

A few minutes later it all appears exactly as he said it would.

When she kills the engine, the sudden silence feels like a weight that pushes in on all sides of her. In another second, the headlights wink out. Her eyes begin adjusting to the darkness. The parcels on either side of the twisting two-lane blacktop are massive; their fences enclose grassy hills and the occasional lone farmhouse and barn.

"Parked," she says.

"Do you have a flashlight?"

"I do. Is there anything else I'm going to need? Or will that be a surprise, too?"

"A flashlight and some short-term memory will do fine."

She pops the trunk. A pickup blows past her so fast, she realizes the driver probably didn't even see her parked on the shoulder. From the earthquake emergency kit Luke put together for her, she pulls out a halogen-bulbed flashlight. It's slender as an ink pen, but it shines something fierce.

"Ready," she says.

"Walk back to the drainage ditch and then into the drain pipe where it runs under the road."

"Into it?"

"Yes. It's winter, so you won't need to worry about snakes."

"I'm not afraid of snakes. I'm afraid of you."

"Still?"

The ditch isn't terribly deep, certainly not as deep as the arroyo where she used to do target practice behind her place in Arizona. She descends the grassy bank by occasionally reaching out and gripping the side of it that's level with her shoulder. With her other hand, she angles the flashlight so that it floods the bottom of the ditch with light. Maybe her former psychiatrist got the details confused, or maybe he's forgotten. What passes under the road isn't a ditch, really; it's a culvert. And at this hour, it looks like the great yawning mouth of a subterranean beast.

Fear dances up her spine, sends chills along the tops of her shoulders.

Being alone in the dark like this is not something she's done since she experienced Zypraxon's power, and the return of what feels like an old, childish fear first annoys, then paralyzes her.

"Charley?"

"I'm going. I'm going."

When she steps up and into the culvert's mouth, she knocks the flashlight against the rim by accident. A wavery metallic gong echoes through the culvert's run.

"Reach up to about the height of your shoulder and run your hand along the metal until you feel a handle."

She obeys, but the choice of where to angle the flashlight bothers her. She decides to run her hand along the metal in darkness and angle the flashlight's beam at the opposite end of the tunnel, in case some night predator decides to peer inside and see what all the fuss is about. But the darkness beyond the opening is so total, the flashlight makes the opposite end of the culvert look like a portal into a realm of infinite nightmares. So she turns the beam to the curved metal wall next to her.

Then she feels it.

"Pull," he says.

She does. "It's not doing anything."

"Pull harder. It's been months."

Months, she thinks. *So whatever it is, he could have put this in place himself.*

She'll have to either put the flashlight down or stick it in between her teeth. She goes with the latter. It works. With both hands, she begins yanking on the metal handle. It whines and bucks, fighting her for every tug. If she tries any harder, she might end up swallowing the flashlight and choking on it. Instead, she curses as she bites down on it, which only causes Noah Turlington to say her name again and again.

Then, suddenly, she's flat on her ass in the thin stream of water trickling through the culvert's bottom. Whatever fell to the culvert's floor made an impact that sends vibrations rattling through its length. They tickle her thighs and butt, so startling she almost misses the second loud gong that follows the first—the sound of something big and heavy falling free of the new opening overhead.

It's a lockbox, and it landed on one side in between her splayed legs.

"Charley!"

The flashlight stayed between her teeth, probably because she bit down harder on it during the shock of the metal door coming free. She pulls it from her mouth. "I'm OK."

"Do you see it?"

"Yes. What's the combination?"

"Seven, five, eight, one."

The lockbox is too heavy and big for her to hold in one hand. She rocks up onto her knees, even though it means keeping them in the water, and enters the combination.

The lock clicks open, and she pulls the lid up, and she's shining the flashlight down on a plastic bag of what must be a dozen orange pills just like the one Dylan Thorpe gave her in his office at the Saguaro Wellness Center five months before.

"That should help with your security issue," he says.

37

"How long have these been here?" Charley asks.

"That's all?" he asks. "Not even a thank-you?"

"How long?"

"Like I said back then, I figured if we got separated after Arizona, you'd either run to your lawyer in San Francisco or back to Altamira. It's not quite halfway, but given you picked Altamira, I'd say I chose a good spot."

"These have been here that long? You planted them before you sent Jason to my house?"

"Yes, as a backup."

"A backup," she whispers.

She's surprised by how much this lockbox frightens her.

Yes, she was angry when Cole refused her request for pills today. But when they had first started working together and he demanded she give up the rest of her stash, she had felt relief. Immense relief. A freedom from the responsibility they presented. The responsibility of keeping them secret and deciding how, if ever, they should be put to use. Now she's responsible not just for the three she requested, but for nine more Cole doesn't know about.

"I'm so disappointed," the voice in her ear says.

"This is incredibly dangerous, leaving these here like this."

"For whoever gets in your way, maybe."

"This isn't about me. Someone could have found these."

"Oh, you're right! The local chapter of the Isolated Ditch Exploration Society just had a huge membership drive. What was I thinking? Honestly, Charlotte! Can you not manage to thank me for anything?"

"Now I'm supposed to find a place to hide these?"

"My hiding place is perfect, thank you. Just take what you need and leave the rest for later." Her hands are shaking as she runs her fingers over the plastic bag. It's like the pills inside are giving off invisible vibrations. She feels less like an employee—a test subject, a *host!*—who placed herself, perhaps foolishly, but entirely, in Graydon's care, and more like that frightened woman who had to flee Arizona months before, without a plan, without a map.

"I'm assuming Cole doesn't give you an unlimited supply to do with as you please." He takes her silence as an affirmative response. "OK. Well, there you go. You don't have to use them, of course, but now you have the choice. And someday soon, once you get past your anger, you'll see that's what I'm all about."

"Secrets and hiding places?"

"Choices."

Her phone vibrates in her pocket; she pulls it out, sees a text from Bailey. Busted. Wrap it up. They're onto him.

"Shit," Noah whispers in her ear. "Later, Charley."

What she hears next sounds like a flurry of movement, followed by a door being thrown open so hard it bangs into the wall behind it. Noah Turlington shouts a word or two of what sounds like an overly cheerful greeting to whoever's just burst into his room, then the connection goes dead.

Told u we didn't have much time, Bailey texts. Prolly mins til they figure you're systems offline too. U should head back.

She wants to text him back, but she can't remove her hand from the bag of pills. *Choices,* she thinks.

"Choices," she whispers.

Charley?

Three is what she asked for, so three is what she'll take.

After the drama of the hiding place and the lockbox, the Ziploc bag inside seems surprisingly pedestrian. The pills within look just like the last ones he gave her. Lumpy and cakey, like they came from a meth lab and not an industrial one. That means they'll break easily. She empties nine of them into the lockbox's padded interior, then twists the top of the Ziploc bag into a loose knot above the remaining three so they'll be protected.

Give me a sec, she texts back.

In another few minutes, she has the lockbox closed and back inside its hiding place.

Once she's up the grassy bank and back on the shoulder of the road, she texts, Did you know this is what he was going to do?

Yes, comes the response.

Are you next?

?

They just busted in on him. Are they coming for you next?

They can't.

Why not?

That's not how it works.

She's not about to keep typing in furious responses to his evasiveness in the darkness on the side of the road.

We need to talk. Now.

We r talking. This is how I talk.

Call me. Now.

Ugh.

Now Bailey.

As she settles into the driver's seat, the phone rings. It's an unknown caller, of course. She places the Ziploc bag in the empty cup holder.

"This isn't really necessary," Bailey says when she answers.

She can count on one hand the number of times she'd heard the guy speak out loud when she was a teenager and Bailey was barely high school age. He was a lot younger than her, for one, but he was also a quiet introvert, rarely seen around town; the polar opposite of his athletic, loudmouth older brother. Still, she's surprised by the softness of his voice. It lacks the spark of his text messages.

She starts the car, pulls a U-turn, and heads back in the direction of the 101.

"Did you know this is what he was going to do?" she asks.

"Yes."

"OK. Then you need to also know he can't always be trusted."

"You think the pills are fake?" Bailey asks.

"That's not what I meant," she says. "You just don't know the whole story with him."

"I'm learning. I did a bunch of reading while you guys were chatting."

"Where are you?"

"If I try to explain the Graydon network to you, you'll just get—"

"No, I mean physically, Bailey. Where in the world are you?"

"I don't want you to know."

"And you don't want Luke to know, either, is that it? I'm not keeping this call a secret from him, so please. Give me something I can tell him that will make him hurt a little less."

"I'm safe. He doesn't have to worry about me. He's *never* had to worry about me. I don't know why he does anyway."

"Because you're all he has."

"Not anymore. He's got you. And he shouldn't waste his time with you worrying about me. That's dumb."

She shouldn't be surprised Bailey speaks with the sullen certainty of a seven-year-old who's never had a responsibility. But she is.

"Just give me something I can share with him that will make him feel like you're OK."

After a long silence, Bailey finally says, "Tell him Cole doesn't even know where I am."

"What? How are you working for him, then? Have you guys even met?"

"IRL? No. I don't do anything IRL."

"What about all this raw computing power he supposedly gave you?"

"Ever heard of UPS?"

"I thought he agreed to clear your record."

"So he says. Do you believe everything Cole says? You shouldn't. 'Cause if he told you you had good security, he's lying. You've got surveillance, but that's it. And right now, he doesn't even have that because I threw it all off-line."

"That thing . . . Noah said. About being injected with something that can kill him?"

"Yeah, they've got some kind of tracking system on him. *In* him, it looks like."

"They injected me with all sorts of things during lab testing. Do I have one, too?"

"Yes."

"And it could kill me at a second's notice?"

"I can't tell that from here," he says, as if he's trying to spot a storm front, not discussing whether there's a device inside her that could end her life in an instant.

"What can you tell?"

"With you, it's not just a tracker. It's giving them biometric data. Like blood oxygen levels, cell counts. It's more like a medical monitoring system, and it's putting out twice the information his is. With him, they're just trying to tell where he is and if he's alive."

"OK, so is it tracking me right now?" she asks. "Or did you knock it off-line, too?"

"I didn't knock it off-line 'cause I figured that would trigger some kind of alert. Like they'd think you died or something."

"All right. So they can track me right now?"

"Not really. I played with it a little."

"What does that mean, Bailey?"

"It means, you're not really where you are."

"Where am I?" she asks.

"Graceland?" Cole screams. "How the fuck did she get to Memphis?"

"Also, isn't Graceland closed right now?" Fred asks.

"That's not the point, Fred," Scott barks.

The condition of Fred's house already has Cole on the brink of rage. There's a relatively secure fence, but most of the place is devoted to Fred's living quarters. The room allocated to Charlotte and Luke's surveillance is one tiny closet that can barely fit a chair. Inside, several flat-screen computer monitors broadcast feeds from the house's kitchen and living room. There's no live audio on either feed, and a separate computer's set up to receive an alert if a certain buzzword's spoken inside the house or on their cell phones, an alert that then allows Fred to access the archive of recorded conversations. There aren't even any exterior views on the driveway or backyard. And even though there's a rest area in the back of Fred's house for the microdrone crew, their feed, when they're dispatched, goes directly to their van.

He's going to destroy Ed Baker. He's going to destroy him, then drag his destroyed pieces through the streets whereupon he will urinate on them in front of his entire security team.

But for now he has to focus on Scott's words, even though the effort's a struggle. "There's no way she got to Tennessee since we saw her this afternoon. The closest airports are both three hours away, and then on top of that's the flight, which is, what, four hours?"

"And they've never played Elvis in that house once," Fred says.

"Shut up, Fred," Scott says.

"I'm just trying to lighten the mood."

"Someone's playing with her blood trackers," Cole says. "And they're doing it so we'll have a long, stupid, useless conversation about how to get from Altamira to Tennefuckingsee."

Someone being my independent contractor.

He refuses to beat himself up over this.

He'd had no choice but to hire Bailey, and given the amazing job Bailey did finding Richard Davies, Cole isn't ready to regret the decision yet. He never thought handling the kid would be easy, or entirely possible; he's too brilliant and too unattached. But the way Cole saw it, he didn't have a choice. No way in hell he could let a hacker with Bailey's incredible skills just hang out on the edges of Project Bluebird 2.0, servicing Charley and Luke's needs whenever he felt like it. Still, the terms of his deal were hardly favorable to Cole, and now he fears the reality of that is going to sink its teeth into his backside and take a nice, big bite.

"Playing with her blood trackers," Fred says, as if each word is so heavy it pulls on his bottom lip. "That can't be good. For her, I mean."

"They're not weaponized," Cole says.

"Still, they're in her blood, right? I don't want anybody *playing* with something in my blood."

"What's the ground team relayed about her house since there are no fucking cameras on the exterior?"

"The lights are all on, but her car's gone. When they noticed, they called in."

"How did they not see her pull out?" Cole asks.

Fred says, "Because the car tracker's also off-line, and the ground team was using that and the blood trackers so they could stay out of sight up the street."

"Well, apparently they weren't using both, because they didn't see her blood trackers suddenly went to Tennessee. Why's that?"

Scott looks him right in the eye. "They're not our best people. These are the guys who are supposed to hang out in restaurants and bars and eavesdrop and file a report if they hear any interesting gossip."

"Thank you, Ed Baker," Fred says quietly. "Wild guess is her cell phone surveillance has gone dark, too."

"Digital service just confirmed that's a yes," Scott says.

Fred says, "So we're being hacked? Is that what's going on here?"

"We're not being hacked," Cole says, "technically speaking."

Scott says, "I'm not sure I follow."

"The call is coming from inside the house, gentlemen," Cole says. "What? Nobody here likes horror movies?"

"My job's scary enough, thanks," Fred says.

At least he didn't say my boss, Cole thinks.

"Launch the microdrones," Cole says with a sigh.

"They're useless at night," Scott says.

"They're not useless. They just don't have night vision, which means they're harder to navigate, especially when there's tall buildings around. We're not in Seattle anymore. Follow light sources. Stay in the valley. Avoid the mountains. Sweep Altamira until we find her Volvo."

"What if she left town?" Fred asks.

"Then we'll catch up with her when she comes back. In the meantime, this amazing crack-shot ground team who didn't notice her leave, how many are there?"

"Four."

"They each have a vehicle?"

"Pretty basic, but yeah."

"Send one to the 101 off-ramp now. Put another one at the intersection of their street with the mountain road."

"What do you want them to do?" Scott asks.

"Notify us if she comes back, and never look me in the eye again."

"What if she's not coming back?" Fred asks.

"This isn't a jailbreak. She just went somewhere and she didn't want us to know. That's all."

"So *she's* the one who hacked us?" Fred asks.

Cole says, "Somebody get me a satellite phone. Now."

"How bad is it?" Charley asks.

The traffic heading south on the 101 is much lighter, probably because she's leaving the necklace of communities south of Salinas in her wake.

"So he *did* tell you there was good security?" Bailey asks.

"He said nobody was safer anywhere."

"That's ... not an accurate description. I've been scanning the personnel files of the people he's got in town. Only one has military experience; the rest are just lackeys who file written reports about the gossip at the Copper Pot that are putting me to sleep right now. They've got a microdrone crew that's in a mobile van, but I seriously doubt any of those nerds are skilled at hand-to-hand combat. And there's something called the Med Ranch—"

"I know that. I'm supposed to go straight there if I have a stomachache or my arm suddenly falls off."

"OK," Bailey says.

"So they're just watching us? They can't do anything if something bad happens?"

"It doesn't look like it, no. So, um, this security threat? The one he didn't want me to know about? How bad is it?"

"Oh, that old thing? Yeah, your brother just found a domestic terrorist network that's setting up shop in our backyard. That's all. Oh, also, the woman who gave us the flash drive proving all of it has been missing for two days."

"So like by backyard, do you mean, like, the backyard of your house, or are you referring to—"

"That's just not funny right now, Bailey."

"I'm not trying to be funny. OK. Well, I'm seeing emails from the local security director there that look like he's reassigning people. Fast. It's a lot of code words I don't understand, but it's also travel instructions and arrival times. But ... none of these guys are going to be there until tomorrow. They're coming from different parts of the world."

In her mind's eye, she sees Luke's house—*their* house—an island of light amid the dark sloping lawns, in a neighborhood with wide, grassy lots. A peaceful, quiet neighborhood on the lower flank of a mountain. Or a lonely one, depending on your point of view. Only now can she appreciate the extent to which her mind ran wild with Cole's comforting words—*safer than anyone anywhere*! She imagined cameras in the trees, snipers in the bushes, vans full of mercenaries always on the ready nearby. Scary if you're plotting an escape, comforting if your boyfriend's making trouble with possible terrorists. But apparently there's nothing of the kind anywhere in town, and now she feels as if they've all spent the last twenty-four hours, Luke included, acting with reckless confidence against a vicious menace in their own backyard.

Because, after all, if Jordy Clements is who they think he is, he won't see Luke as anything other than a small-town sheriff's deputy with a big mouth. And it's possible Jordy's already made one troublemaker disappear.

There's a half-empty bottle of water in one of the cup holders. Before she can stop to wonder if the lid's been closed tightly enough to keep out bacteria, she uncaps it. Without looking, she reaches into the Ziploc bag and pulls out a pill as if it were just an aspirin. It's on her tongue when she hears a strange chirping from Bailey's end of the line. It sounds like a ringing phone, but not quite.

"Uh-oh," Bailey says.

One swig of water, down the hatch.

Decision made.

No second thoughts.

She'd hoped the fear would evaporate, but it hasn't. Now she's full of the very real fear that comes with responsibility. If something goes bad in Altamira tonight, she'll have to be the one to stop it.

"Guess who this is," Bailey says.

"Cole?"

"Calling on our private line."

"What happens if you don't take it?"

"I don't know. Maybe he kicks me out of his system."

"Can he?"

"I could probably make my way back in. But I'd be at war with his digital services team, and that would take some time."

"Can you find out if he's actually doing anything to investigate Jordy Clements? Maybe he's found something bad, and that's why he's reassigning people."

"Who won't be there until tomorrow morning," Bailey says. "So Jordy's a terrorist maybe?"

"The ringleader, maybe."

"I better take this," he says.

"Sure."

She fights the urge to close her eyes, just so she can think. But then she might end up having to think about what to do now that she's driven off the road.

Either Cole flat-out lied about their security situation, or he was too lazy or distracted to know the facts. Both prospects are terrifying.

And in another few minutes, Bailey, the closest they have on the inside of a system that's failing to protect them, might get kicked out of the network.

To say nothing of the terrorists in their backyard.

Not bad for a Sunday night in a small town.

She dials Luke's cell.

Charley likes to leave all the lights on when they go out, so Luke's not surprised when he comes home to find they're all burning, even though her station wagon's gone. But when the burglar alarm only lets out a weak two-tone chime as he opens the front door, he stops in his tracks.

The lights are one thing; the burglar alarm's another. She likes that extra layer of security. So does he. And if she'd set it before she left, the thing would be squealing holy hell right now until he punched in the code.

He checks the panel, scans the log. Every time he spends more than a few seconds futzing with the system, he remembers how Bailey used it to first make contact with them months before. And Bailey's the last thing he wants to be thinking about right now.

Apparently Charley left a little over an hour ago, long after he went to the station.

So she just walked out the front door and didn't set the alarm?

He's getting ready to call her when his cell phone rings; it's her.

"Hey, where are you?" he asks.

"So lots of news to discuss. Are you at the station? I should come there."

In the kitchen, he undoes his gun belt, sets it on the counter. "No, I just got home. Hey, why didn't you set the alarm? I mean, not like it matters with Cole's people all over. Still, it's probably not a bad idea to have an extra layer of—"

"Luke, stop. They're not all over. That's just it. We need to talk. In person."

There's a cold breeze on the back of his neck. He turns. The window above the sink is halfway open. More than halfway open. He's moving to it when the darkness just beyond it lurches toward him. There's a sharp, high-pitched buzz, then a fiery bloom of pain erupts in the center of his chest. The shock of it sends him skittering backward, reaching for the edge of the counter nearby. His hand misses, and he hits the floor ass-first.

He's screaming Charley's name, but his voice sounds far away, and he sees his phone spinning away from him across the linoleum. Maybe it's shock. But it's not a bullet that struck him. It's something small, and it's somehow coating his throat and his arms with a sensation that combines hot and cold.

The words coming from him are hopelessly mangled. *Charldontcum DontcomeCharley . . . Chaurrrlleee.* Then it feels as if all his bones have been swiftly and effortlessly removed from his body. Having lost control of his limbs, his upper body hits the floor, vaguely aware the final impact should have hurt more than it did.

Poisoned, he realizes.

Everything around him goes dark.

At first, he thinks he's losing consciousness. But there's a shrill, insistent beeping in the darkness, the sound the burglar alarm makes when a power failure forces it to use its reserve battery.

Someone's cut power to the house.

Then there are other sounds: the front door opening, footsteps—heavy, but moving swiftly and determinedly. Inside, he's screaming, but whatever the dart was tipped with has paralyzed him. He tries to shout, hears only a snotty gurgle in one nostril.

There are shadows over him. Two, he thinks. One's so tall and broad, he wonders if he's imagining it. They lift him by his shoulders and limp ankles as if he weighs nothing. As if all of this is normal, routine. He can't feel the material that's suddenly being pulled up around him. Only when he sees it closing over him does he realize it's some sort of bag. The sound he hears next is so ordinary, in another circumstance, he might laugh. A zipper. He's being zipped inside of a bag the size of a human body. The size of *his* body.

Blinded, his limbs useless, he's hoisted up into the air. It should hurt, but it doesn't. His body's numb; his eyes feel hot and wet. There are tears coming from his eyes he can't blink away.

Then a siren starts to scream, and the men carrying him jump with surprise.

It's the burglar alarm.

Whoever these men are—Jordy's? Cole's?—they cut the power to the house, but someone managed to set off the alarm regardless. There's only one person he knows who might be able to do that.

Bailey, Luke thinks, and then darkness takes him.

When the top of the steering wheel cracks in her grip, Charlotte realizes she's been triggered.

She's been screaming Luke's name ever since he started crying out to her in that horrible garbled voice, and now, the sensation she hasn't felt since she jammed one foot into Richard Davies's bear trap is back, up and down her body. *Bone music.*

She hasn't broken the steering wheel entirely. She can still drive, thank God.

She widens her grip, sucks in the kind of deep breaths required to focus Zypraxon's power so she can perform ordinary actions.

Thread the needle, thread the needle.

Then she realizes her foot's pressed the gas pedal all the way to the floor. She's been doing 120 ever since hell broke out on the other end of the phone.

A flurry of texts from Bailey have lit up her phone's display. GO TO HOUSE NOW. ATTACK. SOMEONE'S TAKING LUKE.

The Pearson Road exit's within sight.

She accelerates.

38

She meant to open the car door like a normal person, but when it goes flying across the sidewalk and the man and the woman who were just running toward her Volvo start backing away in terror, she realizes she failed.

Both people on the sidewalk look vaguely familiar. She's seen them around town, trying to blend in while they casually study everyone and everything. The woman wears a baby doll dress and a blue-jean jacket; the man, acid-washed jeans and a baggy polo. So when they both pull matching Glocks on her at the same time, the effect is jarring, like two everyday humans revealing their lizard-like alien faces.

When she starts walking toward them, their eyes get wide. Their gun hands shake.

"Where is he?" she says.

In a trembling voice, the woman says, "Ms. Rowe, please, if you just calm down we can—"

Charlotte keeps walking toward them. "We're past that. Where's Luke?"

The man in the polo shirt's apparently looking for a promotion. He takes up a post in front of the half-open front gate, raises his gun so that it's aimed directly at her chest. "The rest of the team's on its way. We're handling it. You need to—"

"*Team?* There's no goddamn team. You're it, and someone got to Luke, didn't they?"

"Mr. Graydon will be here any minute and then—"

She closes her fist around the barrel of his gun. He doesn't have the courage to fire. It wouldn't matter if he did.

"Nobody's coming who has what I have." She crushes the gun barrel in one fist, then tugs the resulting misshapen mass from his hand and tosses it to the sidewalk.

"Move."

He obeys.

The house is dark. The alarm system's sounding out two different alerts: one that says it was recently triggered, another that says it's operating off reserve battery. Someone cut power to the house, and just this house. The neighbor's lights were on when she pulled up.

Unfamiliar male shouts come from the guest bedroom, the one where she sometimes sleeps when Luke's snoring keeps her awake. The memory of Luke's snores, of his sleeping, peaceful profile, are hot pokers prodding the flames of rage in her chest.

Brief flashes of light come from the same room—the erratic jerks of a flashlight.

It's two voices, she realizes. One's shouting questions; the other's chanting the same thing over and over again. The chant sounds like a Bible verse, and the guy giving it sounds remarkably peaceful and content. But his words run together, as if he doesn't really care if anyone hears aside from his crazy idea of a god.

Slowly, she reaches out and gently presses the door open. Like the guards out front, she vaguely recognizes both men from around town: the one down on his knees is from the Clements tunnel crew; the one holding a gun on him is a plainclothes spy like the two out front. Jordy's guy is a stout fireplug of a man, but right now his nose is bleeding and the flashlight the security guard's shining down on him from above gives his face a misshapen cast. He rocks back and forth on his knees.

"Where? *Where* were they going?" the man standing over him screams.

This desperate interrogation is the best these idiots can do. And they've dragged the guy back inside the house because their primary concern is what the neighbors might think.

When the terrified guard sees Charley standing in the doorway, he shines the flashlight in her direction.

"Ms. Rowe, you need to leave immediately." There's a breathless tremor in his voice. Like the folks outside, he's terrified and overwhelmed and not cut out for this. "Ms. Rowe, please, go wait outside. The rest of the team is coming."

"There is no rest of the team," she says.

"Ms. Rowe, please, when Mr. Graydon gets here, we'll regroup and figure out what—"

"Who is he?"

"He was the lookout. We caught him. The others . . . the others got away."

"Luke?"

He doesn't answer, doesn't even shake his head.

"Did they get away with Luke?"

He doesn't answer.

Charlotte punches her fist through the wall next to her. The sound's loud enough to stop their captive's prayer. His eyes open, and along with the security guard standing over him, he watches Charley gently remove her forearm and fist from the deep hole. She extends her hand in front of her, opens it, and releases chunks of drywall onto the floor. Then she twirls her fingers so they can see her hand's in great shape.

"Give me the flashlight," she says.

His hand shaking, the guard extends the flashlight, leaning forward onto one foot, as if he's afraid of her gravitational pull. She takes it from him gently, then shines it in their captive's face. His expression is a fixed mask.

"Get out of here," she tells the security guard.

Practically falling over his feet, he complies.

"Where is my boyfriend?" Charlotte asks.

The captive doesn't answer.

She gives the open door behind her a gentle kick with one heel; it slams shut with enough force to shake the walls. The man before her flinches, squints into the flashlight, but he still doesn't answer.

"You work for Jordy Clements?" she asks.

He doesn't answer, so she sinks down to the floor, onto her knees, flashlight angled at him.

"I asked you a question. Two questions, actually. Why aren't you answering me?"

She balls her free hand into a fist, slams one side of it against the floor. The center of the indentation buckles the wood, sends out a jellyfish of cracks. His jaw tenses and he shakes his head slightly, as if he's denying what his eyes are telling him.

Then he leaps to his feet, bolting past her.

Any attempt to touch him might accidentally snap his neck. So she moves to the spot he just left, grabs one corner of the bed's headboard, and sends the entire bed sliding across the room and into the bedroom door, instantly blocking his path.

When he realizes he's trapped, something inside the man snaps. His back hits the wall and he slides to the floor, pumping his hands in the air in front of him like a toddler having a tantrum. He's wheezing like the wind's been knocked out of him. If it has, it's terror that's done it.

Charlotte sinks down on the floor next to him. When he sees how close she is, he screws his eyes shut. "What are you? What are you? What the fuck *are* you?" he screams.

"Someone who needs you to tell the truth. What's your name?"

His sobs have kicked ropes of snot from his nose. He spits them from his lips before he can speak. "T-Tommy. My name's Tommy."

"Where did they take him, Tommy?"

"I don't know," he whines.

She punches through the wall next to his head. He lets out a choking, wheezing cry.

"I think that's a lie, Tommy. And if you tell me another lie, I'm going to break your legs. Slowly, all the way up the bones, every few inches."

Struggling to catch his breath, Tommy says, "They're gonna move him. If . . . if they don't hear from me, they're going to move him and I don't know where."

"Oh, OK," she says. "Well, it sounds like they need to hear from you, then. I mean, that makes perfect sense, doesn't it? They need to hear you tell them you're fine and you just ran in a different direction when the alarm went off. But you got away and you're on your way to them now and they should wait for you where they are. Right, Tommy? Doesn't that make sense?"

"Wh-what if they don't believe me?" he sobs.

"You're going to make them believe you, or they're going to listen to you scream. Where's your phone, Tommy?"

"It's in my po-pocket."

"Good. Get it out. And no sudden moves. I'm very jumpy."

He straightens as much as he can in his seated position and pries his cell phone from his pocket. Then he looks at her like a frightened child.

"Deep breaths, Tommy."

"What are you?" he whispers.

"I'm very angry you took my boyfriend away. But the good news is, that makes me easy to understand and easy to please. So do both. Make me happy, Tommy. Make me happy and this won't get any worse."

"You w-want me to t-tell them I'm OK and I'm coming to meet them."

"That's right. And find out where. If they're moving him, find out where they're moving him to. And if they're not moving him, make sure it's the same place they told you before. Got it?"

"Ye-yes."

"Good."

Tommy starts to dial.

It rings, and rings, and then finally goes to someone's automated voice mail greeting.

"There's no reception. They're up the mountain."

She reaches out and gently lays one hand on top of his head.

His eyes meet hers. His entire body shudders beneath her palm.

"Are you telling me the truth, Tommy?"

"I am," he sobs. "I am. I am. Please."

"Where are they?"

"There's se-seismic stations . . . set up just down the mountain. It's four miles up mountain on 293. It comes up on the left r-real fast. You gotta be careful. It's a service road. But they cut it themselves. It's still dirt and if you keep going . . . about twenty yards . . . you'll come to a storage shed. That's where they said they were taking him, b-but . . ."

"But what, Tommy?"

"Since I didn't come back, they might have moved."

"Where?"

"I don't know. But all our firepower's up there. And M-Milo. He likes to work in secret, but the shed . . . The shed is . . . The shed's where they had Lacey."

"When?"

"Before they shot her . . . But I think he worked on her some-where else."

Worked on her. These words alone have her monitoring every tick of the hand she's still resting atop his skull. His fragile, breakable skull.

Her mind races through the list of all the possible hideouts along 293's lonely, twisting passage to the sea. There's an old Buddhist temple up there somewhere that was volunteer maintained until it wasn't. It's a ruin now. Then there's a spread of ruined limekilns surrounded by redwoods. The ones she visited with Marty when she was in high school; it was a long, grueling hike without a clear trail.

And then there's the mountain. A mountain covered with long slopes of pines and redwoods where they could be doing god knows what to Luke far from anyone who could hear.

"Why did they take him, Tommy?" she asks.

"They want to find out what he knows."

"And then what?"

"Make sure he never tells anyone."

She was about to release the top of Tommy's skull, but this news keeps her hand in place.

"How are they going to do that?" she asks.

"I don't know. But you better get there before they do. Milo's . . . intense."

"Intense?"

"Sick. He's . . . sick. On the inside."

"You better hope I do, too, Tommy, because we're not the police."

She gets to her feet, backs away, and pulls the bed away from the door by one hand.

When she steps into the hallway, several flashlight beams hit her face at once. They outline the barrels of at least two guns she can see; one's real big.

"Looks like someone has a secret stash," Cole Graydon says.

"Back up," Charley says.

Cole says, "Why don't we take a breath and just—"

"*Back the fuck up!* Right now!"

Just then, the lights throughout the house flicker back on. There are hums and whirs, and even a few warning beeps, as power meets appliances in every room of the house. Now she can clearly see Cole and two of the security team members who brought him to the boat launch earlier today. They're standing just a few feet away from her. The younger of the two holds a formidable-looking shotgun aimed right at her chest, but his stance makes clear he's more interested in defending his boss than taking her down. The older balding guy's got his Glock out.

In the sudden glare, none of them looks as confident as Cole first sounded in the dark. As for the man himself, he's winded and glassy-eyed. It's the first time she's seen him truly frightened.

"They have Luke," she says, as if she's speaking to dumb children. "They have Luke because you either fucked up or lied to us. You told us we were safer here than anywhere, and now those sick fucks have Luke, and they killed Lacey Shannon a few hours ago."

Nobody says anything.

"Get out of my way," she says. "Get out of my way or I'll blow this whole thing apart."

"What are you going to do, Charley?"

"I'm going to get him back."

"What are you going to *do* to get him back?" Cole sounds gentle, conciliatory. She gets his meaning. He'd probably show her a picture of Richard Davies's corpse right now if he could. But he can't. So he better get the hell out of her way.

"Whatever it takes," she says.

Cole nods, reaches out to the shotgun held by the guy next to him, and encourages him to lower it with several quick taps on the barrel.

"No matter what happens, I'll clean up the mess," he says quietly. "It's the least I can do."

She takes a step. Shotgun Guy lowers his weapon. The older man with the Glock takes a few steps back, but he keeps his aim on her. His right shoulder looks like it's magnetized to Cole's left one. She takes another step, then another, then at the last second, she spins, bringing her face as close to Cole's as it's ever been. To his credit, he doesn't flinch or look away.

"The *very* least," she whispers.

Then she's out of the house. Outside, everything seems normal, except for the fact that the driver's side door is missing from her car. The two plainclothes security guards are both engaged in cheerful-sounding conversations with different neighbors, probably delivering some bullshit story about what all the fuss was about earlier.

She slides behind the wheel of her Volvo and peels off into the night.

39

Jordy's willing to die for this, he realizes. He's been crouching in the brush for a while when this realization sweeps over him with the quiet, bone-filling certainty of God's truth.

Before he started on the road to righteousness, he had nothing but disdain for the suicide bomber's rush toward martyrdom. He thought it vainglorious, lazy. Arrogant. Who was he to determine that God only had one job for him? Strap a bunch of explosives to your chest the first time out, and you were just letting yourself off the hook for a lifetime's worth of ministry. To be truly faithful, he was sure, was to lead the longest and most productive life you could.

But now he gets it. It isn't arrogance. It's pure faith meeting desperation. Hidden in the shadows just uphill from the seismic stations and the storage shed, waiting for possible invaders, Jordy Clements feels like he's inhaling the suicide bomber's despair, their sense of being cornered, of having no time left to enact God's will on earth.

The only thing he can be proud of in this moment is that he made all his foot soldiers abandon the clearing and the storage shed after Tommy Grover didn't come back from the Prescott snatch. That was a smart move, even if Milo thought he was overreacting.

He also ordered Bradley Kyle, their best driver, to evac with the black Econoline van that's been their main transport all day. Bradley's the one who brought all the foot soldiers up from town before Jordy and Milo went and picked up Henricks; he's also the one who brought Jordy and Milo back up the mountain after they dropped off Milo's truck. Now he's heading over the mountain and then south on PCH, putting as much distance between him and Altamira as possible.

Before the team left to get Prescott, they'd already used their ATVs to move Lacey and Pete's bodies. All evidence from Lacey's brief stay has been scrubbed from the shed, which was easy, because there was barely any to begin with. In the hours just before he brought her down to meet Pete Henricks, Milo had been using narcotics on her, not fists, so she'd arrived with no open wounds.

Now, the same ATVs they used to relocate the corpses have taken Milo, Prescott, and three foot soldiers up the mountain to Milo's workshop of choice.

Meanwhile, Jordy and two of his best guys are sitting stakeout just upslope from the clearing to see if Tommy's absence is going to signal the arrival of law enforcement.

Sure, it's possible Tommy could come wandering through the woods any minute, disheveled, a little worse for wear, but not under the thumb of whoever popped out of the woodwork down at Prescott's house.

Jordy doubts it.

Jordy wasn't there, but based on the description Milo and Manuel gave of how quickly things went to shit, he knows someone important was watching the place. And that means Prescott must have talked to someone, and that means Prescott knows something, and that means Jordy waited too damn long to send the guys after him.

And why was that? Because of Lacey, dammit.

Because of his weakness for Lacey.

If any other dumb bitch had jammed them up like this, he'd have let Milo use his typical methods, and they probably would have got something out of her in a few hours. But instead he made them slow down and wait while he gave them bullshit speeches about patience and steadiness and resolve. Remembering those words now gives him the urge to throw himself off the nearest cliff.

Of course, Milo's acting like it can all be saved. And parts of it probably can be. But Milo always gets chipper and optimistic when he's about to unleash agony on someone. Torture makes him feel useful.

The more time that goes by without any disturbance from the woods below, the more Jordy finds himself getting a little optimistic, too. There are some best-case scenarios, even if he's afraid running through them in his head might weaken his resolve.

For one, Tommy might have escaped.

Also, he might have been killed, which means he won't say much.

Or, despite being in restraints, he might prove faithful enough to keep his mouth shut.

If only he knew Tommy better. If only Tommy was one of his guys and not Milo's.

The guys sharing the brush with him now are his—Bertrand Davis and Mike Frasier—former Recon Marines like him who also saw shit in Afghanistan that reshaped their view of the world. Things they can't share with people stateside because they know they'll just feed into the pansy liberal view of America as some great invader and corrupter of barbaric shithole countries. They know the truth is different—America's moral decay is weakening its fiber, its very spine, and the country's sliding downhill as a result. You don't fight the kind of barbarism they've seen by trying to understand it. You only try to understand it if you don't want to fight the unchecked sin within yourself, and if that's the case, you aren't out to save anything but your pride—a state that describes most citizens of this once great country. The country's would-be heroes are being weakened a few years out of the womb. They grow up questioning Christ because they're taught to question everything from the very idea of patriotism to their own God-given gender. Freedom and self-indulgence are not the same thing. No man who gives in to his every instinct is free.

The only solution to this, Jordy knows, is the single unifying fear of a greater power. This fear has to be instilled in all those who believe their sole purpose is to service their every craving, no matter how childish or perverse. And for it to be effective, this fear must be constant. True freedom, the freedom that saved nations, will come when people are liberated from their own base instincts. Only then will they have the clarity to pick up the sword of truth. Until then, their self-indulgence lays the country open to ceaseless corruption from outside its borders and endless, unwinnable wars in culturally inferior hellscapes.

Jordy is breathing deeply now, even as he adjusts his sitting stance.

There's hope for their plan. Hope for the bones of it, at least. If Luke Prescott's gone, he can't testify to whatever Lacey told him about what she might have seen on his computer. If the dummy seismic maps haven't been exposed, they can still use those to justify the orders for the explosives. The rest he can operate from the shadows.

But if Lacey passed Prescott something real, if the guy has evidence and he passed it to someone else, someone who was watching his house . . .

Then they would already be here, he realizes, with the first twinge of hope he's felt in two days. *They would have been watching* us, *not Luke.*

But they haven't been. If the feds were staking them out because Prescott had passed on damning information, they wouldn't have just sat idly by while he put a bullet in Lacey's brain or when Milo snapped Pete Henricks's neck. They would have been tailing them earlier today when they drove Henricks up the mountain. They would have exploded out of the woods, guns drawn. But they weren't.

He wonders, suddenly, if Luke's not just a troublemaker but something else altogether.

Some sort of criminal who was under surveillance.

The thought speeds his heart, actually has him nodding at the shadows.

Is this a test, God? he prays. *Are you enlisting us to wipe out a minor pestilence before our reign of fear brings your will to the country at large?*

When he hears a low rumble, he believes, for a few blissful seconds, that God's sent him an instant answer. Then headlights flash far downslope, silhouetting the pines and the redwoods briefly, before some sort of station wagon slowly makes its way up the service road toward the clearing.

A Volvo.

He's been expecting an Altamira sheriff's cruiser or maybe a black sedan that screams FBI. Instead, he gets a Volvo station wagon. *What the fuck?*

The car's drifting in a way that suggests the driver's lost control. It's not going very fast, so when it slams nose-first into a pine trunk, the collision isn't too jarring, but the tree dents.

The horn blares.

The impact canted the headlights so they're shining slightly uphill. He's not blinded, but he can't see what's behind the windshield. With the horn going the way it is, there's no doubt someone's slumped against it. Someone badly injured, possibly losing life. Tommy Grover?

Slowly, he gets to his feet.

A few yards away, Bertrand Davis does the same, eagerly looking to Jordy for a signal. The guy's not Milo's size, but he's still a linebacker type. He's turned his baseball cap backward, and even though it's chilly up here in the mountains, his black T-shirt's sweat stained, possibly thanks to the long, anxiety-producing wait.

A yard or two beyond him, and a little ways downslope, Mike Frasier rises from the brush as well. He's about half Bertrand's height, but thanks to a serious Napoleon complex, he's got about ten times Bertrand's courage. Frasier's the kind of guy who'll run into an enemy hideout with a grenade between his teeth while his bigger comrades come in hot behind him. Shortly after they first met, Jordy nicknamed the little dude Bottle Rocket.

Frasier starts walking toward them in a crouch, which says maybe he's seen more of the Volvo than either of them.

Once they're in a huddle, Frasier whispers, "Thing's got no door on the driver's side."

"What?" Bertrand asks.

"No door. It's gone. Like it's been torn clean off."

"It's Tommy, man. It's gotta be," Bertrand whispers.

Jordy looks downhill. The horn's still blaring, the headlights shining slightly uphill. Everyone else who was at the Prescott snatch has gone up the mountain with Milo. A strategic mistake, he realizes now, because there's no one to ID the car. But none of them mentioned a Volvo. They said it was two different plain sedans, both black, that sped up out of nowhere, not a station wagon.

"He got hit, I bet," Frasier whispers. "He's bleeding out down there, man."

Jordy shakes his head, which causes Bertrand to add, "Someone could be after him. He could tell us who, how many. Jordy, come on. We can't just stand here."

Jordy says, "I'll head in the direction of the road till I'm a few yards past the wagon, then I'll cut down around the back and come up on it from the other side. Bertrand, I want you to follow me, but stop directly behind the car, back up out of sight, and wait. Frasier, you come downhill on the passenger side. But you keep eyes on the woods behind me as I approach the vehicle. You see anything coming up on me from behind, shoot it dead. And nobody moves in until you see me close on the car."

They nod, start to move. Frasier's the smallest and the stealthiest, but they're all doing their best to beat him in the light foot department tonight.

Once he's safely past the car, Jordy starts downhill, Bertrand right on his tail. When they reach the service road's fairly level ground, Bertrand falls back. Jordy keeps going, gun out, crouched, dodging low branches before he comes parallel to the station wagon in the cover of the trees east of the road.

No shadows dart from the wagon as he circles it from behind.

Frasier was right. The driver's side door is gone. There's not even a mangled piece of it left. It's like the damn thing was torn right off the car. Once he's away from the headlights' glare, the wagon's silhouette is easy to discern.

Something's leaning on that damn horn, though. Something as heavy as a human body.

In a crouch, Jordy sweeps the woods behind him, then the stretch of pines off to his left that leads to the storage shed. The headlights give off enough of a glow that he can make out the general outline of each tree trunk. None of the shadows seems human. And he has to go by sight because that damn horn's drowning out every other sound. It's up to Frasier to keep him covered from his vantage point uphill.

Gun raised, Jordy starts toward the car. His skin prickles when he steps out from the trees, but there's a deliciousness to the feeling as well. He's approaching the chance to prove himself again after his screwups these past few days. Off to his right, he sees Bertrand coming up on the car from behind, and then he sees Frasier's shadow coming downhill.

Then, finally, he sees what's behind the wheel. He stops cold.

Because nothing is behind the wheel, and still the horn's wailing.

Something, he realizes as he blinks, is *in* the wheel.

Something that looks either metal or plastic and is almost as slender as a pen. It's been pushed through the center of the steering wheel as if the wheel's rubber center was just a tub of butter. The amount of pressure required to do this would be formidable, but also precise in a way he's having trouble understanding.

And that's when the back end of the station wagon jumps several feet off the earth and flies backward.

Gunfire explodes.

Jordy realizes Bertrand just shot at the Volvo as it lurched toward him. But because he assumed it was being driven by someone, he didn't calculate for the fact that the damn car was being dragged toward him by its back end by some invisible force, so his bullets went straight into its trunk and not through the back windshield as he'd hoped.

Jordy's thinking of crazy defense contractor bullshit, of some kind of giant magnetic ray that can lift station wagons off the ground and send them flying through the air, because that's the only damn thing that might explain whatever the hell he's seeing.

He stumbles backward, far enough to see the Volvo slam into Bertrand's chest—not his waist, his damn chest, because that's how high off the ground the car is—then Bertrand goes down and suddenly the Volvo's back tires crash back to the earth, and everything seems normal again. Until Bertrand's dragged under the car.

Bang, bang, bang. Jordy's not sure where these gunshots came from. Then he sees Frasier upslope. The little dude just fired three shots through the Volvo's windshield. They've spiderwebbed the glass. But maybe Frasier can't see what Jordy already saw—nobody's behind the Volvo's wheel.

Someone's under the Volvo. Someone lifted it.

And now Bertrand's under it.

And that someone's under it *with* Bertrand.

His mind is trying to stretch to accommodate this impossibility, but everything else inside him is fighting it. Then something spits out from under the station wagon, sliding through the dirt toward his feet. He jumps backward, fires, then realizes he's been frightened by a mouse. Not literally, but close. The thing's hand-size, a misshapen mass of metal. At first, he thinks it's a piece of the car; then he recognizes the barrel of Bertrand's gun, bent at a ninety-degree angle.

The Volvo rises into the air again. Much higher this time. And higher. The nose drops to the ground suddenly, but the back end keeps rising.

Too late, Frasier starts firing like mad, bullets punching through the Volvo's upturned roof. Then the entire station wagon flies forward roof-first six feet, ten feet, and smashes into the trees Frasier's crouching behind.

Thrown, he thinks against his will. *Something just* threw *that damn car at Frasier.*

Jordy's so stunned he almost misses the patch of darkness rushing toward him. It's darkness in the shape of a woman.

He lets out a scream that fills him with shame, then he runs like hell.

Branches scratch and claw at him.

He hears more gunfire behind him. Frasier. He must have been able to skitter backward away from the flying Volvo in time. The gunfire's closer to him than the station wagon. Frasier's pursuing whatever this thing is—*demon, demon, demon,* his mind screams. The brave little fucker lets out a warlike yell, and that's when Jordy realizes he's got a gun just like Frasier does, but he's running like some dickless little shit, and so he spins, gun raised, ready to face the demon behind him.

He spins in time to see Frasier rocket backward through the air, over the road, cracking and snapping the branches with his back, until he lands against one with a sickening thud. When the little dude suddenly goes limp ten feet off the ground, Jordy realizes he didn't land against it; the branch went straight through him, and that's why he's screaming.

Jordy fires once, twice into the darkness, convinced it'll be useless but just as convinced he's got to do something on behalf of his friend. His screaming, dying friend.

There's a riot of snapping branches in the darkness. It's coming toward him. These aren't twigs or leaves crunching under foot; these are thick limbs and maybe even the trunks of small trees, and whatever's coming for him, it's breaking them like kindling as it claws its way through the dark.

The shed's his best hope; the shed and its fuel and weapons and God knows what else he might be able to use to defend himself against this demon. If he has to give his life for this, maybe this is the moment, the moment when he and this demon bitch go down together in a marriage of flame, all so Milo and the others can get away.

He throws himself against the shed's door, grabs the handle, then he's ripped backward. He makes the mistake of holding on to the handle as hard as he can. His shoulder pops out of its socket. It feels like his entire torso's caught fire. He lands face-first in the dirt. After the terror of the chase and now the fresh agony of his broken shoulder, the single tap of a foot against his lower back feels almost comical. Then the foot braces itself against his right side and pushes him over onto his back like a spatula.

Not a foot, he reminds himself. *A hoof, a cloven hoof.*

Jordy blinks madly, prepares himself to behold some of the grotesqueries of Revelations, the face of a true demon. Instead, he finds himself looking up into the eyes of a vaguely familiar woman with a plain, baby fat–padded face and straw-colored hair and an expression on her face that comes from some feeling between rage and focus for which he doesn't have a name.

"Where is he?" she asks quietly.

Jordy laughs deliriously. *His girlfriend. Prescott's fucking girlfriend.*

"Is he in there?" she asks. "In the shed?"

Jordy wants to stop laughing, but for that he'd have to be breathing, and he can't do that, either. Apparently, she takes the resulting struggle as an insult because she raises her right foot high, then brings it down into the earth several inches from his face. When she withdraws her foot from the crater it just made, the sole of her tennis shoe has a fissure running down its length, but wedged in the dirt is the misshapen mass that used to be his gun.

Studying him, she brings her foot to the center of his chest, gives the center of his rib cage a tiny little tap. "Where is he, Jordy?" she asks again.

"Got something!" the tech yells.

The microdrone crew's van is speeding up the mountain road so fast Cole's thrown one arm out to his side so he can brace himself against the inside of the sliding door. It's the only way to keep from being knocked off the bench that runs the length of the cargo bay. The microdrone feeds are on three flat-screen computer monitors affixed to the bay's only solid wall.

Scott's riding up front with the driver.

They've kept the microdrone cloud as high above the mountain road as they can, searching for any light source, and now they've got a hit.

"It's some kind of light source, and it's pointing skyward," the tech says, pointing to the screen.

Cole leans forward. "A signal?"

"Let me descend," the tech says, "but I'm not promising I can avoid the trees."

"I heard you the first dozen times," Cole says.

The tech seizes the tiny control stick next to him. The microdrones operate like a swarm, bouncing off each other's electromagnetic waves in a way that allows them to flock together and move as a unit without needing one operator for every tiny little drone. They provide hundreds of different feeds, which are processed through a central computer that amalgamates them into three different angles that are relatively easy to monitor, albeit with some occasional headache-inducing distortion.

"Uh-oh," the tech says.

That's when Cole sees what the light source is—the headlights of Charley's Volvo. And they're pointing directly skyward. Which is not good. But they're also shifting to one side.

The entire car is slipping loose from whatever's holding it up at a ninety-degree angle. Cole figures it's trees. They're probably breaking under its weight.

As the microdrones descend, the Volvo goes over sideways, landing on one side, headlights vertically stacked, blasting light onto two men with frighteningly large guns who are running directly toward the spot where Charley stands over a prone, fallen man.

One of the running men raises what looks like a shotgun.

"Give me that," Cole says, then he gently closes his hand around the control stick.

There's a sound like a single clap of thunder.

The demon bitch is blown sideways.

Ears ringing, Jordy lifts his head off the dirt, sees Manuel Lloya lowering his sawed-off shotgun as he races toward them up the road. Ralph Peters is next to him, armed with an AR-15 on a chest strap. They're supposed to be guarding Milo's workshop. But Greg Burton's not with them, so maybe he stayed behind. The guys must have come speeding downhill on the ATVs when they heard all hell break loose. Now, they're running directly under the spot where Frasier's pinned to a tree trunk ten feet in the air. They don't notice the poor son of a bitch. Maybe because he's not screaming anymore.

Jordy goes to call out to them, to warn them this creature's not what they think she is. But just then, the tree branches above both men explode, as if a flock of invisible birds just took flight from them all at once.

Manuel Lloya freezes, spins, and raises his shotgun to the sky. Then his body jerks in a dozen different places. His shotgun is thrust to the dirt at his feet by an invisible force. Then he hits the dirt, too, ass-first, like he just needed to take a little break. The rest of him collapses with dead weight and when his head rolls back, Jordy can see pieces of his face are missing. Ralph Peters is still on his feet, but his AR-15 hangs loosely from the sling at his chest, and he's staring dumbfounded at the shredded flesh on his palms as he spins in place. When he turns in Jordy's direction, one leg bends under him. As he goes down, Jordy can see that one of the man's eyes is missing and arterial spray's also pumping wildly from his neck.

Then Jordy's would-be rescuers are just two bleeding corpses.

Three, if you count Frasier dangling from the tree branches overhead.

All three computer screens go dark, then they're filled by bright-blue squares and the white words TRANSMISSION INTERRUPTION, which bathe the cargo bay in a sudden wash of blinding light. Cole thought maybe one or two of the drones might survive, but apparently they're all shattered or have embedded themselves inside a human body. At least they're not offering live close-ups of broken bones and spleens.

Cole releases the control stick and sits back on the bench. The two techs are doing their best not to look at him, but the screens before them are so bright now, they're going to have to eventually, if only to protect their eyes.

"There," he says, "that should help."

"But now we can't see anything," one of the techs finally says.

"Neither can they."

Jordy knows he shouldn't be surprised when the demon gets to her feet.

He shouldn't be surprised to see the lacerations along her right cheek and jaw healing right before his eyes. The wounds should be oozing blood, but instead they're closing up, and what blood they've spilled is left behind in a drying smear along her jaw.

But it's her eyes that get to him. Eyes as focused and alert as someone who's just had their third cup of morning coffee and is ready to tackle the day. It's not the expression of someone who was just blown sideways by a shot from one of the most powerful guns there is, a blast that turned the right shoulder on her shirt to black shreds.

As if recovering from a light shove, she regains her balance.

There's a strange whirring sound in the dirt a few feet away. Something hand-size and metallic is spinning in circles, like a mad fly with a broken wing. But it's some kind of machine. A small, bug-like machine unlike any he's ever laid eyes on before. The sight makes him think of godless films like *The Matrix*, of tears in the fabric of reality that recognize no distinction between heaven and hell, and he soothes himself by telling him those are the very type of things a demon like this bitch would want him to see. First she'll snap his bones; then she'll take his faith.

It's one of those things, he realizes, *one of those things that came out of the sky and tore my guys to shreds.*

The demon's standing over him again. Once again, her foot's centered over his chest.

"Where is Luke Prescott?" she asks.

"If you're gonna take my soul, you're gonna have to break it first, bitch."

"OK."

The pain is so sudden and total at first he doesn't realize where it's coming from. Then, when she once more centers her foot over his chest, he realizes she just shattered his right knee with what in a normal world would have been a light tap.

"Fuck you in hell, cunt," he groans. "Fuck you in *hell.*"

He's prepared for it this time, at least as much as anyone can be prepared for pain so bad it sends sounds from your throat like your tonsils are being torn out. When he stops gasping and wheezing and letting out guttural groans, he sees the demon's face inches from his. The bitch isn't even sweating.

"I am running out of patience with you, you pathetic, caveman piece of shit. And you have a lot of bones in your body for me to play with. So tell me where your sick friend took my boyfriend or I will break you again and again while the only thing you can do is watch and scream."

"Fuck you, you—"

Real quick, one after the other, like she's snapping twigs, she breaks both of his ankles in a two-handed grip. He smells his own piss before he feels it wetting his underwear. Shit, too, it smells like. Everything. He's lost all semblance of anything anyone might call control. His mind gropes for words to express his agony, but there aren't any. The pain is so total and complete, he feels skinless, like a raw nerve writhing in the dirt, and then he realizes his screams are organizing into words against his will.

One word, over and over again.

Limekilns. Limekilns. Limekilns.

It's possible she's flying, but she doubts it. She's just going faster uphill than any human can because there's barely anything in her path that can stop her. Some of the redwood trunks slow her down a little, but mostly her shoulders gouge chunks from the ones she fails to avoid.

She's tempted to try some running leaps, but those usually end with her feet cratered in the earth, which might slow her down or throw her off-balance. Instead, she keeps her arms thrust out in front of her so that the branches and the occasional tree limb break across her chest as if they're light snowdrifts and her body's a locomotive.

These men have cut a crude uphill trail, probably for use by the two ATVs she saw parked just uphill from the clearing. She's not sure where else the little trail could go except the old ruined limekilns, but even though they're isolated and overgrown and there's no clear trail there from 293, they're listed on a bunch of hiking maps and outdoor adventure blogs. So whatever torture shop this Milo has managed to set up there has to be either highly portable or temporary. No way would he leave equipment or evidence behind to be discovered by some intrepid backpackers during the day. And that's good, because it means his fortification will be flimsy at best. By her current standards, at least.

When she smells smoke, she goes still.

There's a small lantern glowing through the trees up ahead. She almost missed it. And that's because someone's turning it off, someone who probably heard her approach. The thing must be electric; it doesn't gutter as it fades.

If memory serves, the limekilns are actually four structures, one main kiln with a large brick base and a metal chimney about as thick and tall as a Mack truck turned on one end, and then three smaller outbuildings, all with tall metal chimneys, but none of them as big as the main structure. Now, she wishes she'd paid more attention to

Marty's lecture about the place when they hiked here years ago. But she's got eyes on the entire site and can make out the structures she remembers. That'll have to do.

The lantern on the ground was in front of the largest structure, the one with the fattest chimney and the giant crumbling brick base. She can't be entirely sure, but she's willing to bet it's also the one putting out the smell of fire. It's too dark to see smoke, and the steel chimney's relatively intact, so there aren't a lot of holes that could give off light within.

Priority one is not alerting anyone who's close to Luke to her presence before she's got eyes on them. All the strength in the world won't allow her to stop what she can't see.

As quietly as possible, she snaps off a nearby branch in one hand. Then she turns to her right and throws the branch with all the force she can. It spears a tree trunk with a loud thwack. A shadow lurches forward from the spot where the lantern just went out. Just one.

She had plans. Plans to crush the guy's windpipe or try to knock him unconscious without breaking his skull, but as soon as they both hit the dirt, she realizes the sheer force of her impact was enough to knock him out cold. But he'll be a problem if he wakes up, so she rolls him onto his back. He's not wheezing, or coughing, or groaning.

She places her fingers to his throat and feels what must be the last beats of his pulse.

The impact killed him.

Once she sees what he's been guarding, maybe she'll feel guilty. But she doubts it.

She crawls up onto the main kiln's brick base, going for speed over silence, reminding herself of her main priority: eyes on Luke; eyes on this Milo fucker. Then unleash whatever hell necessary. The base has got one ruined entrance, but it's filled with piles of bricks she'd have to crawl over, and the remaining frame of the entrance is too narrow for her to leap through without making a noisy impact.

One thing she can remember about that long-ago hike is that the main kiln's chimney has the metal rungs of an old access ladder running up the side. Marty had yelled at some random kid who'd been about to climb the thing, and the kid's parents had thanked him profusely.

The chimney's steel wall is warm. The fire smells stronger now, which says the top of the chimney's still open. Even better, the fire brings no strange or putrid smells; just woodsmoke, and some chemical smells that suggest accelerant. Nothing on the order of the stench that used to come from the Bannings' incinerator when she was a little girl.

Nothing that might be the smell of burning flesh.

Milo's sick, she hears that kid Tommy saying. *You better hurry.*

She climbs. A rung snaps off under her foot. She pushed too hard. She places the center of her palm flat against the rung overhead and pulls slightly. It does the work of a solid strong-armed grip.

She's halfway up the chimney when the rungs suddenly stop altogether.

A few of them must have broken off over time. She places one hand against the steel and squeezes gently. There's a low metallic whine, but nothing as loud as the noises she accidentally made in the culvert earlier that night. Within a few seconds, she's made a handgrip in the steel, which she uses to throw her other arm up over her head. She repeats the process with her other hand. If whoever's inside can hear her, maybe they'll assume it's just the metal responding to the heat from the fire inside. The kiln hasn't been used in God knows how long.

When the rungs start to appear again, she's relieved.

She grips the next one gently, tugs lightly, and swings her arm up to the one after. She keeps climbing until she's got her feet lightly resting on the first rungs that showed up after the gap. The edge of the chimney's roof is within reach, but if she tries to pull herself up the old-fashioned way, she could end up tearing a section of the roof away. So she balances her feet gently on the rungs, imagines that she's floating underwater as she rests both palms delicately on top of the roof's edge.

Heat blasting her face, she peers down the chimney's opening.

The chimney's about eight feet across, but most of what she can see below is fire. It fills what looks like a portable metal firepit. The pit looks too new to be part of the ruined kiln. They probably brought it in for just this purpose. An impossibly tall man in a black stocking cap feeds more fuel into it. One Duraflame log, followed by another, followed by another. Then he steps back, moving out of the frame offered by the chimney.

Luke's been stripped down to his underwear and lassoed to some sort of hollow metal platform that's raised off the ground vertically. It looks like a bed frame. The best she can see, it's been upended, elevated, and attached to some wooden contraption that looks vaguely like the base you'd see on a catapult in a medieval fantasy epic.

The fact that she can see this much of Luke is a really bad sign; he's as close to the fire as possible without being in the flames themselves. His wrists are tied to the top corners of the bed frame, his ankles to the bottom, and the frame's got long struts running down its length that are probably being heated by the nearby fire.

She forces herself to breathe deeply. Panic isn't likely in her given state, but rage is. And the real gift of Zypraxon isn't just strength, it's the clear focus that comes from knowing you have it. She can't waste that gift. Not right now.

She tries to adjust so she can get a better look at the wooden platform. There's a winch on one side, and with churning in her gut, she realizes what it's for. It's attached to a wheel hidden inside the wood that can lower the metal frame, and Luke, across a ninety-degree axis until he's facedown, right over the fire. Or in the fire, depending on how far it goes.

She knows it's a bad idea, knows it won't help her swiftly end this, but she can't help it. She looks at Luke's face.

His face and chest are bruising in an orderly pattern that suggests his beating was methodical and precise, and his eyes are slits. Is he actually crying, or is it just the heat making his eyes tear up? His expression makes him look like he's trying to retrieve a lost thought or he just took a bite of something strange that fell into his food by mistake. Pained, but distant. Like his mind's left his body. Or it's trying to.

Standing on the other side of the firepit, Luke's captor holds up a photograph in one hand and lifts a hot poker in the other. He slams the side of the pit with the poker to get Luke's attention. Then he drops the poker, holds up the photograph even higher, and mimes the universal signal for *talk* with his other hand.

Luke just stares at him. It's a picture of Lacey Shannon.

His captor repeats the signal.

Slowly, in a halting voice, Luke says, "Is th-that the girl that broke your . . . your heart?"

The captor lowers the photograph slowly, shakes his head in a dramatic fashion to let Luke know he's not happy with this response. And she's terrified by the thought that he's been reacting to his captors with too much swagger because he's got no idea how bad their security situation is and he's sure Cole's sent a small army of Navy SEALs to his location.

She knows what's coming, knows the guy's about to walk over to the winch and lower Luke closer to the flames. And she knows if she hesitates, she'll overthink what she needs to do next, and nobody ever improved their aim through overthinking.

She holds the edges of the chimney on either side of her waist, then she tucks her feet up onto the rim.

Should she try to stand before she leaps?

She tries it, but at the last second, she loses her balance. Still, she manages to pitch herself forward headfirst, which was the objective. As she falls, she extends her arms in front of her like an imitation Olympian and drives straight for the kettle drum's bed of flame.

When her hands strike the firepit's metal instead of the dirt floor, she feels a surge of relief. *Bull's-eye.* Then, just as she'd hoped, her impact flips the firepit up over her back, dumping burning logs and branches down onto her body. There's no pain at first, but her vision's spotting madly. The surfaces of her eyes are being burned. The sensations all along her back, arms, and hands are like stinging needles, enough to make her cry out if she weren't triggered. When she is triggered, that's a sign she's actually on fire.

But she's got one freshly warped edge of the firepit in her left hand, while she braces the empty bottom against her right. Blinking madly, hoping her eyes will heal quickly enough for her to get her vision back, she stands, holding the upturned firepit over her head now like a giant helmet.

She blinks, sees a pair of black boots several feet away. They must be Milo's, and she's struggling to her feet.

She lowers the firepit some, spins in the direction of the boots, and runs at him with all her strength.

First she hears unfamiliar, piercing screams as the scalding-hot steel meets the body on the other side. Then she hears snapping sounds that are either bones or the bricks in the wall behind him as they crack under her impossible pressure.

She keeps pressing. She tells herself she's doing it because she can't see him and so she has to be sure she's got him. But really she's doing it because the man on the other side of the burning-hot steel is a man who loves torture, because he derives pleasure from the agony of those who get in his way, because his way is fire and hate and he tried to defile the only man she's ever loved. She does it because she wants him to feel pain. Deep, constant pain like the kind he's caused to who knows how many others. So she keeps pressing until there's nothing but silence from the other side of the hot steel.

When she releases the firepit, it doesn't come free from its fresh crater. The imprint of the man's body pushes up through the steel, including a lump in front of his chest that suggests he'd crossed his arms in front of him to stop her assault and failed.

All around her feet are scattered flames, and when she looks down at it, she realizes her jeans are on fire.

She turns. Luke's bare, bloody chest rises and falls with labored breaths. His eyes are so wide it's as if she's changed size before his eyes and he's struggling to take in all of her. Either that, or she's just become an incomprehensible mystery to him.

The metal frame could still be burning his back. But she can't untie him while her clothes are burning, so she tears off her jeans and her shirt. The top of the frame's too high for her to reach without jumping. If she does that and misses, she could knock the whole thing off its platform and break Luke's neck. Rotating him flat on his back, his face to the ceiling, might press his flesh more tightly to the hot metal. She drags the wooden base away from where the remains of the fire burn like little bright islands on the dirt floor, then she starts turning the winch, lowering Luke face-first to the floor. It makes her stomach knot, turning the winch in the direction meant for torture, but it's working.

"Charley." He sounds like she's not really there and he's asking for her.

Her words pour from her in whispers and coos—any tone she can think of that doesn't sound like the voice of a human monster.

Once he's parallel with the floor, she cuts the flex-cuffs around his wrists by sliding a finger under each one and tugging outward. He braces his hands on the dirt as she does the same thing to his ankles. Once his feet are free, he lowers his knees to the earth. Something about this new posture unleashes a series of phlegm-filled, hacking coughs. On all fours now, he looks at her, eyes bloodshot and watering. For the first time, she sees the grill marks along his back. They're bright red and blistering.

"Charley." There's no denying the confused, broken tone in his voice. He still sounds like he's not sure it's really her.

He crumples to the floor, curls into the fetal position. One hand's extended in her direction, but there's no life in it, so she can't be sure he's reaching out to her. She takes it as gently as she can anyway. What she wants to do is take him in her arms, but she can't; not with the burns on his back so fresh. And in the silence that follows, she's reminded there's nothing in Zypraxon that protects her soul from the things she does while she's on it.

What she wants to do now is run. Not alone. With him. She wants to take him in her arms and carry him down the mountain, as far as Bayard Rock where she'll bathe him in the sea. And then they'll keep running to somewhere isolated and safe, where she'll never have to be this kind of avenging angel again, a place where they won't have to rely on anyone rich and powerful and deceitful to keep them safe. Maybe she'll change her name again. Maybe he'll change his. And she'll never let Zypraxon touch her lips again. Never hear the names Dylan Cody or Noah Turlington or Cole Graydon again. Except in her nightmares.

She's got a little less than two hours of strength left. The other two pills were destroyed when her jeans caught fire, she's sure. But why should that stop her?

And there's always the culvert, she thinks before she can stop herself. *There's always your secret stash.*

And that's when she realizes there's no running. That's when she realizes they've got their hooks in her in more places than she wants to admit, that no matter what comes next, her first thought will always be of Zypraxon and what she might be able to do with it.

She doesn't want to run from what she had to do tonight; she wants to run from what Luke might think of it. And those are very different things.

Maybe the horrified look in his eyes and the shock in his voice were both responses to watching her kill, and maybe they're signs he's never going to come back to her. She won't know until his shock comes to an end, until he's back inside his battered body again.

She tells herself it doesn't matter.

What matters is that she saved him.

What matters is that he was worth saving.

40

When one of Graydon's black Suburbans comes charging up the dirt road toward the Med Ranch, dawn has just started to break over the rolling hills to the east, mingling with their flanks to create a gradually ascending curtain of gold. Charlotte ignores the SUV's approach. For an hour now, she's been sitting on the house's front porch, listening to birdsong and trying to find the space between her breaths. She figures the SUV's just carrying some of the hired mercenaries Cole scrambled to relocate the night before. At this point, she could not give a damn.

Too little, too late, she thinks.

Then the Suburban rolls to a stop a few yards from the front porch, and Marty steps from the back seat, looking tired, but freshly showered.

Charley shoots to her feet.

He must have gone to sleep last night with no sense of what was unfolding at their house or in the mountains above town. Now Cole's brought him here. Maybe it's a peace offering, or maybe Clements has more men out there and Cole wants to keep Marty safe. There's no asking Cole. He doesn't step out of the car after Marty, which means he and whatever cleanup crew he's managed to put together are probably still up on the mountain, picking through the bloody mess she left behind.

Whatever Marty sees on her face causes him to rush toward her up the front steps. As soon as she's in his arms, the entire night before comes rushing out of her in whispers.

Marty's never set foot inside the Med Ranch, so he can't hide his reaction to the stark contrast between the house's exterior and interior. Outside, it's a one-story ranch house with solar panels on the roof and a spread of drab-looking trailers in back. Inside, several windowless state-of-the-art treatment rooms run down the center from front to back, their perimeter walls creating two narrow hallways along the sides of the house. Any footprint suggesting the house's old livable spaces is gone.

In the trailers behind the house are the implements and laboratories required by a basic trauma center.

In short, it's a miniature hospital, built just for her. But the only patient today is Luke. He's been out cold since they brought him in, thanks to a potent combination of painkillers. He sleeps sitting up in bed, his chest resting on the type of cushion designed to allow pneumonia patients to rest upright so their lungs don't fill with fluid. In Luke's case, it's their best way of keeping him from rolling onto his injured back. For most of the night, she sat vigil next to him. The nurses and doctors, some of whom she recognizes from her last checkup, kept giving her long, frightened looks as they walked past her, fully aware that, for a while at least, she was capable of crushing their skulls in one fist even as she sat there quietly. Of course, they weren't too scared to take their vials of paradrenaline from her when she first came in.

Maybe if she had put up a fight . . .

There's a bench outside Luke's room, just beneath a window that was probably once framed by frilly lace curtains. That's where she leads Marty as she finishes the story.

"Where is he?" Marty finally asks.

She had just told him Luke's on the other side of the nearest door, so he has to mean Cole.

"Cleaning up, I think. Probably up in the mountains. I figure they'll want to get as much of it done before sunrise."

"Well, time's almost up." There's an angry tremor in his voice.

"I think . . ." Her breath catches in her throat. She clears it, but that somehow makes her eyes wet and she has to blink a few times. It works. The tears are gone for now. "I think we're gonna need to change things up a little."

"What does that mean, Charley?"

"I think I'm going to let them put me up somewhere."

"Like a hotel?" he asks.

"No, longer than that. Like . . ."

"Like what?"

"I just don't think I can stay here, Marty."

"What, the ranch?"

"Altamira," she answers.

He just stares at her for a while. Biting his tongue, she realizes.

"Why not?" he finally asks.

"It's not safe."

"What are you saying? Where are you going to stay if you don't stay here?"

"Someplace they can . . . I don't know. Do a better job of taking care of me."

"Their labs? You're just going to go live in their labs?"

"I don't know."

"You're going to become their prisoner? *That's* your response?"

"How do you think I should respond?"

"I don't know, but not like it's your fault."

"It's not?"

"You didn't bring those psychos here."

"I didn't? Cole brought them here, and I brought Cole here."

"Cole followed you here!" Marty shouts. "That's different."

"Marty, lower your voice."

"I will not!" Marty shoots to his feet, looks to the ceiling over his head as if he's searching for hidden microphones. "I will not lower my voice. I will not let you take the blame for this because some rich asshole's decided to scare us with hidden cameras and helicopters and *for-shit* security! This is Cole Graydon's fault, and I don't care if he or his minions hear me say it. It was *Cole Graydon* who told us on that boat dock yesterday that we were safe like no one else.

"He didn't say, *Sit tight but stay sharp, I've got good people coming. In the morning!* He said we were safer here than we were anywhere. And if he'd said otherwise, I would have been out in front of your house with a gun on my lap and Rucker and Brasher backing me up just like we did when we watched over you before. And we would have caught those sick sons of bitches when they were moving *in*, not when they were moving out!"

"Marty, please. Just sit."

"No," he answers. "I won't sit and I won't quiet down, and I don't care who's listening in on a hidden microphone or a goddamn toaster oven. This is not your fault, Charley. It's not your damn fault!"

When no one comes running to put him in restraints and fly him off to an undisclosed location, Marty sucks in a deep breath and flounces down onto the bench next to her. He clasps his hands in front of him, elbows resting on his knees. It looks like he's chewing on dip, but he quit doing dip years ago. There's no misinterpreting his pose and his expression; she's known him too long for that. His outburst didn't satisfy him, so that means there's a lecture coming.

"Your grandmother used to tell me that she thought if she'd just feel guilty enough about something she could end it somehow. No matter what it was. If she just shouted to the universe that it was really her fault, the universe would say, *OK. Thanks, Luanne. We get the picture. We'll take it off everybody's plate now.*

"It was driving her crazy, doing this. It was part of why she drank so much. And the thing she kept wrestling with when she first got sober was she really, she *really*, thought that if she stopped hurting for you and your mother every hour of every day that it was as good as breaking up your bones and throwing them down a hillside. As if they'd never been part of a person.

"Those were her exact words. And do you want to know, when they found you, baby girl, is when she sobered up. When she stopped torturing herself every damn hour. Now, I'm not saying those two things aren't connected, but what I'm sure as hell saying is that the first two things aren't. She wasn't keeping you alive by refusing to live.

"But God help me, you are just like she was, Charley. You take the hit for something you shouldn't because you think you're gonna absorb all of it and nobody else will get sprayed. But you can't. You're not that powerful even when you're triggered, and if you keep doing it, all you're going to be is in more pain than you deserve."

"Marty . . ."

"You're in love, Charlotte Rowe. You're in love for the first time, and under the craziest damn circumstances I can imagine, and this is how it feels. And that's what you want to run from because when you're in love with somebody and they get hurt, you hurt just as bad. If you don't, it's not love.

"It's true, darling. Don't deny it."

"Marty, he saw me do things. Terrible things."

"You did them for him."

"Still, if he wakes up and he looks at me like he doesn't recognize me because of what I did on that mountain, I don't know if I'll be able to take it."

"If he does that, then he's the one who should ditch Altamira."

"I killed people, Marty. I killed them and I didn't think twice about it."

"You did what we expect men to do for their women. What we expect parents to do for their children."

"No, Marty. Not the kind of things I did."

"You didn't stop until the one you loved was OK, and you stopped the people who tried to stop you. You just did it with a tool nobody else has got. That's all. That's the only difference, Charley. And if Luke can't see that, he doesn't deserve you."

She's not sure if she can't argue with him because deep down she believes he's right or because she's just too damn tired.

After a while, her head meets his shoulder, then she loses her sense of time and slips into that shallow sleep where you're not sure what's real or what's a dream. Maybe the low murmur of Marty talking to the doctors and nurses is real, but sometimes it sounds like their words are quiet, whispered versions of the vicious things she said to Jordy Clements. Then the sunlight on the other side of her eyelids feels brighter, and she figures day is breaking fully outside. Someone pulls the window shade above her, but it sounds kind of like the winch on that horrible torture device did when she turned it. Is she lying flat on the bench now? Is someone—Marty? A nurse?—bringing a blanket up over her?

Then there's a loud crash, and when she jerks awake, she sees Marty standing a few feet away, staring through the doorway into Luke's room.

"Howdy, podnah. How'd you sleep?" There's no answer, but she's got no doubt who he's talking to.

She swings her legs to the floor, shoves the blanket aside.

Marty enters before her, which means he's blocking her view of Luke and Luke's view of her.

Then he crosses around the foot of the bed, and she sees what made the crash. When Luke started awake, he pushed his chest-support pillow off the bed and it knocked into a supply table next to the bed as it fell.

Luke looks dazed, disoriented, and frustrated.

"What was that thing?" he asks in a voice still scratchy from smoke.

"It was supposed to keep you up off your back," Marty says. "Got some burns there, son."

"I couldn't breathe," he says.

"Well, that's fine. You can breathe now, right?"

Marty's looking back and forth between her and Luke, probably waiting, just as she is, for the dreaded moment she described earlier.

Charlotte's heart feels like it's hammering faster than it does when she's triggered. And she can't bring herself to step entirely inside the room yet, so her hand's gripping the doorframe next to her.

Then Luke sees her. His mouth goes slack and his eyes widen. Her heart drops. It looks like the sight of her makes him numb. For a second, she thinks it might be possible he really doesn't remember her, that he suffered some terrible head injury before she got to him.

"Charley . . ."

He says it the way he said it inside the limekiln. Soft, but also distant and confused.

"Charley."

Is it tears or smoke damage choking his voice? In this moment, does it matter? He's reaching out for her, for real this time. She starts for him and when their fingers finally touch, he pulls her to him quick and forcefully. She's about to throw her arms around him, but then she remembers the bandages covering his injured back. So she cradles his head in her hands instead as he embraces her as hard as he can.

"You saved me, Charley," he says into the fabric of her shirt.

And that's when she starts crying harder than she ever has in her life.

313

This time when she wakes, it's dark again, and she has the feeling she's being watched.

Earlier, around dusk, the nurses saw her trying to sleep beside Luke in the narrow wedge of bed left over after he rolled onto his stomach. They took pity on her and brought in another hospital bed they put right beside his. Around that time, Luke complained of more pain, so they hit him with another dose of painkillers. That's probably why he doesn't even stir as she sits up in bed now.

There's a shadow close to the open door, sitting in a chair that wasn't there before.

Marty senses it, too; he starts awake in his chair, his snore turning into a hacking attempt to clear his throat.

The smell coming from their visitor combines body odor with dirt and green things. She hits the light switch on her bed. Cole's sitting just far enough away for it to send a soft glow over him. But she can tell he's wearing the same clothes he had on the day before, and the product that usually styles his hair into a side part has lost its hold. The scratches on his cheeks look like they were left by small branches. His slacks are dirty and his expensive-looking dress shirt dirt smudged. He didn't just supervise the cleanup effort. It looks like he actually took part in it with his own two hands. No doubt he wants her to see this, and that's why he hasn't showered or changed.

But there's a feeling more severe than exhaustion in his look of glaze-eyed shock. He's seen the bloody evidence of everything she'd left up there. Not just seen it. For Christ's sake, it looks like he touched it.

Nobody says anything for a while. When she glances at Marty, she sees his expression is a tense mask that betrays traces of anger, but he seems just as startled by Cole's appearance as she is.

"How is he?" Cole asks.

She glances down at Luke to see if he's still asleep; he is. "Resting."

"Good."

"How did it go?" she asks. Cole looks at her, confused. "The cleanup," she says.

"The less you know, the better."

"There were a few things we should have known yesterday," Marty says.

Cole's face displays none of the jaw-tensing arrogance he showed them on the boat dock.

"I didn't come to justify my decision," he says. "I fucked up. I failed you. All of you."

She's so startled by this admission she's not sure what to say. Neither, it seems, is Marty.

For a while, no one says anything.

Cole gets to his feet, crosses slowly toward Luke's hospital bed. His eyes are focused on something, but she can't tell what exactly. Then, when he reaches the bed, Cole reaches out and runs his fingers along the bandages on Luke's right wrist.

"Rope?" he asks.

"Flex-cuffs," she answers. "Plastic, I think." She leaves out the part about how they had started to melt into his skin by the time she got there. The bandages say that for her.

"Rope is bad," he says quietly.

Marty straightens in his chair like a cat hearing a strange sound.

She waits for Cole to explain this strange statement further, but he doesn't. Is he drunk? He doesn't smell like booze. Just sweat and dirt. And smoke, a scent that takes her back to the limekiln with a sudden speed that makes her head spin a little.

"They were going to kill him," Cole says. "You know that, right?"

"I figured there was a pretty good chance . . . yeah."

"It's not a guess. I saw what they were using. You don't use that to scare someone into being quiet. You use it to extract information before you get rid of them. They weren't going to return him to his normal life covered in third-degree burns."

"How much else did you see?" she asks. "During the cleanup, I mean."

He looks into her eyes for the first time since she woke up. "Everything," he says. "Nice work, even if it was technically unsanctioned."

She's so unprepared for this, so surprised Cole hasn't blown in and tried to take her to task for everything, she's not sure what to say. For Christ's sake, he hasn't even asked her where she got the pills. Maybe he already knows.

Across the room, Marty seems equally surprised, but not satisfied. When it comes to Cole, Marty will never be entirely satisfied. And maybe she shouldn't be, either.

"I'd like you to stay here for a bit," Cole says. "There was another guy. Their driver, apparently. He ran, but we just caught up with him in Morro Bay. He was trying to get rid of their van. But let me make sure we've covered everything before you and Luke go home. We have real security here now. New people, good people. People who trust me and believe in what I'm doing. What we're doing. But just stay for now, please. I'd hate to make the same mistake twice."

Now she's the focus of Marty's intense stare. Either he's pissed that Cole's passing the buck down onto the people who work for him, or he's waiting for her to make the same proclamation she made to him that morning. To ditch Altamira, as he put it. To hand herself over to Cole's constant custody.

She doesn't. The urge is gone. The need to run is gone. Maybe Marty's lecture did the trick, or maybe it was the need in Luke's eyes when he woke. But there are moments, she realizes, when her past will make her feel like she doesn't deserve attachments and the messy complexities of love. Everyone deserves them. Everyone. But when you cut yourself free of the possibility, you forget.

"Jordy Clements?" she asks, remembering the howling man, broken in more ways than one, she'd left in the dirt beside the storage shed.

"The less you know, the better," he says. "About this part anyway. Besides, as we agreed last night, it's the least I can do."

There's a sudden quickness to his step. She's pretty sure he's about to leave, so she calls out to him. Startled, he turns. Maybe he was trying to make this quick because he thought she'd never want to lay eyes on him again.

A few hours ago, that was the case. But her only thought now is that she's never seen this version of Cole Graydon before, and it's too erratic and off-balance to be a put-up job.

"What did you mean, *rope is bad*?" she asks.

His stare seems blank, but it's also steady. Steady in a way that makes her unsure if he's distracted or just stalling.

He looks at Luke again, at the little carpet of bandages on his naked back. Cole's silences have surged with all sorts of thinly repressed emotions, but never this kind of sudden acute pain.

Like her, Marty's frozen in anticipation of whatever Cole might say next.

"When I was thirteen, my father sent me to this wilderness adventure camp in Colorado. The goal was to toughen up rich kids like me. I hated it. Every minute of it. I bitched and moaned and whined like a spoiled brat. Because I was a spoiled brat. And at the time, I had no desire to be anything else. We hiked five or six miles every day. At night, we camped with these plastic tarps that would barely do anything if it rained. We didn't even have tents.

"But even as I hated it, there were beautiful things. I remember one day before dawn we hiked to the top of a mountain so we could watch the sunrise from several thousand feet. There were animals that came so close it was like we were . . . I don't know. Siblings.

"The hike was two weeks long, and the last day, we were supposed to rock climb. They took us to this little cliff face, and really, the cliff itself was only about twenty feet high, but it was on the edge of a mountain, so when you were at the top, looking down, the perspective made it seem like you could fall thousands of feet. They kept saying it was just a trick of the eye, but I didn't give a shit. I wasn't doing it. And this one counselor, he practically came at me with the harness. He'd had it. He'd had enough of me and my mouth. Well, I'd had enough, too. I took off running.

"I was a good runner. Thin, light. They didn't catch up to me. We weren't that far from civilization, so I had a pretty good sense of which way I needed to go. We'd all been hiking for two weeks. We couldn't carry the rock-climbing gear the whole time, so we'd stopped off at the lodge before and the lodge was pretty close to a town. So anyway, my plan was just to walk until I got somewhere, and then I'd get to a phone and call my father and say that I had done as much of his little camp as I could and it was time for me to come home."

Cole nods, and for a second, she wonders if that's where the story will end.

"It turned out I wasn't on the road I thought I was."

He chews briefly on his bottom lip. He hasn't looked away from Luke once since he started to tell the story; he doesn't now.

"I heard the truck when it was pretty far away. And I knew it wasn't from the lodge because it was . . . well, those cars were new, and this one was making a hell of a racket. I thought about trying to wave it down, but there was plenty of day left and I figured I'd be fine. If the guys in the truck knew anyone from the lodge they might turn me in, and God forbid they make me go back to that fucking cliff.

"At any rate, I was going to ignore the truck. That was my plan. But at the last second as it was driving past me, I turned and looked, and the guy in the passenger seat was . . . He had the prettiest blue eyes. They were like crystal. And I remember, I smiled like I'd never let myself smile at another boy. That was my mistake."

Her stomach's gone cold, and across the room, Marty's jaw is set, his deep breaths flaring his nostrils.

"They pulled over. There were three of them. I guess they were in their twenties. And they started out helpful. Asking me if I needed a ride, where I was going. And I told them I was good and not to worry about me. And then it was like they all smelled something on me. Probably from the way I talked or the words I used. Maybe they saw a city boy or maybe they just saw a faggot who could have been from anywhere. They all came at me at once. Like a *force*. I just remember it felt like my head was on fire all of a sudden. Then I was in the back seat of the truck and they'd tied my wrists up . . . I just remember being astonished by what was happening. Nobody had ever lifted a hand to me, ever. Nobody at my school fought. We were too damn rich!"

He smiles so broadly all of a sudden, Charley almost returns it on reflex. But it's not that kind of smile, and she knows it.

"I remember as they drove me, I spit out a tooth they'd knocked loose. Then they took me to a shed and . . . the rope. The rope was maybe the worst part because I could *see* the rope . . . on my wrists. They'd pressed me facedown on the floor, and my hands were out in front of me. The rest I could just hear and feel. But the rope I could see." Again, he looks to Luke, to the bandaged evidence of his injuries, and it's no longer any mystery to Charley why this memory's come bubbling to the surface now. The platform, the limekiln, the woods. Brutal men who move like a single, hateful force. "It's funny, how many porn stories there are on the internet about the type of thing that happened to me. But the thing they never get is that the people doing it to you are doing it because they're sure it's the worst possible thing they can do to another person. And you feel that in everything they do. When you scream, when you beg them to stop, they push harder. That's the thing people don't understand about rape. It's the feeling of having hate, someone else's hate, inside of you, and you try to gather every part of you into the space that's left over, and the longer it goes on the space gets smaller and smaller."

After a long silence, Cole looks from Luke to her, and whatever expression's on her face causes him to give her a sympathetic smile. As if he's pitying her, when really it should be the other way around, she figures.

"I realize at times I've made a deliberate effort for you to see me as less than human," he says, "but believe me when I say I have my own reasons for wanting to see this drug do some good in the world. And you can also believe me when I say, I'm going to get everyone responsible for doing this to him. Everyone."

Before she can respond, he leaves the room.

For a while, she and Marty just stare at each other, as if Cole Graydon's humanity is a bitter pill neither one of them is ready to swallow.

This time it's a helicopter that wakes her.

In the hallway, she moves to the window and sees a bright light appearing out of the night sky to the south, sweeping low over the black waters of Lake Patrick as it approaches the ranch. Cole's helicopter; she'd recognize it anywhere. She took a fateful ride in the thing a few months before, and its details are emblazoned in her memory, from its retractable runners to its leather-padded passenger compartment.

As she emerges onto the front porch, she finds Cole close to the front steps standing in a huddle with the younger security guy from last night and three black-clad men she doesn't recognize. Cole has a new outfit on—a black T-shirt and jeans so similar to what his security guys are wearing she wouldn't be surprised if they're borrowed from one of them. Freshly showered, with no product in his hair, he looks startlingly boyish.

When the group sees her, they fall silent. The new security team members retreat, headed in the direction of the helicopter, which is coming in for a landing just down the dirt road.

Cole starts toward her. He doesn't look as exhausted or dazed as he did earlier, but there's an openness to his expression that startles her. As if he thinks they've shared something that makes them friends. And maybe they have.

If the story's true.

"Are you leaving?" she asks.

"Yes."

"And the less I know about where you're going, the better."

"Probably. Is he still resting?" She nods. "Good. They'll take good care of him. They'll take good care of both of you."

Better care than you did, she thinks. He smiles as if he knows she's thinking it and is grateful she didn't say it out loud.

"I'll be back," he says.

When he turns for the helicopter, she calls out his name. He turns.

"Why did you tell me? About what happened to you in Colorado. Did you want me to think we were the same?"

"Oh, no. Not at all."

"Why?"

"Because we're not the same. You've never been raped. You've never even been beaten or held down against your will. The one time someone broke into your house, you were able to knock him to the floor in ten seconds flat. And when you were abducted by Pemberton, it was by your own design, remember? You've had horrible things happen to you, no doubt. But they're not the same as what happened to me. Or Luke. Or your mother. I mean, that's Noah's theory, isn't it? That Zypraxon works in you because you haven't undergone severe physical trauma. That the emotional shock of such trauma deformed the neural pathways in all our other test subjects, and that's why they went lycan."

"It's just a theory," she says quietly.

"We'll see. The point is, I didn't tell you what happened to me so that you'd think we were the same, because we're not, Charlotte. We're not the same at all. I told you so that you'd know I see you as something other than dollar signs. Or a subject. Or a project."

"And what do you see me as?"

"Hope." His smile strikes her as a little too cheery and forced. The raw and vulnerable person he'd been in Luke's room a few hours before is being covered up again, piece by icy piece.

"Did Noah know, back when he was Dylan?"

The question startles the smile off his face. "He had his suspicions that there was some . . . trauma in my past, as he put it. He knew one of my front teeth isn't real."

"And did he tell you that you could accept that what happened to you made you a better person without celebrating the people who'd done it to you?" Cole's answer is in his shocked silence. "And is that how he got you to let down your guard and do things that maybe you shouldn't have? Like swallow a strange new pill without stopping to Google it first? Or send four test subjects to die horrible deaths one after the other in some lab somewhere?"

He doesn't answer; she doesn't need him to.

"Then we're the same," she says.

"Well, then," he says quietly. "If it makes you hate me a little less . . ."

She shrugs, and he laughs.

He's turned for the helicopter when she says, "Did you ever tell your father about what happened in Colorado?"

"Yes."

"What did he do?"

There it is again, some flash of the authentic Cole, the one she met for the first time just a few hours before. She can't tell if he's studying her or coming to some sort of decision. Eventually, he looks to the dirt between them, then takes a few steps toward the porch.

"I'm going to send you a package tomorrow," he finally says quietly. "The contents will be familiar to you. And the instructions will be clear."

"Instructions or orders?" she asks.

"Neither, really," he says, smiling. "More like an invitation. For you and only you."

"An invitation where?"

"I'm going to pay someone a visit," he says, "and I'd like you to see how it goes."

TruGlass, she realizes. Apparently he's planning to wear a pair, and he is going to give her a monitor and a code for it, just like the ones he sent her five months ago, before they'd ever met in person.

When his helicopter rises into the air a few minutes later, the branches of the nearest trees dance in the downdraft, then the headlight swings south into the dark toward Altamira. Charley stays on the front porch, waiting until it's out of sight completely so that she can pretend, just for a moment, that the ranch house behind her is a peaceful and ordinary one, and that the small town just to the south is once again only a tiny, forgotten little village in the middle of nowhere that waited patiently for her inevitable return.

Then she goes back inside to be with the man she loves.

41

When Donald Clements hits the light switch in his dining room and sees Cole sitting at the head of his long hardwood table, he raises his Glock 17 in both hands. Cole smiles, holds up the fifteen rounds they removed from the gun earlier that day while Donald was watering the lawn, and passes them to Scott Durham, who pockets them inside his jacket. Donald glances toward the front door, where he probably notices two more shadows blocking the nearest exist. Or maybe he's looking to his alarm panel to wonder why it didn't alert him to the presence of intruders.

"Have a seat," Cole says.

It's a peaceful, chilly night in the Blue Ridge Mountains, and there's not so much as the sound of a car engine audible anywhere nearby. His breath making low growls in his throat, Donald starts for the other end of the table.

Cole says, "No, no, closer," and waves him forward.

Donald releases the back of the chair and shuffles down the length of the table. His night clothes constitute a T-shirt with a design so laundry faded Cole can't tell what it was in the first place and boxers that ride up his stout, hairy legs. Before he sits, he checks the chamber of his gun just to be sure Cole wasn't bluffing. His worst fear confirmed, he sinks into the chair closest to Cole's, sets the Glock on the table, and thrusts it across the wood as if it bit him. It thunks to the floor on the other side.

Then, just as he's been instructed, Scott sets an open beer bottle on the table in front of Cole. When Donald sees it, he laughs.

"I guess we're going to end up sharing a beer after all," Cole says.

"You could have called first."

"I did. Three days ago, remember?"

"I meant before . . . this."

"I'm on a schedule. I needed to visit while I had time. I figured you'd understand."

"A schedule?"

"I've got a lot of work to do. Your son's made quite a mess."

Donald nods.

"Where is he?" he asks. "I've been calling him for three days."

"You two speak a lot, do you?"

"Where's my son?"

"I just want you to know, it's possible I'm more sympathetic to your cause than you might realize."

"I don't have a *cause*. Where's my son?"

"I don't know if I believe that, Donald."

"I don't know if I care."

"You were so protective of Jordy when I called you the other day."

"He's my flesh and blood. What did you expect?"

"Some business sense, perhaps. Some sense that even family has to be stopped before it endangers profit. Our contract, it's heavily in my favor. I can stop the project and pay you only half of what you're owed for the work you've already done. But for you, this tunnel isn't about work. It not even about getting paid. It's about something else, and whatever that is, your son's so in the middle of it, there was no moving him, no matter what I wanted. So you can't blame me for thinking his cause is also yours, Donald."

"And what cause would that be?"

"Men like you. Men like Jordy. You're being rendered irrelevant. It's not your fault. You're being automated out of existence. Today it's drones replacing fighter pilots. Tomorrow it'll be the soldiers, true American heroes like Jordy, who are replaced by . . . something. I don't know what. Yet. But it's coming. Look at the drilling machines you use now. The manpower and explosives they replace. These forces are unstoppable. We all know it, but only a few of us admit it. But what does this do to men like you? Men who made their living with their hands and found ways to master brute strength. Who relied on clear, fundamental beliefs. Men like you. Jordy. Mike Frasier. Manuel Lloya. Ralph Peters. Greg Burton. Bradley Kyle. Bertrand Davis. Tommy Grover."

With each name, a little more life seems to go out of Donald.

"Milo Simms," he adds, saving the worst for last. "Who did I miss, Donald? Did I miss anyone?"

Cole's never seen someone go quite as still as Donald Clements has gone in this moment. One arm's resting on the table next to him, so it's conceivable he might try to pick up the beer bottle and use it as a weapon if Cole doesn't move it. But even when Donald's not acting like a statue, the man seems to lack quick reflexes.

"Where's my son?" Donald Clements whispers.

Cole reaches for the beer bottle, takes a slug, then sets it down a few inches closer to Donald than it was before.

"This might not make much sense to you, Donald, but I've learned something recently. Something important."

"Oh yeah?"

"Incredible things happen when a predictable monster stumbles into the middle of something he doesn't understand."

"My son is not a monster," Donald said quietly. "And neither am I."

"What are you, then?"

"Faithful," he whispers, but it's the kind of whisper that sounds like the person's just preserving their breath so they can spit in your face once they're done.

"I see. Who else shares in your particular faith?"

"You think I don't know how this ends? Why should I tell you anything?"

"It's what comes after this ends that you should worry about. Believe it or not, you do have a choice."

"Oh yeah? What's that? The choice between a Glock or a Luger?"

"No, the choice between dying peacefully in your home of what will appear to be natural causes or being exposed to the world as the mastermind of a domestic terrorist network that planned persistent small-scale bomb attacks targeting places of value in communities they despised. In the first choice, you leave the world as a respected, but divorced, business and family man, distraught and perhaps stressed to the point of cardiac arrest by the car accident that killed your younger son.

"In the second, the minute the story breaks that you were a terrorist mastermind, the press finds a way to worm its way into your mother's assisted-living facility in Nashville and get the first garbled, incoherent statement they can out of her, which they will then edit into the sound bite they want for the story they've already written. And your other son, well, he'll probably have to move his family out of Minneapolis, because it's a big city and the exposure will be too much. He'll also have to leave the insurance firm where he works. Maybe go into a business where he doesn't constantly come into contact with people who recognize his last name. He'll tell his wife that they're just pulling the kids out of school for a little while. But a while will probably turn into a few months, then a year. Then homeschooling, if his wife can manage the stress of it. If she can manage the stress of being married to him at all after a year. Maybe less. This is all provided, of course, that no other members of your family were part of your insane plot. But don't worry. I'll find out for sure."

"Who are you?" Donald whispers.

"You really should have asked that question before."

"Before what?"

"Before you brought this shit to my doorstep."

"Yeah, I can see that now."

"Your son and his friends did terrible things to people who are incredibly valuable to me."

"Who? *Lacey?* What are you, her billionaire faggot brother?"

"You'll never know, Donald."

The man's sneer fades.

"You want more names, is that it?" he asks.

Cole nods.

"They only made contact with four men. Their goal was twelve. But they had sit-downs with four. They met 'em through chat rooms. But they didn't even have their targets yet. They were just testing them to see if they could be trusted. It was early. All of it, it was real early. So I don't have their damn names because they never gave 'em to me. You can torture me all night long, I still won't have 'em. As for all the guys you mentioned, sounds like you got the lot. Milo brought some of them to the table, Jordy brought the others. All the names you just said, I recognized."

For a while, Donald stares at the table.

Cole glances at Scott to see if he believes the man's statement; Scott's curt nod says he does.

"Well, Donald, it goes without saying that if that turns out not to be the case, no matter how things end tonight, the scenario I laid out for you a moment ago can still come to pass."

"If it goes without saying, then don't fucking say it."

"A story, then."

"A story?"

"Yes, it might answer the question you just asked me."

"Which one?"

"The one about who I am."

Despite his furrowed brow and wild eyes, there's no real strength to Donald's glare. It's a mask worn by a man who's collapsing on the inside. His lower lip's even started to tremble a little.

"When I was thirteen, my father sent me to this wilderness camp in Colorado. He was trying to toughen me up. Make me less of a spoiled brat, I guess. Anyway, on the last day this counselor and I got in a fight. The details are not important. The point is, he was sick of my mouth, and I was sick of being made to do stuff that scared the shit out of me. So I took off running and believe it or not, nobody caught up with me. My plan was to walk back to the nearest town, call my dad, and get him to come take me home.

"Then this beat-up old pickup truck came down the road next to me, and I think I stared a little too long at the boy in the passenger seat. He was real pretty, you see. So they pulled over suddenly, got out, and asked me if I needed help, and when I said no, they all came at me at once. The next thing I knew, they'd tied me up and thrown me in their truck. They took me to this shed in the middle of nowhere, and they raped me one after the other. Real rape, not movie rape. Not desire boiling over and not being able to hear the word no. The kind of rape where someone uses sex to inflict as much pain and humiliation as they can. I'd stared too long at that boy as they drove by, you see. That was my mistake. When they were done with me, they let me go. That was theirs.

"I guess in their little world, they thought the shame of it would keep me silent. But when I finally got back to town I found a phone and I called my father and told him everything that happened. He got there as fast as he could. He even brought a doctor with him so I wouldn't have to go to the hospital. They treated me in a hotel, took my blood so they could test for everything. And then, about the third day, I realized there'd been no police. I mean, I was being taken excellent care of. My father was there. Doctors were there. And I was fine to travel. We could leave, but we weren't leaving, and yet no one had called the police."

Cole reaches out and takes another sip from the beer bottle sitting between him and Donald.

"That afternoon, my dad knocked on my door. He asked me to get dressed. He told me we were going somewhere. We got in a car with some guys just like the fine gentlemen who came here with me tonight. And he gave me this little pill and told me to swallow it. I didn't think twice about it. He was handing out pills all the time. That was his business.

"And then I realized we were driving to the shack where those boys took me. He told me to be calm and that everything would be all right and that he was there for me no matter what happened. And there they were, all three of them. Inside. They'd brought in a little round table and they were all sitting at it, scared out of their minds. But my dad, he just acted like we were there to talk things through. He actually asked them to explain themselves. To explain why they'd raped me, but he asked like he was asking them to explain why they stole five dollars. It was so insane.

"They just blubbered. They just sat there and they blubbered. And they apologized. And they blamed it on sin and the devil. And my father just nodded sympathetically like he understood. You know, like we can all get so caught up in our sin, we end up raping thirteen-year-olds in the woods. I couldn't believe what was happening. I'd been in a fog for days, but I could feel rage coming up in me. Pure rage. Was my dad really going to allow these bastards to explain it all away?

"Then he made all three of them get down on their knees, one after the other, and apologize. And I thought, well, that's something. I liked seeing them on their knees. Then, we all sat down at the table again and they're still crying, but now they're doing it like they're relieved, you know? Like it's wrapping up and now that they've made it through, they'll never make the mistake of raping a child for fun again. Promise.

And that's when my dad starts passing around this bottle of Dr Pepper and he says, *Let's share a drink together to show all is forgiven.*

"And he drinks out of it, and then I drink out of it, and then they drink out of it, one after the other. And then, about thirty seconds later, all three of them are dead. The pill he gave me, you see, it protected me from the poison. He took one, too. It was quick, the poison. Real quick. Painless. At least it looked that way to me. I mean, those boys went down like a bag of rocks, each one. No thrashing. No seizures. No foaming at the mouth."

Cole reaches out and takes a sip from the beer bottle. Donald's eyes follow its journey from his mouth and back to the table again.

"You see, he was trying to teach me two things that day. One, that I would always be his son, no matter what. That he would always protect me no matter who I was on the inside or no matter how long I looked at a pretty boy in a pickup truck. But the second part, that was harder. He wanted me to sit at the table with him and see those boys, hear those boys, remember them as something more than my rapists, so that I could see the weight that would pull on his soul from that day forward. The vengeance that day was his, not mine. He was getting back at them for hurting his only son. But he was showing me what he'd have to remember for the rest of his life after he took theirs. Their sobs, their lies, their pathetic, desperate talk of sin and the devil. *Vengeance is always possible,* he said, *but only if your memory can endure it.* My father taught me a lot of valuable things in my life, but that was one of the best."

He's told this story as much for the father of Jordy Clements as he has for Charlotte Rowe. No doubt, she's watched all of this through the TruGlass lenses sitting in his eyes, hopefully from someplace quiet and private in the closest thing she's ever had to a hometown.

He lets the story settle, then he reaches out and pushes the bottle a little closer to the man sitting across from him.

"Drink your beer, Donald."

IV

The less I know, the better, Cole said.

Fine.

But here's what everyone thinks they know about the men who came to build a tunnel on the edge of our town.

A black Econoline van registered to their company and carrying Jordy Clements, Milo Simms, Bradley Kyle, Greg Burton, Peter Henricks, and Bertrand Davis was discovered crashed at the base of some cliffs halfway between here and Cambria. Evidence of a wild party, complete with drug paraphernalia, was discovered at a work site just off State Mountain Road 293. The assumption is they got good and wasted and then decided to go for an ill-advised joy ride, maybe to do a little barhopping down in Morro Bay or San Luis Obispo. On the way, they veered off the cliff and plunged hundreds of feet to their deaths.

According to the descriptions in the Tribune, *the nearest local paper, the van was all but destroyed by the fall, and most of the bodies were blown out of it on impact. So it's assumed that Mike Frasier, Ralph Peters, Manuel Lloya, and Tommy Grover, who are also still missing, were inside the van when it crashed, but it's possible they were swept out to sea. The* Tribune's *coverage has made no secret of the fact that Peter Henricks had recently quit the Altamira Sheriff's Department and had been seen regularly in the company of Jordy and his crew. The implication is that he fell in with a bad crowd and ended up plunging to his death with them.*

Here's what I know that the papers don't.

Mike Frasier, Ralph Peters, and Manuel Lloya were probably never placed inside the van because it would have been too hard to explain away their injuries by car wreck. Mike was speared by a tree branch, and Ralph Peters and Manuel Lloya were mutilated by technology that most people don't even know exists.

And then there's Lacey. I know they found her body in the same place they found Peter Henricks's, but for some reason Cole's men thought it was too big a risk to place her in the van as well. Which probably means she was shot, just like Tommy Grover said. No one seems to be looking for her. Not her family. Not old friends. Not old friends of Jordy's. The ones that didn't die with him in that van, that is. On balance, it sounds like she didn't live what anyone would call a good life. But when she discovered a horror show in her backyard, she tried to stop it, and so she deserves some credit, goddammit. She deserves to have her memory honored even if it's just by me.

In a few days, Marty and I are going to go up the mountain and say a few words for her near the shed. Maybe Luke will come, too, but we're not going to pressure him. Not after what he went through up there.

But for now, Lacey Shannon has shuffled off to the same place Richard Davies's victims will have to live thanks to the fact that I ended his life. A purgatory of the missing and the lost who have no graves and no obituaries, who veered out of visible life in a tailspin of addiction and bad choices. Presumed dead by the natural causes of self-destructive destruction, not the hands of a psychopath.

Back to what the world knows.

The night after the Econoline was discovered, Jordy's father, Donald Clements, suffered a massive heart attack at his home in North Carolina. The Tribune speculated that the stress of finding out about his son's death might have caused it, but I know better.

I watched him die.

After the transmission ended, I walked the Med Ranch for hours in the dark, searching for an easy-to-understand reaction to what I'd *just witnessed. But the question of why Cole wanted me to see it was foremost in my mind, and so the endeavor felt analytical and cold in a moment when I thought I should be feeling guilt, anguish, or, God forbid, vengeful satisfaction.*

For someone who talks as much as he does, Cole says almost nothing about the things he does that are of actual consequence. I could trick myself into believing I have some insight into how he works, but what benefit is there to knowing that he inherited his immense capacity for psychological manipulation from his father? It's like knowing where a suspect stores his weapons in a house you can't find.

The more important question is, why did he ask me to watch him murder Donald Clements?

The cynic in me believes he wanted me to feel implicated, partly responsible.

The optimist wants to believe he was showing his devotion. Making up for his decision to leave us dangerously exposed as he scrambled to protect us with the security he'd claimed we'd had all along.

It's probably both.

But maybe, just maybe, it was his response to the things I'd said to him before he flew off in his helicopter that night. Maybe he was saying, Yes, you're right. *We are more the same than he first realized. Thrown together against our wills by a man named Noah Turlington, himself a victim whose every attempt to reject victimhood has claimed more lives.*

Over time, I'll probably come to regret what I did to save Luke's life less and less, so long as Luke is in my life, his very presence reminding me of what I was fighting for that night. Luke.

It's different with Richard Davies. Try as I might to learn up on them, his victims are abstractions. Words on paper. Social media posts from their few grieving relatives. They'll never lie beside me in bed, and so when the demons of doubt and self-guilt come for me, they'll use Richard Davies against me, not Jordy and his men. And if the voices of the demons overpower Cole's, he'll have a much harder time getting what he needs out of me.

Consensually, of course.

And so, for now, he has to make me think some degree of killing is essential, obligatory.

And that is what frightens me.

It's one thing to become numb to the value of life by taking lives to defend yourself.

It will be another if Cole succeeds in making other people seem expendable.

We are on hiatus, Cole says.

A necessary break.

It's such a bland, corporate word. Wholly inappropriate to describe the kind of emotional recovery Luke and I will need.

In another week, once they've finished making it, Cole's people will bury a vessel just under the earth, off 293, a vessel they claim will be fireproof, earthquake-proof, and possibly even volcano-proof for all I know. Inside of it will be the additional nine pills Noah Turlington directed me to the night of the attack. For now, Cole has allowed me to keep them on my person at all times. Originally, I'd wanted the vessel to be placed at the limekilns so that before I accessed it for whatever reason, I would be forced to remember what I had done there. But even the handful of visitors the place might get in a month poses a risk of discovery. So I've selected a spot just uphill from the service road Jordy's men cut through the woods, not far from where I killed Mike Frasier.

Beneath several layers of soil will be a keypad for which only I know the code. The catch: if I choose to open it, an alert will be sent to Cole's people right away, and I will be obligated to either explain my reasons for doing so or ignore their request and simply let their security teams respond in the manner they think most appropriate given what they're seeing on their surveillance.

I partly suspect that Cole's called a hiatus because he needs time to deal with Noah. As for how he's going to do that . . . the less I know, the better.

When it came to Luke's recovery, Cole gave us only one set of instructions.

Don't let anyone learn that he'd been burned on the same night the Econoline allegedly plunged over a cliff.

To do that, we gave Luke the flu. Not a real flu. But a call-in-sick flu and, wouldn't you know it, he didn't get the damn vaccine, so it lasted about ten days instead of five and no way could he go into work because the last thing he wanted to do was spread the virus. Apparently, Mona and her boyfriend managed to patch things up, just in time for another brutal round of chemo, so she'd stayed with him in Santa Ynez as much as she could the day everything went down. Her information about the wreck of the Econoline all came thirdhand. But Luke has said, and I agree with him, she'd be a fool if she doesn't suspect something eventually.

And Mona's no fool.

Luke's going back to work tomorrow, so tonight we went out to dinner at the Copper Pot for the first time in I can't remember how long. Most of the talk in town was fear that the tunnel project might get canceled altogether after the terrible tragedy that befell the Clements crew. The company's big signs had already been taken down at Trailer City and at the site of the first grading on the edge of town. Out of respect, people said. And now, apparently the ownership of the entire company's in dispute. Donald Clements's sole surviving heir has no desire to run it, and so he's considering selling off its assets to another firm. Graydon Pharmaceuticals has used that as cause to cancel their contract and start the search for another tunnel company.

But Altamira's been knocked down before, and so people aren't that hopeful the tunnel will happen now, and there's a sense of grief hanging over the town that's shot through with self-interest.

As our server, Carla, shared these details with us, Luke and I just chewed our food and nodded and made various noises as if we were hearing it all for the first time, what with Luke having been so sick for so long and all. Then, once Carla left, the two of us sat in silence that felt like a strange blend of contentment and astonishment. We're two people who have seen the giant hand that sometimes moves the earth underfoot. But how long, I wonder, before the hand moves the earth so many times, there's nothing left for us to stand on anymore?

During his recovery, Luke has been gentle and needy. It's as if some of the hard edges have been rubbed off him. They'll probably mend or grow back, I'm sure. He's still Luke Prescott. But with Project Bluebird 2.0 on hiatus for the time being, there's been no further talk of him joining the team. Maybe he's too tired to discuss it. Or maybe he no longer feels qualified. Or maybe he just doesn't give a damn after what he's been through. We'll see.

When we make love, the sense of urgency or playfulness has gone out of it. But it's been replaced by something different. Something steady and intense.

I could have lost him.

I realize this now.

I think, in some sense, I became so fixated on the idea that he would reject me when he woke up that it distracted me from what I was really feeling: the fact that he could have died, or suffered some unspeakable debilitating injury before I managed to get to him, in which case our new life together might have been instantly and forever changed. And so now, when we make love, we take our time. He has to always be on top, of course. Until his back fully heals. But I don't mind. And when we're finished, we lie there for a while in such a way that I can breathe, in a way that feels like the weight of him is steadying my breath, not shortening it.

I can't remember which one of us said it first, but it's been said many times over the past few days. And neither one of us made a big deal about it. We're not teenagers, for God's sake. What's the big deal? They're just three words.

I was thinking of saying them out loud, right there at the Copper Pot, when Luke's eyes caught on something outside and his fork froze halfway to his mouth. Then he was rising to his feet and leaving the table, and I had no choice but to follow him. I had to apologize to Carla and swear we weren't skipping out on the bill, but she looked more worried by the expression on Luke's face.

When I caught up to him, he'd stopped just outside the door, and that's when I saw the little guy about a half block away, holding the straps of his tattered book bag. Short and slender, with Luke's same color hair but brushed forward over his head in a big, thick mop that almost hid his eyes. It'd been years since I'd seen him. Not quite as long for Luke, but close. And as they stared at each other, I got nervous. I'd never expected this reunion, not this soon, but there he was. Looking bashful and uncomfortable in his skin, which made sense, given he can never stay in one place and rarely steps outside.

"Hey," the guy said.

And then I saw all of it in the little guy's eyes at once—the fear and the regret and the need for something. At least I hoped there was need. I hoped he'd stay for a while, because as Luke stared, he didn't seem angry or poised to vent years' worth of frustrations. He seemed like a man experiencing some great relief, and I wondered if this was exactly what he needed.

Then he ran to the guy and took him in his arms, and the two of them hugged like straight men always hug when they want it to last for longer than a few seconds, like two bears wrestling.

And then Luke looked at me with tears in his eyes because Bailey was home.

42

When Scott Durham raps on the car window, Cole realizes the plane carrying Noah Turlington has just touched down outside the hangar. He steps from the SUV.

A few minutes later, the hangar door ascends just enough to allow Noah and his security team to walk under it. Noah's dressed in the jeans and T-shirt they provided for him and flanked by six of the best security personnel they could find. If he's excited to have been released from the cell where they've kept him for the past three weeks, it's nowhere in his expression. His stance is another story, however. He walks with a skip in his step, his head erect.

Then he sees the two large vessels parked off to the side of him and comes to a sudden stop. Like coffins, but bigger, they sit on wheeled platforms, but their bottoms extend almost to the floor, and the low and steady hum of life-support equipment comes from each one. Maybe he's afraid he'll have to make the next leg of his journey inside one of them. Cole opens his mouth, preparing to disabuse him of the notion, then decides to hold off for a bit.

Noah looks from the transport pods to the gleaming, brand-new Boeing 737 parked nearby; it's painted a blend of silver and light blue, the color of a daytime sky.

"Nice plane," Noah says. "I take it we're back in business?"

"You think you'd be here otherwise?"

Noah doesn't answer.

"Feel free to thank me at any time," Cole says.

"Give me a few more days aboveground and I'll think about it."

"I thought you weren't a fan of Stonecut Ridge."

"I'm a fan of daylight."

"You're also a fan of breaking the rules, and we're not going to be able to go forward without a few. Hence, your brief punishment."

"Brief. OK. Is she all right?"

"She's fine."

"And that boyfriend of hers?"

"He's recovering nicely. His injuries were minor."

"Sounds like I broke the right rule, then."

"Well, then, the cell was worth it. Right? I mean, it had a toilet."

"What about the kid?"

"What kid?"

"The hacker. Luke's brother. Did you throw him in a cell, too?"

"I made a terrible mistake with their security, and I couldn't fix it in time. Luke's brother responded. I can't fault him for that."

"I was the response, and you just faulted me for three weeks."

"Maybe I just don't like you, Noah."

"It's Dylan you don't like. You don't even know Noah."

"Small blessings, then. Come now. This is a happy day. Don't ruin the mood by reminding me you're a sociopath."

Cole walks up to the transport pods and knocks on the titanium outer shell of the nearest one. Then he runs one hand over the unmarked sensor in its side. Part of the top goes translucent, offering a square view of the young comatose man inside. An oxygen mask covers the lower half of his face; it hides the feeding tube that's been forced down his throat.

Noah approaches slowly, making no effort to hide his interest in its occupant.

"This is Tommy Grover, a veteran of the United States Marine Corps who fell in with a very bad crowd after his honorable discharge. He's believed to have been killed and swept out to sea after a car crash on PCH that also killed most of his friends. But the truth, as you can see, is very different. He's very much alive and in one piece and here with us today. You see, the real story is that Tommy was the lookout the night his friends abducted and tortured Luke Prescott. And unfortunately, he didn't get away in time, which means he was interrogated by Charlotte. After she'd been triggered by the drugs you gave her."

Eyes wide, Noah looks up at Cole for confirmation this isn't a joke. When Cole nods, he feels, for a moment, like they're back to being partners again. In business, at least.

"So unfortunately, given what he's seen, Tommy Grover will not be integrating back into society at any time in the foreseeable future. And given that he was rather enthusiastically participating in a plot to repeatedly bomb targets of value to various marginalized communities who had earned the ire of his very special group of fellow bigots, I don't really think any of us will be shedding a tear for Mr. Grover anytime soon."

Cole moves to the next transport and repeats the same ritual, revealing the partially obscured face of the man inside. This man's older.

"And this is Richard Davies. If he has any loved ones, which I doubt he does, they recently came across the smoldering remains of his property in the mountains just south of Seattle, and given his history as a loner and generally unfriendly individual, they probably assumed he burned the place to the ground on purpose and fled into the next phase of his nomadic existence. He's got no family that we can find, probably because what little family he had destroyed itself when he was a boy. His father lost the family farm. His mother descended into addiction and prostitution, before his father shot her right in front of him when he was a kid.

"Maybe this is what eventually triggered his career as a serial killer. I'll leave the messy psychology of it to you. But what we do know for sure is that he murdered several women and turned their skin into personal items. Wallets, belts, that sort of thing. We hope he did it after they died, but we're not sure. We haven't bothered to wake him up to find out. We figured we'd leave that to you."

"We?"

"You asked me to reactivate The Consortium, and I'm proud to say I have. And these two men are a gift from all of us. To you."

"To me," he says.

While Noah eyes Davies's transport pod with something that looks like hunger, Cole wonders if the man inside will survive a long plane flight. Surely Noah has more patience and self-control than that; surely he can see the greater potential.

"Your name isn't going to be the only thing that's different this time, Noah."

As if he's been caught studying the cover of a dirty magazine by the parent holding his hand, Noah looks up.

"This time out, you're going to follow a dual track," Cole says. "Now, none of us want to deprive you of your great dream of turning Zypraxon into something marketable that increases competence and effectiveness in the wake of what would normally be paralyzing fear. We share in this dream, even. We do. Truly. But we don't know how long it's going to take you to get there. And given the strange, twisting path we took to get where we are today, I'd be the last one to give it an end date.

"So this time, you're going to pursue another path concurrently with your chosen one. You're going to make a study of the minds, the behavior, the brain matter, pretty much any part of them you want, of the type of men who *cause* the paralyzing fear Zypraxon is supposed to protect us against. You're going to see if you can isolate the neurological, the biological, the physiological origins of what we, for the purposes of our study, are calling pure evil. And you're going to do it without messy restrictions and the sort of scientific ethics you never really paid much attention to anyway."

"I see," he says quietly. "You do realize that for any study to be effective you need more than one subject. More than two, even."

"You'll get more. Many more, if all goes as planned."

"I see."

Just as Cole hoped, Noah's so sidelined by the offering of two live subjects, he's temporarily forgotten about paradrenaline altogether.

"Good. I'm glad you *see*. See this, too."

When Cole comes within inches of Dylan, the security team seems to straighten all at once.

"There's no recording of the phone call you had with Charley the night of Luke's abduction. So I have no idea what other secrets you might have shared or if you took her into your confidence about anything besides your secret stash. And honestly, I don't care. I'm not going to make her miserable over it. Not right now. Not after everything she's been through. And you? You have way too much work to do.

"And besides, you and I now have a secret that's far more important than anything you could have shared with her. And so, if you ever go around my back again, if you ever try to earn her confidence, try to make her into the sister in darkness and grief that you probably fantasize she is during your private moments when there's no one around for you to crack wise with or fuck into doing your bidding, I'll let her know. I'll let her know that you're hard at work on the very serial killer I let her believe she murdered by mistake. And then I'll take him away from you, close your labs again, and destroy everything you've done."

"Then you won't have my hard work, either," Noah says.

"I have paradrenaline and you don't. It's a remarkable chemical, the medical implications of which might be so vast they probably won't all be revealed within our lifetimes. And for the time being, you're not going anywhere near it. You can't make it without her, and you have no access to her without me. Make no mistake, Noah Turlington. You're my employee again. I've rehired you, despite everything, and that means this time, I've figured out the best way to be rid of you if things go off the rails again."

"I see." His smile seems genuine and affectionate. Maybe he just likes the attention. "How long? How long before I can study paradrenaline?"

"Gosh, I'm not sure," Cole says. "You were pretty close, to be honest. Then you went behind my back, and I had to start the clock all over again. Maybe while you're doing all this work, you can make an effort to earn my trust."

Cole taps Richard Davies's transport pod. To his security team, he says, "Load them in, please."

Noah steps back as the team advances, but it looks like it's a bit of a struggle for him, as if the presence of Richard Davies exerts a magnetic pull. He seems so thoroughly pleased with his gift, it looks like Cole's threats and ultimatums have gone right through him. That was the plan. Part of it, anyway. To leave Noah so excited by the prospect of unfettered experiments on a subject like Richard Davies, there will be almost no chance he'll ever break any of Cole's rules again.

The threats were fun, though.

Either way, the rules have been established. The jet is gassed. The transport pods are being loaded into the plane, and in just another moment, Noah Turlington will follow them onboard, albeit from a different entrance. They've already wheeled the staircase to the forward loading door.

Noah turns his back to Cole and starts walking toward the shiny new plane, staring up at it with a look of wide-eyed wonderment.

"You're pleased?" Cole asks.

"Very."

"Good."

Those security team members who aren't helping load the transport pods are standing in a circle around the two of them now. A circle they've shifted and at times widened as they've moved closer to the plane. Cole can tell that every minute the two of them spend together, the surrounding men will spend on edge, trigger fingers at the ready. Maybe it's because they know their history; maybe it's the energy they give off.

He's so distracted by these thoughts he doesn't notice Noah's been looking at him with a broad smile for a long moment. "You seem different," Noah says.

"Different?"

"Yeah. The way you're carrying yourself. I don't know. It's more confident."

"Well, I haven't changed my hair, and I haven't been to the gym in weeks."

"No, it's something else. Don't worry. It's a good thing."

"Oh, OK then."

"Oh, yeah, absolutely. Murder looks good on you."

Many impossible things have become possible in Cole's life of late, but there simply isn't any way for Noah to know what he did to Donald Clements. There just isn't. He'd spent the last three weeks buried in a concrete cell under the earth with no electronic devices of any kind. The cell guards and the team that brought him here played no part in Cole's visit to Donald Clements's home in North Carolina.

So Cole must entertain, for a moment, at least, the possibility that Noah truly did detect evidence of this crime in Cole's very presence. His bearing, his mood. Perhaps, given who he is and where he's been, Noah Turlington can detect the scent of murder the way a former smoker can smell a lit cigarette from a block away.

Or he made a wild guess.

If that's the case, the length of time it's taken Cole to respond has let Noah know he scored a direct hit. That's for sure. Cole's face is hot. He forces himself to maintain eye contact until Noah's smile becomes cartoonish.

"Have a nice flight, Noah." He starts walking toward the awaiting SUV. "And get to work."

He makes them drive the Suburban out of the hangar before Noah's boarded the jet. Then, once they're a short distance away, he makes them pull over and park. That's where they stay until the 737 taxis into the desert night, taillights winking against the dark curtain of mountains on the horizon. They wait until the plane charges down the runway and rises into the star-filled night sky.

It's relief he feels when the plane banks and then vanishes from view. Contradictory, ironic relief, and, if examined too closely, it will fall apart. *Out of sight, out of mind* is a preposterous phrase to apply to Noah Turlington. The man's done his worst while being both. But still, Cole feels like he's finally banishing Noah, and both versions of Dylan, to a distant island prison where his mad genius will be channeled and contained.

Maybe the relief comes from somewhere else.

From the day he took the reins of his father's company, Cole knew he'd one day take a life. His father had been preparing him for this since he was a young boy. True, most likely he'd do it in service of some noble, world-changing endeavor, but no matter the reason, Cole never thought he'd have to pull the trigger himself. And yet, in a way, he has. Which shouldn't surprise him, either.

Eventually he'd have to kill. He's known this his whole life.

Maybe he's just relieved to finally have it out of the way.

43

The last thing he can remember is the satisfying sound of his tannery blowing skyward, followed by dark shadows leaping forward out of the wood like spirits released by the explosion. But while swift, their motions were purely human as they raced toward him with firelight at their backs. And they brought darkness with them. A darkness so total it hasn't left him, even though a cascade of physical sensations is now alerting him to the fact that he's suddenly awake.

His throat is raw and burning. Both of his nostrils are full of something rubbery. Fiery pinpricks run down both of his exposed arms. He has no real sense of where his body ends or begins, save for those parts of it that feel like they've been invaded by inanimate objects.

Then, very slowly, light appears. First, a vague halo, right in front of his vision. Then the halo begins to spread, like a time lapse of ice melting from a windowpane. He's blinking what feels like layers of sand from his eyes. But he doesn't feel any on his cheeks. His eyes are just terribly dry; that's when he realizes he must have been out for some time.

He's only been on a plane a few times in his life, but he has no trouble recognizing the low thrum of jet engines beneath him. Then a face appears just on the other side of the suddenly translucent glass. A face like Superman. Impossibly handsome, studying him with cheerful curiosity. The man's eyes meet his. The man smiles.

"You and I," the man shouts, just loud enough to be audible, "are going to have a lot of fun together, Richard."

The glass starts to turn opaque again. But the impossibly handsome man keeps smiling. As the window shrinks, what he glimpsed of the man beyond the window gives him a sudden sense of space and perspective that makes him realize how confined he is. He's not floating in some dreamlike space; he's naked and stuck full of IV lines and trapped inside some vessel he doesn't understand. Immobilized and helpless inside something that has the shape of a coffin. And that's when he starts to scream.

Richard Davies screams until there's a burning sensation inside one of the IV lines feeding into his arm. A sharp, acrid smell fills the mask covering his nose and mouth. He starts to lose consciousness, knows he's no longer making a sound, but it doesn't matter, because he's already screaming in his dreams.

ACKNOWLEDGMENTS

Liz Pearsons of Thomas & Mercer and Caitlin Alexander offered this book wonderful editorial direction, making the writing of Charlotte's second adventure a supremely gratifying endeavor. Also, big thank-yous to my agents, Lynn Nesbit at Janklow & Nesbit and Elizabeth Newman at CAA, and my attorney, Christine Cuddy.

A huge thank-you to Dennelle Catlett with Thomas & Mercer publicity and the wonderful team at Little Bird, namely Sarah Burmingham and Claire McLaughlin. Kyla Pigoni and Gabrielle Guarnero are the best marketing team ever, and they also have great taste in macaroons. And, of course, Grace Doyle, Thomas & Mercer editorial director, who's given her full support to this series from day one. Barbara Peters at Poisoned Pen in Scottsdale, Arizona, and Bea and Leah Koch at the Ripped Bodice in Los Angeles were both very supportive of the first book in this series, and I thank them for that.

For research help, a big thank-you to Kim Ullrich for putting me in touch with her brother, Jeff, who helped me navigate some of the complex science around tunnel engineering and construction. Also thanks to engineer Cory Haeder for providing additional resources. Any embellishments or errors relating to these topics belong to me alone and not these highly skilled experts.

Whenever I finish a novel, I always feel compelled to thank my regular support system, including my best friend, the very talented writer Eric Shaw Quinn, as well as my always wonderful mother,

Anne Rice; my aunt Karen O'Brien; Sandra Lassalle; my amazing webmaster Cathy Dipierro at The Unreal Agency; and her crack-shot graphic designer Christine Bocchiaro.

And now a standard disclaimer: Altamira can't be found on any map. Neither can most of the roads and highways mentioned as passing through it. That's a shame, because once they get some of their issues sorted out, I think it could be a pretty great place to live. We'll see.

ABOUT THE AUTHOR

Photo © 2016 Cathryn Farnsworth

Christopher Rice is the *New York Times* bestselling and Lambda Literary Award–winning author of *Bone Music* (the Amazon Charts bestselling first novel in the Burning Girl series), *A Density of Souls*, and the Bram Stoker Award finalists *The Heavens Rise* and *The Vines*. He also coauthored *Ramses the Damned: The Passion of Cleopatra* with his mother, *New York Times* bestselling author Anne Rice. Christopher is currently serving as head writer and executive producer of *The Vampire Chronicles*, a television series based on his mother's bestselling series of the same name. He also cohosts the YouTube channel *The Dinner Party Show* with his best friend, *New York Times* bestselling author Eric Shaw Quinn (#TDPS). Christopher lives in West Hollywood, California. Visit him online at www.christopherricebooks.com.